The Girl from Kandahar

James Ward

COOL MILLENNIUM BOOKS

4

Published in the United Kingdom. All rights reserved. No part of this publication may be repro-
duced, distributed or transmitted in any form or means, without written permission.

Copyright © James Ward 2012

First published by Lulu 2012.
This edition published 2021.

A CIP catalogue record for this book is available from the British Library.

ISBN: 978-1-913851-22-4

Cover photo shows Piccadilly Circus.

This novel was produced in the UK and uses British-English language conventions ('authorise'
instead of 'authorize', 'The government are' instead of 'the government is', etc.)

To my wife

Chapter 1: Joy Turns to Sorrow

George V Restaurant, Thames House

Ruby Parker and the man who styled himself 'Toby Copthorne' sat opposite each other at a table by the river-view window with an A4 document wallet in between them. They hadn't ordered lunch, nor were they intending to. The staff here were supposed to understand such things, and knew to keep their distance. She was the head of Subterranean One, a black woman in a grey skirt-suit. He might or might not have been the Blue Maiden. He looked to be in his late fifties, and his camel overcoat, immaculately ironed white shirt, navy blue tie and trimmed moustache all gave him an air of gravitas, possibly bluff or triple bluff. It was midday and six swans serenely battled the current.

She removed the inserts - a mixture of memos, reports on 80g/sqm paper and aerial reconnaissance photos - and perused them in silence. He ordered a bottle of pinot noir, largely, she calculated, as a means of maintaining his insouciance - she suddenly realised he wasn't the Blue Maiden after all – and leaned back: yes, another affectation.

"You're saying she's dead?" Ruby Parker said eventually.

"I'm very sorry," he replied.

"Talk me through it," she said coldly.

"It's all in there."

"I'm very busy and, for what it's worth, I know you're not who you'd like me to think you are. Tell your boss you've still a lot to learn."

He sat up a notch.

"Dead or missing?" she said.

"Missing presumed killed."

"And you're returning her to me because you want me to tell her parents, I take it."

He looked at the tablecloth and tried to affect an air of humility. "You're supposed to be very good at that sort of thing, yes."

"I don't expect you to be subtle. I know that's not your department's speciality, but I do need something to go with. Apart from the necessary case-transfer documents, which I'd like on my desk by this evening, please."

"Yes – yes, of course." He cleared his throat. "She was posing as the third wife of a village chief in Dhur al-Khanabi, Pakistan, about fifty kilometres south-east of the Durand Line. Her job was to identify high-profile insurgents and co-ordinate them for drones, or if necessary liquidate them herself. Sorry to say, well ... she proved fruitless. She made no identifications at all, not one. We – I admit this was remiss of us: I'm not sure how it happened – we temporarily lost sight of her – there are lots of things happening out there, you understand. The CIA unloosed an MQ-9 and she and her controller plus his two real wives were killed. In our defence, there were at least six high-level militants among the casualties. We've confirmed that through a variety of sources – militants Marciella Hartley-Brown herself probably *could* have identified, but failed to. But it seems that she ... herself ... didn't survive ... the effects of what was otherwise a remarkably successful sortie."

"When you say you 'lost sight' of her, I take it what you actually mean is you lost interest. That it wasn't as if she ... wandered off."

He swallowed. The pinot noir had arrived and the waiter uncorked it. Copthorne waved him away before he could pour anything. "No one's underestimating the seriousness of the blunder. It's one of the reasons we're asking you to take charge of the family side of things. The Blue Maiden's almost certainly for the chop."

It was her turn to sit up. "I'd heard. I didn't realise this was the pretext."

"Celia Demure's influence, partly. She's furious. And of course, the victim was Sir Anthony Hartley-Brown's daughter. The Secretary of State for Defence may not have heard yet – it was three weeks ago, we've only just joined the dots - but it'll certainly help him come to terms with matters if he knows heads have already rolled."

"*Three weeks ago?*"

2

"As I said, no one's underestimating the extent of our - "

"You say she proved 'fruitless'. Are you sure you were even paying attention?"

"I believe there's to be an internal inquiry. The next level down's taking charge. If it's any consolation, there will probably be a significant cull in Blue."

"Actually, it isn't."

"It may interest you to know Celia Demure doesn't believe she's dead."

She sighed. Typical Celia. "Based on what?"

"As far as we can tell, wishful thinking. I don't know how much you know about Pashtun culture, but women tend to stay indoors. The chances of her having survived the blast when her controller and his other wives died instantly are negligible. And three weeks later she hasn't contacted us. The Tehrik-i-Taliban certainly haven't captured her, or we'd know about that too. Admittedly, we haven't been able to send a forensics team to examine the debris, but it's probably too late now. No, I've long experience of this sort of thing. It's one of those times when you're entitled to assume the worst, and anything else just prolongs the misery."

"Couldn't she be lying wounded somewhere?"

"First thing we considered. But no. We put a spy in two days ago to do some discreet asking around. As far as anyone's aware, there were no wounded, only fatalities."

"So I'm to tell her parents we know she's dead."

He half-shrugged, half-nodded. "That would probably be kindest. But it's not really for me to say."

She flicked through the documents without focussing on them. He was right. If she hadn't been killed, she'd have found her way to Kandahar by now. The border wasn't exactly watertight. And if there were no wounded, then that was the end of the alternatives.

But she wouldn't tell her parents she was dead. She'd supply the details exactly as she herself had been supplied with them and let them draw their own conclusions.

Not that there was a range to choose from.

St. Mary's Church Hall, Hertfordshire

Joy mounted four steps to the stage, took up position behind the table and read falteringly from her notes. She'd never mastered the art of public speaking. It didn't help that it was what her husband did for a living, since she could never conceal the comparison from herself, nor, she guessed, everyone else. Above her, a 'Fund4Darfur' banner hung half the width of the building illumined by a row of spotlights from above, not quite masking the audience where it was dark. She was dressed in her tweed skirt and jacket, with a cashmere sweater and a cameo pendant.

In the front row, her husband was flanked by their two adopted Darfurian daughters, Anya, nine, and four year-old Hawa, asleep with her thumb in her mouth. Next to them, as well as behind, sat Sir Anthony's six bodyguards. They alone wore suits and ties. The rest of the audience – six rows out of a possible fourteen – was made up of men and women of all ages and styles of dress, united chiefly by their earnest faces and a passion for justice.

She'd read out four out of her six pages, and judged she had another three minutes to speak, when she chanced to look to the back of the hall and caught sight of a black woman she vaguely recognised making her way to one of the rearmost seats.

Ruby Parker. Her throat dried up. She made two attempts to restart, but began to tremble. There were a few concerned noises from the audience, her eyes met the newcomer's, in which – her first instinct had been deadly accurate – there was anguish, and she left the stage by the wings.

She descended six concrete steps to a fire door and emerged woozily into an empty corridor. Somewhere she heard the polite commotion she'd created, but she'd lost all sense of direction now and had no idea whether it was in front, behind, or even above or below. She saw herself in a desert village with explosions and women hurling imprecations in a foreign language. She had to run. She had to get away from Ruby Parker's news. But she also had to hear it, she had to stay. She swayed back and forward. Why had she let Marcie *go*? She couldn't have stopped her. But she'd never thought – yes, of course she had -

"Joy!"

She turned to her husband and his bodyguards, two of whom were carrying the children.

"What's the matter?" he demanded, walking over. "Are you *ill*?"

Behind his right shoulder, Ruby Parker suddenly reappeared like the Danse Macabre, impossible to shake off. He registered Joy's sight-line and turned.

"You!" he gasped. And then it seemed to sink in. "Oh, no, *no*," he said weakly. "Please don't tell me – *no* – is this what this is ...?"

"We need somewhere to speak in private," Ruby Parker replied softly.

Seven days later, after consulting with as many people as the wide-reach of his job permitted, Sir Anthony asked the coroner to file a report to the Justice Secretary requesting an inquest without a body. Nicholas Fleming, Marcie's fiancé, was informed and paid a brief, emotional visit to communicate his condolences. Anya and Hawa were told. Joy spent that week travelling between her bed, where she lay in silence with her daughters either side of her, and the estate chapel, where she lurched from one prayer to another without remission. She felt God to be unspeakably powerful and malevolent, and she was terrified. She didn't dare imagine what He had in store for the two children, let alone for her. She begged His forgiveness for whatever she'd done as if she was demented.

On the eighth day, however, she unexpectedly took herself in hand. She awoke early, showered methodically and put on her make-up. She left Geraldine in charge of Hawa, then sat Anya on the piano stool in the living room and told her the family secret. She spoke much more fluently than she had at St Mary's Church Hall, and she was conscious of God's mouth beginning to turn up just a little at the corners, even as the portraits of her ancestors glowered in the afternoon gloom. As she explained that it would only mean a difference of one remove in their relations, and that in a deeper sense they were even more closely linked than before, Anya showed neither pleasure nor displeasure. It was as if she'd known for a long time. Joy wondered if Marcie had divulged it in a moment of weakness but, no, she didn't think so.

They had lunch together in the dining room – the first full meal Joy had eaten in over a week – then put on their best dresses, shoes and coats. Joy asked Geoffrey to bring the car round to the front and inform Benjamin and Jolyon, the security guards, that the house would be empty for the afternoon and to switch on the alarms. Then they drove into Hertford.

Three-quarters of an hour later, they stopped in front of an Edwardian semi in a silent suburb with London Plane trees on the verges and bird baths on the lawns. Joy asked Geoffrey to park nearby and wait, since she didn't anticipate being long.

She took Anya's hand and accompanied her up the garden path to the freshly painted front door of number thirty-one. They looked solemnly at each other, squeezed fingers, and knocked.

After a few seconds, the door swung open and a bald black man in his late forties stood in an old stripy shirt, jeans and bare feet. He looked blank for a moment, then his face filled with recognition – a mixture of indignation and displeasure.

"What the hell do *you* want?" he said.

"Marciella's dead," Joy replied.

He looked as if she'd punched him. "Wh - *What?*"

"She joined the army, she was posted to Afghanistan and she was killed in action. Once upon a time, I'd have said it was what you wanted, but I can't bring myself to believe that any more. I'm here to insist we bury the hatchet. I'm fed up of waiting for you to see sense and I'm prepared to go to a lawyer and ask for a contribution to Anya's upkeep if you remain obdurate."

He half-turned to the interior. "Penny! *Penny! Come to the front door now!*"

A stout black woman appeared behind him in a print skirt and black tights, wiping her hands on a tea-towel. The same sequence of blankness then recognition was repeated on her face, only this time the expression was of contrition. She put her fingertips to her mouth and came forward, slightly bent.

"Oh, thank God, *thank God!*" she said. "We knew you'd come back. John, didn't we?"

He grunted unhappily.

"We've been through this," she told him, straightening. "If you really want me to leave you, *then just put one more foot wrong.*" She turned to Joy. "I'm sorry, truly, for everything we said - and did. I know you probably think it's far too late, but believe me - "

"It's okay," Joy said. She felt her cheeks flush and she found herself looking through a film of lacrimal fluid.

The black woman knelt in front of Anya and started to cry. She looked imploringly at Joy. "Can I ..."

"Of course you can hold her," Joy said, getting a grip on herself. "She is part of your family, after all. Anya, meet your other grandmother."

Chapter 2: A Murder in the Village

Zaituna forgot exactly how they became lovers – what gestures, touches, conversational inflections preceded that icy morning in Ordibehesht when she kissed Reshtina's fingernails over a glass of chai. They sensed they'd been dumped in the vortex of a dust storm with no exit. They touched chests and hips and Reshtina stood with her toes on Zaituna's as if to say You Are Mine. The canvas billowed, the voices of the men haggling over a leg of mutton intensified, and the breath of the two young women grew hot.

Afterwards, it wasn't easy for them to find openings. In the early, reckless stages of their lust, luck was all that stopped them being discovered. Male homosexuality was brusque and desultory here because the Qur'an forbade it, but women didn't count for anything, and oddly, this made them relatively immune. After a while, they even thought the men – Gharsanay, Reshtina's brother-in-law, a fleshy fifty year-old with hooded eyes and a wild beard - and Khushdil, Zaituna's uncommunicative husband - might know. Maybe they saw it as an infantile pastime – because children were all women were, in the end. Providing you were obedient, nothing much else mattered. At other times, the two women fell asleep and dreamed they'd been discovered *in flagrante* and buried alive because stoning was too honourable for them.

All their encounters took place indoors when Khushdil came to visit Gharsanay or vice versa. There were fifty-three mud houses in the village, each an interlocking network of rooms housing between six and thirty-six people. To be alone, you had to get away from the men, but that was easy. It was the grandmothers, aunts, sisters and daughters that posed the problems.

Reshtina was somewhere in her mid-twenties, no one knew exactly how old: after what had happened to her in Dhur al-Khanabi, not even her. She had pale skin with cracked lips, a tiny nose like a toy and eyes that defied the neutralising effect of the niqab. She walked with authority, almost as a man would. At twenty-three, Zaituna was already plump and splay-footed. You could hear her laughing two tents away – or crying. As a matter of policy, Khushdil beat her when he left for Helmand, and caressed her when he returned. A hard-faced, taciturn man with a snub nose and gaps between his teeth, he claimed both things put him in the right frame of mind for the succeeding day.

No sooner was their relationship established than Zaituna began to worry about it ending. Reshtina's first husband had been killed, along with her two co-wives, in a drone attack, and she'd travelled the hundred and six kilometres to Gharsanay's family with two village elders and a caravan of Baloch tribespeople, to claim *nanawatai*, the Pashtun right to refuge. She was expected to re-marry soon.

There were rumours that al-Queda fighters were seeking war widows as a way of gaining influence, so that was one way she might be spirited away, but Zaituna wasn't overly anxious on that front, because there were better opportunities closer by. Faridun, for example, was twenty-five, handsome as a *mala'ikah* and the unofficial leader of a tribe within a tribe of militants with shaven armpits, six-inch beards, AK47s and mopeds. He'd studied in Peshawar and now he wanted to found a dynasty. He had the men, all he needed was four wives and forty children. And Reshtina was young, devout, illiterate and hard working. A perfect woman. According to Khushdil, his aunt and older sister had already called on Gharsanay's mother to express an interest.

But if Gharsanay had given a reply, it was no. For it was obvious he had his eye on her himself. The problem was, Durkhani had been his only wife for so long it was unlikely she'd quietly accept what was effectively a demotion. Nevertheless, thanks to *nanawatai*, nor could she take pre-emptive action. So for the time being Reshtina lived in a kind of status-less limbo. She seemed happy that way and in Zaituna's eyes it made her even more alluring.

Then one day in the month of Shahrivar, there were three of them. Ghatola Rahman was thirty-two, taller than

most men, with black and white hair and digits like buzzards'
claws. She was the sole wife of the most important Khan in the
district, Zaituna's cousin, Balay. Balay was forty-eight years
her senior and his three other wives had died of old age. He
wore a grey karakul hat, a dark blue chapan that was too big
for him, and still walked with a pugilistic gait. Nowadays,
though he didn't know it, his wife controlled every aspect of
his existence and, by extension, of her village and its relations.
Almost the first thing she'd done after marrying was have herself elected *qaryadar*, local head of women's affairs.

On one of her rare visits to Gharsanay's house, she insisted on preparing a Kadu Bourrani for Reshtina and Zaituna
– an honour for them, given her wealth and standing - then lit
herself a cigarette and told them calmly she knew what dirty
thing they did every week on the mud in front of the cooking
pot. But when they fell down weeping, she only laughed and
demanded entry. Reshtina stood on her left foot and Zaituna
on her right, and they had a peculiarly methodical type of sex
that served to affirm their mutual entitlements.

It turned out Ghatola was an acolyte of Shaytan, and a
sorceress. She quickly initiated two more women into the
group, Ambrin and Badrai.

Ambrin was nineteen and childless. Her husband was
away so frequently on American-killing missions they hardly
had time for sex, she said, but he refused to take the blame and
was considering taking a second wife. Ambrin's fingers always looked dirty, the result of an untreated medical condition that also made her face faintly blotchy; otherwise, she was
the prettiest of the five.

Badrai's main feature was her taciturnity. She sometimes became hysterical during sex and afterwards wept in-
consolably. Her eyes were rheumy and her mouth sagged – no
one could remember seeing her smile, not even her parents.
She'd been taught to read the opening surah of the Qur'an in
Arabic by the village Mirab when she was seven, a feat she still
performed at public ceremonies, moving her finger under the
calligraphy in perfect synchronisation with her recitation.
Two years afterwards, he married her. At twelve, she miscar-

ried and came within a brush-stroke of dying. Rumour had it she was on opium nowadays, which her husband – who finally wanted rid of her, but respectably – gave her in the form of pellets from Kandahar, wrapped in sweet-paper.

Then one day, Ghatola declared herself the leader of the group. She expected all four women to obey her without question, she said, for if she denounced them to her husband they'd die the same day. Any counter-accusations would go as unheard as an insect's wings, because he considered her beyond reproach. In short, they were her slaves.

But they probably would have been anyway, because she had the jinns under her heel. She could make people remember things they'd never seen or done, and forget things they had. More importantly, she could make people behave in ways completely contrary to their natural inclinations. She proved it one Panjshambe morning by making Ambrin bleat like a lamb at the end of every sentence her husband spoke, until he almost broke a pot over her head. The rest of the family laughed to the point where they gasped. Afterwards, she had no memory of doing anything remiss.

One morning just after sunrise, as Reshtina led the children's first daily prayer, someone banged hard on the door. It was still dark outside. No one had noticed till then but, when they all stopped what they were doing: somewhere nearby, shouting, wailing, gunfire. Gharsanay grabbed his fleece and ran into the street. His uncle followed.

Durkhani pulled her burkha on and went too, flapping her arms like a bird. "Take your rifle! Take your gun!"

The children and their grandmother barged in from the adjoining room. "Bolt the door!" the grandmother yelled, implementing the emergency procedure they'd once half-discussed, but almost gulping mid-sentence with fright. "It's the Americans! *The Americans are here!*"

They'd been expecting something like this for ever, how on earth could it still find them so unprepared? Reshtina's brain hovered over a mental map of her surrounds, clutching for somewhere, anywhere safe to take everyone.

11

No hiding places in this house, though. Think, *think*. Women and children, they – would they shoot them? Where else to go? Outside? That was worse.

Then the useless scrap of an idea. "Hide in the kitchen. If they come in here, I'll fend them off, and if you hear me scream, run into the alley."

The children huddled round their grandmother. Durkhani's sister arrived, pale as a cloud. Reshtina could see what they were all thinking now, written in their faces: *no need for grandma to take the helm: Reshtina isn't a blood-relative; she's expendable.*

Hide in the kitchen, Reshtina had said. They nodded and swallowed at the same time. Angeza, the youngest daughter, cried.

"But what if they come from the alley?" the aunt hazarded.

"Gharsanay wouldn't have run out the front if they were round the back," Reshtina replied. "I'll use his rifle if need be. *Hurry!*"

Suddenly, they almost fell over each other to get away. The grandmother tripped onto one knee as she turned, then scurried upright, dragged by the aunt. The children clasped each other and juddered out of the room as a unit, mewling. They closed the door behind them.

Silence. Outside, a dog barked. In the emptiness, the two kerosene lamps on the shelf hissed as if they'd just come into being.

Then a figure slipped in from the street and closed the door. A hard cold descended like death, two massive shadows, one from each lamp, and Reshtina's whole body fizzed with terror.

Then she saw it was a woman.

Zaituna, *thank God.*

But something was wrong. Zaituna shook. Her eyes bulged and she staggered backwards. She removed her veil, cast a knife on the ground. Her eyes met Reshtina's.

"Take it and get rid of it!" she whispered.

Reshtina picked it up. It was sticky. Blood? "What - " She stopped herself. *What is it* was stupid. "Where did it come from?"

"Gh – Ghatola. *Hide it!*"

Everything was becoming normal in the way events in nightmares become normal once you're amongst them long enough. Your lover's in trouble, the Americans outside, blood-covered dagger. Overcoming the desire to freeze, she laid the knife in her vest, picked up Gharsanay's rifle, donned her chadri and went out. A group of villagers five or six deep gathered about a focal point, kicking, spitting and flinging abuse, while others furiously appealed for calm. An enemy soldier, presumably. *Nothing to worry about then, we're winning.* But where did the knife come from? What did it mean?

She dashed to the back of the houses and carried on fast-walking to where the settlement met the scrub. A tyre, sheep's bones, a ragged sheet of polythene caught on thorns, all just visible in the first glimmers of sunshine.

What about if the rest of her family had come out here too? Then, trouble. Don't think, just do. Focusing all her pent-up horror, she hurled the knife into the dark.

Maybe the thud of it landing. Too dusky to see. Please, Allah. But no way to check. She didn't want to … Or she did …

She blinked slowly and turned to go and crashed into Zaituna. For a second, she could gladly have murdered her. Then they whimpered and separated for home. Reshtina swilled her hands in one of the water pots by the drain, let herself back into the house and sat up with the rifle pointed at the door.

Half an hour later, Durkhani came in.

"It's over, it's okay," she said calmly, as if she was personally responsible for averting whatever crisis. "I don't know what happened. Or rather, I can't say. But it's not the Americans. We're all safe. Everyone's safe."

Reshtina put the gun away, hugged her and gave the all-clear. The rest of the family came out crying and laughing manically.

Five minutes later, Gharsanay arrived with a face like thunder. "I don't want any questions. I want something to eat, and the house needs cleaning. Get doing something. No arguments, no questions, or I'll lose my temper. And definitely no gossip. *Spy not neither backbite one another.* I want to eat, then lie down."

Only later that day, as the men put on their best clothes for a shura council meeting, did it gradually became clear what had happened.

Or what nearly everyone thought had happened.

No one disputed that, at sunrise, Badrai lay dead in the open courtyard of her house, outlined by a pool of blood. Nor that the stab wounds in her chest meant she was murdered, nor that, because there were three separate wounds of different sizes, there might be more than one perpetrator. The only possible dispute was about who.

Luckily, the uncertainty didn't last long because, shortly after the attack, Ghatola had seen Faridun, the village's eligible young militant, haring down the main road with two of his friends. They were carrying knives, she told her husband. They were laughing.

Shortly afterwards, the murder weapon itself – or at least one of them – was found in the house Faridun shared with his parents, tossed into the courtyard that ran by the alleyway.

And hadn't he always ridiculed Badrai's reading? Everyone knew women's education was his bugbear. He was proud of his two-man-per-moped excursions to Kandahar and Kabul to throw acid in girls' faces as they carried their exercise books to or from school.

The nearest Afghan Local Police station was the district one, ten miles away, but Balay wanted everything dealt with speedily, before old resentments had time to take sides and too much "deep thinking" got started. The shura reorganised itself into a Shari'a court, with Balay – the Khan's prerogative, everyone agreed - as judge.

Given the weight of the evidence, Faridun's chances of an innocent verdict were slim, but they dwindled to nothing when it transpired that four of the most important villagers were already against him. Badrai's husband had long hated Faridun for insisting he should never have educated his wife. Ghatola was convinced by the evidence of her own eyes. Balay had no opinion about Faridun's ideology, but, even at eighty, felt threatened by his dynastic ambitions, and, in addition, saw the integrity of his wife's testimony at stake. And Gharsanay saw Faridun as his rival for Reshtina. After a perfunctory court session three hours after sunrise, he was found guilty of murder, a *Qisas*, or retaliation, offence.

Badrai's husband wasn't in the mood for mercy. Faridun was bound and gagged and dragged weeping to a pit outside the village. He was buried upright to chest-level. His father and uncle cast the first rocks in a bid to restore the family honour.

Six out of eight of his friends left for Kandahar the same morning. Three were never heard of again.

Four months later, the others returned to inflict a vengeance from which the village never recovered.

Reshtina discovered the truth in scraps from Zaituna and Ambrin over several weeks. Ghatola supplied the entirety when the two women sat alone on the kitchen floor one afternoon. The children were in the street, the aunt and grandmother were at the market, Durkhani was outside cutting Gharsanay's hair.

"Badrai had a room of her own," Ghatola said, lighting a cigarette. "Why? Because the rest of the family knew she was an addict and liked her out of the way. She said she felt ill that night and as usual she asked for Zaituna and I to sit with her. The men took us over there – weren't pleased about it, but never are about anything - and as soon after we sat down by her mattress, she stopped breathing. Pulse, heart, nothing.

"'Zaituna.' I said, 'sneak out and fetch Ambrin'. Luckily, the men were elsewhere by now, I don't know doing what, who cares. Anyway, we each put a knife in Badrai's chest. I insisted, me, it was all my idea. Afterwards, I hid them, the knives, in my burkha and Zaituna and I came out and asked to go home, leaving Ambrin still in there. She pretended to be Badrai when her husband said goodnight, then climbed out the window - probably having puppies, you know what she's like.

"I re-entered the room the same way, through the window. When I was sure the family was asleep, I did Badrai's morning chores and dragged her corpse into the courtyard. I replaced the bloody blankets, took the soiled ones home and burned them, and planted the knife on Faridun. Finally, I returned home and got into bed with my husband. I'd put something in his tea ages before to make sure he slept. End of dull story."

Reshtina sat for several moments, looking at her fingers.

"Don't you want to know why I did it?" Ghatola said.

"I suppose Faridun must have done something to you. Something you didn't want your husband to know about."

"Good guess."

"Did he ... make advances to you?"

Ghatola laughed. "He'd have died a lot sooner if he had."

Reshtina shrugged. "Then I don't know. You must have had something against him."

"He was desperate to marry you, did you know that?"

She felt herself blush. "I heard he'd asked Gharsanay. Is that why you killed him?"

"Partly," Ghatola replied. "Of all my lovers, you're my favourite. You're worth more than Zaituna, Ambrin and poor, pathetic Badrai put together. Zaituna tells me you threw the knife away."

"It's what she told me to do."

"Have you thought of going to retrieve it? It'll have your fingerprints on, which may not be a problem now, but if the Kandahar police decide to get involved, they'll easily be able to make a match. There can't be any more than fifteen hundred people in this village."

Reshtina took a deep breath. As usual, Ghatola saw well ahead.

"Part of the reason I did it," Ghatola went on, "was to implicate you four. It's a Russian idea, I believe: unity through corruption. We're even closer now we share this guilty secret. We may not have murdered Badrai, but we certainly killed Faridun." She gathered Reshtina's hands and kissed them. "Who cares, anyway? I love you more than I've ever loved anyone or anything. If I could, I'd cut a gash in my side and sew you in so tightly you'd never be able to escape. And all day long you'd have to listen to my thumping heart."

Reshtina was excited and horrified at the same time. She forgot about Faridun. "But – but I'll *have* to marry soon. I can't stay single for ever!"

"Your stinking brother-in-law then. You must relish the idea. I know Durkhani's looking forward to it," she added sarcastically.

"But I'm just a widow, a nobody. I haven't any choice - "

"I've taken care of it."

It took a second to sink in. "What?"

"Tomorrow, Balay's coming to make Gharsanay an offer - "

"*Balay?*"

"Don't look so appalled, Reshtina. This is my husband we're talking about. Anyway, it's not Balay you're going to marry. Apart from anything else, the demands of another wedding night would probably kill him. No, he's received an offer from my cousin. Anoushirvan's your age and he's homosexual, so there's no need to have relations with him, you don't even have to splash goat's blood on the sheets, because you're a widow. He knows how you stand - "

Reshtina laughed nervously. "But I don't want to be married to a homosexual. I want children."

"And we'll *get* you children, my beauty. There are plenty of men available to do that. But they'll be *our* children, don't you see?"

"I – I'm not sure - "

17

Ghatola wiped away Reshtina's tear. "It's already been decided, sweetness. You don't have a choice."

"Oh. Oh, yes, I see." It happened every day, of course it did.

"Balay always gets his own way, and Gharsanay won't dare stand up to him. Now, marriage is always a big step, but there are a lot of pluses. You'll have to live in a big city, because Anoushirvan's lifestyle is difficult enough as it is: in a village it'd be impossible. But we'll see each other every weekend. Look, Balay's eighty. He hasn't long left, and I might be a big shot now, but I'm childless. When he dies, his sons are going to clean his house out and throw me into the gutter. Then we'll run away together, okay? Somewhere far, far away. Somewhere European maybe, where they'll accept us for what we are."

"If that's true, why can't we go now?" Reshtina put her head in her hands. She didn't want to say everything that was on her mind. She wasn't even sure she was a lesbian. She liked the affection, and she loved Ghatola and Zaituna and Ambrin, but could she live a completely homosexual life? She didn't know.

Ghatola was having difficulty restraining her own tears. "Because there are still men like Faridun around."

"I don't understand."

"I'm going to tell you everything now. I used to be a teacher in a girls' school in Balochistan. In 2008, it was blown up by the Haqqani network. No casualties, just the building and the books, not that they'd care either way. I don't have any relatives nearby. The people Balay thinks are my relatives are all members of the Afghan Women's Reparation Brigade or its sympathisers."

"The what?"

"It's a civil war, Reshtina. Gender against gender. Faridun isn't the first man I've killed and, Allah willing, he won't be the last. My only regret is that I didn't use the other two knives to nail his slimy little friends. But it's too late now."

Reshtina wasn't feeling at all what she should be. She felt elated.

18

"And now I want you to fight alongside me," Ghatola said, as if she'd thrown away her last chance of sympathy but these were the words she'd practised. They emerged in a croak.

Reshtina picked up her hands and looked deep into her friend's eyes. Outside, the children argued, an old woman scolded them. Argue, scold, argue, scold, tears. A cool breeze drifted beneath the doorway.

"God is great," she said calmly. "I will."

Chapter 3: A Marriage of Convenience

Reshtina dressed in green and white. She sat still while her female relatives put kohl on her eyelids, henna on her hands, slipped borrowed bracelets onto her wrists and rings on her fingers. She travelled to Kandahar by bus accompanied by Balay and Ghatola, a sullen-looking Gharsanay, Durkhani, Zaituna's and Ambrin's families, and six of Balay's labourers, his bodyguards for the occasion. The Majestic Hotel, their destination, was a four-storey turbaza, built during the Soviet occupation on the northernmost outskirts of the town. The bus crawled and the harsh scenery was mostly hidden by billows of dust.

Anoushirvan, the groom, was thin and pock-marked. His sticking-out hair, regular taper cut and pointy beard made his head seem triangular. His fingers left the sleeves of his jacket like wires. Such was his aura of unwholesome frailty, Reshtina wondered if he might be ill. Not that it mattered, since they were never going to have sex. He smiled when he first met her. He asked disinterestedly how her journey had been, then, exactly six minutes later, they entered a room with his father and mother and an even more dejected Gharsanay and Durkhani, and signed the *nikah*, the marriage contract. The mullah held the Qur'an over their heads and recited an Ayah from Surah 30: "Among His proofs is that He created for you spouses from among yourselves, in order to have peace and contentment with each other, and He placed in your hearts love and care towards your spouses. In this, there are sufficient proofs for people who think."

Anoushirvan's family was so wealthy the whole of Kandahar seemed to be at the *Walimah* party. The couple sat side by side on a yellow chaise longue mounted on a dais at the front of the hall while the guests brought them presents for a full thirty minutes. They performed the tradition of looking at each other in a mirror. Reshtina noticed he looked bored and a little contemptuous.

Afterwards, the men sat on one side and the women on the other. A group of musicians at the front played the Ashesta Boro and Agar Sabza Boodam and at eight-twenty, five of the younger women got up to dance and show off their dresses while a nineteen year-old seamstress from Aybak painted Reshtina's toenails. The chandeliers glistened, the air filled with cologne and Chanel. Ninety minutes later, the buffet admitted the guests to all imaginable pilaus with every combination of chicken, lamb and eggplant, and at eleven-thirty, the married couple retired to bed.

The bridal suite overlooked the tennis court illumined by a harvest moon and gilded silhouettes of the far mountains. There was a double bed with a canopy, an ensuite bathroom, a dresser and TV, all in pastel blue and cream, the same colours as the carpet.

The gun was under the mattress like Ghatola had said. Reshtina changed into gloves and shalwar kameez, descended two floors via the internal fire escape onto a spot-lit corridor, and slipped into the first door on the left. She strode across a worn Persian rug, aimed the barrel at a grey-haired, bearded man as he fumbled with his shoelaces, and pulled the trigger. A string of blood shot out of the front of his head and sprayed the bedclothes. Breathing heavily, she tossed the gun on his corpse and retraced her steps until she was back in her room. In the ensuite, she doused her face in cold water.

Five minutes later, she tried to climb in bed with her new husband but he shrank and stood up. "You sleep on the floor," he said.

She found a fleece and coiled up on it. She waited for him to throw her a blanket, but nothing came. She put her clothes back on and got some sheets from the wardrobe.

"How did it go?" he asked her sleepily after about twenty minutes.

"Satisfactorily," she replied. She hoped it was the right man. But she had a feeling it was. Somewhere, she'd seen him before. As she went to sleep, she reflected that the Americans or the British would probably get the blame – he was almost certainly on one or both of their Most Wanted lists - and there might even be reprisals. But she didn't care about that. She hated the Americans and the British.

The next night, Anoushirvan left her alone and went out to an assignation. And the night after. She realised that this was how it was going to be until Balay died now – if she was lucky - but also that it was what she'd signed up for.

Anoushirvan's home was a sixth-floor flat in Aina Mena overlooking a strip of wasteland and a chicken coop, with a bed for himself and a cot for her. He went out every night to meet his lover, confiding his woes to Reshtina when things went wrong. Otherwise, he was silent. He expected his meals cooked and brought to the table, his bath run, his bed made, his washing done, his cigarettes lit. But he didn't beat her nor did she ever wake up wondering how, given what had happened to her eyes, bones and skin, she was still alive. She was merely a slave, and in this sense, happier than some wives she knew of.

Ghatola came to Kandahar every weekend. Anoushirvan diverted Balay while the two women lay in bed or went shooting. Their walking out alone wasn't as scandalous here as in the country, and they soon discovered that, if they chose a man at random, shadowed him three blocks, then switched to another, they could obviate even this peccadillo.

Their targets were always men who murdered women as a warning to other women. Their routine hardly varied. (1) A chadri for the gunshot, then run into the doorway of a public building; (2) remove chadri to reveal second-level disguise - a man with beard; (3) enter said building, wash, change, apply make-up, let hair down, leave via the entrance, a glamorous Western-style woman. For indoor killings they took turns, one the lookout, the other the assassin. The pistols always came through Ghatola, different makes and models according to the task in hand: front loading, fixed cylinder, top break, single action, double action, automatic, semi automatic, with or without silencers. Reshtina never met Ghatola's contacts, nor did Ghatola ever encourage her interest. Six months after the wedding, they'd killed twelve men between them. They celebrated with a ginger cake.

Everyone commented on how marriage had changed Reshtina, no one ever said for better or worse. Ghatola considered it simple but unsettling: she'd assumed the queen's mantle. As Ghatola had eclipsed Zaituna, so Reshtina had eclipsed Ghatola. Some weekends she even felt afraid of her. Her plan that they elope after Balay's death started to fade. It was too difficult to imagine Reshtina living without violence. At some deep level no one had discerned till now, hatred clung to her like rain to dry soil.

Yet nor could Ghatola imagine living without her.

Twice, she hypnotised her to discover where the malignity's source lay, but she couldn't reach behind the drone attack. Of that time, all Reshtina said was gibberish. According to Balay, who had it from Garsanay, who had it from the village elders who'd dumped her on his doorstep, it had taken her two days to regain consciousness after the blast. She had to be told what her name was, who the dead were, what a drone was, the meaning of the Shahadah, how to go to the toilet, wash, boil water. Her wounds became infected, so she perched on the border-wire of death for a further fortnight. All things considered, it was a miracle she was still alive, let alone fit to re-marry.

The second time she put her under hypnosis, Ghatola was tempted by Shaytan. She'd been his handmaid so long she'd forgotten how to resist, so she asked Reshtina if she was in love. When she replied with her usual string of baby-talk, Ghatola brought her round and sat looking out of the window, blank-eyed, smoking a Marlboro. Reshtina asked her what was wrong, Ghatola told her and they argued. That night, the two couples – Balay and Ghatola, Anoushirvan and Reshtina – went to a Sufi gathering in a second floor apartment in Zoar Shar, the two women still at odds. The sheikh retold the story of Ibrahim's temptation by Iblis, and during the Allah Hu, Ghatola wept so hard they had to bring her away.

The next day, one of her regular contacts from the Afghan Women's Reparation Brigade called her mobile. The

Taliban had found her guilty of the murder of Faridun and they were planning to ambush Balay's chauffeur-driven Corolla just before he reached home. What they would then do to her was both complicated, insofar as it would involve lots of stages, and simple, in that it could only have one ending. Balay had already been informed through other, equally concerned, channels.

Ghatola knew her husband. He was bullish enough to relish the challenge. He'd imagine he could buy in lots of mercenaries, go on the counter-attack and give them a taste of their own medicine.

Her suspicions were confirmed when she came home to find him sitting on his bed in the wallpapered room Anoushirvan had supplied for their stay-over, holding court with two men she'd never seen before, both young, vicious-looking and solemn. They looked at her as if she was intruding.

"Have you something to tell me?" she asked her husband.

"What do you mean?" he asked.

"I heard in the market the Taliban are planning to attack us."

Balay looked as if he'd been stung by an insect. "Wait outside," he told the two men.

When they'd closed the door behind them, he gestured for his wife to sit on the floor. She obeyed.

"Who told you?" he asked.

"Someone I've never seen before. A woman. It's true, isn't it?"

"There's nothing to worry about," he replied. "It's taken care of. As far as they know, we don't suspect a thing. I'm going to unleash the forces of hell on them."

Ghatola put her head in her hands.

"What's the alternative?" he said. "We can't run away. Where could we go?"

She sighed. "Are we fighting because we think we're going to win, or because we've no alternative?"

"Both."

"You realise it's me they're after? They think I'm responsible for Faridun's murder."

"And are you?"

"No!"

"You were the only eyewitness. The other boys you said you saw carrying those knives are still around. If they feel aggrieved, maybe that's because - "

"I *did* see them!"

He shrugged and smiled. "I must admit, I had my suspicions at the time. Never mind, it suited my purposes to get rid of the slimy bastard too. Anyway, it's irrelevant because it's gone way beyond that now. It's a family uprising."

"I'm not sure I follow."

"The Taliban want you dead because of Faridun. My sons want both of us dead because they're tired of waiting for the house and all that goes with it. And they're all working together."

Her heart fell over. "Then – then we're finished! We can't possibly stand up against all of them!"

"Not through force alone, I admit. Cunning has to play its part."

"Sorry, I'm not following."

"What do you really think of Anoushirvan's wife?"

There were so many twists in this conversation, her head felt airy. "Reshtina? What's she - "

"Because I think she's a bad influence on you. And Anoushirvan says she's disrespectful to him too. Anyway, you can wave goodbye to her."

"What do you mean?"

"No one in the Taliban knows what you look like. She's going to stand in for you, and hopefully they'll stone her so hard she'll be unrecognisable. Anoushirvan's agreed, because I'm the only one who can save his life. Turns out he's queer. Garsanay's been watching him, believe it or not. Now don't get me wrong, Ghatola, that sort of thing's all right when you're a young man, unmarried maybe, but he's a newlywed, for God's sake. Anyway, I've put it out all over the city, so the mujahideen are on their way to get him as we speak."

"Oh, my God."

He chuckled. "Don't worry, it won't come to that. I happen to know there's a vacancy for a warlord's *batcha* in Daykundi. It won't be quite the lifestyle the greasy bastard's been used to, and it's the opposite of what he deserves, but Ustad Abdul Baru will give him what he's been used to and more. Anyway, Reshtina should pacify the Taliban. Which just leaves my sons." He laughed. "They'll shit themselves when they realise their backup's all gone."

She got to her feet, still reeling. "When you say she's 'going to stand in for me' ... "

"I don't mean she knows. No, I've got some friends coming round tonight to bind and gag her. They'll cut her tongue out first, because we don't want her denying she's you, and that'll mean putting her to sleep so she doesn't bite any fingers off. Anoushirvan's department, that. His brother's a doctor. Until then, keep out of her way. After this has all blown over, we'll pretend you're someone else and we'll 're-marry'. It'll be as if it never happened."

She sat down on the rug again, feeling she'd faint if she didn't put more of her viscera closer to the floor.

Balay got up. "You just stay here. Try to get some sleep. The next twenty-four hours are going to be very busy. And don't fret. I've looked it over from every angle. Nothing can go wrong. And don't brood on Reshtina. She should probably have died in that bomb attack on her village. She survived for this, if you ask me. It's God's will."

If she never heard another man talking about 'God's will' again, it would be too soon. She waited till he'd left the room, counted to twenty and tried the door. Then again.

Locked.

Of course, why wouldn't it be?

She had to have a cigarette. Waves of nausea swept over her like blasts of acrid air and she wasn't even sure a chestful of nicotine would help. She opened the window in case she needed to vomit. Bloody hell, the cigarettes weren't in the wardrobe. Never mind, she needed a plan, a plan.

The room contained the wardrobe, a bed and side-table - where the Marlboro were, thank God - a rug and a large tilt window with white curtains. Whatever her scheme, it would have to involve some combination of these. And there was a sensor in the corner, too small for a camera, and what would a camera be doing in here anyway?

Then her pulse raced. Obviously not a camera, stupid. A smoke alarm.

She gathered all the chadris from the cupboard, piled them up next to the door and thrust the lighter beneath them. They caught fire as if they'd been made for it, and she took the bedclothes and heaped them on, then pushed the wardrobe over.

In a minute the alarm would sound and if they didn't think to rescue her, the door would burn down and she'd be free. She lit a cigarette and moved over to the window so she wouldn't choke. It was a long way down and jumping wasn't an option.

But suddenly, it wasn't just a bonfire any more. The wardrobe had caught now – everything was happening at three or four times the speed she'd anticipated - and flames crept along the floor as if they were chewing the rug up and spitting it out red hot. She screamed – part of her plan from the start, but much easier now she was actually frightened. The alarm began to sound and the door caved outwards, taking the fire with missionary zeal into Anoushirvan's hallway. She could hear men shouting and suddenly a bucketful of water came into the room like a joke. It fizzled and the flames ate it as if it was a delicacy. She screamed again.

What had she done? Suddenly, its whole horror sank in. She'd set an entire building alight and the only way she wasn't going to get cooked was if she threw herself out of the window, which was suicide. She'd have to climb through the inferno if she was to survive. Then what?

The ceiling was on fire now. She coughed and retched and tried to huddle into herself. A fireball leapt across the room and set the curtains alight. She yowled in terror and suddenly she could only stop screaming to resume coughing. At the same time, she was getting woozy and all she could think of was Reshtina.

That was what all this was for: Reshtina. She had to attempt an exit, then find her.

She threw herself at the doorway and clambered over the scorching embers into what she thought would be safety. But the fire was out here as well and she'd already been in it too long. She felt her clothes on fire and her flesh blistering like a mad itch. The whole hallway was ablaze, but at its end she could see Reshtina shrieking at her.

She tried to run but buckled. It suddenly struck her that she was probably close to death and no human could help her any more. She cried out to Allah and the words of the al-Fatihah – those read to all good Muslims on their deathbeds - rang through her head over and over. She fainted.

Then she was in the corridor. Six men she'd never seen before were carrying her downstairs in a panic, while Reshtina – looking sooty and ragged, but no worse – was patting her hand tearfully, bouncing alongside as they took the stairs awkwardly and saying what sounded like a du'a prayer.

She had to get them to stop. They'd take her to Balay or Anoushirvan, then it would be too late. She started to wriggle and scream, making the men bellow indignantly.

She heard Reshtina order them to put her down, next an altercation – she could see smoke wending its way down from the upper floors, it was no wonder they wanted to get a move on – then they put her down grudgingly on one of the landings.

Reshtina knelt over her and kissed her. Then she apparently realised what was wanted. She put her head close again. Ghatola brushed the hair aside and whispered directly into her ear.

"You've got - to get away now. Balay's going - going to kidnap you. And hand you over. To the Taliban. It's all - arranged. I can't tell you – any - more, but you'll die. If you don't run away. It's why - why I started the fire. There's a gun and some ammunition. Waiting for you in - Shahre Naw, thirty-two - Ashraf Hotaki. They - know who you are. Now, go."

Reshtina drew back and looked at her as if she thought she might be delirious.

"*Go!*" Ghatola screamed.

Only when she was absolutely sure she was being obeyed did she allow herself to slip from consciousness again.

Balay stood by his car with his hands on his hips glowering at the ground when the rescuers laid his wife before him. He looked at her and sneered. His chauffeur leaned on the bonnet. Two young men in grey shalwaar kameez and turbans slouched next to a motorbike, smoking cheroots. In front of them, Anoushirvan's block of flats billowed thick wreaths of black and grey smoke.

"Looks like the queer might have burned to death," one of the mujahideen said, as the rescuers turned around and dispersed, apparently put out at not having been thanked.

"Saves us a job," the other said. He chuckled.

Balay let out a cry of rage, making the others jump. He booted his wife in the side as she lay moaning, then he spat on her and kicked her repeatedly until she rolled over.

"It'll *have* to be her now," he said. "Stupid, *stupid* bitch! I should have known. Get her in the car then, no point in hanging around. The Taliban can do what they damn well like to her, it's nothing to do with me any more. She's a disgrace to her sex. When all this is over we'll come back for her friend and we'll see to her ourselves. She'll wish she'd never been born too."

Chapter 4: The Rescue Mission

Kandahar International Airport

Four senior officers in combat fatigues – three Americans and a Briton - scoured a map on a table in a windowless room lit by a strip lamp. A fifth, more junior, stood straighter than each and tried unsuccessfully to engage them in eye-contact as he answered their questions. The room smelt of sweat.

"It's unlikely they'll be out in numbers," the Briton said.

"How extensive is his bodyguard?" asked one of the Americans.

The junior officer turned square to face the questioner and spoke in an Oklahoma accent. "According to our source, he rarely travels with more than six armed men, sir."

The door opened and a US Colonel entered, a tall man with grey hair and a lined face. The others turned and saluted. He removed his hat and stood over the map as if he wasn't sure whether it was time to start examining it.

"Fill me in," he said.

"It began about an hour ago, sir," the junior officer said. "A local man called Anoushirvan Sarbanri arrived at one of our checkpoints accompanied by his brother, one of our approved medics, seeking our protection from persecution for his ... sexual orientation. In return, he said he had information regarding a Taliban ambush on a local chieftan just north of here. Nothing remarkable so far, but if the victims are people working for us, we thought it might be politic to get involved on some level. Anyway, we took him to one of our secure units in the old town and showed him the usual missing persons files, as per protocol, while we did the checks and prepared our report. It turns out the ambush is targeted at a British agent" – he put a photograph on the table – "who disappeared on active service a year ago, presumed dead."

"Name?"

"Marciella Hartley-Brown."

"How does our source know her then?"

"He's married to her."

The colonel flicked his eyebrows and a grin, as if this was a story too far. "No shit."

The junior officer put three more photographs on the table, side by side. "These are the wedding photographs his brother took six months ago. That's her, there."

The colonel swiped them up and looked at them, tucking them beneath each other till he'd completed the loop. "Uncanny, I admit. Of course, it may simply be a matter of some people look like some other people. What else have you got?"

"Only that the Taliban are apparently desperate to get their hands on her, sir. We've checked his story from our other sources. And we've satellite pictures of a large group of insurgents accompanied by six known ISI operatives moving in from Pakistan. He's not bluffing."

"I'm missing something. What's wrong with her? If she's alive, why hasn't she contacted us?"

"We don't know. We're guessing she may be suffering from amnesia. It's - "

"Bullshit. How and when did she go missing, Lieutenant?"

"A drone attack on the village she was working in, sir. The CIA didn't know the Brits had operatives in there, apparently it wasn't told."

The colonel scoffed. "So much for 'intelligence must be intelligent'."

"She was posing as the third wife of one of NATO's best sources. The source himself was killed, and we assumed his three wives were too. We haven't been able to penetrate the area to do forensics, so we can't be certain. It is possible she could have survived."

"Maybe she's gone native."

"Working for the Taliban, you mean?"

The colonel smiled sourly. "We both know this country well enough to recognise that, however much we may despise them, the Taliban aren't its worst nightmare."

"She married Anoushirvan Sarbanri, an urban office-clerk, sir. If she was intent on ingratiating herself with a warlord like Saleh or Baru, she could probably have done so. She has the skills."

"'Has' or 'had'? Are we so certain this is her?"

"Sir, it's difficult to imagine how it might go down in London and Washington if we decide not to mount a rescue operation, and we later discover we made a mistake. Her father's a member of the British Parliament."

The colonel swallowed air. "I wasn't suggesting – wait, are you making fun of me, Lieutenant?"

"No, sir. Absolutely not, sir."

A few moments passed in which no one knew what thunderbolts might pass from the palms of the colonel to the naked heart of the lieutenant, then the colonel decided to let it pass. "Sounds like it was our drone that caused the trouble. On the other hand, the British should have told us. Group Captain, you'll need to provide helicopters. We'll cover the ground."

The Briton nodded, as if this was such a given his mother had told him it at birth, then all six fell to discussing the finer points of the map.

Garsanay sat in his living room polishing his rifle while Durkhani darned the hole in their youngest son's trousers. The children sat in the corner, playing with a box of marbles. Their grandmother had gone to bed only a few minutes earlier. Outside, it was dusk.

"Be careful," Durkhani said for the fourth time. She yelped as the needle slipped and pricked her finger.

"Where's Daddy going?" the youngest girl asked again.

"Just *out*," Gharsanay said tetchily. "Stop asking."

Durkhani sucked her finger and looked at it. "I don't know why Balay can't just stay in Kandahar a bit longer. He must have contacts there."

"Not like he has here."

"Assuming he even makes it back home."

"That's the whole point, woman. If he does, he can bargain from a position of strength – he's always got favours to call in – and maybe even talk them out of it. They must have made a mistake. They're the Taliban. They're not unreasonable."

"What if they haven't?"

Gharsanay expelled his breath through his teeth as if this was no time for academic questions. "You weren't at the shurah, neither was Ghatola. How the hell could a *woman* be to blame for something like Faridun's death, anyway?"

She sighed. "She's not normal."

"She's the *qaryadar*, so you don't like her. Anyone who does that job mustn't care about being unpopular. And you know how women are. They're each other's worst enemies. You're no different."

"She isn't a good person, Gharsanay. I don't know why she arranged Faridun's death, but I'm fairly sure she did."

"Do you also know *how*?" he asked sarcastically, pulling his boots on.

"She was the only one who saw him. What if she was lying? Faridun's friends would know that, and they'd want revenge."

He stood up and grabbed his gun. "What are you trying to prove? Are you trying to weaken my resolve, make me think I should leave Balay to his fate?"

"If Ghatola really is to blame, they won't rest till they've got her. They'll keep coming back. And if you stand in their way, they'll get you too."

She was right, of course. She always was. He wondered if Reshtina would be as concerned for his welfare when they were married. Or as perceptive. Despite everything – all his spying on Anoushirvan, on Reshtina, all his mad jealousy, his sterile night-lusts - maybe he'd be better off sticking with what he'd got. Even now, all he had was the ambush and his rifle. Useful conditions for a murder, but only if they were properly used. He still wasn't sure he could manoeuvre Durkhani to a place he'd be able to dispatch her.

Balay tied what was left of his wife up and sent word, through men he knew were in contact with the Taliban, that he was happy to hand her over unconditionally. To be on the safe side, he hired six empty gravel trucks with reinforced sides, and fifty gunmen. After attaching two white flags to each cabin – the Taliban's known ensign, symbolising purity - they started out at dusk for his village, minus headlights. Luckily, the moon was full and the sky was relatively cloudless.

They were within two miles of his destination when two men in black turbans stepped into the convoy's path with their palms out. He breathed a sigh of relief. They'd got his message. He reached under the dashboard for the gifts – six flagons of orange juice and a basket of cakes, not that they couldn't buy such things themselves anywhere, but gesture was everything – and stepped out of the cabin. As Khan, it was incumbent on him not just to be courageous and generous, but to demonstrate it.

He gave the order for his men to disembark, hands on heads, and the plain came alive as Taliban fighters – at least fifty, maybe as many as eighty – got to their feet and leisurely closed in.

"Bring her out!" Balay shouted as theatrically as he could. In these sorts of cases effect was of the essence.

Ghatola's body – dead or alive now, no one knew – was dragged from the middle truck by three of Balay's henchmen, and tossed into no man's land between the two sides. It looked like an elongated sack. The men replaced their hands on their heads and backed away as slowly as dignity allowed.

Then there was a sustained crackling whose significance everyone recognised at once, and which, as usual, immobilised them for a second, redoubling its effects. Of the fifty or so Taliban, Balay saw at least three quarters slump or lunge backwards. Men screamed. Others whiplashed in silence like a cobra had snapped their throats. No one knew how or from where, but suddenly a helicopter approached, then descended. Americans poured out, shooting methodically. Balay crawled under one of the trucks as the firing went on.

Then to his astonishment, he saw what they were up to. They grabbed Ghatola, six of them, and knelt down. Six more arrived with a stretcher and eased her onto it. All twelve crouched down solicitously, then bore her onto the helicopter. Someone shouted. Its rotors roared louder, it ascended, and it was gone.

The firing continued for some time. This would go down in the annals of the enemy as a stupendous victory, and in those of the Taliban as a blank. When, after about an hour, he was sure it was safe, he crawled out.

He swallowed his bile and felt himself vindicated. So she'd been working for the enemy all along!

But then he realised how that would look.

The two brothers, Anoushirvan and Aarmaan Sarbanri, sat on a bench in the second-floor room of the office-block they'd reached in company with two US soldiers through a tunnel and a series of staircases one hour ago. The floorboards were stained and loose, the white paint on the walls was flaking, six hardboard ceiling tiles hung at an angle as if they might drop at any time. This was the waiting room. The conference room - where the Americans discussed the trustworthiness of Anoushirvan's witness statement, presumably – was on the other side of a glass door with Arabic letters etched into it. He stood up and told his brother he had to go to the toilet.

Aarmaan grunted his acknowledgement. They'd hardly made eye-contact since coming in.

It was obvious why. Anyone's guess how violently the rest of the family would react. They'd probably say Aarmaan should have killed him as soon as he learned. Instead, he'd accompanied him to some sort of safety.

So what, he had other things to consider. Balay's men were probably slaying his lover right now, making him want to retch and cry at the same time. He prayed to Allah that Reshtina would massacre the bastards with her bare hands.

It made sense of a sort, her an American spy. What sort of a woman knowingly marries a homosexual? Answer: one whose interests lie outside marriage. For the first time, he felt proud of her. He'd never thought about her much before. Odd, given that she was his wife. One more cause for regret.

He knew the Americans couldn't be relied on to give him long-term sanctuary, whatever they promised. Reshtina was probably dead already, so she couldn't help him, and he'd run dry of things they wanted to hear. No matter, at least he'd done some good – assuming they'd actually listened to him, and - small hope - Reshtina was still alive to be rescued.

Now it was time to resume responsibility for his own destiny.

He walked down past the toilet into the street – as part of its cloak the building was guarded only against entrants, not leavers – and, fifteen minutes later, climbed three flights of moulded concrete stairs to his lover's apartment by Kokaran Park.

The door stood ajar. The corpse of the man he'd re-clined alongside during six evenings out of every seven for the last two years lay face-down on the bed, naked, punctured and bloody. Save that the assassins were long gone, everything was roughly as he'd expected.

He left the room, and doggedly climbed the remaining ten flights of stairs. On the final landing, he climbed the main-tenance ladder, pushed open the trapdoor and hauled himself onto the building's flat roof.

In the sun and the warm, clean breeze, he gazed around at the horizon, savouring the peculiar beauty of Kandahar's landscape on all four sides. The hills shimmered as if they were melting. The trees whispered to each other about everything they saw and heard and felt that no human could. Above him, a shelf of hard azure.

Exquisite! No one knew Afghanistan like he did! It was the most beautiful place on earth and nothing Allah offered in the hereafter could possibly compare with its tiniest, most ragged morsel.

Still, no good to be thinking that. Too late, far too late for thinking, all exits sealed but one.

He strode to the parapet and threw himself off.

Gharsanay arrived on the battlefield a split second too late to be of any use to anyone. He hit the ground as soon as he heard machine guns, lying static throughout the carnage and long afterwards, trying to stifle the sound of his breathing.

A helicopter swooped in, flew away and left a pro-longed silence during which he guessed the Americans were scouring the area with night-vision equipment. One man shouted from the easternmost edge of the combat zone – Gharsanay had seen something similar twice before, in different parts of Zabul – and another replied from the western. Ten minutes later two more helicopters arrived, much bigger. The troops boarded without incident and were gone.

Then he saw Balay emerge alone from beneath one of the trucks. It couldn't be anyone else. The outline of the eighty year-old Khan was unmistakable.

Gharsanay felt the adrenalin gallop to every part of his body. It was obvious Balay would have to leave the village now. Anyone who had a problem with the Taliban was sign-ing his death warrant by calling the Americans in. They'd be back for him post-haste.

... So if, say, he was to be found shot dead at home in the midst of his packing, everyone would 'know' what had happened. And if the murder weapon was one of those now strewn about the desert, that would end the matter.

But what about what the Qur'an said? If Gharsanay's understanding was correct, Allah didn't like murderers.

Maybe he'd got it wrong, though. Murder never seemed to bother the Taliban, and they were religious schol-ars.

Anyway, killing Balay was in everyone's interests. It would save the mujahideen a journey and thereby shield the village from their wrath. He – the valiant and noble Gharsanay – would have set out to protect his Khan. He tried to see the assassins off, but in spite of his efforts Balay was killed, and of course, poor Durkhani just happened to be caught in the crossfire. The gallant, tragic widower, of course he has to re-marry, a man of his standing, and with Anoushirvan out of the way, as he surely was now ...

He waited till Balay had covered a good five hundred metres, then prised an assault rifle from the stiffening hand of one of the corpses, put it under his arm next to his own gun, and set off in pursuit. The moon kept appearing and disappearing behind clouds, making Balay look as if he was a walking mirage. Just before they reached the village, the old man wheeled round to the right, a manoeuvre that would bring him to the rear of his house after a long detour through camel-thorn and laburnum. Presumably, he'd worked out that someone might already be lying in wait for him back home. Gharsanay took a left turn.

When he got in, Durkhani was sitting in the living room with a set of subha beads. She'd been crying. She ran over and hugged him.

"I couldn't go to bed," she said.

"It's not over," he said roughly. "We've got to go out."

"*We?* But what have *I* got to do with it?"

"We've got to go and protect Balay. All his men have been massacred and the Taliban are coming for him."

"All his men? What about Zaituna's husband? And Ambrin's?"

He shrugged. "They went too, did they? I didn't see them."

"How did you get away?"

"We haven't time for this. Just – here – take my gun and come with me."

She took the rifle as if it was a tube of volatile explosive and followed him into the street. He heard her behind him, breaking into little trots to keep up, and suddenly, miserably, against all his expectations, knew he couldn't kill her. Partly, it was her obedience. It would be like shooting a toddler.

Maybe she could be brought to accept Reshtina as his second wife, after all. At least she deserved a chance.

But he couldn't kill her even then. *Think not that Allah doth not heed the deeds of those who do wrong. He but giveth them respite against a day when the eyes will fixedly stare in horror.*

He was fifty. Too old to start going wrong, if he really knew what was best for him. *And those whom Allah hath cursed, thou wilt find, have no one to help.*

They were outside Balay's house now. A step further and it would be too late to turn back. He stopped and turned, causing Durkhani to bump into him with a little squeal.

"Go home," he said. "I shouldn't have asked you to come."

"But – but you didn't have any choice. You said: all the men Balay took with him are dead. There's no one else for you to call on."

"It's not a woman's job."

"You're my husband, our children's father. What becomes of us if you die?"

"I won't."

"I think we should kill Balay," she said.

It took him a moment to match the words to her. *"What?"*

"If we don't, his enemies will come looking for him. They'll want revenge. And if he's not here, they'll go on a killing spree. It's not just the Taliban, anyway. His own sons have turned against him. He hasn't even got any friends any more. What have we got to gain by allying ourselves with such a man?"

He slapped her across the head, making her fall. *"What's the matter with you? Haven't you any sense of loyalty?"*

She got to her feet, rubbing her scalp as if she'd been expecting this. "At least, come home," she croaked. "You've done what you could. Anything else is suicide."

He hesitated. There was undeniable logic in this. And since he wasn't going to murder her any more, the whole excursion was pointless, they might as well turn round.

But if they did, he'd look a coward. She wouldn't forget, she'd dredge it up every time they had a row.

Anyway, what about the Khan's other sons? "Balay has about twenty sons," he told her. "They can't all have turned against him."

She was weeping now. "Then leave him to them! He'll know where to go! It's a family thing! It's not our business any more!"

He sighed. He couldn't let himself be swayed by a female. He wished he'd thought of her objections before. Or that she was the sort of wife – he'd heard there were such, maybe Reshtina would be one – who had the decency to let you think *you'd* come upon her ideas first.

But it was too late now. Forward was the only way to salvage his honour. "Come on," he said. "We'll see what happens when we're inside the old man's house."

The door was ajar. It was dark within.

Then they saw two flashes and it was as if they'd been hit by something kind enough not to hurt too much.

Balay lit an oil lamp and bent over the corpses. They'd died cleanly, which was more than they deserved. Presumably, Gharsanay had seen the ambush, and he'd brought his good-for-nothing wife over to loot the place. They wouldn't have been carrying guns if they'd come to help.

He forgot about them in his haste to pack his belongings. He'd left his car in Kandahar – no way of retrieving it now - but he had a horse and six donkeys to hand. No one much bothered you if you were on a donkey, he'd take one of those. His brother would look after him for a while, up in Wardak. He'd decide what to do next after he was safe.

He thought he heard someone stir in the darkness and he raised his gun. But before he could squeeze the trigger, someone hit him. His last thought as he exited consciousness was that this was a shabby way to go, ambushed in the dark from behind. He didn't expect to come round again.

He was therefore surprised – he wasn't sure how much time had passed, but he was in agony – to awake in bright sunlight, sitting on a donkey. As the world came back into focus, he saw he was flanked by three women in identical black chadris, also on donkeys. For all the world, the four of them were travelling together. He had no idea who the women were, or where any of them were, other than that a plain extended to a range of mountains in the distance. He tried to scream, but he couldn't open his mouth. The pain was so intense his body began to jerk involuntarily and he fell off his mount.

The last thing her recalled was one of the women punching him.

Chapter 5: Nangial

When Ghatola explained about Balay and shouted *go*, Reshtina realised both their fates lay in doing exactly that, no questions. She half-ran, half-walked to where the older woman's gun supposedly awaited her, bobbing in and out of the shadows, attaching herself six paces behind a succession of men, keeping her head down to make herself small. Her heart banged, her breathing accelerated, her mouth became clammy.

Ashraf Hotaki: one of the high-rise blocks in Shahre Naw, the newer part of the city. Thirty-two, on the third floor, was the last flat in a concrete corridor with lights in protective cages. It smelt of cigarette butts and bleach. She took off her chadri and bundled it under her arm, ran her hand nervously across her hair, knocked.

A dark-skinned woman in a cloak answered and stood leisurely to one side. "You must be Reshtina Sarbanri," she said in a Pakistani accent. She showed no surprise. She was about forty-five, thin and hunched but not small. "I'm Saira Mohammad. Please come in."

"I need a gun," Reshtina said. This wasn't the time for introductions.

"Go through into the living room and sit down. I've just made some tea."

She brushed past her into the hallway. "Ghatola - Rahman - said you had a gun. I need it now or they're going to kill her."

"Relax. Your husband's gone to the Americans. He's probably told them everything he knows, which, since he's a lynchpin in Khan Balay's plan, is probably enough for them to save her. Or try to. You see, we're fairly sure they know what she is."

"Ghatola? How do you mean?"

"She's a top-level assassin, just like you. She knows things the Americans probably don't and which they'd certainly like to. I imagine they'll think they can co-opt her. So not only will they cross the seven mouths of hell to rescue her, they'll also treat her like royalty."

"I'm not a 'top-level' anything. I hardly even know who I work for."

Saira Mohammad gave a condescending smirk. "Not very bright then, are you?"

"Are you going to give me that gun or not?"

They stood in a cool, brown-painted hallway with a pine telephone table and a wall mirror. Saira Mohammad turned round without answering and walked through the farthest door, forcing Reshtina to follow.

The room they emerged in contained a sofa, two wooden chairs, a TV and a sleeping bag in the corner. A quartered window framed the Mosque of the Hair of the Prophet, and an Arabic-inscribed plaque indicated what was presumably the *Qibla*, the direction of Mecca. A man of about forty with a fundamentalist's beard, expensive clothes and oiled hair sat on the sofa with a glass of tea in his lap. He was the only other person in the room, and, Reshtina guessed, the whole flat. He gazed at her as she entered in a way she couldn't read. It wasn't hostility. Lust?

Two cups stood next to a teapot on the top of the TV. Saira Mohammad filled them.

"Milk?" she asked. "Sugar?

Reshtina waved her hand dismissively and turned about. "I have to leave. If you're not going to give me that gun - "

She heard a rifle cock behind her and she froze.

"Sit down and have some tea," Saira Mohammad said, firmly. "You'll enjoy it. It's *zhu cha,* what the English call 'gunpowder'."

Reshtina turned round. The bearded man pointed a rifle at her and sipped his tea. "I've heard a lot about you," he said. He put his glass down and wiped his mouth. "Now, little girl, I don't want to shoot, but it would be kinder than letting you fall into the hands of the mullahs, which is what will happen if we give you a Makarov and set you free."

The voice didn't fit the speaker. It was about fifteen years too young.

Realising, in any case, that she was trapped, Reshtina sat on one of the wooden chairs, and Saira Mohammad thrust the cup in her lap. Why were they so eager for her to drink? Made sense to think they'd laced it with something: they were holding her at gunpoint, after all.

"Just out of interest," Saira Mohammad said, "do you have a plan?"

Reshtina shrugged. No comment.

"Balay has to be heading home by now," the man said. "I imagine Reshtina thinks she'll overtake him and kill him if necessary."

Saira Mohammad laughed. "Just like that? Some idea."

"What's wrong with it?" the man asked.

"How does she intend to travel? By car? Steal a motorbike? Because a lone woman in the driver's seat of anything isn't a common sight round here. They'll probably spot her a mile off. Even assuming, by some miracle, they don't, how does she intend to deal with Balay's bodyguards? Or his assailants? Because she'll have to get through both of them to get to him."

"It's only Ghatola she wants," the man said.

"Come, come, the same applies."

Reshtina sighed and saw the matter with fresh eyes. Of course they were right. "But I can't just sit here, drinking your stupid tea," she said.

"Yet you see our point?" the man asked rhetorically.

She nodded. The room became silent like a hole had opened. Reshtina saw Saira Mohammad nod almost imperceptibly to the man. He put his rifle on the sofa, stood up and began to remove his clothes.

So that was it. He was going to rape her, how sordid.

Well, he was in for a shock: she hadn't drunk anything yet and she was perfectly capable of taking his eyeballs to Jahannam with her. She began to look casually for makeshift weapons. His rifle was an obvious choice, but there was also the teapot and that mirror in the hallway. The TV screen, once smashed, would probably work. She wasn't sure she'd win, but she'd give them a run for their efforts.

"This isn't at all what you're thinking, my dear," Saira Mohammad said, sipping her *zhu cha*.

The man turned his back when he'd removed most of his clothes. He took off his underwear and socks – the final items – dropped them in a little pile with the rest of his things and turned to face them.

Reshtina took a second to adjust to what she was seeing. The bearded man wasn't a man at all. She was a woman.

"But ..."

"You'd never have believed it if we'd told you," Saira Mohammad said. "You had to see it with your own eyes. Just as everyone does when they have work to do and they're as important as you are. You can put your clothes on now, Nangial."

"It's a long story," Nangial said, as she re-dressed. "I was a *bacha posh* as a child. My parents used to dress me as a boy and treat me like one, and, as is customary, everyone in our village played along. Later on ... well, let's just say my husband regularly beat me and one day I shoved a nail through his eye. Obviously, I'm wanted by the authorities. He messed up my insides too. Not only can I not have children, I was actually incontinent for a while. Till Saira got me into hospital, that is." She guffawed. "The steroids come through my *hijra* friends in Lahore, incidentally. It's amazing how much better life gets when you grow a beard. If someone was to say to me, beard or breasts, I'd say amputate my breasts no hesitation: I'm holding on to the face-fur. In any case, there's no turning back now. I can get you some if you like."

"Nangial's one of eight of our 'escorts'," Saira Mohammad said. "So-called because they accompany our assassins to and from gigs. It deflects suspicion if you look respectable. And of course they're absolutely essential for long-distance commissions and rural areas."

"And now I'm going to escort *you*, my dear," Nangial said, finishing her tea and standing up. She picked up her rifle. "If Saira's right, the Americans intend to abduct Ghatola.

Which is bad news. Either she'll talk and they'll find out all about us – which exposes people like me to the possibility of blackmail or worse; or she won't talk and they'll slam her in Guantanamo; or they'll fail entirely and she'll end up in the hands of the Taliban, where again, she'll either talk or she won't. Four options, not one of which bears thinking about."

"So we're going to rescue her?"

"We'll do our best. Otherwise, we're going to kill her."

"What? But I - "

"It's what she would want," Saira Mohammad said. "There are my other women to think of, many. We've always known it might end this way. It's not for you to judge."

Reshtina gave the kind of smile that comes with conflicted emotions. Naturally it didn't matter if Nangial killed Ghatola if that was a last resort. If the rescue attempt failed, she wouldn't be left to see it. Otherwise …

"Can I have that gun now?" she said.

Nangial and Reshtina dressed as Talibs and Saira Mohammad wished them luck. They set off on a motorbike for Reshtina's village, arriving two streets away from Gharsanay's house just after dusk. They double-backed on foot to hide behind a rock they'd selected, two miles south of the settlement, where they knew Balay's convoy would pass. They'd overtaken it on their way in, when it had been too sunny to do anything. Reshtina had an Ots-33 handgun, Nangial a high velocity rifle. They sat in the shade and prepared for twenty minutes' wait, sharing a canteen of water.

"Ghatola and I talked of going west when Balay died," Reshtina said by way of passing the time. "She reckoned his other wives' sons hated her."

"Probably right. Often happens. You mean Iran, or Turkey?"

"Farther than that. Italy, maybe, or France. Perhaps even London."

Nangial smiled. "London's not a country, bonehead. Anyway, what do you want to go there for?"

"Because it's supposed to be not so bad for women."

"Sure. The men make us walk round naked in London, did you know that? In public. And that's 'not so bad', eh?"

"I didn't know."

She laughed. "It's just like here, of course. The men have invented something degrading for the women to do, and the women not only think they're doing it of their own accord, they think they invented it. The prettier ones get money for it, and maybe a husband. The plain ones can't even get husbands."

"You don't *have* to take your clothes off there, though, surely?"

"They sure as hell don't like it if you go round in a chadri, put it that way."

"Yes, but the chadri's ridiculous."

"You've killed quite a lot of nasty people in your time, Reshtina. How successful do you think you'd have been had it not been for that one specific garment?"

"It's got its uses, but it fills with dust, and you can hardly see – come on, you know that as well as I do!"

"What do you think it's natural for a woman to wear then?"

Reshtina frowned. "I don't know what you mean."

"The chadri and the niqab give us invisibility. They can't have been devised by men. You don't control slaves by putting them in interchangeable disguises. At some point in history, they must have been invented by oppressed women as a tool of engagement. They've just been turned against us, that's all."

Reshtina froze. "I heard something."

They forgot what they were talking about and got on their haunches. A man with a rifle, about five hundred metres to the west, slithering towards the road. And another, and another - scores of them. Taliban. Balay's convoy was just visible in the south, approaching at a crawl, decked with white flags.

"Shit," Nangial whispered. "Now what?"

"We're going to have to sneak past them and meet the convoy before they do. We're dressed as they are, after all.

There are lots of them, and it's not as if they're focussed on each other right now. We can probably do it."

"Then what?"

Reshtina frowned. "We hold Balay up before they do."

"Two of us."

"We've just got to be quick."

"Even assuming we get hold of Ghatola, how do we get her away?"

Reshtina suddenly realised Nangial was here solely to terminate the captive. Everything else was bunkum. "We hijack one of the lorries," she replied caustically.

Nangial shrugged: whatever you say, bonehead.

They put their heads down and broke cover, trotting unremarked through the Taliban lines at an angle. When they judged they'd passed the last fighter, they broke into a sprint, arriving about a hundred metres from the convoy's left flank just as it ground to a halt.

"We're too late," Nangial said.

Two men in black turbans stepped into the convoy's path with their palms thrust out.

Balay barked an order for his men to disembark, hands on heads, and at least fifty Taliban fighters got to their feet and leisurely closed in.

"Bring her out!" Balay shouted.

An elongated sack – presumably Ghatola – was dragged from the middle truck by three of his henchmen, and tossed into no man's land between the two sides. The men replaced their hands on their heads and backed away.

Nangial was about to shoot. Reshtina whacked her in the face with the butt of her pistol, and banged her skull hard as she went down. She hit the ground and lay still.

Then there was a sustained crackling from the direction of the convoy and Reshtina flattened on the dust, expecting to die. She heard men screaming and yelling and a helicopter arriving.

When she gathered the courage to raise her head slightly, she saw a coterie of enemy soldiers loading Ghatola onto a stretcher and then the helicopter. As it flew away, she realised it wasn't American. She didn't know how she knew, but it was British.

Then quiet. The battle was over. She lay motionless for a long time with her pistol underneath her while the enemy patrolled, looking for things to loot probably. Finally, two men shouted to each other and a pair of helicopters swooped in, American this time.

As far as she could tell, that was it. Done.

Then she saw Balay emerge alone from under one of the trucks. She watched him go with a loathing so intense it was almost a creature within her. Then she had an idea. She had to go to Britain now, retrieve Ghatola from the beast's jaws. And he was her ticket.

She was startled by a woman's cry somewhere nearby. It wasn't Nangial, she was still out cold, the bitch. She could stay that way forever for all it mattered. She looked across the plain and fixed on the silhouette of a chador about a hundred metres west. Then another, running, screaming. Wives of the one or more of the dead. One of them yelled *why, oh why*, over and over, and Reshtina recognised Zaituna, then Ambrin. Her heart leapt with as much joy as the night allowed, and she ran to them.

But there was no time for sentimentality, she realised that immediately. She had to be firm.

"Pull yourselves together," she said once the reintroductions were over and their grief had subsided. "You have to think about what will happen now."

"My husband's dead!" Ambrin screamed. *"Don't you think it's a bit early for that?"*

"You never loved him," Reshtina replied, trying to infect them with some of her calm.

"There are a hell of a lot worse men than Babrak and Khushdil!" Zaituna said.

Reshtina raised her voice. "That's right. Bad, bad men, who call you names and beat you, and to whom both of you might be re-married in a week's time!"

No one spoke. They looked out over the plain of corpses.

"At best you'll become servants in someone else's house," Reshtina added.

"What's the alternative?" Ambrin asked, her voice halfway between resignation and sarcasm.

"We can unite," Reshtina replied. "This can be a new beginning. Remember, we love each other. This is our only chance. We've got to flee the country, start anew. In Europe, we'd be accepted for what we are."

"I don't want to go to dirty, nasty Europe!" Zaituna yelled. "I want my husband!"

"Keep your voice down," Reshtina said. "He's dead, remember? We can't afford to stand round grieving. If we're to cut and run, we've got to do it now."

"That's so easy for you to say," Zaituna said. "You haven't lost anyone."

"*I can't think!*" Ambrin wailed.

"You don't have to think," Reshtina said. "I'll do that. Firstly, the reason your husband's dead is Balay, right?"

"That *bastard*," Zaituna said, rubbing her eyes. "I told Khushdil he didn't care. I hope he rots in hell."

"Not until he's dead he won't," Reshtina replied. She kissed Zaituna's hand then her elbow. Ambrin wrapped her arms round her and wept some more.

"You don't mean to say he's still *alive?*" Zaituna gasped.

"And laughing," Reshtina said. "Listen, we're going to London. The British have kidnapped Ghatola, I don't know why. We're going to rescue her. Then we can be together, all four of us."

"The only reason I'd ever go to London is to *bomb it to bits!*" Ambrin yelled. "Do to them what they've been doing to us for the last ten years!"

Reshtina shrugged. "I don't care what excuse you need, beauty. The point is, we'll be together, either there or in Jannah. First, though, we've got to see to Balay."

Ambrin looked at Zaituna and sighed. "What have we to lose?" she said miserably.

They both turned to Reshtina. "Lead the way," Zaituna said.

They broke into Balay's house just too late to stop him killing Gharsanay and Durkhani. Reshtina knocked him out, then she cut off his thumbs and big toes, and sewed his lips together. They loaded four asses with provisions from his pantry. They sat him on one of his donkeys and took three more for themselves.

Then they and set off for Herat province and the Iranian border, taking turns to prop him up, in between them.

Two hours later, six men ascended the stairs of Ashraf Hotaki in Kandahar with a flat-pack of empty holdalls and a stainless steel canister. They found number thirty-two on the third floor at the end of a long, dirty corridor with a concrete floor.

Four of the men were Pakistani Talibs in turbans with black beards. The other two - Idris Kakahel and Haider Chamkanni - were renegade ISI agents in kurta shirts, jackets and scuffed brogues.

They knocked politely on the door and when it opened an inch, the taller agent kicked it hard, causing the occupant – a thin, dark-skinned woman in a cloak - to flip backwards and land in a daze.

Her eyes filled with horror as she seemed to realise what was happening, but the foremost mujahideen kicked her jaw and she fell unconscious. He tied her hands and feet, dragged her into the kitchen, and joined his colleagues in the living room. They made themselves a pot of tea.

An hour later, after a thorough search of the premises, they found everything they were looking for and more. Five of them exited the way they had come in, their holdalls stuffed with documents and cash. The sixth waited till they were clear. He emptied the gasoline over Saira Mohammad, dropped a match, and followed them at speed.

Chapter 6: Badrai's Beliefs About the Afterlife

Ambrin and Reshtina carried white pennants inscribed with one of the few Arabic words which, thanks to a visit to their village by the Red Crescent a year ago, everyone in the village knew how to recognise: 'leprosy'. When travellers in the opposite direction saw it - as they all did somewhere on their approach - they mostly gave them wide berth.

Balay regained consciousness on day two as they neared the red mountains of Ghor. His mouth poured blood as it fought the stitches. He wriggled off his saddle and crashed, teary and twitching, beneath the belly of his donkey.

Reshtina dismounted, turned him on his back, and punched his face. Then again. He stopped struggling and lay supine. Zaituna and Ambrin got off their donkeys and leaned over him.

"I know what he did to Gharsanay and Durkhani," Zaituna said, "but I can't help feeling he's suffered enough. Look, he's soiled himself."

"Of course he has," Reshtina replied. "It's been two days. Helmand River's not far away. We can wash him there."

Ambrin stroked his cheek. "What if you've killed him?"

"Then he can count himself lucky," she replied.

"He looks like my father," Zaituna replied emotionally, stroking his cheek.

"We'll have to make him some sort of stretcher," Reshtina said, "and tie him to it. The donkeys can pull it."

"That'll make him queasy," Ambrin said. "He'll vomit."

Reshtina shrugged. "So?"

"Where's it going to come out? He'll have to swallow it and he'll choke. Bang goes our insurance."

Reshtina smiled. At last they were beginning to think like men. "Maybe we should cut his stitches and remove his teeth. At some point we're going to have to feed him or he dies.

52

How are we going to do that if we've sewn his mouth shut? It'll be difficult enough to put a straw in his mouth, let alone a spoon."

"You were the one who insisted on it," Zaituna said.

"I'm not infallible. Who is?"

Zaituna shook her head. "He's eighty. Do you really think women of our age should be doing that to men of his age?"

"He's going to hell," Reshtina said, "and we're headed for Paradise. He can do some of his suffering on Earth, or not. For every punch he receives here, that's one less in Jahannam."

Zaituna laughed. "Bullshit."

"I don't think it is," Ambrin said. "I think it's right."

Reshtina sighed. "Either way, we've no choice. Balay may be old but he's got it coming to him. Has had for a long time."

"I still think it's immoral," Zaituna said. "His age. And a man."

Reshtina picked up a rock. "Let's just stop nattering and get on with it, shall we? Ambrin, bring me some scissors."

They were expert seamstresses so it took them less than an hour to rig up a stretcher and suspend it between two asses so it didn't trail on the ground. Reshtina cut the stitches and bashed out Balay's incisors and canines. They collapsed surprisingly easily. The women bound him securely, remounted, raised their pennants and continued. They stopped at Helmand River then again at Khash to sluice him.

They passed an American army convoy on its way back to Kandahar at a crawl, a gang of youths on motorbikes, a succession of displaced people in threes and fours, businessmen in tinny cars without exhaust silencers. There were craters and burned out vans where IEDs had been. They crossed roads rather than following them and whenever they inspired curiosity it was nearly always deflected by their warning tags. They avoided the villages. They crossed vast plains where Zaituna or Ambrin suffered panic-attacks: they'd hardly ever been out of the house, so open spaces frightened them. They ascended and descended mountains where cedars grew alongside almond trees and honeysuckles. The sky was white, black or pink, orange, blue, silver, according to the climate and hour, and in the deserts the full moon projected their shadows glass-sharp. Every moment they expected to stand on the landmines they knew littered the country, yet they rarely stopped conversing, except when they were dog-tired. Balay didn't regain consciousness. His breathing became fitful and he whimpered as if Shaytan was already digging his claws in.

"I saw an American soldier killed by a mine once," Zaituna said, when they were ascending a mountain track flanked by pines and junipers. She stopped to catch her breath. Before them, a distant path climbed steeply to a snowy summit; a thousand metres below lay pastures, scrub and hillocks, shimmering through a heat haze. "I expected to feel glad, but it was like seeing my little brother. He didn't even have a beard. He had spots. His lips were red like a woman's."

"When we reach London, we're going to blow it up," Ambrin said.

Reshtina sighed. This was the pretext under which she'd persuaded her to come along, but she wasn't convinced. "Why don't we just concentrate on finding Ghatola?" she said.

"I never liked Ghatola," Ambrin replied. "She thought I was stupid. Remember that time when she made me bleat like a sheep?" She suddenly became tearful. "I didn't have all that much time with Babrak, and *that's* what she made me do?"

"I don't think she knew how he'd end up," Zaituna said.

"She made a complete fool of me in front of my husband!"

They rode on in silence for a kilometre. Ambrin suddenly drew her ass to a halt.

"What's the matter?" Zaituna asked her.

"If we're not going to bomb London, I'm turning back."

Reshtina laughed. "The village? How do you think you're going to explain your absence? They'll stone you to death the moment they clap eyes on you."

Ambrin took her donkey through an about-turn. "I'm homesick. I don't want to go to on unless I can become a martyr and be with Babrak. I'll think of something."

"All that martyrdom stuff's Bin Laden flycrap," Reshtina said vehemently. "The Qur'an says suicide's a sin."

Zaituna hooted. "How the hell do *you* know what it says in the Qur'an? You can't even read!"

"Badrai told me."

Ambrin laughed. "Badrai couldn't read the Qur'an either. That was just a trick her husband taught her. She was nothing more than a performing monkey."

"Even if that's true," Reshtina replied, "and I'm not sure it is, she was married to the village Mirab. They probably talked about the holy book all the time - "

"Sure, when she wasn't out of her mind on smack," Ambrin interrupted.

"He was the one who really killed her," Zaituna added. "I hardly think we should respect his authority, Reshtina. Where does it say in the Qur'an that you're allowed to murder your wife with drugs when she loses her looks and, thanks to what you did to her when she was a child, she can't bear your sons? I can't read the Qur'an either, but I'm pretty sure the Prophet Muhammad, peace and blessings be upon him, wouldn't have sanctioned that!"

Reshtina shook her head. "Badrai's husband could have got rid of her a hell of a lot sooner if he'd told her suicide was *mustahabb*, recommended."

"I'm happy to bomb London," Zaituna blurted out. "I want to. For Khushdil's sake."

Reshtina swore under her breath. She'd seen this before, everywhere: widows reassessing their autobiographies so as to beatify their husbands. If they both felt like this, her only hope was to persuade them they'd got Khushdil and Babrak wrong. That was going to take time.

"Hello, ladies!" exclaimed a voice they didn't recognise.

They turned to face the front and the speaker. In their distraction, they hadn't noticed the arrival of four young men on motorbikes, toting guns. They were dark-skinned with short haircuts and uneven teeth, dressed in Western-style jumpers and jeans. Dacoits. They grinned as if congratulating themselves on a rich haul.

"Where are you going with your grandfather?" the foremost said.

"How old are you?" the second said. "Show us your hair."

"We're transporting a leper," Reshtina replied, with lowered eyes. "It's catching. You don't want to become infected."

"Sexy voice," the foremost said. "Where are your husbands, *naaz*?"

"They're dead," Ambrin muttered.

Reshtina cursed Ambrin's stupidity for the second time in as many minutes. The four men switched off their engines and gathered in congress. The women brought their donkeys together for safety.

"What are they saying?" Zaituna whispered.

"They don't believe us about the leprosy," Reshtina said. "They're discussing how to force sex on us." She reached into her saddlebag, calmly removed the pistol Saira Mohammad had given her and secreted it under her chador. If they were going to be raped, they'd be killed afterwards. Anything less might, from the rapists' viewpoint, conjure male relatives looking for retribution.

The four men seemed to reach a decision. They sat upright and puffed up their chests. "Dismount and lie on the floor," the foremost said. "We're not going to hurt you. Much."

The others chuckled. "It'll be over before you know it," one of them said under his breath.

"Remove your chadors," a third said.

Reshtina did a quick assessment. None of the men thought they were in the slightest danger, hence they held their guns limply. She checked the safety was off hers – she hoped she'd got it right – then dropped her chador as instructed and fired. Two of the men died instantly. She saw the third as if in slow motion. In normal circumstances, he could probably have fired before she did, but – and she'd seen this before – he was so shocked to find a woman attacking him, he had to make a mental adjustment, and in that split second, a bullet ripped his heart. She missed the fourth man. He thrust his rifle to his shoulder and would undoubtedly have despatched her but then there was a crack and he lunged backwards with a death-yelp and fell in a heap on the earth.

She swung round to find Ambrin lowering Balay's rifle, as brazenly as if she was in a Bollywood film.

Then there was silence. The women put their chadors back on, remounted and sat motionless for a full ten minutes, avoiding eye-contact, trying to digest what they'd just done. A pair of American warplanes passed at high altitude. Balay moaned.

"You saved my life," Reshtina told Ambrin eventually, almost in a whisper.

"I killed one, that's all," Ambrin said. "You saved my life three times over."

"Shouldn't we be moving on?" Zaituna asked as if she was emerging from a trance. "If they're part of a bigger group, their friends might be coming. They'll probably have heard."

They pulled their hoods down and listened. "I can't make anything out," Ambrin said.

"They might not have motorcycles," Zaituna said. "They might have horses. Or even be on foot."

They dragged the bikes and the corpses into the undergrowth on opposite sides of the path, and found a clearing where they fed and watered the donkeys. They ate before sundown so their campfire wouldn't give them away. Then they pitched their tent, removed Balay from his stretcher and slept huddled against him and each other for warmth, three rifles to hand. But no one came.

The next day, Reshtina awoke early. She dressed in shalwar kameez, recovered one of the motorbikes from the undergrowth and wheeled it onto the path. She mounted and pushed its stand away with her foot. She had no idea where or how, but she felt she'd been here before. Maybe her dead husband had owned one, although why he'd have shown her how to ride it she couldn't imagine. Maybe he'd been in love with her. Besotted men did crazy things. They nearly always came to their senses a few months later.

She turned the key and the engine came on. She tried turning the handles and squeezing the gripper things but she couldn't get it to go anywhere. There were some levers where her feet were, so she tried them. The one on the right didn't do anything and the one on the left was stiff as a rusty pump. Then she squeezed the grip and the lever rose, propelling her an inch forward where she stalled. Her heart nearly turned inside out and she laughed involuntarily.

So it was something to do with the left foot-lever and the gripper. She turned the key again and the engine resumed.

Zaituna heard it first. She gasped with horror, grabbed one of the rifles and shook Ambrin awake. Ambrin sat up with wide eyes and looked straight at her as if this might be their last view of each other. They scrambled out of the tent into the bright sunlight, squinting, and scrambled to where the undergrowth met the path, pointing their guns to where the sound of the motorcycle was. They couldn't see it yet, but it was receding.

"Where's Reshtina?" Ambrin hissed.

The answer didn't bear thinking about.

Then they saw it. Fifty metres above them where the dirt track climbed to the summit, a motorbike emerged from a clearing. Zaituna swallowed as it slowed and did a U-turn.

"Do you think we can hit it from here?" Ambrin asked.

"It's too fast," Zaituna replied, as it disappeared back into the clearing. "There's no rush, though. He's on his own."

"Where the hell's Reshtina?"

"Just keep watching the bandit. We'll work that out later."

All they had to do was keep their eyes on the road further down the slope, where the trees thinned. Suddenly, bike and rider emerged there at speed. They raised their rifles, peered along the sight-lines and jumped in unison, electrified. They turned to each other and grinned.

"I wonder who taught her to do that?" Zaituna said.

They spent the next three days learning to ride the motorbikes, performing the five daily prayers and lounging in the sun. Their provisions were almost spent, but they weren't worried. Hospitality was a given in this country: providing they came in peace, travellers were never turned away. Balay's alleged leprosy would simply mean they'd have to encamp outside any settlements. Even then, *pashtunwali* or its equivalent wouldn't fail them.

For the first time in as long as she could remember, Reshtina felt happy. If it pleased Allah to admit her to Paradise, she hoped she'd find it like this. Her friends, copious sunshine, the odour of pine and rue, and twenty thrills a day. She listened to the cicadas, watched dragonflies veer by, grew light-headed staring at eagles hovering above the mountain peaks. God spoke to her in words she remembered vaguely from a past life: *Seest thou not that it is Allah whose praises all beings on earth celebrate, and the birds of the air with outspread wings? Each knows its own mode of prayer and praise!*

Zaituna brought three mugs half-full of dried fruits and nuts, and three glass of water. "Balay's awake," she said. "I gave him some water and a little semolina."

"Did he take it?"

"A bit. He's fully conscious, I think."

"He's not talking, is he?"

"I don't think he can. He may be recovering. I hope he is."

"We'll probably be able to ditch him before we enter Iran or Turkmenistan."

Zaituna ate her nuts and washed them down. "Assuming we're not turning back. Ambrin's still pretty determined."

Reshtina scowled. "We might as well just shoot her in the head if that's how she feels. Probably anything's better than being buried waist-deep in a pit and having an entire village lob rocks at your head. It took Faridun nearly half an hour to die, so Gharsanay said."

"Yes, but Ambrin's not as strong as he was."

"Oh, that's all right then."

Ambrin pulled up on her motorbike, switched the engine off and pounced on her share of fruits and nuts. "What are you talking about?"

"Balay's conscious," Zaituna said.

"I don't know how you can possibly talk about bombing London!" Reshtina burst out. "That's exactly what they're doing to us, and we call them all the names under the moon and sun for it! And don't give me that, 'Yes, but they started it' shit, because that's the sort of thing children say. And don't tell me Muhammad – peace and blessings be upon him - said suicide's *mustahabb*, because that's blasphemy. We're talking about killing innocent people here. I don't want any part of it."

"Zaituna and I have decided to bomb London," Ambrin said calmly. "We're going on. You can do what you like."

Zaituna blushed. It took Reshtina a moment to realise she'd been both outflanked and stabbed in the back. She shot a wounded look at her two companions and got to her feet. "Fine," she said, brushing the dust off her chador. "You two go ahead without me then."

She crawled into the tent, grabbed her revolver and a canteen of water, then untethered and mounted her donkey. As she passed Balay on the way out of the encampment, she considered putting a bullet through him. That would show them. They'd be finished then. But she was pretty sure the Qur'an didn't approve of killing defenceless people either, innocent or not. *God is oft-forgiving,* she thought, *most merciful.*

"Stop right there, Reshtina," she heard Ambrin say behind her. She heard a rifle load.

She didn't think Ambrin had the guts to kill her, but she wasn't sure. In any case, she wasn't going to give in to threats, no matter how serious. She carried on riding.

Suddenly, they were both running alongside her, wailing, telling her how sorry they were, they hadn't meant to hurt her, she was their leader, they loved her, begging her to stop. She drew her donkey to a halt.

"So no more 'Let's bomb London'?" she said.

"We don't have to be suicide bombers," Ambrin said, clutching her hand and wiping her eyes.

"Please, let's just talk about it," Zaituna said. "Please come back."

"There's nothing to talk about."

"*You* don't understand," Ambrin said. "*Your* husband's sophisticated and you're really pretty. He's rich and he's probably crazy about you. They have different standards in the cities. I bet even if you were to go back tomorrow and say, 'Anoushirvan, dear, the reason you haven't seen me for a while is I took a lover from Kabul' he'd still forgive you. It's not the same for Zaituna and I. If we go on, we're finished, if we go back we're finished."

"I don't understand," Reshtina replied. "You could ask the British to take you in as refugees, let you live there."

Zaituna gasped. "Go begging to our enemies?"

"Even if I wanted to, I wouldn't," Ambrin said. "Afghanistan's full of people who've run away to London and been sent back. My cousin's brother-in-law, Awalmir, went to London through Turkey and some other country after the Northern Alliance knocked his house down and raped his wife, and they just sent him straight back. He says the same thing happens to everyone. So going there's no different to going back to the village, don't you see?"

Reshtina shrugged and sighed.

"Come and pray to Allah," Zaituna said. "We'll build a fire and make some rice pudding and tea, then we'll decide what to do."

"Please," Ambrin said.

Half an hour later, the sun went down and Reshtina began to overcome her feelings of betrayal. Zaituna lay before the fire gazing at the flames. Ambrin cupped her tea and hummed a lullaby.

"Maybe we should have let those bandits have us," she said. "They might have taken us for wives if they'd liked us. Maybe it was silly to kill them."

Zaituna drew her chin into her neck as if she'd never heard anything so stupid.

"We haven't that many options any more," Ambrin added. "We have to take our chances, however slim."

"If a man rapes you, he dishonours you," Reshtina said coldly. "If you're dishonoured, you're not only unmarriageable, you're trash. They'd have killed us as soon as they'd pulled their trousers up and felt virtuous about it for the rest of the week."

"I suppose so," Ambrin replied dejectedly. She swallowed. "It's a funny world."

"We're all three of us finished, really," Zaituna said. "If we go on, we're dead, if we go back we're dead ... But we're also dead just sitting here. Our lives are over, whatever we do. We're ghosts."

"Have you forgotten about Ghatola?" Reshtina said.

Zaituna scoffed. "Is that really what we're going to London for? Really? We don't know anything about the place. From what I've heard it's got millions and millions of people in and it's bigger than Helmand and Kandahar put together. Added to which, the British have probably hidden her. She might not even *be* in London for all we know. She might be in Afghanistan still. She might be in Guantanamo. Or she might be dead. None of us speak English, so we can't ask anyone, we can't knock on doors. You might as well face it, Reshtina, she's gone for good and there's nothing we can do to bring her back."

They sat in silence for a while. Reshtina saw as if by inspiration how right Zaituna was. Why hadn't she noticed it before? Because she'd been so preoccupied with the bother of getting across the country, that's why, and lately she'd been so concerned to quash the Bomb London heresy. She felt a surge of bitterness like nothing she'd ever known and suddenly bombing London didn't seem like such a bad idea after all.

"Reshtina's crying," Ambrin whispered to Zaituna.

Zaituna put her arm round her. "I'm sorry," she said, "Really. I shouldn't have said anything."

"Reshtina feels the same way about Ghatola as we do about Khushdil and Babrak," Ambrin said.

Zaituna wiped Reshtina's eyes with her chador, then her own. "Maybe we should think of another country to go to," she said. "Somewhere where they treat women well."

Ambrin laughed hollowly. "Like where?"

"There are supposed to be some places in Europe. Except they're full up. And they don't like you if you wear normal clothes."

"There isn't anywhere," Reshtina said. "There isn't anywhere in the world. Women are just talking animals as far as most places on earth can see. Ambrin, tell me about your plan to bomb London again."

Ambrin drew a sharp breath. "But I thought we'd given up on that?"

"I'm just asking, that's all."

Ambrin clasped her hands. "We'd be suicide-bombers, I think, because otherwise they'd be bound to catch us afterwards, then they'd torture us. This way, it'd be quick and we'd be with our husbands, and you'd probably be with Ghatola, because I'm pretty sure that's where she is now."

Zaituna put her hands on the ground behind her and leaned back. "I agree with you, Reshtina, it's probably *not* recommended in the Qur'an, but I shouldn't think it's condemned either. I used to sit with Badrai a lot in the months before she died, and I think I got a proper perspective on all this."

"Go on," Reshtina said.

"Badrai said she could see things other people couldn't; into *Barzakh* where the dead live. She said there's only a very thin curtain separating this world and the next one."

"Of course, she was a druggie," Reshtina remarked drily.

"I know that. She knew that. But there are drugs that hinder and drugs that enhance."

Reshtina clicked her tongue. "And you're saying Badrai gained special powers from taking heroin?"

"I'm not saying everyone gets them, but she did. She predicted the exact date and hour of her death, for example. She told me Khushdil would be killed by the Americans. She said you'd marry a man from Kandahar, even though we knew Gharsanay wanted you and everyone thought he was the only possibility at the time. And there were other things, even stranger."

"And she said we'd bomb London, is that it?"

"Of course not."

"So what, then?"

"She said Allah sees the dead and the living as one country. We see death as the end, a tragedy. He sees it as no more important than opening a door and walking from one room into another."

"Except you can't walk back again," Reshtina replied. "You've no further chance to repent."

"Think about all the awful things on the earth," Zaituna said. "All the suffering. A leopard munching a sheep to death. Why would Allah allow that? Badrai said the sheep doesn't actually die, not the real one. It just turns into a *jinn*. It probably doesn't even know what's happened. Sometimes you think, how can Allah have created all this? But if we're only seeing one half, it makes sense!"

"Yes, *if*."

"Think about when a mullah sees someone that's done something wrong and he issues a *fatwa* ordering him to be killed. He isn't saying 'snuff him out', he's just saying, 'I'm not qualified to judge him. Send him through the air to Allah, and let Him decide'."

"Let's say we do bomb London," Ambrin said, "and a thousand people die. We're not *doing* anything to them, Reshtina. If they've lived good lives, they'll just pass gently through the door and Allah will welcome them into Paradise. He'll probably be extra merciful to them because they didn't expect to die at that precise moment, so He'll give them the benefit of the doubt on Judgement Day. Yes, the people they've left behind will grieve, and that's sad. But human life's so incredibly short in comparison with the eternity they've got in front of them that ultimately, it won't matter. Even if they go to Jahannam, they won't stay there forever. No one does."

"In a thousand years," Zaituna said, "they'll all look back on it and wonder what all the fuss was about. Most of them will probably thank us."

Ambrin smiled. "Meanwhile, we'll have brought the war to an end and we'll be with Khushdil, Babrak and Ghatola. Everyone wins."

Reshtina rubbed her forehead and bit her lip. She dug her fingertips in above her eyebrows and pushed them gently onto her eyelids. "I need to think about this," she said. "We'll talk about it again in the morning, if that's okay."

Chapter 7: So You Want to be a Suicide Bomber?

The threat of bears and leopards meant Reshtina had to get inside the tent but she lay apart from the other three, who slept with their limbs intertwined. Zaituna used Balay's chest as a pillow. Ambrin tossed and turned, snored and wheezed. Occasionally, she stood up in a trance and went outside to relieve herself. Like most women who'd married early, she had bladder problems.

Reshtina lay with a set of *subha* beads thinking about Badrai. How was it possible? Allah was undeniably *al-'adl*, the equitable, but how could you reconcile that with this life of justice and injustice, health and disability, strong, weak, rich, poor? Only, perhaps, if this was some sort of shadow-place - a dim reflection of a better world where everything was reversed. In that case, the bigger picture would contain no evil, because whatever resembled it would be redressed elsewhere, somewhere out of view. Which would be consistent with there being the flimsiest of boundaries between here and the hereafter. So maybe Badrai *had* been a seer after all.

She remembered when she and Ghatola first went to a Sufi gathering in Kandahar together, and afterwards they met a beardless man who'd spent the evening spinning in the middle of the floor while the congregation chanted God's ninety-nine names. He told them his hat was his tombstone, his cloak his shroud. In the deep sense of complete detachment from the world's goods, he was deceased. *Oh you who believe! Let not your riches or your children divert you from the remembrance of Allah. If any act thus, the loss is their own.* How could that be unless Badrai had been right?

Reshtina guessed there were two hours till sunrise. She was starving, notwithstanding the provisions they'd filched from Balay's pantry. She ate some more fruits and nuts, but afterwards she was still hungry and now she was thirsty too. Her mind soared. She saw arabesque in the air and heard Allah stroking her hair and it crackling in response.

Bomb London. Nothing mattered. Earth was a realm of confusion and ignorance in which evil was good, good evil, and in all this muddle only noble intentions counted. There was nowhere else for them to go. Turkmenistan, Iran, Uzbekistan, Tajikistan, China, Pakistan - all equally closed to self-reliant women. No place in the world to receive them. She had nothing against London especially ... except that it had killed Ghatola.

But that was enough. Perhaps it deserved to die. If anything did, yes, yes, it was London.

She heard something outside the tent. A rifle loading.

She sat up rigid. The bandits were back and this time they had them as entirely at their mercy as a litter of kittens in a sack.

"Come out with our hands up," a man's voice commanded. "We know you've got guns in there, so leave them be otherwise we'll blow you to bits. You won't even see us."

All three women sat up. It was obvious from their eyes Ambrin's and Zaituna's hearts were beating as hard as hers.

"What should we do?" Zaituna hissed.

"They'll have heard you ask that," Ambrin said shakily.

Reshtina closed her eyes to rummage in her brain. Whoever was out there could have killed them already if that's what they wanted. Surrendering themselves as rape-fodder at least gave them an extra ten, twenty minutes of life. They might just be able to swipe someone's gun and go down fighting.

"We're coming!" she said in her most feminine voice. "Please don't shoot us, we're only women!"

They crawled out of the tent, Reshtina first then Zaituna then Ambrin. Ambrin's teeth chattered loudly. They expected to be pounced on but they managed to stand up with their hands raised without seeing anyone. A thin moon hung over the mountain, the stars were losing their sparkle and the sky was turning from black to indigo. The air hung cold and still.

"Take off your clothes," the disembodied voice said. "And don't try anything stupid."

They removed their outerwear and undergarments and stood shivering in the dim light. Now they'd been ritually dishonoured, they'd deserve whatever happened to them next. That was how most men's minds worked.

"Where are you going?" the voice said.

"Nowhere!" Ambrin exclaimed wretchedly. "We never moved, I swear!"

"I meant, where are you headed for?"

Reshtina did a quick reassessment. *I meant where* ...: 'we' had become 'I'. So there was only one of them, not a gang. Even with a gun, he'd find it difficult to rape three of them unless he was going to shoot them first. But then why would he be keeping them talking? His voice didn't sound right, either. She had a vague notion she recognised it.

"Are you hungry?" he said.

They nodded. "Yes," Zaituna said. "Very."

A sack of provisions crash-landed at their feet, nearly scaring them faint. A burly man with a beard emerged from the undergrowth in a sheepskin jacket and high boots with his gun lowered. Reshtina could just about make out his features in the dim moonlight.

"Nangial?"

Nangial grinned and threw her gun down. "I owed you a scare after you nearly broke my jaw, Reshtina Sarbanri. You can put your clothes back on now."

They embraced not quite passionately, but with sufficient joy to demolish their remaining resentments.

"Surely Nangial's ... a woman's name?" Ambrin said as if she wasn't quite sure if such a remark might still get her shot, but she couldn't help it.

"There's enough food in there to keep us going a fortnight," Nangial said, ignoring her. "Let's get a fire going."

The sack contained rice, a hemp satchel of red onions and three kilos of lamb packed in salt and stuffed into gashed plastic water bottles. Nagial provided water from a canteen strapped to her mule. They showed her Balay then built a fire and cooked and ate in silence, watching the sun rise. Afterwards, Nangial stripped naked, exactly as she'd done for Reshtina a week and a half earlier, this time to reassure Ambrin and Zaituna.

"Isn't that against the Qur'an?" Ambrin asked when she'd finished.

"I've been forced into this position by men behaving like Kafirs while claiming to be exemplary Muslims," Nangial said. "I'm closer to Allah than they'll ever be."

"Oh."

She pulled up her trousers. "I asked you last night where you were going. I'm not going to insist on knowing, but I might be able to help you. Three women alone are likely to meet a sorry end in this part of the country. With a man, it's a different story."

"We're going to London," Reshtina said without looking up, poking her bare feet with a stick. "We're going to set off an explosion there."

She felt Zaituna and Ambrin turn to her in astonishment. Nangial laughed.

"What's so funny?" Zaituna said.

"With or without your donkeys?" Nangial asked. "Have you any notion how far away Britain is?"

"She didn't say 'Britain'," Ambrin replied acidly. "She said 'London'. Yes, we know it's quite a long way."

"Ambrin, London *is* Britain," Reshtina said self-consciously.

Nangial sighed. "So you're planning on a suicide bombing mission, yes?"

"What's wrong with that?" Ambrin said. "It'll help bring the war to an end. And we'll be with our husbands again. Even you, Reshtina, you'll be with your first husband. I know you don't remember anything about him, but he'll recognise you, and Allah won't let you be deceived."

"You probably think it's all a big hoot," Zaituna told Nangial coolly. "I can tell you're a 'big city' sort of person."

"What's that mean?" Nangial said.

"It means you think you know better than us. We're superstitious and stupid because we come from a village."

Nangial chuckled. "That's right, it's nothing personal. Do any of you know how to make bombs?"

"I shot a man on a horse the other day," Ambrin said.

"You put a lot of gunpowder in a box with a fuse," Zaituna said. "Then you light it. We're not idiots."

"What's the English for 'gunpowder'? Do you know?"

"We'll find out," Zaituna said heatedly.

"How?"

"Ask!"

"In what language?"

Reshtina rubbed her head and stood up. "Stop it. Zaituna, Ambrin: Nangial's right. We haven't the faintest idea what we're talking about." She walked off to one side, staring at the sky over the mountaintop as if she'd only just noticed it. She turned to Nangial. "What do *you* think we should do?"

Nangial shrugged. "If you want to tell yourselves you're suicide bombers, who am I to contradict you? Whatever helps you cross two continents, that's what I say. Believe me, though: it is a pretext. Once you get into Britain, you'll be praying on asylum just like everyone from here who makes it there."

"What's 'asylum'?" Zaituna said.

"How can you help us?" Reshtina said. She walked over on her knees till she was in front of Nangial. "I realise we still hardly know each other, but I'm begging you."

"You want to blow London to pieces that much?" Nangial said. "I don't believe you."

"We're deadly serious," Ambrin replied. "We really do. We've worked out there's no such thing as real evil. It's just make-believe."

Nangial laughed. "You'd make very good Hindus, you know that? There's no such thing as good and bad, it's all just *maya*, illusion. God knows what the ISI would say if they could hear you. You know how paranoid they are about India 'encircling' them."

"What's the ISI?" Zaituna asked.

"The Pakistani intelligence service," Nangial replied in a tone that suggested he knew she'd be making them none the wiser.

Ambrin blushed and looked resentfully at the ground. Zaituna clicked her tongue as if she'd never met anyone so rude.

"I won't believe you unless you all say it," Nangial replied seriously. "Say it together. Say you want to bomb London."

"Why?" Zaituna said.

"Because I *can* help you," Nangial replied. "I promise."

Reshtina, Zaituna and Ambrin looked at each other with varying degrees of conviction and incredulity. "We do," they all said.

"You're handing yourself over to Shaytan, you realise that?"

"What do you mean?" Zaituna asked.

"I can get you to London with the help of men who'll be only too happy to work gratis, on the understanding that your intentions are what you say they are. Three Pashtun women up for trekking and suicide-bombing – they'd see that as a priceless commodity. But God help you if you change your minds."

The three women exchanged looks again.

"Not that you will," Nangial added. "Contact with such men will change you. You'll eventually become who you say you are now."

Zaituna and Ambrin frowned. "We *are* who we say we are now," Ambrin said.

"Even you, Reshtina?" Nangial said.

Reshtina looked at the ground and shrugged. "I'm not entirely convinced, I admit ... Therefore it would be a good idea for me to meet people who can convince me, wouldn't it?"

"So it's decided," Nangial declared. "I'll have to come with you, of course. You'll get nowhere without a man, or the appearance of one, and Balay's no use. I've always wanted to go to London. There's nothing left for me in Afghanistan."

"I thought you had an important job here," Reshtina replied.

"Saira Mohammad's dead, and the information she kept has fallen into the hands of the Taliban, the ISI and all the endless conglomerates of women-haters. I don't know for sure, but I suspect they're looking for me."

Reshtina got to her feet and dusted her chador down. "So you need us?"

"Until we get over the border into Iran, my life depends on you. Afterwards, you're my three would-be suicide-bombers, hence my free ticket to London. If it's any comfort, one way or another, I need you all the way to our arrival."

Reshtina sat down facing the moon. So it was decided. They would bomb London. Whatever her doubts now, they'd have been removed when she arrived.

The four women sat in the red light of dawn without speaking. Zaituna went into the tent and came back with the news that Balay was dead. They all went to check. An hour later, they wrapped him in his own Payraan Tumbaan and buried him facing west.

After they'd completed the prescribed prayers, Nangial took out a pellet from her pocket, smashed it between two rocks and put it in an empty cigarette casing. She smoked it with her eyes closed, emitting sighs of pleasure.

Reshtina felt her outlook darken. It didn't bode well that they were entrusting themselves to a druggie, but it was too late. She wondered how much of an addict Nangial was, and how often she'd let them down in the coming however-long-it-might-take. Because let them down she definitely would, sooner or later.

Then again, heroin was so plentiful in Afghanistan nowadays, it's use was normal. Raising it as an issue probably wouldn't get her anywhere.

She tried to imagine how many mountains they'd have to scale and plains they'd have to cross before they reached Britain.

Chapter 8: Tasneem Babar

Ruby Parker sat behind her desk opposite Toby Copthorne –
his real name, after all – with Celia Demure to one side. Her
office marked one of the terminals of the first underground
floor of Thames House. It contained a portrait of the Queen, a
variety of potted plants and a tropical fish-tank whose fizzing
aerator served to fill awkward silences. Since the debacle with
Marcie Brown, Copthorne had been assigned to Red Section,
and he'd supposedly brought new information with him. It
was what they were here to assess. Celia Demure leaned her
chin on her walking stick. Her white hair and paisley dress
gave her a deceptive air of dotage.

"We followed it up with exemplary speed," Copthorne
said, "but it turned out to be a false lead. There were no casualties on our side. The Taliban suffered between seventy and
eighty fatalities according to the subsequent body-count."

"Could you take us back to the beginning, for Celia's
sake?" Ruby Parker asked. "I know most of this from your report, but it'd be good to get a fresh perspective."

Copthorne turned slightly to face his new audience.
"Last Tuesday in Kandahar, 3pm local time, a homosexual
man by the name of Anoushirvan Sarbanri turned up unan-
nounced at one our safe centres accompanied by his brother,
an ISAF-approved medic. He claimed a group of tribesmen
were on their way to execute him. As a matter of routine, we
showed him the log of missing persons photos while we completed the paperwork, and he selected Marciella Hartley-
Brown's from the pile. He claimed she was his wife and that
the Taliban were poised to abduct her as she travelled back to
her home village that night in company with one of the tribal
elders."

Celia Demure leaned forward. "His *wife*?"

Copthorne nodded. "Rather far-fetched on the face of
it, I know, but he had no reason to select that particular picture
and nothing to gain from the deception. We've since obtained

wedding photographs of the couple. The resemblance is uncanny."

"An honest misidentification, then," Celia Demure said. "Everyone has a doppelgänger, so they say."

Ruby Parker passed the wedding shots across the table. "Apparently, that was everyone's first thought. It was certainly mine. Now I'm not so sure. You might mistake the face of a neighbour or an acquaintance, but your own wife?"

"He's a homosexual," Celia Demure said. "Presumably, he uses her to conceal the fact. You wouldn't expect the same intimate familiarity with every line, blemish and mole you might find in someone who's infatuated with his spouse. What's her name?"

"Reshtina Sarbanri."

"And how does he say he met her?"

"He doesn't. He went awol shortly after identifying her and was found dead two or three streets away."

"So much for our safe houses. And his brother? What does he say?"

"He's also missing."

"What about the other people in the photograph?"

"Those we've been able to trace claim ignorance," Copthorne said. "All on his side of the family. We can't trace anyone from her side."

Celia Demure sighed irritably. "For what it's worth, I don't think the woman in this photograph looks much like her anyway. However, let's get to the point. Your 'false lead', Mr Copthorne."

"As I said, Anoushirvan Sarbanri claimed his wife was due to be abducted by the Taliban that evening as the village elder drove her home. So we intercepted the convoy *en route*. However, it wasn't Reshtina Sarbanri we ended up saving, it was another woman entirely. Badly burned, currently recovering at NATO Role 3 Multinational Hospital, Kandahar airport. Name of Ghatola Rahman."

"Why was she badly burned?" Celia Demure said. "Just out of interest? No, on second thoughts, don't answer that. Just tell me if this story of yours is going anywhere. As far as I can tell, we've identified a lookalike, and now we've lost her. I thought we were all agreed that Marciella Hartley-Brown couldn't have survived the blast. According to your own former department's report, Mr Copthorne, we sent a spy into her village to ask if there were any wounded and he was told, no, only dead. That strikes me as fairly conclusive."

Ruby Parker smiled wryly. "It seems we read rather too much into that, didn't we, Toby? Do you want to explain, or shall I?"

Copthorne shifted uncomfortably in his chair. "In Pashto, 'Did anyone survive the blast' can be taken to mean, 'Did anyone *important* survive the blast'. In other words, it can be taken to refer only to male survivors. In addition to which, the existence of female victims may not have been universal knowledge, even very locally. This is a culture where it's sometimes considered iff-y for a man to know the name of his best friend's wife."

Celia Demure shook her head incredulously. "And your spy didn't know that?"

"Rather, it took *us* a while to twig."

"How about the intended abductee? Have you any information confirming Anoushirvan Sarbanri's claim that it was meant to be this ... 'Reshtina' woman?"

"Quite the contrary," Copthorne said. "All our sources say the Taliban intended to capture Ghatola Rahman."

Celia Demure's eyes narrowed and she nodded. "I see."

The aerator filled the silence for a few seconds. Finally, Ruby Parker said, "What are you thinking, Celia?"

"Reading between the lines of what you've told me, Mr Copthorne, Reshtina Sarbanri herself is nowhere to be found. She's disappeared into thin air. Doesn't that strike you as rather odd in a country where women are kept as close as men's shadows? Where do you think she's gone?"

"I – I don't know. There have been a number of inexplicable murders of women in Kandahar in the last week, but we don't think she was one of the victims."

"I didn't know that," Ruby Parker said reproachfully.

"I didn't think it was relevant till now."

"Is there anything connecting them?"

"It's only a working hypothesis, but we think they may all be members of the Afghan Women's Reparation Brigade."

"Which is?"

"According to the consensus, a radical feminist cabal dedicated to extrajudicial capital punishment, possibly a remnant of the country's Marxist era. Anyway, if that *is* the common denominator, then something's happened. Its membership list's fallen into hostile hands. Which probably makes it a matter of time before one of them knocks at our door begging for protection. Then we might have a little more to go on."

"Back to the question I almost asked a few moments ago," Celia Demure said. "Why was Ghatola Rahman badly burned?"

"We don't know that yet," Copthorne said. "As soon as she regains consciousness we're hoping she'll tell us herself."

Ruby Parker and Celia Demure exchanged glances.

"Here's another working hypothesis, Mr Copthorne," Celia Demure said. "Ghatola Rahman's a senior member of the AWRB. She was captured by local men and tortured by fire, in the course of which she betrayed many of the organisation's secrets – all of which explains why the Taliban were so keen to talk to her. Seventy fighters keen, in fact. Reshtina Sarbanri was in league with her. She used marriage as a cover, and, as a practising homosexual in a country where homophobia's rife, I'm sure her 'husband' got as much out of that arrangement as she did. In the course of being tortured, Ghatola Rahman betrayed the Sarbanris' secret, and that's why he ended up soliciting refuge. His 'wife', however, fell back on her network of friends. She's on the run. Have I left anything out, Ruby?"

"Of course, it explains why Anoushirvan Sarbanri thought his wife was the intended abductee. Either of the two women would have been suitable. And it does indicate that Marciella Hartley-Brown – I don't think there can be the slightest doubt it's her now – is suffering from some sort of deep memory loss."

"What's our next step then?"

"I need to think. Obviously, no word of this must reach the Hartley-Brown family. There's no point in raising false hopes."

"So what are you going to do about Nicholas Fleming? It'll be hard to keep it from him."

"Fleming's her fiancé," Ruby Parker told Copthorne in response to his inquiring look. "He's also one of our best officers."

"Except that he's more than her fiancé," Celia Demure said. "They were married in Mannersby chapel the night she left for Afghanistan. I had that from her own mouth."

Ruby Parker rose a centimetre. "Good God. You never mentioned that. And her parents ...?"

"Don't know either. I don't suppose he told them. What about Lieutenant Bronstein?" she said, changing the subject. "Could we bring him in on this?"

"Most likely, but to what end? If Marcie's still alive, she's in Kandahar. As far as I know, he can't speak Pashto."

"Where is he?"

"NYPD requested his assistance with a political homicide. I could hardly say no. Anyway, at this end, it's going to be mainly sedentary work. The sort of thing you and I can probably manage between us."

"Providing we can keep Mr Fleming out of the way."

Ruby Parker put her pen to her mouth. "I believe Serious Organised Crime have an ongoing investigation into a gun-running cartel in Newcastle-upon-Tyne. I'll attach him to that with immediate effect."

"Stress the need for him to work *in situ*. We don't want to be bumping into each other."

"We'll fly Ghatola Rahman to Britain as soon as she opens her eyes. Either that, or one or more of us can fly out there. We'll promise whatever it takes to get her talking. We'll issue Marciella's photo to all our contacts in Kandahar. We'll focus our spies on the Afghan Women's Reparation Brigade, known and suspected. She's got to be somewhere in the city, although she's probably fairly safe in a chadri, providing she's got a man nearby. I never thought I'd have a good word to say for that particular garment, but I suppose there's a first time for everything."

Whenever Ghatola regained consciousness she was in pain. She had no idea why but she was aware of her body encased in plaster. She often awoke in darkness, otherwise she was always somewhere different. Sometimes at home with Balay, sometimes with Reshtina standing over her in a hotel room telling her to get up, sometimes addressing a classroom full of girls, or marking handwriting exercises. Once, she lay helpless in the village street while her school burned down, and men and women sidestepped her, apparently oblivious to what was happening. Two images kept recurring. In the first, she was in a hospital. She could tell that's what it was because there were other beds with women and children in, a smell of disinfectant, and people crying. In the second, Nangial sat next to her, sometimes with a nurse or doctor behind her, sometimes alone, sometimes in focus, mostly blurred.

She'd met Nangial once. She was one of eight bearded women the agency used for dangerous assignments. She'd shaved since they last met, but no amount of foundation could hide the stubble. And – this was how she knew it was a dream – she wore a hijab. Nangial in a hijab!

"Nangial?" she said. She was surprised how it came out. Like a thin whistle.

Nangial didn't respond. She turned and spoke to someone, and somehow in a flash, the bed was surrounded by men in white coats, some Afghans, some obviously American. They muttered among themselves but they didn't look hostile.

"Nangial?" she said again.

Nangial's eyes filled with water. "I'm Tasneem," she replied. "We don't know where Nangial is."

Ghatola sighed and fell asleep. She awoke what felt like a few seconds later, but Nangial was wearing a different colour hijab and the shadows had changed shape. There were lights on.

"Nangial?" she whispered. "Where are we?" She had an inkling this wasn't Nangial. Aquiline nose, high forehead, smooth olive skin – no stubble, after all - eyes surrounded by wrinkles, underscored by dark circles and hooded by thick black eyebrows reaching midway into her temples. "Who are you?" she added.

"I'm *Tasneem*. I used to work for the organisation. You're in the American hospital in the airbase in Kandahar. You were in a blaze and you were badly beaten."

She tried hard to remember, but no fire materialised, nor any beating. She felt light headed. She tried to recall anything at all. She was Ghatola Rahman. She was married to Balay, she was the village *qaryadar*, she was thirty-two, she -

"Where is my husband?" she whispered.

"Shush, now. Have some more sleep. You're getting better, that's the main thing."

The next time she awoke, she was conscious of several days having passed. Tasneem – that's right, not Nangial – was where she usually was. Who was she? Why was she keeping the vigil? Where was Balay? Reshtina, Zaituna, anyone?

"The doctors say you're doing a lot better now," Tasneem said cheerily. "You'll soon be better."

"Where is my husband?"

Tasneem blinked slowly. "You don't remember, do you?"

"Remember what?"

"Your husband tried to hand you over to the Taliban. He's dead now."

Ghatola tried to make sense of this for a few moments. "I don't believe you. Why would he do that?"

"I might as well tell you everything. You know it deep down, anyway. The Taliban found you guilty *in absentia* of the murder of Faridun Jalwaanai. They demanded your husband hand you over. You discovered what he was up to and tried to kill him, and yourself, by razing the block of flats you were staying at with Reshtina Sarbanri and her husband. You didn't succeed. The Americans heard what was happening – Anoushirvan Sarbanri told them – and decided they could usefully co-opt us. Saving you, they thought, would put us in their debt and allow them to kill scores of mujahideen at the same time. It worked up to a point. The only problem is, there isn't an 'us' any more. Not since the Taliban raided Saira Mohammad's flat and burned her alive. Lately, we've been dropping like insects before hungry birds. I've no idea where Nangial is, but I'm fairly sure she's dead. I've no idea where Reshtina Sarbanri is, but I'm pretty sure she's dead. Name who you like, I'm pretty sure she's dead. We're the only ones left."

Ghatola didn't recognise any of this from memory, but she knew it was true. It didn't leave space for questions and *I've no idea where Reshtina Sarbanri is, but I'm pretty sure she's dead* contained all the information she needed anyway. She wondered how bad her burns were, how many bones were smashed, what she looked like. Maybe she'd been fighting to stay alive. Well, she could let go now.

"Listen," Tasneem was saying, "the Americans have offered us a place in Britain – it's one of their provinces, like Helmand in Afghanistan. All we've got to do is tell them what we know about Saira and all the rest. It's history now, so we've nothing to gain from keeping quiet. They'll give us a house and new names if we want, and we can stay there indefinitely. Whereas if we remain in Afghanistan we'll be doused in petrol and burned to crumbs. You don't even have to speak to anyone you don't trust. I'm bilingual, so I'll be your translator."

"What do they think *I* know that you don't?"

"I never met Reshtina Sarbanri. For some reason, it's her they're interested in."

Ghatola's heart leapt half a millimetre. "Do – do they think she might be alive?"

"I don't know. They might do."

"Tell them I'm ready for them now ... I'll talk to them now."

Tasneem smiled. "Tush, you're falling asleep."

Ghatola realised she was right. Her eyelids began to flutter of their own accord and she could feel herself falling into darkness. She tried to fight it.

"Your prognosis is very good," Tasneem said. "In about a week, we're going to travel by plane to London. They'll take all the proper medical precautions, you won't even know you're in the air. Then they'll settle us in, make us very comfortable, after which it'll be a series of gentle conversations and pots of tea. Get some more rest now."

"Tell them ... I'll talk to them ... now," Ghatola whispered. "Tell them ..."

When Ghatola fell asleep, Tasneem Babar returned to her living quarters, put on her make-up, donned a chador and left the compound just as a troop-carrier arrived to fly the latest coffin to the US. There was a breeze blowing north to south. She turned right at the traffic lights and caught a yellow bus to the city centre, alighting twenty-five minutes later at Baghi Pul park, where two men awaited her in a Suzuki Mehran parked against a vending machine. She got onto the back seat.

"She knows something about Reshtina Sarbanri," she said.

Idris Kakahel lit a cigarette and wound the window down a centimetre. "Find out what it is then, and kill her. That's what you get paid for, right?"

"It isn't, actually," she replied. "My job description says I get paid to manipulate social networks, and a hell of a lot more than either of you two. This is mere work experience as far as I'm concerned."

"I want to get back to Quetta," Haider Chamkanni added.

Tasneem rolled her eyes. "Whatever she knows, it'll be well out of date by now. Reshtina Sarbanri isn't stupid by all accounts. She'll know her friend's been captured by the Americans and she'll have put twenty or thirty miles between herself and whatever location she's able to name."

"What's your plan then?" Idris Kakahel asked.

"It's obvious what the Americans are after. They want to resuscitate the AWRB, re-arm it and direct it. With only one of these women on board, such a plan will probably succeed. As they say in the West, if you're going to kill a hydra, you have to sever all its heads."

"Get to the point, Tasneem."

"We've got to keep Ghatola Rahman alive because only she can lure Reshtina Sarbanri. The Americans will arrange the details, don't worry ... with my prompting. Then I'll kill them both. In the meantime, be patient. Go back to Quetta if that's what you want. I'm going to Britain."

"Britain?"

She smiled. "You've heard of it, right?"

"How the hell's Ghatola Rahman going to lure Reshtina Sarbanri if she's in Britain?"

"I've told you, the Americans want to recreate the AWRB. How are they going to do that with its queen bee six thousand kilometres away? No, obviously they'll have to bring her back here. And once Reshtina Sarbanri thinks the fuss has died down, she'll take the bait and come out of hiding. It's what they call the long game."

Chapter 9: Fleming in Newcastle

Ashraf Cassidy, a middle-aged DCI in a windcheater, with black curly hair, brown eyes and a hunched frame, sat on a backless bench under the bus shelter in Newcastle city centre clutching a *Fenwick's* carrier bag. It was ten o'clock on a sunny Monday morning and the flow of passengers was largely incoming, mothers with pushchairs and pensioners making for Eldon Square on walking sticks without a backwards glance. When he judged no one was looking, he reached into his bag, unscrewed the cap of a three-quarters full bottle of Scotch and took another pull, his last. Then another. Soon he wouldn't be able to see single images any more, he knew that. Once the alcohol hit his eyes, it was two for the price of one. No one around. He reached for another swig but changed his mind. With a huge effort of will he lifted the bottle six inches and brought it down hard on the pavement. It broke. Whisky seeped out onto the concourse, and he realised it looked like urine. Since there was no one either side of him, he'd weed himself. He laughed.

Time for action. The new bod was due to arrive at midday. He sprang to his feet like a superhero and caught the 10.21 to Heaton. Once inside his flat, he spruced himself up with a tablespoon of salt, a vomit and a coffee, then showered and brushed his teeth to remove the mingled reek of gastric fluid and Colombian Arabica. He still wasn't seeing double, good old willpower, never ever failed him. Sukie, his tortoiseshell cat appeared through the cat flap. He picked her up and stroked her till she purred. Time: 11.24. He put on his suit and tie, combed his hair and squeezed a spot between his eyebrows. They were too thick, that was the problem. The hair follicles exuded grease. Wash, wash, wash, even prescription cream, nothing helped.

Half an hour later, he stood on Platform Four at Newcastle Central Station wolfing a chicken tikka pasty. He felt a lot better now, although he guessed he was probably dehydrating. He'd just been for his sixth pee in an hour. Should he or shouldn't he put more fluid into his system, a Pepsi, say? Would it make things better or worse? If yes, would he be all right with a Pepsi – all that caffeine? – or should he go for a Sprite? Or maybe even one of those milky things like a Mars drink or a Yop, put a bit more lining on his stomach? Close the gate, the horse has bolted.

The midday train came in. All the doors opened simultaneously as if all the passengers had spent the last three hundred miles rehearsing, then everyone poured towards the exit at roughly the same speed like the show had to go on. One man stood out, it had to be him. A beige slim-fit suit with a matching bowler hat, tall and erect as a guardsman, dark eyes, dark eyebrows, firm jawline, a cross between a male model, a Neanderthal and a contract killer. Cassidy swallowed the last corner of his pasty, turned his back and frantically brushed his teeth with his index finger, then span round with a smile and the offer of a handshake. "Nicholas Fleming?"

Fleming beamed, grabbed his hand and shook it. "The very same. You must be ..."

"Ashraf Cassidy. I'm in charge of the investigation. Or I was. Well, I will be for the next six weeks. I'm going to resign this afternoon. Personal reasons."

"Nothing to do with me, I hope."

Cassidy took a sharp breath. "No, not at all. Why would it be?"

"I assure you my arrival has nothing to do with your competence or otherwise. It often happens that when an MI5 officer's suddenly attached to a case, the people who have put the actual legwork in take it as an indication that someone high up isn't satisfied with the way it's going. The truth is the reverse. At Thames House we rarely come across investigations that significantly raise the disquisitive bar, and when we do we're eager to learn all we can from them, in all humility. And we always do things suddenly."

"But I thought you were coming to take charge ..."

Fleming stopped walking and frowned. "Who on earth told you that?"

"I, er ... I don't know."

"Because I assure you, it hasn't come from our end. I'm not qualified. If that's the arrangement, I might as well get on the first train back to London. This is your case, you give the orders, I take them."

Cassidy shook. He hadn't noticed it, but they were standing motionless, face to face. He was glad he hadn't had that Pepsi. An extra shot of caffeine would probably have sent him through the station ceiling. "But, well, if you don't mind my asking, where exactly *will* you stand in the chain of command?"

"How many people are in your team?"

"Eight. Nine, including me."

"I'm tenth, then. I make an excellent cup of tea, an indifferent coffee and I've a basic knowledge of shorthand. I have other skills, of course, to be put to use solely at your discretion."

"Have you eaten?"

"Not yet. What about you?"

"I know a very good pub. Let's go."

Cassidy felt his heart leap. If Sukie had been here, he'd have scooped her up and kissed her furry little back. He regretted the whisky, but not half as much as the announcement that he was about to resign. How the hell was he going to get out of *that*? He was set to look like an idiot!

The Dog and Roast Mutton had a burgundy carpet, a real fireplace and William Morris wallpaper dotted with watercolours of country cottages. The crowd for drinks was two people deep. They looked at the bar meals blackboard above the one-armed bandit.

"I thought it a good idea to come here because it's noisy," Cassidy said. "Less likely people will overhear us. We do have a staff canteen back at HQ, but you'll see enough of that before we're out. What are you having to eat and drink?"

"The steak and ale pie with boiled potatoes and a pint of stout, please."

"If you find a seat, I'll order."

Ten minutes later, after he'd almost lost his temper fighting his way to the front of the melee, he found Fleming sitting pensively at a table by the window with his bowler in front of him. He set their drinks down – a Guinness and a pint of tap water.

"That's the biggest G and T I've ever seen," Fleming remarked without smiling.

"I've a bit of a headache," Cassidy replied. "I've never seen anyone wearing one of those," he said, indicating Fleming's hat.

"They're due to make a comeback."

"Really? I'll have to get one."

"The trick is to wear it with a matching suit."

"If you spin it across the room, can it cut a man's head off?"

Fleming chuckled. "That would make ordering a meal easier."

Cassidy took a sip of his water. Fleming obviously wasn't much of a conversationalist. He hadn't even smiled at his own G and T quip, although he'd had the decency to chortle at the Oddjob one. It was only a first impression, but it was as if he actually wanted to be tenth in command because he had other more melancholy things to consider. Maybe he was on his way out. If you worked in London, maybe being sent to Newcastle was a polite insinuation that your days were numbered.

Fleming drank, then took out a handkerchief and wiped the foam from his upper lip. "So what's afoot?"

Cassidy lowered his voice and leaned over the table an inch. "You've reached us just at the culmination of the investigation. It's a Real IRA plot to bring explosives into the country. A deal struck in Lithuania, financed by Irish Americans. The carrier – a British citizen by the name of Henry Macintosh – is due to arrive in Britain by ferry next week in a Citroën Berlingo with a false bottom. We're expecting the transfer to occur in the living room of number 4 Armstrong Crescent, Jesmond."

"What's he bringing in?"

"He's the pie. I'm the fish and chips. Thank you."

Two plates were set down in from of them, then cutlery, by a teenage girl in an apron. Cassidy unfolded his napkin and tucked it into the front of his collar.

"Enjoy your meal," she said. She smiled and walked away.

"Military-grade explosives," Cassidy said. "Type 1A Semtex, ASA Compound and Composition C4, plus detonators."

"I take it he's a careful driver."

"It's a Citroën Berlingo."

This was as much as Fleming apparently wanted to know. They weren't going to exchange 'so what brought you here' stories. No point in getting pally, given the short time they were likely to be together.

Something of Fleming's sadness communicated itself to Cassidy, or it may have been the after-effects of drinking a quarter of a litre of 40% proof, and their conversation turned to the cricket match on the screen above the bar. After they'd finished eating Cassidy took him to the station to meet the other members of the investigative team. Solely a matter of politeness since in just over seven days' time he'd be on his way back to London and whatever grim fate apparently awaited him down there.

Chapter 10: A Potentially Fraught Interview

It was drizzling when the BAe 125 touched down at RAF Brize Norton and taxied to a halt. The nurses on board transferred their patient to a wheelchair and conveyed her down a disabled ramp into a specially adapted minibus, where two junior doctors were waiting with earnest faces and forms to be signed. A woman in a hijab and trainers joined them, tucking her ankle-length skirt under her thighs as she sat down. The nurses closed the rear doors and the bus pulled away with its wipers squeaking on the downturn.

Ghatola was conscious nearly all the time now, or that's what it felt like. Only the Nitrazepam helped and she wasn't sure how long it'd be till her system became accustomed to it. Horrible memories kept coming back, mainly explosions of blood, the faces of men she'd shot in the wrong place, one particularly vile man with half his neck blown away, his eyes wide open and mouth popping as if to protest the indignity.

They drove through the perimeter gate, and a billboard featuring a woman dressed only in her underwear came into view across a field. She'd seen such a thing before, but here it was normal. She was the odd one out now. She wondered how long it would be before she got used to the idea, if ever. She wanted to die. She was never going to see Reshtina again, and what would they have to say to each other anyway? Her face was melted on one side like an exhausted candle. She didn't even look human any more!

She felt Tasneem's hand slip between her fingers. The nurses had talked about plastic surgery on the way over. Yet she'd built herself up to die in the field. Balay would die and she'd flee his sons, that was the idea, but she'd always known the chances of making it to safety were slim. If the truth were known, she hadn't expected to survive beyond her fortieth birthday. This was a kind of *Barzakh*, waiting in the grave.

The minibus stopped before a detached house in a suburb in North London and she was taken inside to a ground floor flat with a raised bed, armchairs, a stereo music system, electric fire and a panoramic view of a garden with a pond and an orchard. The minibus driver accompanied them inside and explained everything in English, some of which Tasneem translated into Pashto. When he left, the silence was as thick as heat.

"This is perfect!" Tasneem said eventually. "What a lovely view, I could look at it all day. Would you like something to eat or drink? The kitchen's just next door and they've got some food in for us, isn't that lovely?"

"I'm not hungry, thank you. I'm feeling a little tired."

"Well, don't drop off. They're coming to interview you in a minute. Maybe you should have some coffee, wake you up a bit."

She smiled bitterly. "No, no coffee."

It was well known that coffee was the enemy of Nitrazepam, hence the most expensive commodity in *Barzakh*. Only you didn't pay for it in money.

"I want to practise walking some more," she said.

Twenty minutes' later, Tasneem opened the door to two women: one, small, middle-aged and African, carrying a handbag, the other more Afghan-looking and younger, with long black hair. Both wore trouser suits and had uncovered heads. For a moment, she felt relieved: Ghatola couldn't be that important to them if they'd only assigned women. But then she realised that gender wasn't necessarily tied to status here. Nothing in Britain was what it seemed, she had to be on her guard. She stepped aside with a smile, bidding them enter, although given how sick the country was, this was probably their house.

"Good afternoon," the Afghan-looking woman said in slightly stilted Pashto, "I'm Armaghan Jones. I'm a teacher by profession and I'm here to smooth over any difficulties there might be in your translation. This is Ruby Parker, who'll be asking the questions."

Tasneem recoiled slightly as if she'd been poked. "Why would there be difficulties in my translation?" she said in English.

"It's a precautionary measure," Ruby Parker replied without looking at her.

Tasneem blushed. Despite all her training, she had no idea what a 'precorshun-rimesher' was. Presumably, the African woman had said it just to teach her a lesson. She couldn't afford to alienate them, though. "Just come through," she said in English.

Ghatola was sitting in her armchair when they entered. She got to her feet, made a fist with her right hand, put her wrist across her breasts and bowed slightly without smiling. Ruby and Armaghan Jones responded with bows and they all exchanged names and sat down.

"I'm a member of British Intelligence," Ruby Parker began. "I've been sent to ask you a few questions about your past. We rescued you from the Taliban because we sympathise with what I've been reliably informed are the aims of the organisation you used to belong to. We'd like to airlift more of your members to safety if we can find them. They're almost certainly in great danger."

There was a time-lag while all this was translated, then Ghatola turned to Tasneem and they had a heated conversation.

"She wants to know who told you the aims of the organisation," Armaghan Jones said. "Ms Babar admits it was her. Ms Rahman wants to know why, what else has she told you. Ms Babar's trying to persuade her it's over, there's nothing to gain from concealment, they've discussed it already. Ms Rahman's saying they haven't discussed it. They discussed it in Kandahar, Ms Babar's saying. No we didn't, Ms Rahman's saying - "

Suddenly, Tasneem broke into tears and left the room at a brisk walk. Ghatola looked lividly at her feet.

"Maybe we should return tomorrow," Ruby Parker said.

Ghatola turned to her and spoke at length in a listless tone.

"She apologises for what just happened," Armaghan Jones said. "She would like to hear what you know about the organisation to which she once belonged, and what your intentions are beyond rescuing individuals. As far as she knows, it's not possible to go back in time."

Tasneem rushed back into the room with a plate of cakes. She put them at Ghatola's feet and went down on her knees speaking quickly, emotionally and verbosely.

"She says she's very sorry," Armaghan Jones said.

"Yes, I'd rather guessed it was that," Ruby Parker replied drily.

Ghatola kissed Tasneem on the forehead and said a few words in the same listless tone as a moment ago.

"She says, 'Offer our guests the cakes first'," Armaghan Jones said. "It's impolite to decline, by the way."

Tasneem wiped her eyes. She handed the cakes round and everyone had one. They were jam doughnuts from Morrison's. Ghatola ordered her to make a pot of tea.

Ruby Parker reached into her handbag. "Tell her I'd like to show her some photographs. These are women who have gone missing in Helmand, Kandahar and Zabul in the last eight weeks. We'd like to know if she recognises any of them."

Ghatola took the photographs and flicked through them without reaction until she came to the picture of Reshtina Sarbanri. She started and looked up as if she'd been caught out.

"Reshtina Sarbanri?" Ruby Parker said.

There was no need for a translation. Ghatola nodded and looked at the photo as if she wanted to climb into it. "Is she dead?" she asked.

"Not that we're aware," Ruby Parker said.

"How do you know her?"

"Her husband identified her to the Americans shortly before he died."

Ghatola closed her eyes and sighed.

"I'll be honest with you," Ruby Parker continued. "He told us the village elder was due to hand her over to the Taliban that night. We wondered what the Taliban could possibly want with one poor woman. And when we rescued her, she turned out to be ... you."

Tasneem returned with the tea and poured everyone a cup. Ghatola sat without speaking for so long, dusk seemed to creep in. Several minutes after everyone else had drained their cups, Ghatola's remained untouched. Her eyes filled with water. She exchanged glances with Tasneem and blinked hard, forcing the tears onto her cheeks.

"We were cold-blooded murderers," she began.

Chapter 11: Dinner With a Dumbass

Shadi knew she was taking her life in her hands crossing Tehran's streets with barely a sideways glance, but she almost wished she was dead anyway. The party would be in full swing now, and since the host's flat was soundproofed he'd think she was the Basijis come to give him a lecture on virtue. Too late: she'd missed it now, she might as well face it.

Bloody hell, bloody bastard hell. Old men, where did they get off? *There are no jokes in Islam, there is no humour in Islam, there is no fun in Islam.* She thrust her glasses back onto the bridge of her nose and pulled her Gucci headscarf off. The never-ending exhaust fumes, she wanted to vomit. It was a cold night, dirty, too much neon.

She turned onto Pasadaran Avenue and into New Naples, the coffee shop where she'd arranged to meet Esfandyar three quarters of an hour ago. Brightly lit, noisy as the traffic, full to bursting. She didn't know why she was even bothering. He'd probably gone on to Mostafa's with everyone else now, which would effectively mean she'd been dumped.

She suddenly felt very lonely. He'd be enjoying the host's mini-bar and snogging Farah, probably. Well they could rot in hell. She hoped the Basijis *did* turn up. She had a good mind to ring them herself. Fun, alcohol, snogging, Farah in a miniskirt, they'd probably get twenty lashes apiece.

But then she spotted him, hunched over a cappuccino and a comic book in his grey hoodie, trying to look like he didn't care that he'd been stood up. She immediately forgot her anger and shoved through the crowd as if her life depended on it. She put her bag on the floor and sat opposite him.

He looked up. "Where were you?"

"I'm *so* sorry. I know I've really let you down. I couldn't get away. I did everything."

He shrugged like the world had already ended so it was all academic. Nothing less than a full explanation would do. If she could make him laugh a little on the way, there was the slim possibility he might not chuck her at the end. But she didn't want to look too desperate, that might have the opposite effect. She took out her compact and lipstick and refreshed her lips in the mirror, then leaned over to him like he was everything to her.

Four people – two boys and two girls – suddenly pushed up against her. She didn't know them, but there was an unspoken agreement amongst the bache maruf, the cool kids, to form into groups here. The morality police frowned on isolated couples. "Thanks," she muttered. "An espresso, please," she told the waiter who'd glided up, putting twenty-five thousand Rials down for him.

"What kept you?" Esfandyar repeated.

"Completely out of the blue, we had to have dinner with this dumbass from Afghanistan and his three wives plus their 'interpreter'. He spoke like his balls hadn't even dropped yet, or maybe his wives had cut them off in a row about who should have him that night. And as for them, talk about *javad*. They could hardly hold their cutlery. One of them had this awful blotchy skin – I thought she was just dirty at first, but then it was *obvious* she'd caught something. She was full of stupid questions too: 'How long have you lived here?' 'Do all Iranians live like this?', 'Have you ever been to - I don't know: Loo-loo land', the name of her village somewhere. *Well, obviously, no, we haven't been to Loo-loo land, dummy, there's a war on and we don't want to get the shit bombed out of us.* She'd probably never held a conversation with adults before."

Esfandyar smiled, the start of forgiveness maybe. "I guess he must be fairly well off to have three wives."

"Yeah, or he's some kind of holy Salome. You know how my father is. Picks them up like flies. Like he's got a label on his back saying, 'Guardians of the Revolution, I'm a soft touch'."

"He wasn't always like that, though, was he? I mean, *you're* not like that and you're his daughter."

Her espresso arrived. She took a sip. "Bloody hell, don't let's get into his conversion. It's driving mother crazy, all of us in fact." She held her thumb and finger a millimetre apart. "She's *this close* to leaving him."

"Shouldn't you have stayed with her then?"

"I want to be with you. Anyway, I left Pardis with them, it's more in her line."

"I bet *she* was pleased."

"I'll tell you another thing. No-balls holy-beard was a smackhead as sure as I'm sitting here. Even mother could see it. I know Afghanistan's the heroin capital of the world, but even so, you'd think - "

"Come on, how could you tell that?"

"Oh, stop it. We both know the signs. Anyway, his second wife scoffed everything we put in front of her. 'Ravenous' doesn't begin to cover it. Fat as a tyre and it wasn't like she even leant sideways to conceal her burps. The third one, now she was just strange. Hardly said a word all night, probably not quite right in the head. In fact, I'm sure she wasn't."

"Why would anyone marry a woman who wasn't quite right in the head?"

She grinned. "I'm sure most men could think of reasons to make an exception."

"Was she pretty then?"

"Maybe with her hair done properly, a bit of make-up ... but who am I to talk? Actually, that's a point. None of them were wearing make-up."

"Obviously good Muslims then."

"We didn't talk about religion. I guess that was probably mother's influence. There's only so much she'll put up with. They did all clear off upstairs afterwards for a discussion of the finer points of the faith - or it may have been group sex. They're supposed to be staying overnight. I locked my bedroom door before I left. I don't want them going through my things while I'm out, helping themselves."

"You might find fatty sleeping in your bed when you get in."

"Afghanistan's Next Top Model!"

They laughed. She'd ridden the storm. Now all she had to do was turn him back on to the idea of Mostafa's.

"Still on for the party?" he said, pre-empting her. "I've texted them. They'll switch down the music when we get there. What time do you have to be back home?"

"I didn't say. Not too late."

The boy who'd pushed up next to Esfandyar earlier finished his coffee and leaned over to Shadi. "Can we come? I've got a car and so has my girlfriend. It'll make it easier if we travel over there separately."

She sighed. She'd kind of foreseen this. She turned to Esfandyar.

"Let's roll," he said.

Suddenly, her mobile rang. *Pardis*.

Bloody hell, was *anything* going to go right tonight? She'd only just climbed out of the last hole. She couldn't not answer, there was no anticipating the consequences. She put her finger in her left ear and the phone to the right.

"Hi, Shithouse, what's up?"

"Shadi, you've got to get back here. We've had processions of weird-looking men coming and going non-stop since you left, High Voice collapsed in the bathroom, and to make matters a thousand times worse, I overheard what they were talking about. They're suicide bombers!"

"You mean, you were listening with a glass at the wall."

"It's not *funny*."

"Where are they now?"

"They left, half an hour ago."

"I thought you said no-balls holy-beard had collapsed."

"I revived him. Look, you need to get back here."

"For what reason? What can I do?"

"Aren't you *listening*? I just said they're *suicide bombers!* How about 'go to the police'?"

Shadi sighed. "I'll be back later. They've gone, that's the main thing. Look, everyone knows the government wants a piece of Iraq once the Americans have gone, yeah? Even I know it. And if I know it, the police sure as hell do. This sort of thing gives them more of a pretext. So they're going to turn a blind eye."

"But suicide bombers blow up *mosques!*"

"Not all of them. The point is, if they've already gone we can't do anything about it. Other than get ourselves into trouble."

"Mother's beside herself."

"You didn't tell her, did you?"

"Tonight was the last straw. We've got to get out of this house, Shadi. Father's going to take us all down to hell with him and he's not going to care a fig. If you don't come home right now, you may not see us again. Your choice. Tonight was the last straw."

"*Bloody hell, all right then, I'm coming!*" But Pardis had already put the phone down. She turned to Esfandyar again. "Domestic emergency. My parents are about to split up. I have to go."

"I'm coming with you," he replied.

"What about the party?" protested the boy with the car.

She re-tied her headscarf. "There'll be others."

Chapter 12: A Raid on Macintosh's Hideaway

Midday, the sky overcast, the air chill. Dressed in flak jackets, clutching batons, Fleming, Cassidy and twelve other officers sat in an unmarked van three streets from the epicentre, waiting for surveillance to give the signal. Two further teams were set to swoop elsewhere at locations where incriminating evidence was ready to hand. Everything could still go wrong, but Macintosh had done nothing to suggest he was the overly-cautious type and the team was buoyed by a feeling of optimism mingled with fear. This was the kind of raid in which officers could, and did, get wounded or killed.

The radio screamed *go.* The van did 0 to 60 in starting and everyone gripped their seats as it screeched round three corners in succession. Suddenly, the back doors were agape and they all charged across the road and into the front garden of number four. Two officers screamed the policy-warning and battered the door down. Twelve others piled in so quickly that, except for the fact that they'd trained for it, they should have been in danger of tripping over one another.

There were three targets. Miller, a burly man in leather jacket; Grady, a skeleton whose T-shirt, trainers and facial hair were too big for him, and the prime objective, Macintosh himself, a red-faced baldie with a handlebar moustache and a swastika tattoo on his neck. Miller threw a suitcase at the incomers, but ineffectually. By the time he'd reached the back door, he'd been clutched. Six officers slammed him to the ground and cuffed him. Grady looked like he'd been expecting a raid for a long, long time, and his doctor had forbidden exertion. He was hauled to his feet. Both were read their rights.

"Where the bloody hell's Macintosh?" Cassidy shouted. Four men were already doing the upstairs search, but before they could return the negative, Fleming had already formed a hypothesis. The stairs were right next to the front door so for Macintosh to be on the first floor, he'd have to have gone there

on entry. There was a downstairs toilet, so that wouldn't explain it. The only alternative was that he'd made a first false entry: come straight in, gone straight through the back door to test the waters. Presumably, had there been no raid, he'd have re-entered through the front door again in a few minutes' time, on this occasion for good.

It took Fleming a single glance outside the back door to see that it was easier for a would-be fugitive to go right than left. He was succeeded by four other officers. Yes, there he was, hurdling the neighbours' fences. He'd already gained over a hundred metres.

Fleming left the chase to his colleagues. He ran through the front door into the road and turned right. If Macintosh was cautious enough to make a false entry, he was surely cautious enough to have left a getaway car somewhere. It would be pointing in this direction, so he could drive here if the coast was clear.

Then he saw him. Tearing up the driveway of number sixty-four, knocking two bins over and almost losing his balance. Towards a Peugeot 406, light blue, registration P765 JW1. He rived the door open, fumbled in his pockets, grabbed the steering wheel in his left hand and started the engine. Fleming was already running towards him.

Macintosh seemed to realise what was happening and that here was a heaven-sent opportunity to kill filth. There was a lamppost between Fleming and the car. He guessed Macintosh would try to run him over, and if that didn't work, ram the car into the lamppost. Fleming would be catapulted into it and probably killed on impact.

But foreknowledge was everything. He mounted the bonnet, punched a hole in the windscreen and grabbed Macintosh hard by the collar. When the Peugeot crashed into the lamppost, he used the IRA man to brake his flight, pulling him entire through the windscreen and twisting in mid-air so that he not only missed the post but landed with Macintosh underneath him to cushion his fall. He heard the suspect gasp and his ribs snap. Early days, but he hoped he hadn't killed him.

He climbed unsteadily to his feet, dimly aware of being covered in blood. A policewoman in a bullet-proof vest came running over. Short blonde hair, egg-shaped face, tall, feet succeeding each other on the tarmac like she'd been practising.

"Are you all right, sir?" she said. "There's an ambulance on its way. I'm Yvonne, by the way. WPC Yvonne Grimes. That was spectacular, if you don't mind my saying so."

His James Bond moment beckoned. He'd earned it. "Macintosh broke the oldest rule in the book, Grimes," he said.

"Er, what rule would that be, sir?"

"Clunk-click, every trip."

She put her head on one side and looked at him as if he was unhinged. His 007 moment fell on its side and expired. He'd probably never get another. "It was, um, something my parents used to say."

"I think you're in shock, sir. No offence. Sit down."

He did as she told him. "Well, I suppose I would be. You see, my wife ... she was killed in Afghanistan before I arrived here and ... and ... " He wiped his bloody forehead. "Macintosh should have been wearing his seat-belt, was the gist of my would-be joke. A lesson to boy racers everywhere."

"I'm very sorry about your wife, sir. I didn't know."

"Always belt up, as they say."

She smiled tenderly. "It's a minimum £60 fixed penalty fine with no endorsable points. But if it goes to court, it can rise to £500."

He nodded. "My view exactly."

Six other policemen arrived, including Cassidy. They looked Macintosh over and announced that he was still breathing. Cassidy got down on his haunches next to Fleming and patted him on the shoulder.

"Some of the explosives are missing," he said.

Fleming was discharged from A&E an hour after getting there to find WPC Grimes on a blue springback seat attended by a coffee, a solicitous expression and a Ford Fiesta. She ferried him home to a nondescript high-rise flat in the city centre and cooked him Chicken in Butter Sauce using ingredients she'd bought an hour ago in Waitrose, brewed and poured him another coffee, then grudgingly drove him, at his own insistence, back to HQ. She'd have preferred him to go to bed, she said, and so, she added, would all the doctors.

"We need to find out where that explosive is," he replied.

Grady, the skeleton, was generally considered most likely of the triumvirate to answer sensible questions, so Fleming and Cassidy foregathered with him in an interview room. They sat on one side of the table, he on the other. The problem wasn't his Jolly Roger attitude, as so often in these sorts of cases, but his indifference to gravity and air. But then, without warning, he started to come to life.

"We know what you started off with," Cassidy said. "We've got the inventory. We will find out where you ditched the detonators and the explosives because we've got fairly continuous CCTV footage of your journey north. But it would be nice if you could save us the trouble of scrolling through all those metres of videotape."

"What's the point?" Grady replied. "You'll have to scroll through them anyway if you want to know whether I'm telling the truth."

Fleming nodded. He didn't like Grady, but he could see he wasn't amenable to bribes or the suggestion of them. "Yes, but what DCI Cassidy means is that if you tell us in advance, we'll be pleased with you. And if you give us sufficient background information to help us make an arrest, you might even get a reduction in sentence."

"Why would I want to help you make an arrest?"

"I've just said."

"I don't want a reduction in sentence."

"Members of the Real IRA are never going to be popular in British prisons," Cassidy said. "It's not like the old days when you could count on being sent to the Maze, see your cronies, that sort of thing. Nowadays, you're a nobody nobody likes."

"I wasn't even driving the car," Grady said. "Why don't you ask Macintosh?"

Fleming cleared his throat. "Because he hasn't recovered yet."

"What happened to him?"

"He flew through a car windscreen," Cassidy said. "And a man landed on top of him."

"Is – is he going to be all right?"

"We don't know," Fleming replied.

"Who was the man?"

"Me," Fleming replied.

Grady looked at his hands. "You're probably going to get in trouble for that, you know. We've got lawyers."

"Which raises the question why you haven't asked to see yours yet," Cassidy said. "It's normally the first thing suspects do."

"Because I hate the bastards. They're part of the same bloody system the Irish have always lived under."

Fleming ground his teeth. He'd come across this sort of thing before.

"I take it you're a Marxist then?" Cassidy said.

Grady stared straight ahead like he'd just dragged on a cigarette and was savouring it. "That's right."

"Doesn't it bother you that the explosive you're missing could kill hundreds of innocent people?" Fleming asked.

"What do you think we bought it for?"

"And being beaten up by other prisoners doesn't bother you?" Cassidy said.

Grady shrugged. "I'll be looked after. Even if I'm not, it's part of what being a POW's about."

Fleming laughed. "A POW's if you were in a Stalag or an Oflag. A failed mass murderer sent down for twenty-five years to HM Dartmoor doesn't count."

Grady leaned forward. "You really think I'll get that long?"

"Rely on it," Cassidy said. "Of course, each new morsel of information you feed us means you can get time sliced off."

"I wonder where Ireland will be in twenty-five years," Fleming said. "The way the peace process is going, by the time you get out, you're going to be as utterly forgotten as Alwyn Jones and George Taylor."

"Who?" Grady said.

"Precisely," Fleming replied.

There was a knock at the door. Fleming opened it to find WPC Grimes holding a document wallet to her bosom. She beamed. "We've got fresh news, sir. We've found where the extra explosives were offloaded. We've got it on camera."

"I didn't thank you for coming to retrieve me from hospital earlier, Grimes. Thank you. And for the meal. Where do we have to go to see the footage?"

"This way, sir. You'd probably better bring the DCI. I've asked Throckmorton and Smith to escort Grady back to his cell."

He beckoned Cassidy and they followed Grimes to the analysis room where six officers sat discussing case notes or poring over stills. Whatever they'd seen was obviously inspiring. They showed no sign of noticing the new arrivals. Grimes walked up to the recorder and pressed rewind. Fleming and Cassidy stood as close to the screen as they could get.

The film quality wasn't good. They were looking at a multi-storey car park. A Peugeot 406 pulled into a space with Macintosh vaguely identifiable in the driving seat, and a white man in his mid thirties entered stage left. He wore a sports jacket, jeans and loafers and carried a satchel. Macintosh got out of the car. They looked around but for some reason failed to spot the camera. The man took a packet from his bag. Macintosh opened it and counted what were obviously bank-notes. This went on for nearly four minutes. Then Macintosh handed the man a package, which the latter transferred to his satchel. They shook hands, exchanged a few solemn words, and the man exited walking. Macintosh got into his car, reversed out and left.

"Are we sure that's the explosive?" Fleming asked.

"We're miles from being able to prove it in a court of law, sir," Grimes replied. "It's mainly a case of 'what else could it be' at the moment. Which isn't, by any means, to say it couldn't be something else. Yet we've no evidence to suggest he smuggles drugs. And he's been abroad lots of times. He's had the opportunities."

"Have you any idea who the recipient was?" Fleming asked.

"None whatsoever, sir. We're working on it, as you see."

Fleming looked around. Half a dozen officers flicking through files and gossiping.

"The computers are elsewhere in the building, sir," Grimes remarked drily.

"My apologies," Fleming said. "I wonder if you'd mind showing us it again? 'Yvonne', isn't it?"

She beamed. "Yes, sir, it is. I'll put it on now, sir."

"There's no need to keep calling me 'sir', by the way. I'm MI5. I'm not your superior. Rather, the opposite."

She blushed. Bloody hell, he'd offended her. Stated the obvious. But then it was her fault. All that sir-ing.

"I don't think there's any need," Cassidy croaked.

Fleming realised that until now his colleague hadn't spoken. He turned to him. At some point since entering the room he'd blanched.

Grimes apparently noticed it too. "Is there anything the matter, sir?" she asked.

Cassidy turned his eyes on both of them as if they were ropes and he was falling off a cliff. "I – I'd like to see it again," he said. "But I'm not sure there's any need. It was quite ... drawn out, wasn't it?"

Fleming furrowed his eyebrows. "What's the matter, Ashraf?"

"I think I recognise the man Macintosh gave the explosives to."

"And?"

"And it was the man my wife left me for. Jonathan Butler. Or at least that's what he used to be called. Before he got religion and ruined my marriage. These days he goes by the name of Shahid Abduttawwah."

Chapter 13: Even More Exciting than Cake

Tasneem Babar looked around her for the final time to make sure she hadn't been followed, then entered *Branaghan's*, a no-frills cafe on Islington's Holloway Road. The chequered floor tiles hosted twenty five laminate tables, four seats apiece, fixed into the ground. One of the strip-lights flickered, the plastic wallpaper was in need of replacing, exactly the sort of place Idris Kakahel and Haider Chamkanni would choose, she thought: unambitious, slightly seedy.

And there they were, sitting side by side in new sweaters and quilted jackets at the table farthest from the window, cups and saucers in front of them, the only customers. They looked up as she entered, and straightened, as if to say 'finally'. She slipped onto one of the two chairs directly opposite them with an irritable sigh.

"You said you'd be here fifty minutes ago," Idris Kakahel said. "What would you like?"

"What do you mean, 'like'?" Tasneem replied.

"To eat or drink. You've got to order something if you want to stay here. Even though it's a dump and it's empty apart from us."

"Keep your voice down," Haider Chamkanni said.

Tasneem folded her hands on the table and looked at the menu above the counter. "I'll have a cup of tea and a piece of chocolate cake."

"You can have a cup of tea and that's all," Idris Kakahel said sourly. "The budget doesn't quite stretch to cake."

She shrugged. "How did you get into Britain? And who gave you permission to contact me?"

A stout, bald man in an apron came over and took their orders – three teas – and their money. He fished their change from his trouser pocket.

"One bloody pound *ten* for a cup of tea!" Haider Chamkanni hissed, as if it was the ten that was so offensive.

"It's two pounds fifty for a slice of cake," Idris Kakahel said.

"I'll get my own," she replied contemptuously.

"We don't need your permission to contact you," Haider Chamkanni told her. "As for how we got into Britain: officially, we're here to attend a family wedding. Unofficially, we're here on business."

She put on her bored expression. They were idiots. "I'd kind of guessed the latter, given that you've come to the 'wedding' together when you're not related, and that you saw fit to drag me all the way out here for a cup of tea."

The stout, bald man brought their tea and set it down in front of them. Tasneem took a five pound note from her pocket. She'd teach them.

"Could I have a piece of chocolate cake, please?" she asked, in English.

"Coming right up," the man said. He fumbled in his trousers and set her change on the table. She scooped it up.

"I might have a piece of orange cake too," she said, switching back to Urdu.

"You bloody miserable bitch," Idris Kakahel said.

She laughed. "I take it you didn't budget for this trip, boys, and that you're finding it difficult to scrounge from your non-existent relatives. I don't understand. Islamabad's normally pretty generous when it comes to funding foreign operations."

The two men exchanged uncomfortable glances. "Islamabad doesn't know we're here," Haider Chamkanni said.

"Why, you do surprise me. I wonder how it is, then, that you don't need my permission to contact me? After all, I report to the Director General. I don't report to you two."

Idris Kakahel's face filled with fury. "Because pretty soon, sister, we're going to go down a storm in Islamabad. We'll be successful enough for the Director General to want to take credit. And when he does, he'll have to validate our mission retrospectively. And then we'll be promoted and you'll be out on your fat arse."

The bald, stout man set down her chocolate cake. "Enjoy."

She dug her spoon through the icing into the sponge and put it into her mouth. "Mmm, that *is* good. Would you like a slice between you, boys? Maybe I could treat you."

They exchanged looks again. "We're not here for cake," Idris Kakahel said.

"You're actually starving, aren't you?" she said.

A bolt of pain flashed across Haider Chamkanni's face. He shuddered. "We've found Reshtina Sarbanri."

Tasneem put her spoon down. They couldn't be serious. These two? They had to have made a mistake. "You've *found* her? Where?"

"We first caught wind of her in Tehran. That was a fortnight ago. Five days later, she was in Tabriz. Last night she crossed the Ararat massif into Turkey. She's currently, we think, in Agri."

Suddenly, she wasn't interested in her cake. "My God. Alone?"

"Apparently not. In company with three other women. One of whom is an old friend of yours. Nangial Abdullah."

"*Nangial?*" She thought for a few moments. "Still, that would make sense maybe. They must have worked together at some point. What about the other two?"

"As far as we can tell they've no prior association with the Afghan Women's Reparation Brigade. They're complete unknowns."

She clicked her tongue. "Why aren't you hot on their trail? I thought that was the idea. Kill her and kill Ghatola and that's the end of them."

"Keep your voice down!"

"I *am!* Besides, what's the point? No one here understands Urdu!"

Idris Kakahel sighed. "We're not equipped to cross desert plains and mountain ranges. We don't have the resources."

"Or the stamina," she said. "How sure about this are you? You haven't actually seen them first hand, I take it. How do you know it's not someone in Islamabad playing you for a couple of saps?"

"We've a friend among the people smugglers," Haider Chamkanni replied. "We asked him to keep an eye out for her. He charges, of course, but he's very reliable. We get to find out when she arrives in Britain too."

"And where?"

"We know that already. Dover."

"So – what? You're going to be waiting on the beach with a shotgun? Here, take my cake. I don't want any more."

"You haven't heard the best bit," Haider Chamkanni said. "They're not coming over here to rescue Ghatola. They're coming on a suicide-bombing mission."

She looked at each of them in turn. She grinned, then laughed. "You poor boys. Someone *is* playing you for a sap. How much did this 'source' of yours charge? A packet, I bet. No wonder you're finding it impossible to afford a piece of cake. Please don't mention my name in your report, will you? I'll never survive the indignity." Her face fell as she suddenly saw her predicament. "What the hell am I saying? I *am* associated with you!"

"I know it sounds absurd," Idris Kakahel said. "That was our first thought. But there's a watertight line from the people traffickers to their contacts in Britain. Reshtina Sarbanri and her friends are being passed from A to B to C by paying customers who, once she gets to Z, are going to want their money's worth. Put it this way, if she's thinking about double-crossing them, where's she going to hide while her asylum application's being processed? They'll hunt her down like a pack of jackals chasing a deer on an empty plain."

Tasneem reclined and thought for a moment. "From what I know about her, she's not stupid. She must have realised that."

"So perhaps she's in earnest," Idris Kakahel said.

"At any event, we can afford to let events unfold at their own pace," Haider Chamkanni added with a smile.

Tasneem pinched her chin. "I don't understand why she would genuinely want to bomb Britain."

"It's obvious, isn't it?" Haider Chamkanni said. "The British kidnapped her friend. She's obviously found that out, God knows how. And whatever we might think of them, we all recognise there's no love lost between the AWRB and the British. She must have decided there's no realistic hope of her ever seeing Ghatola Rahman again. She probably wants revenge."

"They must have been pretty close," Tasneem said.

"Probably."

"So you think she's a *bona fide* suicide bomber?" she said, stroking her jawbone.

"As I just said, God help her if she isn't."

She chuckled. "God help her if she *is*. So what do we hope to gain from her if she's the real deal?"

"A quicker end to the war. We all know how sensitive Western governments are to public opinion. They'll timetable withdrawal a whole year, even eighteen months earlier than currently scheduled. And in the resulting melee, we'll re-install the Taliban, set India back a decade, and we all get *Nishan-i-Quaid-i-Azam* medals."

"Really? You think it'll pan out that well, do you? Even though none of that's in your gift?"

"It's common sense. Now why don't you kill Ghatola Rahman – she's of no further use to us – and go home?"

She'd underestimated these two, that was certain. But only a little. "Not so fast. Where's your insurance? If Reshtina Sarbanri does decide to duck out of her responsibilities, who better to take her in than her old friend?"

Idris Kakahel smirked. "How's she going to find her, given that she thinks she's dead?"

"If she makes an asylum application, her name will go onto a computer. After that, it's only a matter of time before MI5 pick it up. They'll do the legwork, believe me."

"Maybe you're right," Haider Chamkanni said reluctantly.

"I am right." She reached into her pocket, took out her billfold and peeled off ten twenties. "Get yourselves something to eat and drink, and probably somewhere to stay. Text me when you need more, and for any assistance. But don't take me for a sap."

She finished her tea, then stood up and walked out.

Chapter 14: Would You Like That Investigation Upgrading, Sir?

It took Cassidy a moment to realise that no, he didn't need to see it again. Some faces you'd recognise anywhere. He'd often wondered how that could be so. A face could age or appear from an oblique angle or blurred in a photo and, providing it had impressed itself sufficiently on you at some unspecified point in the past, you'd still be able to say whose it was. Jonathan Butler aka Shahid Abduttawwah, the man his wife had preferred. He'd recognise him anywhere.

"Sit down, sir, and say that again," Grimes said.

So she'd gone back to calling him 'sir'. To be expected, really, with someone like Fleming in town. He'd never really stood a chance with her, anyway. A single date. One swallow doesn't make a summer.

The six or eight people in the room had put down their case notes and photos and crowded him hungrily, willing him to give up his information. Fleming restrained them, guiding him to the chair Grimes was bringing as if he was a nonagenarian.

Then silence fell.

"Tell us again," Fleming said.

"I suppose I'd better go way back," he said. "Give you the full picture. My father was an official in the Malaysian government in the fag-end days of the British empire. My mother was a native Kuala Lumpuran, twenty years his junior. Rather Somerset Maugham, except that it outlasted imperialism's spell. I was born in Cleethorpes in 1963. My father was a religious indifferentist, and since my mother was a Muslim, that's how I was brought up."

A man in a leather jacket brought him a glass of water. He waved it away."I'm fine. Stop treating me as if I'm in shock. I was just a bit surprised, that's all."

"Go on," Fleming said.

"I met Julie at Exeter when we were both in our final year. She was doing Law and she'd just converted to Islam. I don't know how we met, because I never went to the Union of Muslim Students. As far as I could see, it was just a bunch of Salafis exchanging gripes."

"You're losing me," Fleming said.

"Yes, sorry. Salafi-ism emphasises seventh century Muslim theology. With the support of the Saudis it's slowly supplanting all other forms of Islam. Which is a bit like someone replacing Blenheim Palace with seven acres of bog-standard semis. It's one reason Islam has such a bad reputation in the West."

"I'd dispute that," a man with a shaven head said. "Sorry, I'm a Salafi. I don't consider myself a 'bog standard semi'."

"Everyone's a Salafi," Cassidy said. "Or we will be."

The man with the shaven head rolled his eyes. "Maybe let's just get back to the story, Ashraf, eh?"

"There's not much more to tell. Julie and I married, Julie became more and more zealous, I lost my faith entirely. I guess it upset me to see it being bulldozed. I used to go to Malaysia quite a lot when I was a kid. Muslims there were reasonably tolerant. Not so much nowadays. And then she met Jonathan Butler stroke Shahid Abduttawwah. Like a lot of converts, he uses his original name with his old, non-Muslim acquaintances."

"When did this happen?" Fleming said. "I mean, when did she leave you?"

"A year ago. I should have foreseen it, really. Converts are the same in all religions. They feel they have to prove themselves all the time."

"Let's concentrate on Butler, shall we?" Fleming said. "Anyone know where we can pick him up?"

"We've just received an address, sir," Grimes said. She handed him a slip of paper. He handed it to Cassidy.

"Let's not go in with all guns blazing," Cassidy said. "If he's got explosives, it could be dangerous. But in addition he's probably working with others. We'll bring him in for questioning, but it has to look to his friends as if he's suddenly taken a long holiday, yes? They mustn't know we've got him. What do you think, Fleming?"

Fleming pinched his throat. "I'm not sure I agree."

"Why not?"

"He may have passed the explosives to someone else by now. If we bring him in, he'll clamp up, because that's how ideologues work. And every hour he says nothing brings us closer to an explosion. Surveillance and phone taps in the first instance, that's my advice, try to net some of the other fish. But I'm not in charge."

"Yvonne – I mean, Grimes, would you get me a still photo of Butler, a print-off of the footage?"

"I'll pick them up from the reports office. We've several already."

"What's your plan?" Fleming asked.

"It's time for another chat with our man in the interview room."

Grady sat where they'd left him, but with his arms dangling and his chin on his neck like his batteries had run out.

"Wake up," Cassidy told him.

Fleming put five stills of Butler on the table side by side. "Recognise him?"

Grady yawned. "Might do."

"Where's he fit into the structure of the Real IRA? Commander? Divisional commander?"

"Why would I tell you?"

"But he is one of you, isn't he?" Cassidy said. "That's him accepting a consignment of explosives, after all. Jonathan Butler."

Grady smiled. "Looks like the party's back on."

"The 'blowing up defenceless men, women and children as they're minding their own business party', you mean," Cassidy said.

"Yeah, that one."

"Except that Jonathan Butler doesn't belong to the Real IRA," Fleming said. "His other name's Shahid Abduttawwah."

Grady sat up. "What? Like a Towel Head?"

"We discovered his real identity half an hour ago," Fleming said.

"Sure. You're bluffing. I want to see my lawyer now."

"I think that's an excellent idea," Cassidy said. "Get some independent verification. If we can't persuade you, he or she will be able to. What's the name?"

Grady blanched. "Fogarty. It's in my jacket pocket."

Cassidy leaned outside the door and instructed someone to find the card and call the solicitor.

"We all know that, where explosives are concerned, time's of the essence," Fleming went on. "It's only fair to warn you that if Abduttawwah uses what you've given him to mount an attack on an US airline – always popular targets for Islamists - you might find yourself on a one-way voyage to Guantanamo Bay. At which point you can wave goodbye to your hope of being 'looked after' with POW dignity. If the reports are to be believed, you'll be tortured. Indefinitely."

A middle-aged man with a mug of tea poked his head round the door. "Mr Fogarty's on his way, sirs."

Grady put his head in his hands. "Bloody shit."

Cassidy beckoned Fleming outside. They closed the door behind them.

"What's up?" Fleming said.

"We're wasting time. If Grady thinks Abduttawwah's Real IRA, it's highly unlikely he knows much about him. The best thing we can do is get Fogarty to confirm the truth then let him stew. Anything he does know should come to the surface naturally. He obviously doesn't want a trip to Cuba. In the meantime, let's see how the surveillance team's shaping up."

Grimes met them on the way to the incident room. "We've got a couple of plain clothes detectives outside his house now."

"I want to know everything about him," Cassidy said. "Friends, family, background, where he sleeps, eats and defecates."

Two hours later, they stood in team operations room looking at a diagram of Abduttawwah's mobile phone contacts, complete with dates and times of incoming and outgoing calls and texts for the previous fortnight. Sixteen were regular contacts – once or twice daily – and all young Muslim men; a further twenty-three, posted round the diagram's periphery, were irregular contacts, once a week or less. Abduttawwah's mobile lay at the centre. The further away you went, the more irregular the contact. Each name was attached by a pin so that it could be moved in or out as fresh information required.

"You realise Abduttawwah's almost certainly in the wrong place?" Fleming said.

"What do you mean?"

"He's the go-between. The Islamists realise they'll never get men like Macintosh to part with their Semtex if an Asian guy's involved. It has to be a caucasian. But that's probably Abduttawwah's only significance. It would be too much of a coincidence if he was both the fence and the main player."

"We'll know a bit more once we start listening to his conversations."

"We need more manpower. We should be watching nearly all these individuals. Contacts of contacts."

"Taken care of. The Chief Constable's drafting a hundred extra personnel in, some from other authorities."

Fleming smiled. He liked Cassidy a lot. "A hundred ought to take care of it."

Chapter 15: The Man on the Unicycle With the Cinnamon Footballs

When the show started, sixty-seven year old Beşir Davutoğlu was sitting on a high stool in his kiosk overlooking the Bosphorus Bridge, handing out newspapers, Istanbulkarts and change. Three women in black chadors rounded the corner where the cafes were, preceded by one of those fine traditional men with thick beards. The midday sun made the pavements glister; the sea flashed, the traffic roared, the tourists gazed at the ground like cattle, alternately revealing what was happening with the bearded man then hiding it. Easterners, obviously, dressed like that, possibly not even Turkish. Maybe an apartment somewhere in the city. Wouldn't stay long.

Suddenly, the man stumbled and fell over. Contrary to what Beşir Davutoğlu expected, the women stopped like they were used to it and gathered for a little conference. They came forward leisurely and got their husband – he couldn't be anything else – to his feet. You could feel the heat of their embarrassment even through their thick garments, even in the roasting sun.

That bastard, Egemen Dinçer, unicycled by them with his cinnamon blobs on sticks and didn't even pause for breath. Typical. Mind you, no one else stopped. Sadness broke out in Beşir Davutoğlu like a rash. Prophet Muhammad, peace be upon him, would have helped. *Helping a person mount his animal or load his baggage onto it is charity, a good word is charity, to remove obstacles in the street is charity.* The world was in its last days, a fine traditional man like that with a thick beard left to fend for himself, even his worthless curs of wives keeping their distance.

Still, they were all right now. Beşir Davutoğlu picked up his *Hürriyet,* and refolded it at the sports news. Another good result for Beşiktaş, back at the top, although it was early days and their next few matches weren't against pushovers – Gaziantepspor unbeaten this season, and Manisaspor on a mini-run. He wondered if he could get a ticket. Yiğit could probably get him one if he asked nicely. But then there was that thing his wife had planned – was it Saturday or Sunday? If Sunday –

There went the man with the beard again, down hard on his hands and knees. That bastard, Egemen Dinçer, obscured them from view for a moment, up and down like a monkey with his cinnamon excrescences, poking his disgusting purple face at the tourists. Had it not been for the way his wives reacted – again with mingled mortification and disdain – Beşir Davutoğlu would have rushed to help. But there was no telling how three ruffled women might react when confronted with public awareness of their shame. For the time being, providing he stayed behind his *Hürriyet*, and the passersby pretended not to see, and that bastard, Egemen Dinçer, remained preoccupied selling his cinnamon-coated balls of crap, perhaps they could persuade themselves they were still within the realms of propriety. Odd things, women.

They had another conference and pulled him upright again. There was a bench nearby, where a young couple were feeding the birds. Room for four more people, at a pinch. Beşir Davutoğlu hoped they'd seen it. Their poor husband ...

Then it occurred to him what was really happening. Of course! Up from the countryside for a few days – probably a family wedding or an *aqiqah* – suddenly he'd developed a taste for the local Raki. So it was the wives he should feel sorry for. Of course, as good Muslim women, they still had a duty of care, but he could sympathise with their predicament.

They'd seen the bench, thank God. They helped their husband over to it, and almost threw him on there. The young couple stood up and left. The wives stood in front of him and berated him with barely concealed fury. Beşir Davutoğlu wondered what life would be like for them all once they got home. Would they forget all this ever happened, or would it mark the beginning of a new era in their mutual relations? It was a shame to see such a fine Muslim man reduced to a nonentity. Not much of an advertisement for the faith. All those smug Westerners, out in their bathing tops, going home with stories about what hypocrites the traditionalists were. *Do you know, dear, they're supposed to avoid alcohol, but we saw this man with a big beard and three wives in chadors, and he was actually drunk in the street, in broad daylight!* Of course, they were all pretending not to look, but they were looking all right. It was probably the best thing they'd seen since the Blue Mosque.

The man sat and fondled his beard and nodded his acknowledgement of his disgrace. Then the women seemed to run out of insults. The whole group remained virtually motionless for a few minutes, the wives standing, the man sitting pensively looking at the young couple – two benches down now – feeding the birds.

Then something outstanding happened. Egemen Dinçer rolled up to them and held out one of his cinnamon shitballs. They barked at him so hard he nearly had a puncture. He tried to reply in kind but he was no match for three frustrated women. He did a three-point turn and cycled off then hit a bump or something and went splat on his face, crashing on his tray and smashing it all over the pavement. The 'cinnamon footballs' or whatever he called them nowadays went skidding off in every direction. He struggled to his feet rubbing his forehead and left side.

Beşir Davutoğlu was alone, so he didn't have anyone to share the joke with, but he laughed so hard the tears ran down his face. He sold three *Hürriyets* to customers who clearly wished they'd gone to a different kiosk, not one with a giggling maniac, and eventually he had to crouch down below the counter to recover. When he picked himself up, there was a queue. Then he started laughing again. He completed the sales and re-submerged.

Those fine old traditional country women, he thought, as he crouched in the dust. The world needed more, many more.

Chapter 16: Change of Command

Grimes washed, Fleming dried, and since it was her flat and she knew where everything was, she did the putting away. Then they went back into the living room to watch *My Best Friend's Wedding*. She'd seen it ten times, it was her favourite film and she wanted him to see it too because she wanted it to be his favourite film. He'd never quite understood why anyone would want to see a film eleven times, but he'd met lots of women in the past who felt the same way about *Titanic* or *Love Actually*.

She wore a pink mini skirt and flesh tights, and her make-up. He'd never noticed she was attractive before, but then, he reasoned, probably no one looks attractive in police get-up. He wore chinos and a striped tailored shirt. Her flat was like her: neat and unpretentious. A lounge suite and a dining table in the same room, a small fitted kitchen and one bedroom with a single bed and a teddy bear, her sole concession to kitsch. Fleming had agreed to dinner on the understanding that he was too recently widowed to want another relationship and, assuming she was intending to cook for him, he'd buy the ingredients and either keep out of the kitchen or help with the chores. She'd agreed to his terms and conditions and opted for him to stay out of Chef's way. When she said she wanted her favourite film to be his, though, he began to have doubts about her long-term intentions. In addition to which, she'd lit candles.

"How long is this movie?" he asked.

She took his hand, looked at the case and sat down on the sofa, making him sit next to her. "A hundred and five minutes. Come on, it's not even two hours."

"It's nearly eleven o'clock. We're both supposed to be at work at nine tomorrow."

"There's nothing to stop you staying here. I mean, I'd sleep on the sofa."

"I wouldn't dream of making you sleep on the sofa."

She laughed. "Well, *you* sleep on it."

"All for the sake of *My Best Friend's Wedding*. What if I don't like it?"

"In that case, you can sleep on the floor. Or in the corridor. Or on the streets."

He smiled. "Between us, we've had one and a half bottles of wine. It's inevitable we're going to feel like throwing caution to the wind to some extent. But it would be a mistake."

"Forget about the film. We can watch it another time. If we're going to be friends maybe we should just talk. Find out a little about each other."

"What's to tell? I've already said, I was born in Gloucestershire, one of four children, schooled in Harrow, two years in the Coldstream, two in the Met, two in MI5, to be continued."

"I'd like to tell you something about myself, if that's okay."

He shrugged. He had a feeling he knew roughly what was coming. "Go on."

"Ashraf and I had a relationship."

Some response was definitely called for, and nodding was as good as any. "But it's over now, I take it?"

She leaned forward. "Does it matter?"

"Only that, from the little I know about you both, I think you were probably well suited. He's a nice guy, you're a nice woman."

She frowned. "Oh, *no*, we weren't suited at all!"

"Good job it's over then, I suppose."

"Don't you want to know about it? I mean, as a friend?"

Catch-22. "Only if you want to talk about it," he replied.

"I just feel you should know. You see, it may be that he's a bit frosty with you from time to time. I don't want you to think it's anything you've done."

"It was you that ended it, I take it."

"I had to. I don't love him. I respect him, but there's no point in me raising false hopes. He'll find someone that loves him, eventually. There are loads of girls much better than me out there. And like you say, he's a nice guy. A really nice guy."

"And he loves you? Tell me when I've reached the point where it's none of my business, by the way."

"He *says* he does."

"He probably does, then."

She sighed. "But I don't want someone like Ashraf. He's safe, predictable and boring. I don't want that sort of life. I didn't become a WPC so I could end up becoming Mrs Humdrum."

"If you crave excitement, why didn't you become a criminal? It pays a lot more, the hours are better and you get to meet interesting people in exotic locations."

She laughed uncertainly. "I didn't want to end up in jail."

"Statistically, you probably wouldn't have to. If you were imaginative enough."

She didn't seem to know what to do with her eyes. "Is this leading somewhere? You're not involved in anything illegal, are you?"

"Would I tell a WPC if I was?"

She edged an inch closer to him. "Anyway, I just wanted you to know that Ashraf and I are history."

He nodded again and smiled bitterly. "It's none of my business, Yvonne. Look, I like you as a friend, but I'm not ready for anything more."

"I accept that. I just want you to know I'll be waiting when you are. And I'm very patient."

He sighed. "I'll be going back to London when all this is over."

"It doesn't mean we have to lose touch. What about phone calls and text messages, Facebook and Twitter?"

He felt like throwing his hands up. "Let's not run before we can walk, eh? We don't even know whether we're suited as friends yet. We might discover unpalatable things about each other. Habits, preferences, opinions, any number of things. Added to which, I'm a raw widower."

"You'll get over her. Everyone thinks they won't when they lose someone precious. But they all do."

"If anything, I'm the sort who idealises the one they've lost."

She sat in silence for a few seconds. He could almost hear her heartbeat.

"What was she like?" she whispered.

The question he didn't want, and yet it had all been leading up to this. Everything had been, since he first heard she was dead. The cliché said Life Goes On. He'd shaken hands with it and tried to make it true by force of arms when he should really have taken time to grieve. Grieving was by nature painful, but his grieving would be agonising, because Marcie was unique. Everyone else was replaceable. There were millions of Yvonnes, although he couldn't tell her that, millions of Flemings, millions even of people the world considered unique: Gandhis, Martin Luther Kings, the whole saintly bunch. Only one Marciella Hartley-Brown.

"You're crying," Yvonne said.

He wasn't, only a little water had gathered on his eyelashes. *What was she like?* It deserved an answer. Maybe Yvonne would stop pestering him then.

"She was about your height, one of nature's rebels, I suppose. She had a criminal record, for what it's worth."

She sat up. "What?"

"She had an ASBO too, although I understand the two things aren't necessarily connected."

"I don't believe it. You're joking."

"I married her because I didn't want to be Mr Humdrum," he replied drily.

"What about your career? There must be lots of opportunities for excitement in MI5 without your marrying a criminal. And you could have anyone you want ... probably. When you said you'd been married, I pictured you with someone horsey and mega-posh."

She turned away, obviously wondering what this meant for her. Did she want someone who not only fraternised with the common enemy, but married into its ranks?

As he watched her eyebrows try to calculate the permutations, he didn't know what to think. On one level, he was deeply impressed with her. She saw the police as good fighting evil, and herself on the front line. On another level, he felt sorry for her. Her eventual disillusionment was inevitable. On a third, he was repulsed by her narrow mindedness. He didn't dare tell her Marcie *had* been 'posh'. That would probably throw her even further.

"I think I'd better be going now," he said.

She stood up. "I'm so sorry. I didn't mean to offend you. I was just a bit shocked. It wasn't what I expected."

He picked up his jacket. "I'm not offended. The meal was lovely, and I enjoyed your company. I'll see you tomorrow."

"Will we – will we meet up outside work again?"

"I don't know. Yes, yes, of course we will. Maybe not like this. Remember, we're just friends, yes?" He tried to think of some way of softening what he was trying to say, but couldn't. "Good night."

He let himself out. He had no idea what she saw in him, other than that he was supposed to be conventionally good looking and he was in MI5. Since she was an idealist either one of those two things was likely to appeal to her. The truth was, he wasn't half the man she took him for. Paradoxically, seeing himself through her eyes made him feel inadequate.

He walked down two flights of steps and onto a deserted street with iron railings on the far side and two yellow street lights overhead. There were no cars, parked or moving. This was a quiet part of the city and the residents had garages elsewhere. He'd come by taxi, anticipating the inevitable bottle of wine. It was time to switch his phone back on.

Six missed calls. Bloody hell, he wondered who could want him at this hour. It had to be work. He scrolled the callers. It was. He heard stilettos behind him. Okay, so she'd decided to come after him. He hoped this was work too.

He turned round to find her edging her hair from the collar of a coat she'd obviously just slung on.

"I should have rung a taxi for you," she said, matter-of-factly. "Another clumsy mistake. I'm not much good at this having-a-friend-round stuff. Anyway, work wants us. Our ride should be along in a minute. They want you to switch your phone on by the way."

"Why didn't they ring you?" he asked.

"They did."

"I mean, earlier."

She narrowed her eyes as if he was doing it deliberately. "I'm not senior enough. And I'm a woman."

The taxi appeared round the corner at a crawl, the driver looking for the address. She put her hand up and it sped up towards them. She got into the front seat, leaving him no choice but to get into the back.

It angered him that she thought he was part of a conspiracy, and even that she thought there was one. The truth was likely much more prosaic: Ashraf was jealous. He wanted to punish her for having dinner with the man from London. Which of course, boiled down to the fact that she was a woman. He wasn't punishing *him*, after all. So she was probably right.

Twenty minutes later, they reached the police station. She paid – he thought he'd better let her, although he didn't feel good about it – and they entered in silence.

He stopped. He didn't take her arm, that would be presumptuous, but luckily she registered his immobility and froze.

"I didn't come here to usurp you or anyone else," he said. "I told DCI Cassidy that at the outset."

"Let's just forget it," she replied neutrally. She walked off.

Cassidy's office was two doors down from the interview room. His wall was coated with drawing-pinned circulars, the floor-space halved by box folders in baskets. He was alone. He'd obviously just come from somewhere because the door was open and he showed no inclination to sit at his desk.

"You didn't both have to come," he said.

"It seemed sensible," Fleming said. "And right." Which was as much as he could say without embarrassing either one or both of them. He noticed Grimes had quietly fallen to the rear. He took a pace backwards to stand next to her, hoping it wouldn't be misinterpreted. "What's happened?"

"We've got a 'Maulana Mousa Badreddin' and his two wives in the interview room."

Fleming whistled. "*The* Maulana Mousa Badreddin?"

"Do you know another one?" Cassidy said.

"I'm sorry, I don't know who you're talking about," Grimes said tetchily. "Maybe I missed the briefing."

"He's one of the names on the Abduttawwah phone chart," Fleming said. "Available for public scrutiny in the Team Operations room. Come on, Yvonne, you must have looked at it a hundred times. We all have."

She blushed. "Sorry, it's very late. I'd forgotten."

"I happen to be good at names, that's all. And tactlessness, sorry. Why's he here?"

"He came in of his own volition about an hour ago," Cassidy said. "He's given us a statement about the explosives, we're keeping him at his own insistence till we've checked out his evidence. The search warrants should come through shortly. I'm putting three teams together. Yvonne, I'd like you to head one. Naziz is taking another. Fleming, you'll be with me."

"Me?" Grimes said.

"I thought you wanted to."

She brightened. "I do. Thank you, sir. Who's going to be with me?"

"Begg, Frostrup, Johnson, Short, Jackson. We're meeting in Operations in twenty minutes' time, on the assumption that the warrants prove a formality."

"I'm sure I speak for Grimes too when I say I'd appreciate you describing how we got to this point," Fleming said.

"Very simple. Like I say, the Maulana came in an hour ago with his two wives. He says he's strong reasons to suspect some members of his congregation are planning a '7/7 style attack' on London sometime in the near future. Thought it was all talk until recently – disaffected white youths become hoodies and ASBOs; disaffected Muslim youths become Jihadis. Symptoms of the same social malaise. However, he overheard a conversation in the mosque this evening that made him suspect explosives in the equation."

"So far, only what we already know," Grimes said. "But it's useful to have the support of the community."

"Crucial," Cassidy agreed.

"If we're splitting into teams, he must have given us at least three names," Fleming said.

"Four men. All on the phone board."

"Including Abduttawwah?"

Cassidy took out his notebook. "Not including him. Which of course makes perfect sense. If your theory's right, it would be stupid to put him on the front line. The suspects are Rizwan Masroor, Faisal Hussain, Lutfur Salique and Abdul-Aziz Al-Hazzaa."

"And you're sure you don't want to prolong the surveillance, put them at the centre?"

"For all we know, they might be on their way to London as we speak. We've got the CCTV footage of Abduttawwah, we've got Maulana Badreddin's statement. If we don't find the explosives, we've got enough to make the suspects' lives very uncomfortable. But if we wait to catch them red-handed, we might well run out of time."

"I'm not sure we're going about this properly," Fleming said.

Cassidy put his palms together in front of his lips and bathed them in a nervous exhalation. He closed the door.

"Would you like me to leave, sir?" Grimes said.

"Absolutely not," Cassidy replied. "What's on your mind, Fleming? This had better be good, by the way, because I've three warrants just popped out of the toaster. I'm not the only one who's psyched up."

Fleming folded his hands behind his back. "We need to ascertain they're home before we rush in. Let's say we raid the premises like we did Macintosh's, and they're not there, we'll have lost them."

"Where else will they be? It's nearly one in the morning. "

Fleming smiled. "If they're planning a major terrorist attack, they could be anywhere."

"But that's useful too, isn't it? We go through the others on the phone list, we put the capital on high alert, we wait - "

"I see what Mr Fleming's driving at, sir," Grimes said. "Assuming they've remained in the vicinity, if their neighbours tell them we called, they'll almost certainly stay away for good and not only that but they'll move all their dates forward."

"Yes, yes, I see," Cassidy said. "Why didn't I think of that? We've got to get plain clothes over there now, make house calls, pretext of some kind of taxi pickup maybe, just check they're all home. I'll sort that now. It'll push things forward another hour or two, but you're right, it's got to be done properly."

"And we've got to go in softy softly, for the same reason," Fleming said. "No disturbing the peace."

Two hours later, a plain clothes officer knocked at the door of a council house with a bay window. Ten yards farther up the street, Fleming and Cassidy sat in total darkness with six other officers in the back of an unmarked van. It was a cold night, but the proximity of so many bodies meant no one felt uncomfortable. The word 'go' hovered in the air, imminent and inevitable, and everyone braced for the shock of hearing it loud after the prolonged silence.

But it never came. Cassidy's phone vibrated and he had a quiet conversation with the officer on the other end. Then he spoke softly in the darkness:

"No one's at home at any of the addresses. Or if they are, they're not answering. If we break the door down, as we may have to, we've given the game away. Suggestions?"

"I'm in MI5," Fleming said. "I know how to pick locks. Tell Plain to meet us in their van. We'll swap clothes and enter through the back."

Cassidy got on the phone and outlined this plan. "They say there's a burglar alarm," he told Fleming.

"I'll deal with that when I get a look at it. Tell them I'm familiar with BS 4737, BS 6799 Class 6 and just about everything in between. A cross-ply screwdriver wouldn't go amiss, but I can probably manage without one."

Ten minutes later, he pushed the back door of the suspect's house open and stepped inside, followed by Cassidy with a torch and the search warrant. They let the others in through the front and closed the door. Everything was neat and tidy, the decor very nineteen-eighties, with large gold framed photos on the wall, cream sofas and ultramarine bathroom units. There was no one at home.

"Time to sound the red alert," Fleming said. "I'll call my boss in London, you call the Chief Constable. We don't want to look as if we thought we could handle something this big ourselves."

To his surprise, Ruby Parker picked up after only two rings.

"I've been waiting for your call," she said. "Before you tell me, I know. You've lost them. I want you to forget about that for a moment and sit down somewhere. As of this moment, you're in charge of the investigation."

Chapter 17: What We've Heard About Marcie

This was the cue for an argument, and he didn't want the other officers eavesdropping. Most were still busy looking for explosives, but it was probably fair to assume they'd enjoy a few minutes' diversion in the form of an overheard conversation. He went into the spare bedroom – already thoroughly searched – and sat on the bed.

"We've already got someone in charge of the investigation," he said.

"DCI Ashraf Cassidy," Ruby Parker replied. "I know. You're not going to be replacing him, and he's not being demoted. You're leapfrogging him."

He stood up and waved someone out as the door opened. "I don't understand. Where's this coming from?"

"MI7's been keeping its eye on the investigation for a long time, specifically White Department. They were content to let the police run with it while it was all Real IRA focussed - "

"Well, that was kind of them."

"At that point, it was a successful operation. Look, Nicholas, I don't wish to be brutal, but, reading between the lines of your last report, had it not been for you, Cassidy would almost certainly have lost Macintosh. Right now, he's lost four suspected terrorists."

"Not 'he', 'we'. Look, I'm not sure how me taking over's going to go down. When I arrived in Newcastle, I effectively told him I was here on an observational basis and that I wouldn't be stepping on toes."

"More fool you, then," she replied. "You have no right to go round providing the world and his wife with assurances about the limits of our entitlement to reassign you as we see fit, unless those assurances are drawn from your job description. In this case, they aren't."

"I try to make working with someone like me easy."

"You're in the wrong, pure and simple. This is how it panned out. White have been working on this for some time, but they realise you've hands-on experience. Plus they all admire you. They asked to take you on secondment for the duration of the investigation. I agreed, on the condition that you head it. I thought I was doing you a favour."

He rubbed his forehead. "I'm sorry. It's just - "

"What's our priority here, anyway? To save lives or to protect Cassidy's ego? White would have taken over anyway, with or without you."

"Point taken. Apologies for my brusqueness. What's it mean in practical terms?"

"More manpower, better surveillance."

"It's a bit late for that now."

"Your suspects are in Leeds. You'll be given a list of addresses, car registration numbers and so on once you return to headquarters. White fitted tracking devices to all vehicles registered to the suspects and their contacts when you were still putting your phone chart together. And right now we've got a car sitting outside the premises. It may interest you to know Rizwan Masroor's just ordered four pizzas from *Domino's*."

"They must have known we were coming for them tonight. How?"

"We've been listening to their phone conversations. They didn't know. You were just unlucky. They'd probably been planning this move for some time. You know how these sorts of things work. Isolating yourself with a bunch of like-minds helps you sustain the illusion that what you're about to do is reasonable and right."

"So power's being transferred to me. Where and when do I pick up the keys?"

"White have two men in a car outside where you are now. They'll fill you in."

"I suppose I'd better go and speak to them."

Ruby's voice went down a gear. "There is one more thing I ought to speak to you about before you go. On a more personal level."

He could see what was coming. *Don't get distracted by the likes of Grimes.* This time he would argue. Good God, there was nothing in his job description about being spied on by his superiors.

"Go on," he said through clenched teeth.

"We think there's a slim possibility Marcie may be alive."

He had to replay the sentence twice in his mind before it sank in. "Er – *what?*"

"I don't want you to build your hopes up, and before you ask, you're barred from the official inquiry, although I'll keep you updated as and when. It's just, I don't like us to have secrets from each other in this organisation unless there's a very good reason. It goes without saying you don't mention anything about this to anyone, especially her parents."

"Of course, yes, obviously."

"It could all be coincidence, of course, but the more time goes on, the less likely that explanation looks. She could also be dead, although not in the way we thought - "

His hand shook. "I need you to start at the beginning. I'm not following."

"We've identifications of a woman exactly matching her description in Kandahar. Not only that, photo identifications. Name of 'Reshtina Sarbanri'. We've also managed to airlift a woman to this country who knew her. She says she survived a drone explosion in Dhur al-Khanabi. Afterwards, she joined an organisation of assassins called The Afghan Women's Reparation Brigade before it was liquidated by the Taliban. A number of women who probably also belonged to it have been found murdered in Kandahar, but she's not among them as far as we can discover."

His head swam. She was alive, he knew it. Sod the bloody suicide bombers, he had to get to Afghanistan.

"Can I ask you a question, Nicholas?" she said.

"Anything you like," he replied weakly.

"Is it true you two married?"

He blinked slowly. "On the night before she left. I know that sounds mad, but it isn't."

"It doesn't sound 'mad' at all. Do her parents know?"

"Not unless she told them. I went round to express my condolences when I heard she'd been killed, but it didn't seem right to bring it up. What would have been the point? How did you find out?"

"She told Celia. Which is a good job for you. We wouldn't be having this conversation if I thought you were just one-time lovers."

"Given what you've just told me, do you really think I'm fit to lead a major operation into a terrorist cell?"

"You're a professional."

He returned the phone to his pocket and went downstairs. The search – as much of it as could be completed at this stage - was nearly over now. Four of the officers had slowed and were obviously rechecking boxes and corners for appearance's sake. The other two were checking the edges of the fitted carpet with screwdrivers.

He found Cassidy in the kitchen looking in a tea caddy. For some reason, Grimes was with him, on the opposite side of the kitchen, on her tiptoes, looking into a cupboard. He thought she was meant to be with another unit.

"Get a chair to stand on," Cassidy told her.

Fleming closed the door. Both officers stopped what they were doing and turned to face him.

"Is something the matter?" Cassidy said. "What have you found?"

"There's no easy way to say this," Fleming replied. "I've been ordered to take charge of the investigation with immediate effect. There are some MI5 men outside waiting to brief me."

Cassidy put the top back on the caddy and offered a handshake. "Congratulations."

"You're not angry?"

"Maybe I would have been when you first arrived, but I've seen how this operation's grown, so I've been expecting it. It was bound to fall into the hands of someone more senior. And I can see you know what you're doing."

"I didn't plan it, if that's any consolation. When I arrived in Newcastle - "

"Well, I think it stinks," Grimes said. "We put in all the legwork, then you swan in with your friends from the south and thrust us out of the way so you can take all the credit."

"No one's thrusting anyone out of the way," Fleming said, "but when an operation grows to this sort of size, you obviously get lots of different agencies involved. You need someone to coordinate them."

She hooted. "Why can't DCI Cassidy do that?"

"I don't know anything about MI5," Cassidy said.

Grimes thrust the teeth of her lower jaw out for a moment and sighed. "It's not about knowing your way round organisations. God, you men, you're all the same. Anything like this, that's all it boils down to for you: organisational structures, technicalities, specifications, acronyms. Can't you see, it's about dealing with *human beings*? So what if you don't know your way around bloody MI5? If people bring you good information, you put them in your team, and if they're in your team, *they* liaise with the acronyms in the corridors. You don't have to know everything, you've just got to be a good leader."

Silence reigned for a few seconds. They all became aware that the other officers were probably on the other side of the door, listening.

"And you're saying I'm a good leader?" Cassidy said.

She clicked her tongue. "For what it's worth, yes."

"I'm afraid it's a done deal," Fleming said. He thought about giving her an, 'If you're going to get on in this profession, Yvonne, you're going to have to learn to roll with the decisions' speech, of the sort Ruby Parker had just given him. But he heard himself saying it and he saw himself through her eyes again.

"If it's all right, I think I'll clock in for the night," she said wearily. "The raids failed, everyone else in my team has gone home, I shouldn't even be here. Probably why I'm in such a strop."

"At least we know where the suspects are," Fleming said. It was his ace. He'd probably never need it more than now.

Cassidy and Grimes exchanged looks.

"You said that like you think everyone's been told," Grimes said. "I haven't been told and I'm pretty bloody sure, no disrespect" – she turned to Cassidy – "you haven't been told, have you, sir?"

"I haven't been told," Cassidy said.

Fleming leaned back on the kitchen unit and grinned. "Look, let's stop leaping to conclusions, shall we? Five minutes ago, I received a phone call ordering me to take charge. It wasn't particularly welcome, actually, but I do tend to follow orders. In the course of that call, I was told that MI5 fitted tracking devices to the suspects' cars. I didn't know that beforehand, and you're the first people I've told. Happy?"

Cassidy and Grimes looked at each other again. Grimes shrugged, turned and left the room.

Cassidy nodded his head. "Congratulations again," he said drily.

Fleming absently returned the nod. His mind was on Afghanistan.

Chapter 18: Four Large Pizzas, Please

Rizwan Masroor, Faisal Hussain, Lutfur Salique and Abdul-Aziz Al-Hazzaa weren't looking forward to a ten-day stint in Leeds, but they did as they were told. At ten that evening, they got in Masroor's Proton Hatchback and drove to the address they'd been given, not knowing what to expect. They arrived two hours later outside a semi-detached house in a part of the town where gangs sat on walls, car alarms sang duets and dogs roamed. Their first reaction was that it looked derelict.

Masroor, five foot ten inches tall, bearded, who worked in an estate agent's, filing customer details and composing property specs, was the first to express his bafflement. But then he realised: it actually was derelict, hence the invitation.

Faisal Hussain and Abdul-Aziz Al-Hazzaa were short-haired with trimmed beards and the latest in casual wear. Hussain's tiny hands and big feet seemed to have been borrowed from different people. Al-Hazzaa had a soldier's shoulders. He preferred sandals to shoes and smoked cigarettes on a one-an-hour basis. Both men were unemployed for, they told themselves, ideological reasons.

Lutfur Salique, the smallest of the four, carried himself so that his pecs were flush with the tip of his nose, and for this reason, looked like he might be good in a fight. His lean face, darting eyes and high, responsive eyebrows gave him an aura of astuteness. He had a degree in Psychology and worked as a Customer Advisor in B&Q.

The house had a bay window, and was surrounded by a six metres wide stretch of gravel and a laurel hedge. It was obviously old, much older than the estate to which it now belonged, and had been split into semis relatively recently. Masroor was used to this sort of place. Prestigious, sixty years later less so, after a century unwanted. It was probably due for demolition soon.

Two men in balaclavas were waiting for them by one of the side doors. When they spotted the car, they approached silently at speed, and gestured for the four men to go into the house. They did as they were told, Salique taking the rucksack with the explosives in. Masroor looked back nervously. The balaclavas were doing a thorough search of his car with high wattage torches. Except for the fact that no one had arrived to read him his rights, he felt like he was about to be arrested.

When they got inside, they followed the thread of light into a spacious living room of sorts. A standard lamp attached to a car battery illuminated a grimy sofa, three non-matching armchairs draped with blankets, duvets and sleeping bags, and a frayed carpet. A copy of the Qur'an stood in pride of place on the mantelpiece, above a *What Car?* on the hearth. The men's exhalations emerged as steam.

They heard the front door close and footsteps. The car-examiners entered, removed their balaclavas and everyone grinned and embraced as if they were close relations who hadn't seen each other for decades. Except for Salique who stood nervously on the edge awaiting an explanation. Masroor took his elbow, still beaming.

"Lutfur, meet Idris Kakahel and Haider Chamkanni," he said. "Remember when we went to Pakistan six years ago? These two trained us."

They shook Salique's hand and hugged him as if he'd been there too, and the four men sat down to business, the two ISI men on armchairs, the four Englishmen huddled side by side on the sofa for warmth. They were already beginning to shiver.

"You're being watched," Idris Kakahel said. "There's a tracking device on the bottom of your car."

Hussain put his elbow on his knee and lowered his forehead onto his hand, as if this was his worst nightmare come true. "Oh, shit, shit."

"So did you remove it?" Salique said.

Haider Chamkanni took out a packet of cigarettes and offered them round. Al-Hazzaa took one, put it in his mouth shakily and caught the box of matches Chamkanni tossed him.

"Not bloody likely," Idris Kakahel said. "We've about an hour's window before they figure out this is where you've stopped. Then they'll bring in the surveillance teams. Since they don't know we know, they'll be off guard, meaning their vehicles will be fairly easy to spot."

"Yeah, like you're forgetting one big thing," Masroor replied bitterly. "If they know where we are, and they know we've got bombs, what's to stop them just making a raid and taking us in? We've got to get out of here, boys," he said, standing up. "We're looking at a thirty year bloody stretch!"

They looked at him in different ways. The faces of the ISI men expressed contempt. Faisal Hussain and Abdul-Aziz Al-Hazzaa wore hangdog expressions of doom and self-pity. Salique looked indignant.

"Sit down, man," Haider Chamkanni said calmly, taking his arm and guiding him back into his seat. "You've nothing to worry about. You're coming home with us where you'll be safe. Back to Pakistan."

"Just not yet," Idris Kakahel added.

"Look, given the texts you've been sending out," Haider Chamkanni Haider Chamkanni went on, "the police are going to know you're expecting someone from abroad. They're not going to want to pounce before he or she arrives."

"'She'?" Hussain said.

"In the plural," Haider Chamkanni said archly.

"So you're safe as anything can be," Idris Kakahel said. "Even if gets on the phone to the police and says, 'Hey, you know that derelict house on Curzon Street? It's got six Muslim terrorists living inside', even then they won't do anything!"

The two ISI men laughed. The four Englishmen chuckled half-heartedly.

Masroor thought back to the conversation he'd had with Al-Hazzaa and Hussain, two days ago. They'd been standing in Al-Hazzaa's kitchen together. Salique was upstairs with the Imam's son, playing *Assassin's Creed II*. His omission from the conference wasn't accidental.

Masroor closed the kitchen door. "I wish we'd never been to bloody Pakistan," he said.

"Too late to do anything about that now," Al-Hazzaa replied.

For a few seconds that seemed to be the end of the conversation, but then Hussain said: "We could just go to the police. Get it over with. What's the worst that could happen?"

"I don't know," Masroor said sarcastically. "What *is* the worst that can happen to three would-be terrorists? You tell me."

Hussain filled the kettle and put it on to boil. "There's going to be no 'would-be' about it soon."

"*Sssh!*"

Masroor went to the door. It wasn't Salique, it was someone next door. Salique was still upstairs pressing buttons.

"He's missing something up here," Masroor said, tapping his right temple. "All he cares about is his bombs. He's not even interested in the cause. It's purely about technical questions."

Hussain shrugged. "That's what all geniuses are like."

"I've been thinking," Masroor said. "These two men we're going to meet? Maybe they'll let us go once Salique's given them the explosives. I mean, what do they need four of us for? It's not like we're going to be carrying the bombs."

"Not as far as we know," Al-Hazzaa said gloomily.

"We could ask them," Hussain said. "'Now you've got the bombs, can we leave?' Something along those lines."

"It would have to be something better than that," Masroor said. "But I see your point."

"We've got nothing to lose," Al-Hazzaa said.

As Masroor sat in between his two friends, shivering in the dim light provided by the car battery, he tried to work out how to put this resolution into action, how to frame the words.

"Now you've got the bombs, can we leave?" he blurted out. He was so cold his brain hadn't time to vet his words.

Everyone turned to look at him. Once again, the ISI men looked contemptuous. He realised he was blushing.

"I'm just thinking, you might need us again some day," he said, hating himself.

Salique laughed. "What's the matter, brother? Lost your nerve?"

Everyone smiled except Masroor.

"Can we have a look at the bombs?" Haider Chamkanni said, by way of changing the subject.

Salique visibly inflated with pride. He reached into the rucksack and pulled out a tube. "Pipe bombs," he said. "Filled with the explosive we conned the Real IRA out of, and ready to be assembled into belts – corsets, even - as per specification. How many females are we looking at?"

"Three," Idris Kakahel replied.

"I can probably have them made up tomorrow, the day after at the latest," Salique said. "I'll construct them in such a way that they can either be detonated remotely or triggered manually by the sisters themselves, yes?"

"Or both," Haider Chamkanni said.

Salique's eyebrows formed a question mark. "I don't think you could have both, brother."

"We'll show you," Idris Kakahel said. "And there's one other feature we'd like you to add."

"I'd be looking to produce about six or seven hundred deaths with three detonators," Salique said, ignoring him. "But I'd probably be happy with five-fifty. Anything less than five would be a serious disappointment. I assume you're look-ing at rush hour. That was my thinking."

Idris Kakahel and Haider Chamkanni smiled at each other.

"You're a good soldier, I take it?" Haider Chamkanni said. "You listen to instructions?"

Salique suddenly looked cowed. His eyes darted between the ISI men.

"There's one other feature we'd like you to add," Idris Kakahel said.

A long silence followed.

"Yes?" Salique said meekly.

"We need the belts made in such a way that they can be padlocked to the wearers' bodies."

Salique nodded. "A padlock would increase the volume of fragmentation. Best would be a round discus, size seventy millimetres. Sorry, I work in that area, so I know."

Haider Chamkanni looked delighted. "We'll get some tomorrow."

It was Salique's turn to blush. "B&Q do them."

Masroor saw his opening. "Sorry, I don't understand. These women you're bringing in, they're good Muslims, yes?"

Again, silence. "What are you driving at, brother?" Idris Kakahel asked.

"They're doing this of their own free will, yes?"

More stillness. "What do you mean, brother?" Idris Kakahel asked again.

"Why do they have to be padlocked in, that's all?"

Idris Kakahel and Haider Chamkanni exchanged looks, but they weren't the theatrical versions of earlier in the evening. They seemed to Masroor to be asking each other for help.

"Because women are unpredictable," Idris Kakahel said. "Let's get some sleep, shall we? Talk about it in the morning?"

"I'm a bit hungry," Al-Hazzaa said.

Haider Chamkanni laughed. "The perfect opportunity to prove to you that the police aren't going to swoop. And for you to persuade them that we don't think they're there."

"Take out your mobile," Idris Kakahel told Al-Hazzaa, "and order four large pizzas."

Chapter 19: Celia Demure Makes a Breakthrough

Ruby Parker adjusted her suit sleeves and folded her arms on her office desk where Reshtina Sarbanri's wedding photo lay. Celia Demure sat opposite her in a tunic and trousers holding a pile of transcribed interviews with Ghatola Rahman on her knee. Armaghan Jones had her feet and knees together, as if she was at a job interview. She wore a peach cardigan. They were alone together in an office sixteen metres below the Thames embankment.

"There's definitely something Ms Rahman's not telling us," Ruby Parker said. "I don't see how she can have decided so quickly that Reshtina Sarbanri was suitable for the Afghan Women's Reparation Brigade unless she was already aware of her background."

"So you're saying she must have known who she really was from the outset," Celia Demure said.

"It's the only hypothesis that works."

Celia Demure shook her head. "Except, of course, that it doesn't. We've seen that she has no love for the Americans, the British or ISAF generally. If she knew Reshtina Sarbanri was a British spy, she'd have kept her at arm's length. Besides, who could have told her? Such a person would surely have betrayed her to others as well, and that would have been the end of her."

"Maybe Reshtina herself told her," Armaghan Jones said. "I mean, at a relatively late stage in their friendship, when she was confident it would be overlooked on that basis."

Celia Demure rubbed her jowls. "But if 'Reshtina' knows who she really is, why doesn't she contact us?"

"The Blue report on her placement in Afghanistan says her contribution to the war effort was negligible," Ruby Parker said. "Is it possible she's become a kind of Patty Hearst?"

"You mean she might have been abused by the family she lived with?" Celia Demure replied. "And then turned?"

"What they call Stockholm syndrome."

Celia Demure frowned. "I don't think that's very plausible at all."

"The fact that she survived at all is deeply suspicious," Armaghan Jones said. "Maybe she assassinated them. It would explain her subsequent life - as an assassin."

Ruby Parker nodded. "Yes, yes, now that would make sense. So her family mistreat her somehow, and she takes revenge by – what? – feeding their position to the Americans? Remember, the Americans wouldn't necessarily reveal their sources to us. They might not even know it's her who told them. She survives because she knows she has to be elsewhere when the strike happens. Then she relocates to another village. Ghatola Rahman works out what might have happened, and confronts her with it, just to see her reaction. She confesses and Ghatola Rahman puts her to work in the AWRB."

"Does she or doesn't she know she's a British agent?" Celia Demure asked. "That's the question. If yes, she's a traitor. Otherwise, I don't conceivably see how she can be held to blame."

"On this hypothesis, she does know," Ruby Parker said. "So yes, she is a traitor."

"It still doesn't add up," Celia Demure said. "That she should arrange for her controller to be killed by a process so clandestine we still haven't heard about it all this time later? Once he's dead, why doesn't she try to contact us? And don't tell me it's because she's joined the Taliban, because someone who's converted to Deobandi Islam wouldn't join an organisation like the AWRB."

Ruby Parker sighed. "It's not a perfect theory, I admit, but have you a better explanation?"

"In need an interview with Ghatola Rahman," she replied. "I'd like you to accompany me, please, Miss Jones and ideally I'd like Tasneem Babar to be present, although, if what you've already told me about her is true, I shouldn't think that'll be a problem."

Ghatola had no idea who the old woman was. She'd been here two hours now – although less than half that length, in real terms, given that everything they said had to be translated - and despite having introduced herself by name, her status remained obscure. They sat at opposite ends of the flat, Ghatola in her armchair with Tasneem cross-legged at her feet, and Miss Demure and Armaghan Jones side by side on a two-seater sofa. Outside, the sun shone.

The fact that Miss Demure was here with the Jones woman indicated she was something to do with British intelligence. Once again, the conversation focussed on Reshtina. They obviously thought Afghanistan could benefit disproportionately from a re-injection of the Reshtina-Ghatola serum and were determined to pursue the idea to the bitter end. Like all the Englishwomen she'd met, she vaguely recognised her babbling from somewhere, but try as she might she couldn't source it. She'd raised the issue with Tasneem, but she didn't know either.

Ghatola liked Miss Demure, despite herself. However, she had the feeling her eccentric forays into intimate territory and sudden changes of subject weren't entirely arbitrary.

And she noticed Tasneem, sitting cross-legged at her feet, was becoming increasingly uncomfortable. Which might not be the conversation. She'd received a Smartphone and charger through the post the day before yesterday – 'It's our best means of keeping an eye on them, Ghatola, I wish you'd trust me' – and she'd hidden it in the kitchen when they arrived. She probably thought they were here to confiscate it, poor thing.

"I'd be grateful if you could tell Miss Demure I feel tired now," Ghatola said. "I'd like to get some rest if possible."

Before Tasneem could open her mouth, however, Miss Demure started talking. "I wonder if you could tell me again how you came to recruit Reshtina Sarbanri to the AWRB?"

"I apologise on Ghatola's behalf," Tasneem said, "but - "

"According to what you said," Miss Demure went on, ignoring her, "you simply got to know her well and selected her on that basis. I'm not sure you're being entirely straight with us."

Armaghan Jones had to speak loudly to make this accusation heard over Tasneem's protests, but she succeeded. Ghatola blanched.

Miss Demure stood up on her walking stick. "We know the Taliban found you guilty *in absentia* of the murder of Faridun Jalwaanai, Ms Rahman. I think you implicated Reshtina Sarbanri so that she had no choice but to join you. But I doubt she joined you reluctantly. I think you were having a sexual relationship."

The shock the allegation made on the three women was compounded by the fact that Miss Demure made it in fluent Pashto. Each of them moved from that to the uneasy feeling that they had no real sense of the extent of her knowledge of their affairs. She wasn't what she seemed, that was clear. Who knew what other nooks and crannies she'd once inhabited?

"If it's any consolation," Miss Demure added with a smile, "lesbianism is regarded without censure in this country. And of course it would make no difference whatsoever to the high regard in which I personally hold you."

"How *dare* you suggest such a thing!" Tasneem exclaimed, clambering to her feet. "Get out, go on, *get out!*"

Ghatola closed her eyes and let her head fall back. She smiled as if she'd long since given up any thought of preserving her dignity or even her life in this place and that, if this was the worst it could do, she had nothing left to fear or keep breathing for.

"She dares suggest it, Tasneem," she replied almost in a whisper, "because it's true."

Celia Demure submitted her report that same day and returned to see Ruby Parker in her office when she'd given her sufficient time to read it. She sat down with a grim expression.

"I now know beyond a shadow of a doubt that Marciella Hartley-Brown has no recollection of who she is. Had she not come to the attention of Ghatola Rahman, she'd probably have married an Afghan man and settled down to live the rest of her life as a former war widow. Wherever she is, she's in very deep trouble."

"I notice your report doesn't include recommenda-
tions," Ruby Parker said. "I hope that doesn't mean what I
think it does, because I'd have to say no."

Celia Demure smiled. "My dear lady, we both know
you're powerless to stop me. I'm no more than a brigádník in
this organisation, and Afghanistan isn't within your jurisdic-
tion."

Chapter 20: Darkness Arrives in La Ville-Lumière

Way up in a high-rise apartment building in Paris's 13th ar-
rondissement, three Muslim women sat on a bed in their underwear tending a dying woman with facial hair and bruises.
The room was cramped and yellow with dirty net curtains,
peeling wallpaper and an infested mattress in lieu of furniture. Daylight barely penetrated, though it was sunny outside.

Since Naples, they'd picked up a new 'controller', a re-
placement for Nangial, whom unknown men considered too
intimately acquainted with their human bombs, and too 'un-
manly', to be anything other than a potential source of vacilla-
tion. Abedrabbo al-Maitami was a Pashto speaker in his twenties, just under six feet in height and built like a minder. His
beard was nominal – a black strap across his chin rising to join
a moustache – and he looked as if he thought clothes and hair-
styles were important. He considered himself a devout
Muslim. Allah valued him so highly He permitted him things
which for other Muslims were *haram*, forbidden. In return, he
wouldn't hear a bad word spoken about Him, to the extent
that he was willing to kill for Him, slowly and with pleasure.
Since Genoa he'd been trying to seduce Ambrin and in Lyon
he'd tried to rape her after half a bottle of *Pastis*. Reshtina, Zaituna and impotence intervened, and in the morning he
seemed to have forgotten the incident. Of course, he'd been
adding something to Nangial's heroin, although Nangial had
been on the way out long before his arrival. It was partly al-
Maitami's presence that persuaded Reshtina to steal a silencer
from a jihadi in Grenoble to add to the pistol she still kept concealed in her burkha. How she knew it would be a perfect fit,
she had no idea. A killer's instinct perhaps.

They'd been living in the 13th for over a week, waiting
for the documents to be forged and the signal to cross the English Channel. This was a cosmopolitan, busy part of Paris, full
of first or second generation immigrants, mostly kafirs from

the Far East. There was a sizeable Magrebi population, but for all the women met anyone or went to the mosque, it might as well not have existed. They ate canned food cold, and washed in icy water. They had to get used to a soldier's discipline, al-Maitami told them, and he was there partly to ensure they didn't weaken. He lived in the flat next door.

Twice, after nights spent drinking, he awoke them not to assault them, but to give them *jihadi* speeches of the sort they'd been listening to since Herat. They were going to be in Paradise soon. Paradise was like here, but perfect. There were no aches and pains, no disease, no growing old or having to struggle with loads, no hunger, no losing your children or husband, no sweat or excretion. Instead, there were sunny days with cool breezes, goods and services so plentiful you only had to think of them to obtain them, tame animals, fabulous landscapes, excellent company, and of course you'd get to spend an eternity with the ones you loved. As he spoke, his eyes filled with tears, as if he was only hearing about all this for the first time. No one really dies, so there was no need to worry about killing.

Nangial hadn't had a fix for sixteen hours. Ambrin and Zaituna sat on either side of her, wiping her forehead as she floated in and out of consciousness and saying the *Salat-ul-Janaza* while Reshtina sat at her feet. The door opened. Al-Maitami looked in with an expression of disgust, and left before the women had time to cover their modesty.

"Was that ...?" Nangial said. Her eyes rolled into the back of her head.

"Was that what?" Zaituna said harshly.

"Don't be like that with her," Reshtina said.

Zaituna shrugged. "It's her own fault. She's brought this on herself. Anyway, she's going to die, which means we'll all be together. I think she was expecting to apply for asylum once she got to Britain, so it's a good thing. She'd only have been unhappy."

"But surely drugs are *haram*?" Ambrin said.

"Yes, but she's got us to plead for her," Zaituna replied.

Nangial opened her eyes. "Was that ... my mother?"

148

"She means when the door just opened," Reshtina said.

They all looked at it. Another silence settled on the room. Zaituna and Ambrin got their prayers in synchronisation and Reshtina joined them. The black under Nangial's eyes seemed to darken, her flesh sank, her lips popped open. None of them dared ask the obvious question, how are we going to bury her? For all his disdain for her, Al-Maitami still had no idea she was a woman. In theory, they had to get the body down twelve flights of stairs, then dig a hole pointed at Mecca. They knew the holy city was just to the right of where the sun set each day, so that was no problem. But they had nothing to dig with, and nowhere sufficiently private to avoid detection. They were stymied.

Nangial opened her eyes again. "Reshtina?"

Reshtina edged up the bed so Nangial could see her. She stroked her hair. "Yes?"

"Where are we?"

"This is Paris. We're in France. It's the capital of France."

"How did we get here?"

Reshtina began to explain the reasons for their epic journey and the route they'd taken, city by city, but Nangial's eyes glazed over.

"I'm dying, aren't I?" she said.

Reshtina nodded. "I – I think you might be. I don't know."

She turned towards the net curtains and looked as if she was about to cry.

"Don't worry," Zaituna said. "In about a week we'll all be together again. I was just saying that, wasn't I, Reshtina?"

These words made no impact on Nangial's expression. "Remember when we first met," she asked Reshtina, "and I said that, given the choice between a beard and breasts, I'd have chosen a beard every time?"

Reshtina smiled affectionately and nodded.

Nangial sighed. "I was lying. All I ever wanted in life was to be a good wife and mother ... But that wasn't permitted me. I didn't want to spend my life fighting a battle ... we're never going to win. I ... I don't want to live any more. I haven't for some time. There's no place in the world for someone like me."

"Don't say that!" Reshtina said.

Yet something seemed to leave Nangial even before these words were out. Ambrin noticed it before either of the others and leaned over and whispered the Shahadah in her right ear. Reshtina broke into tears and shook her, only half-believing it. Ambrin carried on saying the *Salat-ul-Janaza*. Zaituna sat up and put her arms round Reshtina.

They all knew they couldn't permit themselves the indulgence of paralysis by grief. Nangial had to be given the *ghusl*, the all over wash, and anointed with scents and spices, which they'd bought in anticipation. They wrapped her in five unsewn sheets of cloth, also specially procured, and slid her body under the bed, facing Mecca. An hour later, al-Maitami returned.

"Is he dead yet?" were his first words.

The women sat on the floor facing each other and turned to look at him.

He shrugged. "That's good, because I could see he was on the way out. You can consider yourselves my wives now, under the *nikah al-mutah* rule, that's 'pleasure marriage' in Arabic. I'll get someone in here to formalise it before we leave for England." He looked at his watch and smiled. "Which should be in about ... twenty-four hours time."

"If you think we're marrying you, you must be mad," Reshtina said. "You're not even a believer."

He took a step forward with his fist raised, but Zaituna went for him with a lid she'd peeled from a can and dug it deep into his arm. He roared, but swept her out of the way and flew at Reshtina. She parried his blow without effort and elbowed him in the face. As he bent, she kicked his throat. He staggered choking and fumbled for the exit, only reaching the door handle by luck. Suddenly, he was gone.

None of the women was in the mood for mutual congratulations. They were used to Reshtina doing things they couldn't explain. They sat down facing each other again and said *du'a* prayers for Nangial's soul. They weren't sure they'd ever see al-Maitami again or what that would mean for their bombing expedition.

The next morning, however, he came to call on them with a bunch of flowers, an apology and a faint bruise beneath his right eye. "Pack your things," he said. "It's time to go to Paradise."

Chapter 21: Lead Us to the Rave

Fleming and Cassidy sat in a parked car outside an abandoned house on an estate on the edge of Leeds, hugging their overcoats to them for warmth, and watching two ground floor windows and a garage door. Ten other officers were variously positioned to watch the other sides. It was two o'clock in the morning and so cold even the local gangs were indoors.

Cassidy folded a copy of the *Yorkshire Evening Post* over at page 2. Above a portrait photograph of a teenage girl, the headline ran, 'Still No News on Missing Joanne'. He read the article, sighed and returned his attention to the case in hand. He looked towards the house.

"There'll come a point at which we or they have to admit no one's coming," he said. "It's been three days now."

"They must be pretty certain someone's coming," Fleming replied. "It can't be much fun in there. No heating, no lighting, no running water."

"Have you ever seen *Four Lions?*"

"I don't go to the cinema much."

"Textbook stuff. Frustrated young males seeking an outlet for aggressive tendencies. Sort of *The Football Factory* but with religion."

"I haven't seen that one either."

"Well you should. Some of these films ought to be required viewing for people in our line of work. What did you think of *My Best Friend's Wedding*, by the way?"

Fleming laughed. It was an open secret that *Cassidy-Grimes II: The Return* was playing at all good multiplexes. "I never got to see it."

"It's balls."

"To be honest, I actually prefer romantic comedies to action films. I realise that's unusual."

Cassidy chuckled. "I'll tell you what's unusual. You could be sitting pretty back at HQ instead of freezing your nuts off here. What's the idea?"

"I like to lead from the front. Wind the window down a little more, by the way. The windscreen's beginning to mist."

He obeyed. "You see, *Four Lions* psychology would suggest that these four men – interesting congruity, notice – live in something of a fantasy world. As part of that, they've persuaded themselves, or allowed themselves to be persuaded, that someone's coming from abroad to do their dirty work for them."

"The trouble with all those sorts of 'they're just children playing games' theories is that playing games with bombs equals mass murder. It's not about psychology."

"What if the people they're expecting are already in there with them?"

"We've yet to see them if they are. If they emerge, we'll swoop. But I don't think they will. I think they'll come in from the outside."

"I don't understand why the four lions chose to come here at all. Why not stay home where it's warm?"

"My guess is they need somewhere private to assemble the bombs once the carriers arrive. It's not an easy process, and definitely not something to attempt while you've got one ear open for your mum bursting into your bedroom with a cup of tea and a plate of Digestives."

"I guess that would make sense. If only we could get inside, see what's going on."

Fleming shrugged. "We've got their phone conversations. Like you say, we know there can't be that much happening. Three of them went into town yesterday and bought jumpers, pasties from *Gregg's* and a copy of *The Sun*. And we've looked through their rubbish. They're certainly not living the high life."

"I don't think anyone's living the high life round here." He picked up the *Yorkshire Post* and handed it to Fleming. "Joanne Seally, seventeen. Lives just round the corner from here. Or did."

Fleming read the article, though he knew all about it. "It seems a bit of a coincidence. I wonder if there's a connection."

"I don't see how there can be. We've watched every move those boys have made outside that house ever since they got here. Besides, completely different types of crimes."

A noise from the house interrupted them. The garage door opened and Abdul-Aziz Al-Hazzaa emerged with a duvet wrapped round him. They knew what was coming next. The same thing that happened every night around this time. He walked to the hedge, adjusted his body casing and urinated. Fleming took out his notebook. Al-Hazzaa returned indoors.

"Is it necessary to log everything?" Cassidy said.

Fleming smiled. "No, but it makes life a hell of a lot more gripping." He felt his phone vibrate. He took a pair of headphones from the glove compartment. "Go ahead."

"Busby from White Department, sir. We've had a flurry of text messages. And you probably can't see it from where you are, but cars six and seven report lights on in the house."

"Let's hear the messages."

"Bear in mind I'm translating from text-speak. *Meeting confirmed for Tuesday, See you in Southampton, Are the goods available? Yes. How many shall we expect? Five good sisters, Details Monday.*"

"Meeting Tuesday?" Fleming said. "That's three days away."

Cassidy groaned. "Bloody hell, another seventy-two hours of this."

Fleming's eyebrows gathered. He removed the headphones. "What's that?"

It sounded like a large crowd, approaching quickly. Half a minute later, it came into view. A throng of about thirty adults in party mood, talking, laughing and spilling off the pavement onto the road in their hurry to get wherever they were going. Almost without exception they were dressed for a night out, the men in designer T-shirts and trainers, the women with bare midriffs and tight skirts. Someone tossed an empty beer bottle into the road.

The radio crackled briefly. Cassidy picked up the handset. "Go ahead, Four."

"Sir, we've a large gathering of young adults approaching from a southerly direction. I'll keep you informed of their intentions."

"We see it, Paul," Cassidy replied.

"Er, no we don't, Ashraf," Fleming said. "We don't share a sight-line with Four. And this lot's coming from the north."

They realised together that something was about to happen. Suddenly the house was surrounded by the newcomers, all here for reasons unknown and all indignant at finding themselves locked out. One section started chanting. Others split into groups and walked round the house, knocking on the window boards. Six men started rocking Rizwan Masroor's car, obviously trying to flip it.

Cassidy got on the radio.

"Tell them we may need riot shields," Fleming said. "Bloody hell, what's going *on?*"

Suddenly, the front door was open. The four Muslim suspects emerged and started shouting, then fighting. Swathes of people started to pour indoors. A white man threw Lutfur Salique to the ground and four others began kicking him.

Fleming got out of the car and ran over. He pushed his way through the crowd to where Salique lay bleeding, receiving punches and kicks on his way. Masroor was also in trouble. Two Panda cars screeched to a halt and policeman with megaphones and batons emerged. People ran and hurled missiles. In the hallway, a fire had started.

"Clear the area!" Fleming yelled. *"There's a bomb inside the house!"*

Six white youths hurled themselves out of the front door, laughing. Fleming put his hand to his side and brought it back covered with blood. He'd been stabbed - when? Salique, at his feet, looked equally badly hurt. He dragged him to the safety of two officers. Plain clothes had apprehended the other three suspects, which wasn't ideal, but not the worst-case either. Two vanloads of police in protective helmets arrived, preceded by dog handlers.

Then it occurred to him what might have happened. He ran inside the house and found the fire spreading quickly, flames standing up on the floorboards like evil spirits. He judged he had around a minute till it became rampant. He threw himself up the stairs and kicked each bedroom door open, aware that the smoke was beginning to choke him.

And there she was. In what an estate agent would doubtless call the Master Bedroom. Bound in the foetus position, blindfolded and gagged, wriggling on the floor. There wasn't time to unpick the knots and he hadn't anything to cut them with. He had to lift her. Thanks to his stab wound – bleeding quite copiously now, he noticed - he could hardly stay upright. Suddenly, Cassidy appeared, holding his sleeve over his nose. He scooped Joanne Sealy up in his arms, still blindfolded, and grabbed Fleming's sleeve.

"*Hang on to me!*" he shouted.

They stumbled downstairs together and made it outside just as the fire reached the point of consolidating all its advances and guaranteeing complete victory. Fleming fell to his knees. Cassidy passed the girl to two officers in gas masks, and hauled his colleague to his feet.

"We need to make at least another twenty to thirty metres," he said.

It was the last thing Fleming heard.

Chapter 22: The Same But From Camera Two

One hour earlier, Rizwan Masroor, Faisal Hussain, Lutfur Salique and Abdul-Aziz Al-Hazzaa sat on the sofa feeling dirty and depressed, while the two ISI men reclined in the sofas. The pipe bombs were complete now, and Masroor was still hoping they'd get to go home. He was less than ever convinced of the necessity of bombing kafirs and there were moments when he contemplated throwing the front door open and giving himself up to the police. He suspected the others felt the same. They were slowly going mad and there was no indication how much longer they'd have to wait. Even their little excursion into town the other day – exactly how long ago was it? - hadn't improved matters. God, as if things weren't bad enough, he was losing track of time too. It had underscored their predicament. They were prisoners.

And they probably weren't the only ones. Idris Kakahel had warned them not to go into the largest of the three bedrooms upstairs, although he wouldn't say why. He was so confident of being obeyed without question, he didn't even feel the need to make up a reason. In a rare moment of shared privacy, Hussain said he thought they were keeping someone chained up in there. He heard movements in the night, and occasionally noises like someone whimpering.

Masroor was twenty-eight now. He was twenty-two when he'd been to Pakistan. In those days, he believed all that stuff about dying for the cause. It had been new to him then. Nowadays ... well, even a week ago, he thought he still did. Now he was sure he didn't know.

When they arrived he'd tried asking if they'd let the four of them go once the bombs were made. That hadn't worked. Well, the bombs were made now, and he had a question that might lead to a discussion that might lead to an opportunity to re-raise the issue.

"Can I just ask something?" he said, cutting the thick silence.

"Anything you like," Haider Chamkanni said.

"If the police have got the house surrounded, presumably they think there's only four of us in here. They'll know when the bombers arrive, they'll know when they leave, and the minute we leave, they'll pile in. How are you two going to get out?"

Haider Chamkanni and Idris Kakahel grinned at each other.

"We're going to get you out of here, brothers," Haider Chamkanni said. "And don't worry, the police won't be able to pin a thing on you."

Masroor felt a surge of gratitude so strong he wanted to cry. "How - ?"

"Magic, for a start," Idris Kakahel said. "Have you ever seen the disappearing woman act? No? The magician comes on stage with a tall box which he plants on top of a platform. Twelve or thirteen workmen accompany him in overalls and make adjustments to the box. Then the woman gets into the box. The workmen leave the stage, the magician opens the box and – alakazam! – it's empty. Everyone looks to the platform, obviously hollow. But then the girl runs out from the back of the theatre, mounts the stage and bows."

"The key," Haider Chamkanni said, "is the diversion. The woman gets into the box, changes into a set of workman's overalls and leaves the stage with them. Three or four men, you'd probably notice one extra, but twelve or thirteen, no way."

"I'm not sure I follow," Faisal Hussain said meekly.

"We've arranged for a diversion," Haider Chamkanni said. "In about twenty five minutes, over two hundred people will descend on this address, expecting to find a rave. They'll probably become agitated. You're going to run out and confront them. Some of them will run in, and we'll exit via the back door. One: every policeman within two miles – and we calculate there's about twenty of them – will look to you. Two: even if they clock us leaving they'll think we're clubbers. They don't know there's six of us in here."

"Obviously, we'll take the bombs with us," Idris Kaka-hel said. "And as we go, we'll set the place alight. It should go up like dry straw. Hence, no evidence. You came here to or-ganise a rave, you didn't like the look of the punters, you tried to talk some sense into them, get their ticket-money. It all went wrong."

It sounded too good to be true. And it only took Mas-roor a moment's reflection to realise it was.

"What's in the upstairs bedroom?" he asked.

Haider Chamkanni and Idris Kakahel exchanged glances again.

"Tell him," Haider Chamkanni said.

"A dead girl."

Masroor felt like he'd been slapped. "A *what?*"

"She was here when we arrived. Murdered. We weren't interested in the complications of having to take her out and dump her."

"But why haven't they searched this house?"

"Because they know you're in here, dummy," Haider Chamkanni said. "You're an Islamic terrorist, an idealist. You're hardly likely to be an opportunist murderer too. Be-cause that's all this was."

Masroor could feel himself trembling.

"But even if the building burns down," Al-Hazzaa said, "the girl's bones won't burn. They won't even know her body's started to putrefy. They'll recover the bones and they'll think we did it."

Idris Kakahel sighed irritably. "I'll tell you what. I'll go upstairs now and tuck a bit of Semtex in her bra. She'll be va-pourised. They might find a few microscopic bone-particles if they're looking for them, but trust me, they won't be."

"But that'll confirm the explosives!" Lutfur Salique ex-claimed.

Idris Kakahel nodded. Masroor realised that this had been their plan all along.

"That's a good thing, isn't it?" Haider Chamkanni said quietly. "Look, they already know you've got them. This way, they'll think they've got the culprits and the bombs are no longer an issue. Meanwhile, we'll be on our way to London."

"Yes, you'll have sacrificed yourself for the cause," Idris Kakahel said, "but that was always the idea, wasn't it?"

"Boom," Haider Chamkanni said.

Suddenly, there was a sustained knocking at the front door, then at the window-boards.

Haider Chamkanni smiled. "That's your cue, boys. Get going."

"It's been a pleasure working with you," Idris Kakahel said.

The blood drained from the four men's faces and they left the room.

Chapter 23: Prelude to World War III?

Ten minutes after the building exploded, six medics loaded Fleming onto a stretcher and rushed him to A&E where surgeons operated on his wound, saving his life. The police quelled the riot and put a thirty metre cordon round what was left of the house. The only fatality of the evening was Lutfur Salique, already dead of a knife wound to the heart when Fleming reached him. Joanne Sealy, traumatised and severely dehydrated, but otherwise unscathed, was taken to hospital. A press release issued twenty minutes later said she was 'recovering'. There were thirty-two arrests.

It was Grimes who first noticed the anomaly. At ten o'clock the next morning, Cassidy sat in his office receiving reports written and oral and coordinating clean-up strategies. It was Sunday so he'd forgotten to shave. A coffee, a banana and two Paracetamol stood in for breakfast. Yvonne leant over to knock on the open door. He smiled. Not everything in life was miserable.

"I've only just got in, sir," she said. "I suppose it's occurred to everyone by now that there must have been more than four men in that building. Any idea who they were?"

He gestured for her to take a seat. "You're ahead of me. You're ahead of everyone. What makes you – sorry, I'm not in deductive mode at the moment, all this bloody paperwork, it's as much as I can manage just to keep up with it."

A young policeman appeared in the doorway with a sheaf of documents, which he held up with a pleased smile, before depositing it in Cassidy's in tray and leaving.

"The thing is," Grimes said, "we watched everything they did from the moment they arrived in that building. If they'd abducted Joanne Seally, we'd have seen them. Added to which, of course, she disappeared the evening before they arrived there."

"So they weren't responsible for her abduction, agreed. It doesn't follow that her kidnapper was with the suspects.

That house was a good place to keep your victim if you're into the kinds of twisted things some kidnappers enjoy."

"So close to the crime scene? We both know the only reason we didn't look in there was because we knew the terrorists had taken it over. The congruence of the two things struck us as too unlikely."

"They probably found her there when they arrived. Indirectly, they're responsible for saving her life."

"Which would make sense if we had any evidence that the real kidnapper had returned to the house at some time, and been chased off by the new incumbents. But we were watching it 24/7. Not even a milkman."

"I refer you to the half hour interval between their first arrival and our surrounding them. And of course, I know it was boarded up, but not very expertly: even I could tell there were lights on in there from time to time."

"Have we interviewed her?"

"She doesn't remember anything about her abductor. She was attacked from behind and rendered unconscious. Look, I don't mean to be unkind, but where's your motive, Yvonne? Even if they had abducted her: why? She hasn't been raped or even sexually assaulted. No one's even spoken to her. Not that I'm belittling what she's been through - "

"What about forensics? What do they say?"

"Still too early for the results. Give it another few hours."

A voice from the doorway cut over both of them. "I hate to say this, Ashraf, but Yvonne's right."

Fleming leant on a walking stick with a bruise on his jaw. His casual shirt and chinos had obviously been slung on in a hurry.

"Good God," Cassidy exclaimed, "I thought you were in hospital. I thought you were in a 'critical condition'. That's what they said."

Grimes stood up. "What the hell are you doing here, sir? Pardon my French."

"I was never that bad. The knife missed everything of any value. And the great thing about the NHS being up the creek is that no one bats an eyelid if you decide to discharge yourself, no matter how ill they insist you are. The reason Joanne Seally was abducted was because they wanted her Smartphone. That way, they'd be able to set up a Facebook page advertising the 'rave' – which, of course, we missed since we had better things to do. They needed to abduct a young woman, because that creates certain expectations in the minds of investigators and forecloses others. And her mobile needed to be up to spec. Apart from that, she could have been anyone. The crucial point, as Yvonne rightly says, is that, since she was kidnapped the day before our four suspects arrived on the scene, and since the point of the exercise was the creation of last night's diversion, there must have been at least one other person in the house all along. Someone's escaped, almost certainly taking the bombs with him or her."

"You were unconscious at the time," Cassidy said, "but there was an almighty blast inside that house."

"Nowhere near commensurate with the amount of explosive we saw Jonathan Butler receive from Macintosh in that car park, I'm afraid. I've checked with ballistics. What you saw was yet another diversion designed to throw us off the trail."

A WPC stuck her head round the door. "Sir, Rizwan Masroor says he's ready to cooperate. He wants to make a statement. Although he says he'd rather not speak to a woman."

Fleming smiled. "Excellent news, notwithstanding the arrant sexism. Ashraf, I want you to take it. Yvonne, I need you to get a team of five together and get back to the house – or what's left of it – as quickly as you can, and let me know as soon as you're there. Those text messages about Tuesday and Southampton are almost certainly false clues. For all we know, we could already be too late, but we've got to keep our heads up till we've something to go on. Cassidy, meet me back here as soon as you've logged that witness statement." He took his mobile from his pocket and pressed dial. "Forrester? Fleming here. I'd like you to put a helicopter on standby. London or Dover, possibly both, possibly within the hour, please."

Five minutes later, he sat in front of a computer screen in the office he'd been given, an end of corridor affair with bare walls, plastic floor tiles and a desk with neatly arranged piles of papers in labelled transparent sleeves of different colours. His phone rang.

"Fleming."

"Collins here, sir. The photos are in the shared area on the secure drive. After you've logged on, go to G. I've put them in seven different folders, each containing four sub-folders, according to street names and times of day."

"How many were there? And how comprehensive?"

"All the streets leading from the house were more or less minutely covered by footage of police reconstructions. We've got over five hundred local and national press stills, plus CCTV recordings of the areas between Stanwick Street and Evelyn Terrace."

He was already on his way in.

"Anything more you need, sir, just let me know."

"Thank you, Collins. You were very quick."

There were six roads leading from the house. He began with Barker Drive, looking at the parked cars. A Fiat Uno YD51 GHR – no, probably not – a Ford Fiesta K234 FYZ – again, unlikely.

The phone rang again. "Grimes here, sir. What would you like us to do?"

"I need you each to take one of the roads leading away from the house. I'm going to read you the makes and number plates of the cars that were parked there continuously over the last week. If they're still there, we'll cross them off the list. If they're not, I'd like you to make some house calls, see if any-one recognises them. It's a long shot, but I'm hoping the get-away car will appear by a process of deduction."

He finished listing the cars in Barker Drive, and crossed four off as having moved during the time the suspects were holed up, leaving him with just three. One of those looked outrageously apposite. A red Mazda with blacked-out windows, registration LC51 GFD: a London tag – Wimbledon, to be exact. Surely, it couldn't be a case of first time lucky, could it?

He opened the Stanhope Close folder and began listing and de-listing, ending with just two cars. He called Grimes.

"Ask whoever's in Stanhope to check out a silver Nissan, registration DS54 FGH, and a blue Vauxhall Vectra, registration YL05 BHD. If you can ask whoever's in the other streets to call me at five minute intervals."

Twenty minutes later, he was on the last street. The phone rang. This would be Bodie in Sexton Street. Only one car for him.

"Sir, this is Grimes again," the voice said. "That red Mazda? It's gone, and no one round here knows who it belongs to. Not only that, but some of them even remarked on it at the time."

"Bingo. When did it disappear, does anyone know?"

"It was there early evening last night. This morning it isn't. I've had confirmation from several residents. It's Sunday, so everyone's at home."

"Get back to the station. I'll give the final details to Bodie and see what he comes up with. We'll assume provisionally we've struck lucky. I'll submit an automatic number plate recognition request and we'll see what Cassidy's come up with."

Cassidy deputed a graduate sergeant called Clive to act as a scribe and entered the interview room to find Masroor sitting behind the desk flanked by his solicitor, a stout, balding man in his forties in a grey suit. Masroor's black eye, bald, bloody patch where his right hairline should have been and bruised arm were ample testimony to the ferocity of last night's confrontation. Cassidy sat down. Clive opened his notepad and sat discreetly to one side.

"I understand you want to cooperate," Cassidy said.

Masroor looked up as if he'd only suddenly realised the room had a pair of new occupants. "Oh, yeah ... That's right." He looked closely at Cassidy. "You a Muslim?"

"Of sorts. How can you tell?"

"Once a Muslim, always a Muslim."

"Where would you like to begin?"

"Do you know the Qur'an? It doesn't say, like, killing's okay, does it? Not really. Not unless your life's being threatened."

"Islam's been around for fourteen hundred years. I doubt whether any ideology that made a virtue of murder could survive a hundredth of that time. Look, I should tell you before you begin your statement that we know you weren't alone in that house."

"Is it true Lutfur's dead?"

Cassidy nodded. "I'm sorry."

"What about the others? What about Faisal and Abdul-Aziz?"

"They're fine. Hussein's sustained bruises and a black eye, that's all. Al-Hazzaa's leg was broken, but he's expected to make a full recovery."

"And the girl?"

"Alive, but it'll take a long, long time for the mental scars to heal."

"They told us she was *dead!* They told us she was dead when they got there! They told us they'd just *found her!*"

Cassidy shrugged. "Whereas the truth is, they abducted her and left her to burn to death."

"Was there, like, Semtex inside her bra?"

"No. Why do you ask?"

"Because that's what they said they'd done. They said they'd done it so there'd be nothing left of her corpse. Instead of which, they tried to frame us. But you've got to understand, it didn't bother us only because we thought she was already dead."

Cassidy felt his ire rise. "Look, Mr Masroor, as far as we've been able to determine, you're a bomber. So you're happy for people to die. It's part of your stock in trade."

Masroor deflated. "I was."

"And?"

"Meeting those two men again. It was, you know, like looking in the mirror. If you never look, you never realise how skanky you must appear."

"We need names."

The solicitor leaned over. "You don't have to say anything, Rizwan, you know that."

Masroor jerked away as if he was trying to shake the devil off. "Idris Kakahel and Haider Chamkanni. They're Pakistani army officers. We met them six years ago - "

Cassidy felt like he'd been thumped. *Pakistani army officers? My God, this had the makings of a new world war!*

"Sorry," he said feebly, "when you say 'we' met them ..."

Masroor began to shake. "I mean, myself, Faisal Hussain and Abdul-Aziz Al-Hazzaa. We all went to Pakistan together in the heady days when Bin Laden was still a pin-up, and these guys showed us how to shoot RPGs, mortars and stuff. How to make bombs. It was a Taliban training outfit, really. We just slotted in as extras. Mostly, they spoke Pashto, and our Urdu isn't that brilliant, but we were made to feel welcome. We never expected to see them again. Shit, certainly not in England. I don't know about the others, but I've moved on since then. I don't believe in that shit any more. It took me a while to see, but it's got fuck all to do with ..." He broke down.

His solicitor put his arm round him. "Give him a minute."

Cassidy stood up, hardly less emotional than the interviewee, but for different reasons and with different emotions. "I'm sorry. I don't usually abort witness interviews, especially when the subject's being as cooperative as you are, but this has the makings of a major diplomatic incident. To say the least. I'll ask someone else to fill in. We've a Salafi on the staff. Frank. He's ... Excuse me."

Thirty seconds later, he entered Fleming's office.

"I take it you've made a breakthrough," Fleming said, standing up. "If you'll excuse me saying so, you're wearing the standard facial expression. The good news is, we've also made progress."

"It's bad," Cassidy said. "It's very bad. There were two men in that house with them. Both Pakistani army officers. Idris Kakahel and Haider Chamkanni, they're called."

Fleming's face went from pink to white. "They're *what?*" He laughed nervously. "No, no. There must be some mistake. It's not possible. I mean, I know the Pakistani army's been training the Taliban to kill ISAF soldiers - "

"But if true ..."

"If true, it would constitute the first biggest attack by a foreign state on British interests since World War Two. And since we've got nuclear weapons, and Pakistan's got nuclear weapons ... I think I'd better get on the phone to London."

Chapter 24: Stand Down, Mr Fleming, Stand Down

Ten minutes later, a Westland helicopter descended on the green opposite the police station. A cordon of twelve officers kept onlookers at bay while Fleming boarded with a six-man team including Cassidy and Grimes. The pain in his chest was getting worse. His phone rang. Which could be any one of about ten calls he was expecting. He went to 'Next Incoming', diverted it to Cassidy and picked up. Roger Cross-Sykes, head of White.

"We've been in touch with the Pakistani embassy," he said, "and they claim to know nothing about it."

"Is that an 'Us training men to kill your soldiers?' know nothing about it, or do you think it's genuine?"

"Who knows? I spoke to the ambassador, who sounded shocked. But then he may not have been in on it."

"What practical assistance are they prepared to give?"

"They've given us the two men's files and photos, and they've promised anything we ask. At our end, we've brought the whole of Muslims Against Crusades, Islam4UK and the other toy soldiers in for questioning. We've got our best technical experts going through their hard drives with a fine toothcomb as we speak."

"Anything so far?"

"Not a squeak."

"The car?"

"Paid for in cash ten days ago. The seller was a thirty-seven year old bricklayer from Islington. He recognised the two men as the purchasers."

"What about that ANPR?"

"No show. I'll phone you the minute we hear anything. Remind me why you're going to Dover again when the text message said they'd arrive in Southampton?"

"Because that was almost certainly meant to mislead us. Remember, they think they've got away with it."

"Which, of course, is why it may not have been such a bright idea to go telling the Pakistani embassy."

"Not my decision. It's obviously a thoroughly organised, well financed operation. So they'll almost certainly have forged the relevant visas. Unless you think someone's looking out for you, why take the risk of arriving in Southampton, Bristol or Liverpool in a cargo container when you can arrive comfortably, in full public view, just two hours away from your target? I've issued an all ports warning, before you ask, and the airports are on high alert. They're looking at all documentation through microscopes."

"I understand the traffic delays are already beginning to kick in. Surely the Channel Tunnel would bring them closer to London, if that's their aim?"

"Not much, and Eurotunnel's considerably more jumpy about illegal immigrants. I'm guessing it's a risk they won't want to take."

"I hope you're right. I've informed Kent Police. No point in putting them on high alert because everyone's on high alert. All leave's been cancelled. The PM's considering bringing the army in, so I understand, but I don't know. He's meeting the cabinet now."

Fleming put the phone down. Nothing was visible outside the helicopter. On benches either side the police officers were strapped in, looking grim. Screwed to the middle of the floor, a winch with thirty metres of rope and a first aid box. Above everyone's head, sixty-watt lamps, ten each side. Grimes yawned.

Fleming's phone rang again.

"We've found the car," Cross-Sykes said. "It's proceeding west along the A20 towards Folkestone."

"Presumably, it's come from Dover then."

"Your point being?"

"I'm willing to bet when you bring it to a stop, it'll contain a car thief, white, male, between eighteen and thirty. The important thing is, it shows where the suspects are. Don't make too much of a show. For all we know, they're listening to the police radios. It's a speeding offence, not a car-theft, yes? And for God's sake don't mention the ANPR."

"Understood."

"Find out when he stole it."

Cassidy passed him another phone. "It's the Chief Constable of Kent police."

The connection Fleming had asked for twenty minutes ago. He fought off another wave of pain and tried to keep his tone suitably deferential. "Keep the police presence low-key, put all those officers whose leave has been cancelled into plain clothes. You'll require a list of derelict houses and they need checking very discreetly for occupants. Call reinforcements if necessary, only then make arrests."

An hour later, the helicopter touched down on a playing field at the eastern end of Dover. It was windy and overcast and the ground was soggy. He assigned his team to the vacant apartments in Leazes under Cassidy's supervision, and received the Port Chief Superintendent's report. Five minutes later, the Home Secretary called.

"*Would you mind telling why the hell you still think you're fit to lead this investigation?*" he thundered.

Fleming held the phone an inch from his ear. "I'm not sure I understand, sir. It's - "

"I've just come away from an exceptionally fraught meeting with the Prime Minister and his entire cabinet. Thanks to the fact that we need projections of possible casualties and availabilities of beds, the government's chief medical adviser, Sir Randolph Horton happened to be present. The PM had a copy of your last night's medical record to hand, and he passed it over almost as an afterthought. *Believe it or not, bloody Sir Randolph almost had kittens!* Are you aware you could peg out at any minute? What the *hell* were you thinking clocking in this morning? It's a sodding miracle you're still upright!"

"In my defence, I have helped the team make - "

"You're to step down *immediately*, do I make myself clear? If all this goes apeshit, as it very possibly may, there'll be a major inquiry, and one of the things it's bound to want to know is why the hell no one stopped you sooner. It's the sort of howler that brings a government down. The one thing we can't afford, at this stage, is our top man keeling over."

"But sir - "

"You've done a good job in difficult circumstances, Nicholas, really. But effective immediately, the PM's passing responsibility to Robert Skelton, the head of Counter-Terrorism Command. Non-negotiable. Cross-Sykes is briefing him as we speak."

"That's fine, sir," Fleming said. He was fed up with giving orders and hearing reports. He liked to do things his own way and he realised this was just the turn-up he'd unconsciously been hoping for. He breathed a sigh of relief.

"Now hand yourself in at the nearest A&E, and that's an order."

"Yes, sir. Right away, sir."

He told his driver – a constable with red hair and a moustache - he'd been relieved of his position, and the driver offered his condolences.

"I suppose you'd like dropping off somewhere," he said. "Like a hospital? I'm probably going to be wanted back at the station with all this going on. Better let me know quick and maybe I can drop you on the way."

The phrase 'hero to zero' came to mind. He smiled. "It's been a long time since I've been in Dover. I wonder if you could recommend me a car-hire firm."

"Should you really be driving, sir?"

"Constable, until two minutes ago, I was in charge of a nationwide investigation into potentially the biggest terrorist strike on this country since 7/7. Now I may not be capable of chasing a suspect through a busy thoroughfare, but I am used to sizing up my ability to function in different contexts. Please don't patronise me."

The PC flushed slightly. "I apologise, sir. A&M Cars on Alton Road will do you a good deal, especially if you say PC Gerry Thornton sent you. How long are you thinking of staying?"

"No more than a few days. The name of a good guest-house wouldn't go amiss, either, Thornton."

He hired a Mini Cooper and put up at The Dover Elysium on Marine Parade for three days. Six rooms equally divided over two floors all came with a double-bed, TV, en-suite bathroom and a table built into the wall for balancing snacks on and writing postcards. The window looked out onto the sea. The wardrobe would have to go unused. He hadn't brought a change of clothing, which was a nuisance but no more. He had better things to be getting on with that would keep his mind fully occupied.

He'd already decided that the derelict houses theory was a non-starter. Unless Kakahel and Chamkanni were especially unimaginative, it was unlikely they'd pull the same stunt twice. True, they didn't think they were being watched, but they probably wouldn't take any chances. No, they'd come into Dover in full view – the stolen car proved that – and, as part of the same strategy, they'd probably choose an unconcealed base to consolidate the penultimate stage of their plan. They'd have to meet the bombers, brief them, possibly re-inspire them. A hotel or a guest-house, that is, much like the one he was staying in now. They might even be upstairs at this very minute.

He went down to reception and asked for a Yellow Pages, then sat in a deserted lounge with forty tub-chairs and ten coffee tables.

Sixty-four addresses under 'Hotels and Guest Houses'. He'd better get going.

Best to start where he was. He needed a clipboard, two A4 transparent sleeves, a USB cable and a printer. Then a word with the landlord.

Chapter 25: Landing in Dover

At two-fifteen on Sunday morning, Idris Kakahel and Haider Chamkanni, wearing gloves to guard against leaving finger-prints, stopped in a London suburb to pick up a woman stand-ing motionless on the pavement in shalwar kameez and mittens as if waiting for a bus. An hour later all three stopped at an all-night cafe just outside Maidstone for something to eat and drink. They ordered hamburgers plus Pepsis to go and sat in the car - smoking Silk-Cut in between mouthfuls and toss-ing the stubs out of the window - so they could continue listening to the news on Radio 4.

"I understand Joanne's now expected to make a full re-covery," the reporter said. "Police haven't yet been able to speak to her, although they'll obviously want to do so sooner rather than later."

"Any further word on the disturbances?" the news-reader asked.

"The police say they now have the riot fully under con-trol, although I'm told there *has* been one fatality, twenty-seven year-old Lutfur Salique from Newcastle-upon-Tyne. It's not clear at the moment whether Mr Salique was among the rioters or whether there's some other explanation for his pres-ence. Local people I've spoken to report having seen lights on in the house in recent days, although there's been no confirm-ation of that from official sources. What we do know is that, shortly after the fire began, there was an explosion inside the house which the police seemed to be expecting. Meanwhile, a large number of arrests have been made. We have no confirm-ation of the exact numbers, although it's said to be in excess of twenty."

"And the riot apparently started as a result of a Face-book invitation to a rave. I imagine a lot of people listening will be at a loss how to connect the three things: Joanne Seally's imprisonment, this so-called 'rave' and the explosion.

Are the police treating it as a set of coincidences or are there suspicions of deeper forces at work?"

"They're not ruling anything out at the moment, John, and the feeling is that they *must* be connected, although I haven't yet heard any official theory. One member of the crowd told me the rave *may* have been organised by someone who knew Miss Seally was incarcerated in there, but for the moment that's speculation."

"And we still don't have any motive for the abduction?"

"Early reports indicate she wasn't sexually assaulted. The big mystery, of course, is who set up the Facebook campaign to hold the rave which ultimately freed her, and why. Once the police find *that* person, things may start to become a little clearer."

"Joanne could so easily have been killed in the explosion, of course, couldn't she?"

"It was only the quick thinking of one policeman - "

Haider Chamkanni reached over and switched it off. "In short, they haven't a clue."

"Pity about Salique," Idris Kakahel said. "He was pretty good at what he did. Reasonable guy, too. I'm surprised the others survived."

"Do you think they'll talk?" Tasneem asked.

"About us? Who'd believe them? Anyway, I'm pretty sure they're honourable men."

"What did you do with the girl's mobile?" Haider Chamkanni asked.

Tasneem sipped her Pepsi. "Dropped it off Tower Bridge."

"I hope no one saw you," Idris Kakahel replied. "Dropping a two hundred pound phone off a bridge, that's not normal behaviour. It's the sort of thing people remember."

"I'm a woman," she said sardonically, "so naturally I would do something stupid like that. No, I leant it on the girder, knelt down to tie my shoelace, and when I stood up I accidentally knocked it into the water. I looked distressed, put my head in my hands, walked away at speed. At most, it inspired a callous chuckle."

Idris Kakahel shrugged. "I'm only saying, we can't afford to be too careful."

"What time do you have to be back for Ghatola?" Haider Chamkanni said, obviously trying to change the subject.

"I increased her Nitrazepam before I left," Tasneem said. "She won't be awake before tomorrow evening. In any case, she can do without me for a while. She's got used to me going out. She thinks I'm looking for a way for us to get back to Afghanistan, poor girl."

"Mentally, how is she?"

"Oh, she's suicidal. Everyone knows she and Reshtina Sarbanri were a couple of perverts. That's not the main thing, though. The poor dear thinks she was in love" – she broke into song – "and now, my oh my, her beloved is dead."

"I don't know why you have to be here anyway," Idris Kakahel said.

She laughed. "Because it could all be rubbish," she said. "You're men. You enjoy playing commandos. Whereas I can look at this sort of thing with a clear eye. And since I'm bankrolling it, I'm entitled."

"Where do you get your money from, anyway?"

"There are more sub-departments in Joint Intelligence Miscellaneous than you can possibly know. And you're starting to bore me. When are the bombs set to explode?"

"Nine am Monday morning, central London. You'll have to speak to al-Maitami. He's got the details and he'll be accompanying them throughout."

She drew back a centimetre. "So he's a suicide-bomber too?"

"Obviously he won't be *that* near. No, just close enough to ensure they do as they're told."

"Why? Is there an indication they're having second thoughts?"

"Not as far as I'm aware. It's irrelevant anyway, since they're going to be fastened in with padlocks."

She shook her head incredulously. "So really they're not so much committing suicide as being murdered?"

"What's it matter?"

She shrugged. "Just a question. You can't trust them very much, though."

"They're women."

Idris Kakahel started the car. Tasneem gathered all their litter together and put it in a carrier bag before taking it twenty yards to a bin at the far end of the car park. They called in at the petrol station, where she put on a niqab and filled the tank. Then they drove to Dover without stopping, keeping to the speed limit all the way. When they were within a few minutes of arriving, Tasneem put a tilak on her forehead. At four-forty, they checked into the Grand Hotel on the Marina, first Haider Chamkanni alone, then, twenty minutes later, Tasneem and Idris Kakahel, posing as 'Gita and Krishna Desai', a Hindu married couple from Delhi. Mr and Mrs Desai also made advance bookings for four relatives from India, due to arrive sometime early tomorrow for a wedding, and paid for their accommodation in cash. They were given two rooms on the fourth floor. Two more on the third were set aside for the newcomers.

Half an hour after they settled in, Idris Kakahel went downstairs to the car and spent two hours eradicating whatever evidence they'd left. Then he drove it two hundred yards to Dolphin Lane and left it parked, unlocked with the keys in.

At 4.20am on Sunday morning, a five-door Honda Civic rolled off the gangway of the *Seafrance Berlioz* in Dover's east dock. The driver was an Asian man and he was accompanied by three well-dressed women in hijabs, one in the passenger seat, the others seated primly in the back. After a cursory glance at their passports, the border officer waved them through to E Ramp, from where they joined to A2 northbound. They drove to a secluded car park in the outskirts of the town, took out a Qiblah compass and four prayer mats, washed perfunctorily with a bottle of *Evian*, performed Salah, then slept until an alarm work them at nine, when they prayed again. At 9.15, they drove to the Grand Hotel on the Marina and checked in in two groups: Reshtina and Abedrabbo al-Maitami as a married couple from France, and Ambrin and Zaituna as non-English-speaking spinster sisters from India, all in Britain for the wedding. They were shown to their rooms, spacious lounges with beds, easy chairs, and dressers all in cream, and landscape windows overlooking the beach. Reshtina joined Ambrin and Zaituna. They slept together till midday, then awoke, showered and prayed towards Mecca, completing the third of their five rakahs for that day.

Afterwards, they sat on the bed, saying and seeing nothing. This time tomorrow, they'd all be dead. All they saw before them would have passed behind a thick curtain with no possibility of return. Then, when they next awoke, thousands of years would have passed. Only they would remember the cotton sheets, the distant roar of a jet plane, the raindrop stained windows, fleecy carpet, the faint tingle of freshly washed hair. And then they'd forget it in an almighty bellow of glory as the angels dragged them into Jannah.

And then – what? They'd thought about it for long enough to slough off all their childish notions. They would be where there was no consciousness of loss, no having to heave your body everywhere or have it fail you. Floating and visiting friends and giving thanks to God for his infinite mercy, that's all there would be.

It was so beautiful that occasionally, at times like this, one of them would start to cry. Just like Ambrin was now. Zaituna and Reshtina put their arms round her and their heads on her shoulders, and for a split second they all felt terribly cold.

Upstairs, there was a knock on the door and Tasneem donned her niqab again. As expected, it was Abedrabbo al-Maitami. Since he hadn't brought the three women with him, she uncovered her face and waited patiently to one side like a dutiful daughter while Idris Kakahel and Haider Chamkanni embraced him, slapped him on the back and showered him with compliments. She quickly noticed he'd been drinking. She didn't think he was stupid enough to drive with it in his system, so he'd probably started sometime after arrival. A surge of disgust passed over her. For all their shortcomings, at least the two ISI men weren't hypocrites. She wondered whether the three bombers knew, and whether it had affected their morale. She hoped not. An awful lot of money would have been wasted otherwise.

The four of them sat down without anyone having remarked on Tasneem's presence – she was effectively invisible, but also used to it – until Idris Kakahel gestured casually in her direction.

"This is our financier," he said. He didn't give her name, nor would he unless he was specifically asked. She'd been clear about that.

He stood up and bowed an inch with his fists by his side. Perhaps, as a woman, he expected her to stand. If so, he was going to be disappointed.

He sat down again. "I understand we're wedding guests," he remarked.

"The beauty of it is, we've actually booked a wedding reception downstairs for tomorrow afternoon," Haider Chamkanni said.

Tasneem smiled. "Or at least, I did."

Al-Maitami turned to her. "That must have cost an awful lot of money."

"I only paid a deposit. Just enough to cover the alcohol."

Idris Kakahel and Haider Chamkanni laughed politely, al-Maitami less so. She saw she'd hit her mark and decided to move on.

"They're going to be awfully disappointed when no one turns up," she said. "They're expecting two hundred people and of course, they'll probably have signed for all the food by the time it's supposed to start. And then – boom! – nothing."

"I wonder how long it'll take them to make the connection," al-Maitami said.

"Hopefully, never," Idris Kakahel replied.

"When are we going to meet the women?" Tasneem asked.

"Do you need to see them?" al-Maitami said. "Why?"

"Because Reshtina Sarbanri gave us trouble back in Afghanistan. I need to check it's her you're sending to her death so I can close her file."

Al-Maitami laughed as if he was scandalised. "I'm not sending anyone to their death. It's a free choice they're making."

"That's why you're padlocking them in, is it?" she said.

"I think that's to be expected," he replied. "We've spent a lot of money bringing them over here. The last thing we want is them going astray."

"If it boils down to expenditure then you can hardly deny me a glimpse," she told him. "I doubt whether anyone can have spent more than I have."

"We'll be setting off at dawn for a brother's house in Camberwell, our final staging post. You can see them then. I'll introduce you to them. I certainly wouldn't see them now. They're in a very special place."

She wasn't sure from his tone whether he meant to be sarcastic, and whether, if so, he meant to deride the women or the belief. She got the strong impression that he wasn't especially attracted to the afterlife, even if it existed.

"I don't want them to see me," she said. "I'd like fair warning and I'll put my niqab on. We used to be part of the same organisation, a Communist-inspired women's group that used to go round killing pious men. Obviously, I was only there to undermine it. Apart from two women, I've succeeded."

"You'd be embarrassed to see her?" Idris Kakahel asked.

"I'm not sure what effect it would have. I wouldn't want to provoke second thoughts."

The three men chuckled.

"I wonder what's made her change her mind?" al-Maitami said.

"I'm not sure she has," Tasneem replied. "Our guess is she's upset because the British kidnapped her controller and that's her real motive for wanting to blow the country sky-high."

Al-Maitami drew his eyebrows together. He obviously didn't like the sound of this. "You mean, she's not doing it for the sake of Islam?"

"It doesn't have to be one or the other," Tasneem said.

"I didn't realise. In that case, she could be trouble."

"She's come all this way," Haider Chamkanni said. "Surely if she was going to chomp at the bit, she'd have done so before now?"

Al-Maitami shook his head. "It helps if their motives are one hundred per cent pure."

"You're an expert in this sort of thing, are you?" Tasneem said.

He looked at her as if he wanted to slap her and shut her impudent mouth. "I know my job."

She smiled. "I'm sure she'll be fine. It was always inevitable we'd get the jitters round about now. I'm sure there's nothing to worry about. We should exchange mobile numbers just in case of emergency. How long before our friends in Europe start texting?"

"Could be - " There was a quiet fanfare from his pocket. He pulled it out and showed the screen.

And the great tall buildings shall be razed. Q20.111.

Haider Chamkanni frowned. "That's not right. It's 'All faces before the ever-living, the Sustainer of existence'. It doesn't say anything about tall buildings." Then his expression brightened and he smiled. "Oh, I see, yes. Sorry, I had my scholarly shoes on for a moment. I get it now."

"It's whatever gets the job done," Tasneem said. "I didn't realise you had such a thorough knowledge of the holy book, incidentally."

"I went to a madrasah in Southern Punjab after my parents were killed," he said quietly. "Learning the Qur'an was all we did all day."

"That's my childhood too," Idris Kakahel said. "Both my parents were Afghan. My father was killed by the Soviets. My mother died in the refugee camp giving birth to me. My uncle didn't want me. The school took me in."

They both looked at the floor. It was clear they felt no commonality in their matching tragedies, simply a vague sadness and a sense of life's first quarter radically underused. For the first time, she felt more compassion than contempt for them.

"I thought the police were off the scent since the explosion in Leeds," al-Maitami said. "Surely, if texts start arriving from overseas, they'll only sit up again?"

"Two possibilities," she said. "One: they'll know the texts come from abroad, and they'll assume the news hasn't reached there yet. So nothing to fret about. On the other hand, they may have brought in explosives experts. They'll know that what went off in Leeds is chicken-feed, so they'll still be on high alert. In which case, this gives them yet another blind alley to wander up. As the Americans say, it's about covering all bases."

Al-Maitami nodded appreciatively. "And of course we've still got the Southampton decoy to come yet. If they get that far."

She beamed. "I didn't know anything about a 'Southampton decoy'. It's getting more impressive by the minute. Tell me more."

Chapter 26: A Truly Five Star Hotel

Fleming hoped he wasn't barking up the wrong tree, but there weren't that many more trees to choose from. The police were at the bottom of all the others and if they succeeded, all well and good: he'd go home and start planning his trip to Afghanistan.

The pain in his chest was getting worse, almost as if the Home Secretary had jinxed it. His initial plan had been to hook his mobile up to a printer somewhere, run off the photos of Kakahel and Chamkanni from his email and tour the local inns with them, flashing his police ID card. A good idea, but time consuming and probably excruciating. Then he had a better idea. In cases like this, the protagonist was usually limited by a desire to 'work alone'. What if he decided not to?

Grimes and Cassidy were the obvious candidates, since they were his friends. He'd once read a psychological study claiming that paradoxically you're more likely to win someone's fealty if you ask them for a favour. The head of Counter-Terrorist Command couldn't make them work for twenty-four hours, even in the present circumstances. There would have to come a time when he sent them home for a rest. But they wouldn't get one. He'd nab them.

Problem being, it could be quite a long time before they came off duty, and given that they'd probably be exhausted, how effective a job would they do? No, that was a non-starter.

Then he had another idea. Like all the best ones, its brilliance and obviousness shone equally bright. Its riskiness even more.

The first thing he needed was a new suit and preferably a bowler so he didn't look like a company rep or a member of the CBI. He checked the opening times of the local gentlemen's outfitters. He removed his clothes to shower and realised that, with his bandage and the pain, it was out of the question. His dressing probably needed replacing, but it would have to wait. He filled the bath with water and washed selectively.

He wasn't up to driving any more. At three-fifteen, he took at taxi to Phillips and Drew on the High Street and bought a shirt, a brown suit, matching bowler, lace ups and an umbrella. Then returned to the hotel and his room and took out his phone again.

"You in bed?" Cassidy said, when he answered. "I'm sorry you were dumped like that. We didn't even get chance to say goodbye."

"I just wanted to say how much I enjoyed working with you. I'm not in bed quite yet. I heard that The Dover Elysium on the Marina does an excellent lunch, so I thought I'd call in before heading back to London and probably a gurney someplace. I've never sampled Dover before except as a transit-point."

"You'll never guess what. We're all being re-deployed to Southampton. Counter-Terrorism Command thinks the Dover enquiry's a waste of manpower."

"*All* of you?"

"As good as," he replied bitterly.

Fleming sighed. "I suppose it's out of my hands now. Listen, if you happen to pass the Elysium on your way out of town, I'd appreciate it if you and Yvonne could call in just for a moment. I would like to shake both your hands, if that's okay. I appreciate you're going flat out - "

"No, er no, it would be a pleasure."

"Just for the sake of comradeship. After all, we may never see each other again."

"Give us ten minutes."

He picked up his bowler and umbrella and took the lift down to reception. The smoked glass front gave an excellent view of the forecourt and the main road. A twentysomething woman in a royal blue suit and a scarf stood at the desk checking a PC and smiling at guests. Fleming leant heavily on his umbrella. This was where it could all go wrong.

"Could you tell me if the manager's available?" he asked.

"I think – is it something *I* can help you with, sir?"

"No, I'm afraid it has to be the manager. Don't worry, it's not a complaint."

"Sunday's usually his day off. But I think he's around."

She disappeared through a door to the rear. Fleming noticed a police car pull up in the hotel car park. Perfect timing. Cassidy and Grimes climbed the steps in a hurry and pushed the door open. Fleming stood up to meet them just as the manager emerged. A stout, short man in a navy blue tieless suit whose black curly hair had receded to the level of his ears.

"I'm so glad you could both make it," Fleming said.

"How are you, sir?" Grimes said solicitously. "You should really be in bed."

"I'd just like to introduce you to the manager of the best hotel in Dover," Fleming said. "Mr ..."

The manager had blanched. "Ricci," he said.

"I've just had lunch here, and it was outstanding. But of course I didn't call you here to tell you about the food. I'll be on my way back to Thames House shortly. Thanks to the Home Secretary's eleventh-hour intervention, I didn't get a chance to tell you both face-to-face how much I've enjoyed working with you. I'm going to praise you to the roof in my report. Anti-terrorism has a lot to learn from officers of your calibre."

Grimes and Cassidy both flushed with pleasure.

"We've had an excellent few weeks working with you, sir," Cassidy said, in his emotion using the word 'sir' for the first time.

He noticed Grimes was about to embrace him, so he raised his right hand slightly – a trick he used to subliminally suggest the possibility of a salute. It worked. By way of adding a cherry to the icing, Cassidy saluted too. He returned the gesture and shook both their hands.

"I hope you both find what we're all looking for," he said.

There was nothing more to say. The two policemen left the way they'd come, Grimes putting her helmet on and pushing her hair beneath it as she went.

"I, er, understood you wanted to see me," Ricci said meekly.

Fleming smiled. "Have you somewhere we can talk in private?"

They walked to the bottom of the staff corridor behind the desk. Ricci opened the last door on the left and stood aside for his guest to enter and sit down on the semi-comfortable chair facing the desk. It was one of the primmer offices Fleming had been in. Rows of books and A4 ring-binders stood on shelves with potted spider-plants in front of them. The carpet was slightly deeper than necessary and a window facing a brick wall was tastefully veiled by a lace curtain.

He waited until Ricci was comfortably seated behind his desk before beginning. "I need your help."

"Sunday's normally my day off but I'll do what I can. Of course, my staff are very good at dealing with all routine enquiries, even, dare I say - "

"There's nothing routine about this enquiry, Mr Ricci." It was essential to trot out the clichés in this sort of situation. "I need to talk to you about a matter of national security and I'd like your assurance in advance that nothing I say will leave this room."

Ricci sat up and nodded.

"My name's Nicholas Fleming, I'm a member of the Anti-Terrorist Squad and I came to Dover in pursuit of two terrorist suspects who were last night in Leeds. The consensus within Intelligence is that by now they may have been joined by others from abroad. Also that they're planning an attack on London within the next few days. You can help us."

He nodded again then swallowed. "Wh – what do I have to do?"

"First, you could take a look at the register of new arrivals. I'm looking for at least one man of Asian descent who arrived here sometime last night or this morning, possibly but not necessarily in company."

"That's easy. We haven't had anyone in the last twenty-four hours. I looked when I came in. Hang on, I can double check, if you'd like ..."

"That won't be necessary. You can probably guess my next request."

"You'd like me to ring round the other hotels in the area, ask the same question."

"Not quite. It's essential that as little of this gets out as possible. I'd like you to tell them you've had a visit from the Border Control Agency and they're looking for an illegal immigrant or two. Or possibly three. Just to be on the safe side, anyone that's checked in during the last twelve hours."

He laughed. "They wouldn't have to go far to find illegals round here. No, that'd raise too many suspicions. I don't get it. Why don't the police just do the asking themselves?"

"Data protection, plus we're thinly enough stretched as it is. I'm just saying you can help us, Mr Ricci, I'm not suggesting you're indispensible. Although ... you almost are. Even if we get plain clothes to do the asking, it'll start tongues wagging. As manager of one of the most prestigious hotels in Dover, you can probably access all areas and still keep word from getting out. I could ask the proprietor of the Grand instead if it makes you feel uncomfortable, but I assure you I'd rather not move from here. I was stabbed in the chest last night, and walking's becoming increasingly problematic."

"No, no, I'll do it. I hope you won't mind, though, if I ask to see your identification."

He'd expected this. He removed it from his inside jacket pocket and handed it over.

Ricci looked at it with admiration, then handed it back. "You return to your room, Mr Fleming, and lie down. Would you like me to get a doctor to come and look at you? I know a good one."

"That would be very kind although, as I nearly told the Home Secretary a few hours' ago, I'm not prepared to go into hospital until I've tied up the loose ends."

"I'm sure most hospitals can live with that. I've no idea how bad you've got to be to get a bed these days, but I think death's door's about standard."

Fleming went back to his room, half undressed and slept fitfully for two hours. There was a knock on his door. He pulled his trousers on and opened it to find Ricci holding a piece of paper.

"Maybe I should come in," he said. "My God, that is an awful wound. At least, that's how it looks. Firstly, apologies. I tried to get Dr Wilson out, but it's Sunday and he's not prepared to interrupt whatever it is he does on a Sunday."

"He's a good doctor," Fleming replied. "He's not necessarily a good person."

"'If it's that bad, tell him to ring an ambulance', that's what he said. I'm very sorry."

"Never mind the GP. How's the investigation going?"

"Not much, I'm afraid. Quite a few arrivals in the last twelve hours, obviously. The only one that fits what you're looking for is the Grand, just a few doors away. They've had a few new arrivals in lieu of a Hindu wedding. They're hosting the reception there tomorrow afternoon. It's a big deposit and it's already been paid, so I doubt there's much chance of it being what you're looking for."

"How many new arrivals?"

"Seven. Two married couples, two sisters, a man on his own."

"Their ages?"

"Ah, now that is interesting. All under forty, from what Clive tells me. But I wouldn't set too much store by that."

Fleming smiled. "Thank you very much, Mr Ricci. You've been most helpful. I hope you won't be too insulted if I transfer to the Grand for this evening?"

Chapter 27: As Bob Marley Might Have Said (but Didn't)

Fleming took his hire-car back to the depot. He used the refund to buy a holdall from the last luggage shop open in town, and possibly, judging by the demeanour of the man who served him, the world.

It was raining an hour later when he arrived at the steps of his new hotel. Six houses wide and two high, the Grand looked to have been built in the early half of the last century, before creating a profit for one's shareholders became the only civic virtue. The windows were tall and evenly divided into squares, the frontage was grey stone and it had a portico to give visitors a respite from bad weather and a chance to commend themselves to the Almighty before surrendering to Reception. A porter guarded the entrance.

Fleming was glad of his umbrella now, although, once up, it meant he no longer had anything to lean on. The sea roared, the road shone wet and the wind tore at the Swedish Whitebeams. He passed through a set of revolving doors and walked up to the receptionist, a military-looking man in a tourmaline tunic, who stood flicking through receipts.

"I'd like a room for the night. I'm with the wedding party," Fleming said.

"Just you on your own, sir?"

They went through the formalities together and he paid.

"Dinner's between half six and quarter to eight," the receptionist told him. "There's a menu in your room. The bar's open from half seven until half eleven."

"Terrible weather."

"Hardly suitable for getting married. Mind you, they say it might ease off a bit tomorrow."

"Fingers crossed. Have many guests arrived yet?"

"Just seven."

"Any more to come?"

"None that I know of," the receptionist replied. "The rest are probably mostly locals."

"I know a lot of them are. I used to do business with Mr Chaterjee, the bride's uncle."

The receptionist smiled. "Would you like me to put you near the other families?"

"That would be very nice. I wonder if you'd mind introducing us ... I mean, if you see us downstairs together?"

"I'm sure I could manage that, sir."

"If you see them and I'm not around, tell them I might call on them this evening."

"Very good, sir. You'll find Mr and Mrs Desai in forty-five and Mr Asar in forty-six. And we've got Mr and Mrs Ramakrishna in thirty-four ... and the two Misses Satapathy next door in thirty-five. I could put you in thirty-six, if you like. There's not much of a view, though. Thirty-seven's better from that point of view."

"Thirty-seven being the sea-view."

"That's right, sir. Although presently, it's not much to look at."

"I'll take thirty-six. Are the Misses Satapathy at home now?"

The receptionist checked the rows of little hooks behind him. "Unless they've taken their keys out with them."

Forty-five, forty-six and thirty-four were also missing. Of course, they might still be out, regardless. They might or might not be familiar with the convention of leaving your keys in reception. For all he knew, it might not apply in every country.

He accepted his key, picked up his holdall and went to his room to find the usual double-bed, en suite bathroom, matching easy chairs and teasmaid on a built-in dresser. Only the colours ever varied: in this case various shades of pastel blue, with fittings in pine. The existence of the en-suite bathroom was a disappointment. He'd hoped for communal facilities, forcing them to emerge from their rooms at some point. This way, they could stay put indefinitely.

He put a glass to the wall where thirty-five was, and his ear to the glass.

... No, nothing. If they were at home, they had to be asleep. He took his holdall, went along the corridor to thirty-four, and spent a few minutes outside the door pretending to tie his shoelace. Again, no signs of life.

He let out a frustrated sigh. Of course he could cut the Gordian knot simply by knocking on one or more of their doors. But under what pretext? Not the wedding: if they were who they might be, there was no wedding. He could ring room service, order something, and chance to be walking past the door when they took delivery. But again that would arouse their suspicions, and at this stage they were probably jumpy enough to fly the nest at the slightest provocation. He'd seen it before.

There seemed to be no alternative to sitting it out somewhere. Probably the lounge with one eye on the hotel entrance, since there were no seats in the corridors and no plausible excuse for loitering. He suddenly knew what to do as he sat there.

But there were no Hindu temples in Dover, nor, as far as he could discover, in the whole of Kent. It had to be in a church or village hall then, or a community centre. But that didn't make sense either. If you were prepared to have your wedding somewhere like that, why not the hotel where you were holding the reception? He'd reached a satisfying dead end. It was looking more and more like a cover story.

He went to dinner at six-thirty precisely and stayed till last orders at seven forty-five, sure they'd make an appearance at some point – at least if they were who they claimed. Once again, he was disappointed. And vaguely gratified.

Eight o'clock found him in the bar and, apart from two elderly couples and the barman, alone. He read the *Telegraph* in minute detail, in the hope that no one would come over and speak to him, until nine. Then he saw an Asian-looking man rush through reception and down the steps of the entrance without stopping. He had a neatly trimmed beard and a smart jacket, and Fleming had no recollection of having seen him before.

He rose briskly and followed him outside. The rain had stopped now, although the wind was still strong and the sea growled in the black beyond the parade street lamps. The bearded man had turned left and was about a hundred yards distant, almost at the junction with Townwall Street. When he turned the corner, Fleming broke into a jog, reducing the distance to forty. He was just in time to see his quarry turn right into Woolcomber street, where he turned left again.

After ten minutes, it finally became clear where he was headed. A convenience store called Khan's in Dearlove Street. The large front window was obscured by a blind advertising the Kent Messenger and protected by zinc mesh. The door blind gave a category-list of its provisions: newspapers & magazines, lottery & scratchcards, sweets & snacks, fresh groceries and frozen food, tobacco, household cleaning, greetings cards, wine & spirits, stationery. The bearded man pushed the door open and went inside. The bell jangled.

Fleming counted to ten and followed. He half-expected to find him deep in conversation with a contact – possibly even the proprietor – or to have disappeared altogether, but no: he'd picked up a basket and was scanning the shelves with a fixity of interest that strongly suggested shopping was his sole end.

Khan's was much bigger than it appeared from outside. Two aisles of about six categories flanked an open chest freezer with a fridge behind it. Another row of shelves at a right angle housed baking ingredients, preserves and condiments. The bearded man stood by the fridge and put six or seven packets of something in his basket. He moved into the drinks section, picking up three cartons of fresh orange juice, then into cakes and bread where he squeezed a baguette for freshness and put it into his basket. He paid the shopkeeper without speaking or making eye contact and left with a carrier bag in each hand.

Fleming retraced his route round the shop in reverse. A French loaf, three cartons of Tropicana and six or seven vacuum-packed packs of – halal beef.

Which, suggestive as it was, still proved nothing. Desai could be a Muslim name, and it was hardly unusual for Hindus to be friends with Muslims. They might still be guests at a wedding.

He bought a bottle of TCP and twelve paracetamol and took a short cut back to the hotel so as to be there when the bearded man arrived. He stood by the front desk and pretended to read a flyer about Dover Castle. The on-duty receptionist was the same one who had checked him in earlier and who'd promised to introduce him to the rest of the wedding-party should the chance arise. He was doing sums with a calculator and writing figures in a ledger when the bearded man climbed the entrance steps, two at a time. Fleming cleared his throat. The receptionist looked up and seemed to recall his promise.

"Er, Mr Ramakrishna?" he called.

The bearded man ignored him. He walked past, opened the door to the stairs and disappeared.

"Sorry, sir," the receptionist said. "I tried. Why don't you go after him? Or I could ring up to his room."

Fleming smiled. "I'm sure we'll make each other's acquaintance soon enough. But thank you for trying."

Progress on two fronts. First, Ramakrishna wasn't a Muslim name, not by any stretch of the imagination. Second, he'd ignored the receptionist not, Fleming thought, deliberately, but quite unthinkingly. The best explanation for that was that Ramakrishna wasn't his real name.

Of course, the food too. None of the seven had been down for the hotel dinner, and those packets of halal beef suggested forcefully that they hadn't eaten out either. Why not? And why such basic food? ... Unless your mind was on other things.

So what should he do now? The obvious course was to ring in, at least let someone know of his suspicions.

The problem was, he'd been ordered to check in at an A&E and, although it wasn't a proper order – more rhetorical than binding – in many people's minds it would probably count against him that he thought he was part of the chase. His best bet was probably to hang on and try to observe the suspects in the act of leaving their room. Then what? He felt groggy. There could be no doubt his wound was getting the better of him.

He went upstairs, lay down and removed his bandage. The knife's entry point had swollen and the circumference of the bruise had spread since he last looked. He got into the bath, unscrewed the cap on the TCP and poured some over his chest, clenching his teeth and shivering against the pain. He opened his eyes, staggered back into the bedroom and began to re-tie the bandage. Sooner or later, he'd have to act on the Home Secretary's advice: he couldn't postpone the inevitable forever. But not yet.

He should lie down with his door open and a strong coffee inside him. He went to the teasmaid, changed the water and put it on to boil. There were six sachets of Kenco in the dispenser. He emptied all of them into a single cup. Sugar, sugar, yes, he'd like it sweet. He poured the scalding water onto the granules, stirred and put it to his lips. Far too hot.

He'd go to the door, that was a good idea, open it while it cooled. He had to hold on to the walls to get there, but he made it.

He suddenly realised he was about to faint. A wave of nausea overcame him, so strong it almost hurled his stomach into his mouth, and he lay down on the bed and passed out.

When he awoke, he had no idea how much time had passed or even where he was. Then it came back. And there were noises in the corridor!

Still muzzy, he rose to his feet. He staggered into the corridor to find himself face-to-face with four people, who looked at him as malevolently as if he'd interrupted them in the act of a midnight burial. A man – the bearded man he'd shadowed earlier – and three women. The women wore casual gear and looked awkward, as if they weren't comfortable dressed like this. No sooner had they set eyes on him, than all four barged past him. His legs gave way and he crumpled gently against the wall.

They reached the end of the corridor and had a quiet altercation in a language Fleming had never heard before. Then one of the women returned and knelt down by him, showing her palms and lifting them repeatedly upwards as if to suggest she was willing to help him. He had to look away and look back again, so completely did he distrust the evidence of his senses.

"*Marcie?*"

One of the other women arrived. There was more heated discussion and they lifted him into his room, helped him onto his bed and left. He heard them descend the stairs, then silence. He looked at his watch. Four-forty.

He eased himself off the bed to where he knew a cold cup of coffee was waiting and downed it in a single draught. He went to the window. Nothing, and in the darkness he'd probably be unable to make them out anyway. He went into the bathroom, splashed some water on his face and re-emerged.

He heard a car pull away at speed.

Damn, he should have stayed at the window. Still, as Bob Marley once said, spilt milk, no cry. He picked up his phone, scrolled the contacts and pressed dial.

"Hello, Ruby. Nicholas Fleming here," he said. "I think I may have found my wife."

Chapter 28: Merci, Mademoiselle!

Monday, 3.40 am.

Reshtina sat up in bed and switched the alarm off, though the lights were on and she wasn't asleep. Zaituna and Ambrin were awake too, sitting in the chairs looking groggily at the carpet. They hadn't brought changes of clothing, so they'd all slept in their underwear. On the bedside, the remains of the beef sandwiches they'd nibbled at six hours ago, and the empty glasses of orange.

The alarm meant ten minutes till al-Maitami came into the room and they were strapped into their belts. They had to get moving. He'd almost certainly insist on them stripping half naked so he could ensure a proper fit. Their end-realisation was too valuable a commodity for them to be treated as anything better than livestock while they were still in transit. People had invested money in them, they were looking to make a spectacular return.

Reshtina stood up and went into the bathroom. Before she could lock the door, Zaituna pushed past her, knelt down at the toilet and retched. She stood up and flushed the bowl, then Ambrin came in and did the same, except with more coughing and a few tears. Then she shooed Reshtina and Zaituna out so she could have a bout of diarrhoea.

She returned to the bedroom looking haggard. She and Zaituna put their clothes on and sat down with the same haunted looks as before.

Reshtina went into the bathroom. She locked the door, unfastened her gun and silencer from the cord she'd tied round her waist, and thrust them under the bath. If al-Maitami saw them he'd probably take a shine to them. She needed them. She had the strong feeling she wouldn't reach her target without a fight. The last thing she wanted was a degrading struggle, thrashing about on the floor with some Englishman tugging at her as she tried to set her bomb off. She had enough to worry about without that.

She looked in the mirror for the first time in a long while and had the odd sensation of seeing someone else's face. Someone she recognised strongly without being able to name. She stared into her own eyes – although it wasn't just the eyes - in the expectation that it would dissipate, but if anything it intensified. For some reason, she recalled the Sufi meeting in Kandahar that night when Ghatola had cried so bitterly they had to leave. And she had an unsettling feeling the two things were connected. She felt ill.

There was a knock on the door. She unbolted it again and Ambrin burst into and huddled over the toilet bowl for another retch. Reshtina ignored her and walked through into the bedroom as if she was treading on quicksand. She sat on the bed.

"We won't see the sun set tonight," Zaituna said neutrally.

"We'll never see another afternoon," Reshtina replied, standing up and getting dressed. "Yesterday was our last."

Zaituna was trembling like a poorly sparrow. "It's too late to turn back now, I know, but - "

"It won't hurt. You won't even know it's happened."

"I wish we were going to do it together. Can't you ask him again?"

"It's been decided. It's about taking as many people with us as we can."

"I suppose we'll be together afterwards. But what if we can't find each other for the crowds we've killed? I mean, their souls?"

"We've been through this. The angels will be waiting for us."

She closed her eyes. "It's only a few hours away now. I'm scared."

"I know."

She didn't want to talk to Zaituna any more. There was something she had to remember, and the more she conversed the further it seemed to slip away.

The door opened. Al-Maitami entered casually with a suitcase, followed by two moribund-looking men of about middle-age and a woman in a niqab, talking in Arabic so they couldn't be understood. Reshtina sat down without asking who any of them were. She'd met so many anonymous busy-bodies over the last eight thousand miles, she'd lost all curiosity. They were 'investors'. They sat on the bed without making eye-contact with her and al-Maitami showed no inclination to introduce them.

"Get undressed down to your waists," he said, reverting to Pashto. "And hurry up. We've about fifteen minutes before we have to set off."

Zaituna and Ambrin looked at each other and blushed, then at Reshtina.

"Hurry up," he repeated.

The woman in the niqab sighed. "They're Afghan women, Abedrabbo," she said, also in Pashto. "You can't expect them to undress in front of a roomful of men."

"They'll do as I tell them."

"You really think it's worth upsetting them to prove a silly point like that? They're going to be with Allah and his angels in a few hours' time, but only if they keep clear heads. If people go humiliating them, that's a whole lot less likely."

He threw his arms up. "So what do you suggest?"

"Show me how it all works and retire for a few minutes. I'll make sure they put everything on as per spec. And if you absolutely insist, you can then check it over. Happy?"

He shook his head as if he'd never heard such a stupid idea, but was prepared to go along with it to show how accommodating he was. "Fine, yes, okay." He flicked the catches on the suitcase and opened it. He laid three sets of ten metal tubes on the floor, all about half an arm in length, slightly curved at the base and held together with small-link chains and electrical wires. Then a hand-drawn diagram of a woman wearing one.

"They're basically explosive corsets. Lutfur Salique's genius is that the pipes are much thinner than usual, so they shouldn't stand out, and they're contoured to a woman's shape, so not just straight up and down, see? They're filled with Composition C4, so they're extremely stable. You can fall over with them, bash them, even heat them right up: nothing. Only when the detonator – this thing – fires into them will they explode. This switch – here – is how you'll activate them. It's quite stiff, to eliminate the possibility of an accident. But this connection – here – is taken from the inside of a mobile phone, and I can detonate the whole thing remotely, simply by giving it a call. Insurance, yes? These are the padlocks, and this is where they fit – these two links here, see? You'll stick these wires to your bodies, and bring the detonator switch through into your pockets."

"Tape?" the woman in the niqab said.

He placed a roll on the floor. Then three sets of clothes. "Jeans and woolly jumper and pumps for Reshtina. Ambrin: this long skirt, baseball boots and a gabardine, and Zaituna, a Columbia University hoodie, jeans and Doc Martens. You have to look Western."

"I don't see why we have to change into everything now," Ambrin said in a pleading tone.

"Because you have to acclimatise," al-Maitami replied. "Put all your old clothes in the suitcase, plus anything else that might arouse suspicion when the cleaner finds we've gone."

"How are we going to get past reception?" the woman in the niqab said. "Won't it look odd, us all leaving together at this time?"

"We're going to a Hindu wedding. Greeting the rising sun's auspicious."

She laughed. "Is it?"

"Probably. Hindus believe all sorts of things. They have to show their newborn babies the sun, I know that much, like they might miss it if they're not formally introduced. Anyhow, it rings true. And don't worry, I'll do the explaining."

"How long did you say we had?" she asked coolly.

He looked at his watch. "Ten minutes. We'll wait in the bathroom."

The two gloomy men hadn't spoken a word yet. They stood up.

"I don't want you waiting in the bathroom," Reshtina said.

"I beg your pardon?" said the first gloomy man.

"We've been having diarrhoea all morning. Ambrin vomited on the floor. I'm having my period. I'd rather you didn't."

"I didn't 'vomit on the floor'," Ambrin said.

Reshtina let out an exasperated breath. "Please."

"Wait next door boys," the woman in the niqab said. "Remember what I said earlier. Let's just get the job done and get moving, eh?"

"We'll be back in ten minutes exactly," al-Maitami said. "And girls, you'd better be ready."

They left. The woman in the niqab gestured for them to get started and helped them silently when they weren't sure what went where. She taped the wires to their chests and waists as stipulated in the diagram and helped them pull the switches through. She sewed the holes in their pockets shut so they couldn't fall back. She went round polishing the surfaces as she worked to remove fingerprints. Finally, she took the dummy switch al-Maitami had provided and passed it between them so they could all get a feel for it.

"You'd better pack all your old shit away," she said sitting down. "Grumpy will be back any minute. I think he's quite nervous. He's got a plane to catch this afternoon, and he suffers from air sickness."

The belts were almost impossible to bend over in, so they had to keep kneeling down and standing up. Al-Maitami entered with his two companions and closed the door behind him.

"Right, all sit down," he said. He reached into his jacket pocket and handed Reshtina, Zaituna and Ambrin a piece of paper each with the London Underground logo printed large.

"These are your targets," he went on, "and I'd like you to start memorising them now to minimise the possibility of a cock-up. What you have here is a thick red circle with a white middle and a blue stripe across it horizontally. Now I know they all look the same, but it's the English writing in the middle that's different. Just learn the shapes of the letters, that's all. When we get to the departure point, at precisely eight thirty-five, I'll send you in three different directions. You just keep walking until you see the exact sign you're looking at now, understood?"

They nodded.

"I'm going to give you each a ticket. Just walk straight ahead for as long as it takes. Don't communicate with anyone and don't refer to the diagram unless it's absolutely essential and, in that case, keep it well hidden from everyone around you. Reshtina, you've got Oxford Circus, Zaituna you're Regent Street, and Ambrin you're Bond Street. When you locate the sign, you'll see a wide entrance that leads underground. Take the steps down then put your ticket into one of the machines everyone else is using, and go through. Follow the crowds and descend as far as you possibly can. When you reach the bottom, you'll find trains coming and going and crowds of people waiting. Stand right in the middle of the platform, it doesn't matter which one, any. Wait till one of the trains arrives. When the doors open, flick your switch. In case of a hitch, fifteen or twenty minutes after you've left me I'll call you, one at a time, and detonate you automatically. Have you any questions?"

"What if the police stop us?" Ambrin said.

"In the unlikely event that they see what you're up to, they'll have a struggle to get you out of your corsets. Wait as long as you can to detonate, to give the others more time, but if you're in any doubt at all, sooner rather than later. Keep hold of your switches throughout."

"What if we get lost?" Zaituna asked.

"Then go down any Underground. It doesn't have to be yours. Or, failing that, find somewhere with lots of people. Department stores are good."

"What are 'department stores'?" Zaituna said.

He shook his head. "Or malls. Just follow the crowds, be creative."

"What if, for some reason, the bombs fail?" Reshtina said. "After all, they haven't been tested. They could all be duds."

He frowned. "Let's forget about worst case scenarios, shall we? God will provide. What's the point in being pessimistic?"

The woman in the niqab chuckled. "I was just about to ask the same question."

"I'm just asking," Reshtina said.

"Well, since you're locked into your belts," he replied, "and you've nowhere to go, it's probably only a matter of time till the police pick you up. Then you'll be beaten and raped and slung into a hole so deep no one will ever hear from you again. Your best course in that event would probably be to commit suicide. Remember, you meant well. It's the intention that counts in Islam. You'll still go to Jannah. Maybe not the highest level, but high enough."

"How should we kill ourselves in that case?" Ambrin asked. "I mean, what method?"

Al-Maitami scowled. He obviously wasn't happy with this line of questioning. "There's a big river in London called the Thames. If you walk around for long enough, you can't miss it. You throw yourself off one of its bridges. The amount of metal you've got strapped to you, you'll sink like a stone. And that's probably best for us, because we can bring others in to replace you while the authorities are still complacent. Yes, do that."

"Not that that's going to be an issue," one of the gloomy men said. "Don't worry, the man that made your bombs was a genius."

"'Was'?" Reshtina said.

"The British police raped and killed him."

"That's enough questions," al-Maitami said. "We're behind schedule. Put the suitcase in the wardrobe – we won't need it again - and let's go."

202

"Hasn't it got your fingerprints on?" the second gloomy man asked.

Al-Maitami smiled. "I wore gloves. Come on."

The men preceded them into the corridor. When they all stood outside, Reshtina remembered her gun and silencer.

"I have to go back and pee," she said.

"No, you don't," al-Maitami replied.

"Look, I can't go all the way to London - "

"Let her, please!" Ambrin said.

She wasn't going to wait for permission, let him do his worst, what could he do? She ran back into the room, charged into the bathroom and retrieved her equipment without even taking the precaution of locking the door. She fitted the silencer and jammed the whole thing into her corset and flushed the chain. She emerged into the corridor breathless to find everyone looking furious.

And then something happened no one could have anticipated. A man emerged from the room next door, naked from the waist up, covered in bruises and dried blood. He staggered towards them. They barged past him and he slumped by the wall.

God, what was he? A premonition? They reached the end of the corridor and she couldn't go any further. "We can't just leave him there!"

"We bloody well can!" al-Maitami hissed.

"It's nothing to do with us," Ambrin said. "Please, Reshtina."

She could see al-Maitami was on the verge of hitting her and that even the presence of the woman in the niqab wouldn't be sufficient to restrain him this time. But she had no choice. She hurried back and knelt down by him, showing her palms and lifting them repeatedly upwards to get it through to him, in whatever language he spoke, that she was willing to help but she couldn't raise him on his own.

He looked away and looked back. "Merci!"

Zaituna arrived.

"If we just lift him back into his room and put him on the bed," she said.

"What if he's dying?"

"He'll be with Allah. We can say a prayer for him in the car."

They lifted him into his room, helped him onto his bed and descended the stairs in a group. They brushed past reception while the woman in the niqab explained where they were going and paid, and got into the car, Reshtina in the front with al-Maitami and Ambrin and Zaituna in the back.

They pulled away at speed, leaving the three investors to go home and watch the whole thing on TV.

Chapter 29: Copthorne Proves Himself a Sterling Chap

"Listen, Nicholas," Ruby Parker replied gently. "This is very important. Where are you?"

"I'm in a hotel. The Grand, on Dover's Marine Parade."

"And ... what room are you in?"

"Thirty ..." he had to look at the door, still ajar from his excursion "...six."

"Just hold the phone a minute. Don't ring off."

He heard her say something to someone else, a few inaudible lines in a conversational tone, punctuated by short pauses.

"I sent Toby Copthorne to find you six hours ago. His best lead was at the Elysium, but the manager there seems to have sent him off on a wild goose chase."

Fleming smiled. "Excellent fellow. Look, Ruby, we haven't time to chew the fat. I've just seen Marcie, and she's with a group of women – three, I think. I strongly suspect they're our terrorists."

"Nicholas, Toby's on his way now. I'd like you to pause for a minute and listen to what you've just said and think about the condition you're in. You're badly wounded. You should never have gone back to work. And now it's four o'clock in the morning, in Dover, and you've just seen Marcie in your hotel room."

"I'm not delirious. We've got – we had – seven people here, staying on two different floors, on the pretext that they were here for a Hindu wedding. But then blow me if they didn't come down to dinner this evening, and one of them didn't go round the corner for six packets of halal beef an hour or two later. And now, they've all just – left."

"Really."

"Yes, really."

"So your door's open, is it?"

The receptionist stood in the doorway. He knocked gently. "Is it okay for me to switch on the light, sir? A 'Mr

Copthorne' just called, says he's on his way. Asked me to check on you, see if you're okay."

"Fine, yes, switch the light on."

The receptionist's face resolved itself into an expression of shock. "Bloody hell."

"It looks worse than it is."

"Had I better call an ambulance?"

"That won't be necessary." He reached over for his jacket and took out his identification card. "I'm not a guest at a Hindu wedding, I'm a member of the Anti-Terrorist Squad. I'd be very grateful if you could have a look in thirty-five and thirty-four and tell me what you find. I'll be with you in a minute, as soon as I've finished speaking to my employer."

The receptionist nodded mechanically. Fleming could tell he didn't believe the card. His having a gruesome bruise obviously rendered it suspect too.

"I – I'll – "

"Are you still there, Nicholas?" Ruby said.

"I'm still in the land of the living," he replied sardonically. "Look, Ruby, you can believe me or not. I'm coming to London. I don't know what I'm going to do when I get there, but with or without you, I've got to do something."

A camel-coated man with a moustache appeared at the door and knocked in the same tentative way the receptionist had a moment ago. "Toby Copthorne. I trust I'm not interrupting anything deep. I've been looking all over for you."

"They seek him here, they seek him there," Fleming muttered as he pulled his shirt on. "Show this chap your card, Copthorne, and make him accompany you into thirty-four and thirty-five. Then upstairs. He knows the numbers."

"Sorry, sir, I've been ordered not to leave your side for a second once I've found you."

"Bloody hell, just show him your bloody *card*, will you? We'll *all* go."

"Put Toby on the phone," Ruby said.

He passed the phone over. "Here!"

The receptionist glanced cursorily at Copthorne's card and left. Fleming put his tie on and checked his cuffs were straight. He hoped they were going to get him into those rooms. Now he'd put all his cards on the table, he couldn't very well enter on his own, forcibly or otherwise. Not that it mattered. He knew what he knew.

Or did he? Maybe ...

A porter appeared with a set of master keys. "I've been asked to show you into thirty-four and thirty-five, sir. Come this way."

Fleming thanked God and accompanied him to thirty-four, closely followed by Toby Copthorne speaking on the phone. The porter unlocked the door. Fleming was about to fling it open when Copthorne took his wrist.

"What the hell are you doing?" Fleming said.

"Don't touch it." He handed Fleming his phone back. "We've agreed to try and humour you. Ruby Parker's has sent images of Marcie's fingerprints to your phone. If we get some cocoa, talcum powder and a camel hair brush, we ought to be able to resolve this fairly quickly. Then you're coming back to London with me and straight to hospital."

"I'm going back to London anyway."

"I'm trying to help you, man."

Fleming removed his wallet from his pocket and gave the porter a twenty. "You heard what Mr Copthorne said. And two pairs of gloves would be nice. Time's of the essence."

The porter returned forty seconds later with the bits and pieces. They opened the door.

There was an anodyne feel to what met them. Even for a hotel room it felt unloved. The bedclothes were strewn across the double bed and there was a faint smell of vomit. The curtains were drawn, the bin empty. Three empty glasses and three half-eaten sandwiches stood on the bedside table.

"Lost their appetites," Fleming remarked. "Although, to be fair, they do seem to have had upset stomachs."

"Shall we get started?" Copthorne said wearily.

Fleming flashed anger. "You take the bathroom," he said.

He expected a 'do I have to?' but Copthorne was obviously used to being given the bum's job, and he accepted his fate without a murmur. Fleming immediately felt guilty. "Unless you'd prefer me to," he said.

"No, that's all right. Sorry if I seem a bit grumpy. I'm tired, that's all. I realise that probably sounds a bit rich given how you're probably feeling, but I'm no spring chicken any more."

"I appreciate you coming to find me."

They got to work. Within a minute, Fleming sensed déjà vu. He'd been in this sort of situation in the Met: the biggest fingerprint was no fingerprint at all. That the actual prints had been erased so expertly erased entailed a small pool of experts, known and unknown. It was a disconcerting conclusion. There was a suitcase full of women's clothing in the wardrobe. In other circumstances, he'd have packaged it up for DNA-testing, but the three to five day minimum window was pretty hopeless here.

"Eureka!" Copthorne shouted.

Fleming closed the suitcase and went into the bathroom. Copthorne was leaning over a cocoa-dusted fingerprint on the bath rim. "There's nothing anywhere else," he said. "This must have happened quite late on. She came in here because there was something under the bath. Something valuable she wanted to retrieve. There's definitely a disturbance of the dust under there - although don't tell anyone in the hotel that: they'll only use it to sack the cleaners. I can see it now. She comes here at the eleventh hour, having hidden something precious. She leans down to get it, leaves in a hurry, forgets to wipe. Come on, Nicholas, everything else has been eradicated! Don't tell me you haven't found the same out there, because in these sorts of cases - "

"'She?'" Fleming said.

"I apologise for having doubted you," Copthorne replied. "There's ninety per cent congruence, good enough for me any day. I've taken a photo, by the way. Ruby Parker should be looking at it right now."

Fleming's phone rang. He picked up.

"It's not a perfect match," she said. "But then we wouldn't expect it to be. Okay, you've persuaded me. The fingerprint on its own wouldn't have swung it, mind you, and the testimony of a man with a hole in his chest certainly not, but those two in conjunction with the vote of an expert witness like Copthorne – I'm willing to waive my reservations. Provisionally."

"So what now?"

"You're aware of last night's developments?"

"I'm afraid I haven't had much time to listen to the news."

He heard her sigh. "To begin with, Robert Skelton's focus on Southampton appears to have paid off. At eleven-ten last night, a team of border control officers raided an Algerian-chartered container ship after an anonymous tip-off. Deep inside the hold they found a pair of deceased women installed in a conex box with two kilograms of acetone peroxide and a copy of Sayyid Qutb's *Milestones*."

"I'm not familiar with it."

"A kind of Islamist *Main Kampf*, although much more recent. 1964."

"And what about Kakahel and Chamkanni?"

"No sign of them anywhere. The assumption is they've returned to Pakistan."

"Really?" he said sarcastically. "Before or after the discovery of the corpses?"

"The Pakistani embassy's supposed to have put the frighteners on them after someone high up decided to cut their losses. Which may explain why the women were dead. Expendable merchandise, so poisoned rather than suffocated. We'll know more tomorrow."

"Brilliant. So that's the final piece of the jigsaw as far as Skelton's concerned, is it?"

"He's already scaling the manhunt down. As far as he's concerned, the operation's British half was routed at Leeds by you and your men; the overseas half is lying in the mortuary, awaiting post-mortem analysis. To the extent that he feels the need to exercise further caution, he's put a tight security cordon round the tallest buildings in London. Canada Square, Heron Tower, the Gherkin, St Paul's Cathedral and so on."

"On yet more purely speculative grounds, I assume."

"Not this time. Based on texts sent from abroad to the phones of Abduttawwah, Masroor, Hussain, Salique, Al-Hazzaa and several others, indicating that 'tall buildings' are, stroke were, the intended targets."

Fleming smiled. "I guess that's quite a lot of manpower he's committed, especially if he's winding things up."

"You have no idea where Marcie and her companions might have gone?"

"I can make a pretty good guess."

"London's a very big place. I meant, specifically."

"I'm afraid not."

"I'll put our progress-to-date in a report and send a copy to Skelton marked 'urgent', but I don't expect him to credit it. He's not particularly fond of me and he regards you as a rank amateur. He'll want the fingerprint properly analysed, which will take longer than we've got."

"So what are we going to do?"

"Let's just take a deep breath here, Nicholas, shall we? For both of our sakes, I'm happy to err on the side of caution, which means doing everything we possibly can, but let's also look at the evidence as we imagine Robert Skelton might look at it. We have one fingerprint and one dubious witness-identification. At *best*, we have proof that Marcie's in the country. But it's quite a long way from that to accepting that she's about to launch a terrorist attack on the capital. And don't tell me you've got a 'hunch', because we're not in an Ellery Queen novel."

"Most of what I saw up to Marcie's appearance was circumstantial. But I began yesterday morning, before the Home Secretary so brusquely relieved me of post, working on the premise that our terrorists would arrive in Dover."

"And one logical conclusion is that you could now be suffering from an acute case of tunnel vision."

He sighed. "How long are we going to shoot the breeze here, Ruby? Because remember, philosophers have only interpreted the world, the point is to change it."

"Okay, Copthorne's a qualified pilot. He's got a single-engine Cessna parked at Dover St Margaret, a disused airfield four minutes from where you are. The pair of you, get there as fast as you can. It just so happens that Celia Demure's poised to leave for Afghanistan tomorrow afternoon, and we've an appointment with Marcie's mother to discuss 're-awakening' strategies. She wasn't quite expecting us at five am, but I'm sure she'll overlook the inconvenience when she realises there's a chance her daughter's in the country. How good are you at air navigation?"

"I'm willing to give it a go."

"Just in case you're not flying under instrument flight rules, I'll send latitude, longitude and elevation to your mobile. You're looking to land at Panshanger aerodrome. I'll meet you there in about forty minutes and then ... then ..."

He waited for her to finish her sentence. "Ruby?"

"Yes, yes, I'm still here. Stay on the line. Just excuse me a second. Something important's happened."

He turned to Copthorne. "We're to fly to Panshangar aerodrome in Hertfordshire. Do you know it?"

"*Hertfordshire?* But I thought - "

"Change of plan. The good news is you're broadly indispensable in the revised version. We need all hands on deck."

"I know Panshangar, yes, but I - "

"Nicholas?" Ruby Parker said.

"Excuse me, Toby. Yes, Fleming here. What's going on, Ruby?"

"You don't know her, but some time ago we managed to locate a woman Marcie knew in Afghanistan, just before she disappeared for good over there. Name of Ghatola Rahman. We set her up in a safe house in London and we've been discreetly pumping her for information, without ever letting on Marcie was one of ours."

"And?"

"She's gone. Disappeared into thin air sometime last night or early this morning. And she's taken her travelling companion, also an ethnic Pashtun, with her."

He tried to fit this new piece of information into his mental list of strategies, but couldn't because he didn't have one. Or if he did, it was changing so rapidly it was unreadable. "It's a bit of a coincidence, isn't it? Do you think they might have plans to meet up with Marcie?"

"Let's not get carried away. The good thing is, it may not bode well for the notion that Marcie's involved with terrorists. Ghatola Rahman certainly never struck me as that type. According to the little I know, most suicide bombers have children's mentalities. She doesn't."

"So how does this affect the next sixty minutes as far as you and I are concerned?"

"Border Control's been alerted, they're pretty good at finding certain sorts of people, and they know it's a matter of priority. As for you and I, well, we can't be everywhere at once. Let's just go and see your mother-in-law."

Chapter 30: Joy Comes Clean and Copthorne Proves Even More Splendid

Forty minutes later Copthorne's Cessna 172 touched down on the Panshanger grass, taxiing bumpily to a halt in front of a blue Ford Ka. Ruby Parker started her engine and wound the window down to identify herself. Fleming disembarked. The plane turned full circle and took off for Gerpins Farm, just outside London, so the pilot could catch half an hour's sleep before reporting to base.

Fleming eased himself into the passenger seat and the Ka trundled at thirty-five over the uneven surface until it came to a small country road, which it joined without stopping. Morning was arriving fast now. The near edges of the sun threw horizontal rays which singed the lower distance. A few strips of clouds looked like they'd been unsuccessfully washed and hung on the horizon separately to dry. The sky was pale navy, still dotted with stars and stamped with a harvest moon.

"Any word on Ms Rahman?" Fleming asked as soon as they hit the road and the car's suspension settled down.

"Not so far. Like I told you, though, I don't think she's into indiscriminate killing."

"And yet reading between the lines of what you've just said ..."

"You've worked out that I know she's into discriminate killing. She used to belong to an organisation called The Afghan Women's Reparation Brigade. They ruthlessly assassinated selected targets."

"Misogynists, I assume, going by the title."

"Men who raised their hatred of women into a principle, yes."

"And Marcie was part of that?"

"Correct."

He whistled. "I think we need to plan how much we're going to tell her mother."

"We're going to tell her everything, Nicholas. I might as well start by telling you something too. Marcie and Ghatola Rahman were involved sexually."

His mouth popped open. "What?"

"It was Celia who joined the dots. Think about it. Two women in a land where everything's minutely controlled by men, even your daily routine. To be involved in something like the AWRB, you have to be able to depend on each other absolutely, without reservation. What other basis could there be? They had to be sure on every level."

"Were they – in love, do you think?"

"I hate to say this, for your sake, but all the signs are there. At least, from Ghatola Rahman's point of view."

He didn't know what to think now. He could probably cope with amnesia-Marcie loving someone else, but what if amnesia-Marcie and real-Marcie weren't mutually exclusive? What if, once she got her memory back, she wasn't real-Marcie any more, but some kind of synthesis? What if there wasn't a real Marcie? What would that mean for both of them? He loved her.

"Nowadays, most of us take the equality of women for granted," Ruby Parker said, "or at least the principle. But for ninety-nine percent of history, women were no better off than slaves. Even today, vast swathes of the world are so desperate to turn the clock back they'll stone us, shoot us, pour acid over us, dismember us, burn, bludgeon, bury us alive, whatever it takes. Against all the odds, the West's achieved a distinctly an-omalous, highly fragile outpost of feminine liberty. The realist in me says it can't possibly last, so up to a point I share Ghat-ola Rahman's rage. Do you know what Celia used to say, back in her wild feminist days? '"Women" is a religion'."

He sighed. "I'm sure she's right. I'm sorry, I need to think."

"I'm probably way ahead of you in that regard. Marcie is in this country and she came here because somehow she knows Ghatola Rahman's here. Not only that, but she knows where she is, and now she's got word to her. We both know how resourceful she is."

"A theory, right?"

"That's all. But it fits the facts."

"So – so one of those women I saw in the hotel with Marcie: that was Ghatola Rahman?"

"And one of the others was Tasneem Babar, the woman I mentioned."

"Which still leaves four people unaccounted for."

"Marcie scraped together a pile of Euros in France and paid someone to help her. My guess is they're somewhere in London now."

He scoffed. "Explain to me why they won't have gone back to France."

"Because they stand no chance of getting asylum there, whereas we've as good as promised them it. They met up for sentimental reasons, but their next few moves will be entirely pragmatic. I wouldn't be surprised if we hear from them both before noon. Ghatola Rahman knows we need her. Her hand's immeasurably strengthened if we don't have knowledge of her whereabouts."

He shook his head. "It's all sounds very plausible, Ruby. Unfortunately, it doesn't quite mesh with the facts."

"Oh?"

"As I recall, you told me Ghatola Rahman went missing either 'last night or early this morning'. What did you mean by that?"

"It's impossible to be precise. Between seven and two, maybe. No later than three."

"Since all four women arrived at the Grand at least eighteen hours earlier than that, none of them could have been her. They left in a single car at around four o'clock, making it unlikely they'd arrive in London before five-thirty. By which time Ms Rahman would have been loose for a minimum of one and a half hours. If they can get word to her that they're coming, surely they can fix a time? And they've got three men with them, hardly the ideal context for a sentimental reunion. And they've got seven people in a single car – which can be done, but only just. Two more, however, and your chassis's scraping the road."

She shook her head and sighed. "From your point of view, though, there is a worse alternative."

He bit his lip and let it out. "Go on."

"It should have occurred to you by now that, given the patriarchal nature of Middle-Eastern culture, no woman from the nether end of that region could possibly make it here without first attaching herself to a man. And according to you, there were three men with her."

"You're thinking one of them was – her 'husband'?"

"That would be the most natural conclusion. They tend not to go in for free love."

They pulled onto the drive of the Hartley-Brown's mansion and the gravel began to crackle. Mannersby was a listed Tudor building with ten bedrooms and a gallery, guarded by a deep porch with steps up to it. It was surrounded by four acres of parkland with ornamental trees. As they drew to a stop, a herd of deer moved lazily away to their left. Fleming opened his door and climbed awkwardly out.

"How are you feeling?" she asked.

"As well as can be," he replied.

Geoffrey, the Hartley-Browns' manservant – a middle aged man in a plum waistcoat - appeared at the top of the steps to greet them. "Mrs Hartley-Brown is in the drawing room," he said.

He took them along a corridor they both knew and opened the door. Joy stood up as they entered. Her voluminous grey hair was styled so as to frame her head in a globe, and her make-up was fresh and discreet. She wore a knitted skirt-suit and matching court shoes. She shook Ruby Parker's hand and exchanged cheek-kisses with Fleming.

The room was larger than anyone could comfortably live in, and hung with portraits of obscurities from past centuries. The tan and ochre striped wallpaper and the grey patterned carpet seemed appropriate to the time of day, although in an hour's time they'd probably have combined to look moribund. A coal fire was going in the grate, hardly big enough to heat a fraction of the space. A table was set with tea things.

"I sent Geoffrey out to meet you," Joy said without asking them to sit down, "because I wanted to pour you tea. Nicholas, I understand you've something to tell me."

"It wasn't meant to get out," he replied. "Marcie made me promise not to announce it till after she got back. Then when I heard she'd been killed, there didn't seem any point. How did you find out?"

"Aren't you going to apologise?"

He frowned. "For what? It hardly seemed appropriate, when we were both grieving, to be the bearer of what should have been glad tidings."

Joy stared into the fire and sighed. She smiled. "As Marcie would undoubtedly have said, had she been here now ... 'Typical Fleming'."

This caught him blind-sided and he welled with unexpected emotion. "I apologise, then. I suppose partly I didn't want to provoke the impression I thought I had any claim on the family. I don't know."

Joy rubbed her forehead. "How absurd. And how stupid to think I wouldn't find out when it's there in the chapel register for everyone to see. Do you still love her?"

"Nothing would stop me." He remembered Ghatola Rahman. "Nothing."

"Because I understand there's a slim possibility she may still be alive."

"Which is of course, why we're here," Ruby Parker said.

Joy ignored her and addressed herself to Fleming. "You say *nothing* would stop you. Are you quite sure about that? Please sit down, both of you."

They did as they were told, and Joy passed them a cup of tea each.

"As I mentioned on the phone," Ruby Parker said, "we're here because we think Marcie's almost certainly suffering from complete memory loss. We need to know if there's anything you think might have strong emotional associations for her, to maybe pull her up hard. We need a starting point."

"The face of her husband," Joy replied. "I'm not being facetious. And of course, Anya."

"Your step-daughter."

"My grand-daughter."

Ruby Parker leaned forward and put her cup on the table. "I'm sorry, I'm not quite with you. Your *grand-daughter?* You mean - is she Marcie's daughter, or was she Jonathan's?"

"Eight years ago when she was fourteen, Marcie became pregnant by a black boy of her age. Tom. You don't need to know his second name. She insisted on going to term. Tom committed suicide when she was six months in because, tragically, he couldn't bring himself to tell his parents. He was top of his class in just about everything, I believe, and a musical prodigy to boot. Anyway, he threw himself off a bridge. Marcie was beside herself. She loved him, you see. Fourteen. Who knows what anyone truly feels at that age?

"Now it just so happened that, while all this was going on, Marcie's father was on the brink of leaving me for his personal assistant in London, a younger woman hardly much older than Marcie herself. So we were no use to her at all. Tom's father appeared on the estate grounds on three occasions to hurl abuse at her, and the third time we had to call the police. It was probably only because of Sir Anthony's reputation that she wasn't taken into care. They don't inflict that sort of thing on families like ours, you see, no matter how awful the situation. And it was only because of Jonathan's love that she didn't end up killing herself. She did try, twice, I'm afraid, both genuine attempts.

"In any case, she wasn't capable of looking after Anya when she arrived. We agreed we'd pass her off as an adoptee. Marcie was so disturbed at that point she probably believed it on some level. She certainly never thought she was worthy of the responsibilities of motherhood. We cooked up a story about Darfur – a story that's played on my conscience over the years. Hundreds of thousands in donations, hours and hours of campaign work, even adopting a genuine Darfurian orphan – Hawa – hasn't assuaged my sense of wrongdoing."

They sat in silence for a few moments, listening to the fire crackle.

"So where does this leave us?" Ruby Parker asked.

Joy smiled. "Nicholas? Your call."

"She told me all this before we married. The same night, in case I wanted to cry off. It's ancient history as far as I'm concerned."

Joy closed her eyes and took a deep breath. "You – you've no idea how much that means to me."

"You said you think Anya might help get through to Marcie?" Ruby Parker said.

"A photograph, maybe. I've lots of them. You see, her losing her memory strikes me as perhaps a natural conclusion of everything she's done since she became pregnant. She never got over it, not really. The anti-social behaviour, the civil restraining order, they were all part of the same trajectory. And finally of course, after Jonathan's death – which must have affected her more than even I, his mother, can imagine – the desire to go to Afghanistan. She wanted to annul herself. Well, now she has. There *is* no Marcie any more, only a shell, if the reports are to be believed. The only two things that will be capable of penetrating it are Anya ... and you, Nicholas."

"Does Anya know?" he asked.

"I told her very soon after you told me Marcie was dead, Ruby. There seemed no point in pretending any more. Then I took her round to Tom's parents and threatened them with legal action to recover maintenance costs in arrears unless they acknowledged her. I didn't need to. They were all over both of us. Although it's never going to make you forget the loss of a son, eight years is a long time, and they're ever such nice people really. They're taking Anya ice-skating tomorrow, then on to the cinema. They're probably going to have her over to stay next week."

"And Marcie?" he said. "Assuming she's alive?"

"She was just a child. They can see that now. They're as sorry as sorry can be. Look, Nicholas, if we ever do get her back, she needs to start living a normal life. No more lies. It's her one chance."

He smiled. "I'd worked that out already."

"In which case, it's probably already occurred to you that technically, and perhaps legally too, Anya's actually your step-daughter."

"Except that doesn't know me at all."

"We all have to start somewhere. Now, I'll get those photographs, shall I? And I recommend you have some taken of yourself as well. I've written Celia a letter, saying thank you - "

"Which may not be necessary," Fleming blurted out. "We've – I've – I strongly suspect Marcie's here, in Britain."

Joy put the teapot down as if she just passed through a moment of deafness. "Pardon?"

He relayed the story of his stay in the Grand, the discovery of the fingerprint and Ghatola's disappearance. "Ruby doesn't necessarily agree with me. I was badly wounded last night and I discharged myself from hospital. There's a good *prima facie* case for me being mildly out of my mind, even I can see that - "

"And yet you're certain it was her? You *feel* certain?"

He took a deep breath. "I do."

"This changes everything." She left the room and returned with a notepad and pen. She tore off a piece of paper with a number scribbled on. "I'll ring my husband as soon as you've left. If you need anything – *anything* at all – ring this. It's his personal line. I'll tell him to keep it on. It's high time his being Secretary of State for Defence did some good for a change. Cut, cut, cut – that's all he's done so far."

"I should warn you," Ruby Parker said, "that he may find himself at loggerheads with the Home Secretary if he gets involved. For reasons I can't divulge, any large-scale hunt for Marcie is likely to overlap with an already existing investigation into terrorism. Robert Skelton's the chosen man on the ground, as it were."

"I've never heard of him. But in any case, leave that to Anthony. You just do what you have to."

They had another cup of tea and left. Fleming could tell as they walked to the car that he was in for a severe dressing down. He tried to think of arguments. It wasn't just a tactical matter, it was personal; she'd already said she was going to tell Joy everything –

"You realise how much trouble this could get both of us into," Ruby said loudly as they pulled away. "This is the precise *opposite* of how I like to work. It's why I wasn't keen on letting you know Marcie was even alive at one point. It was only because I discovered you'd married her that I changed my mind. Can't you *see*? People who are personally involved are never going to be able to think clearly! But these two aren't just implicated, they're her bloody *parents!* Now there's going to be an almighty row between the Defence Secretary and the Home Secretary, and when it all blows over, they'll look back and remember the two miserable little know-alls that set them at each other's throats in the first place!"

The mobile on her dashboard buzzed and displayed the caller's name: 'Copthorne'. The second time Fleming was grateful for his unexpected arrival.

Ruby pressed the button. "Go ahead, Toby," she said stiffly.

"I've been trying to reach you for a while. It occurred to me after I left you in Hertfordshire, that there's something utterly obvious we forgot to do. I don't blame you, Nicholas, if you're still there, because you're not a hundred per cent. But I should have thought."

"Get to the point, please," she snapped.

"We forgot to question the receptionist at the Grand. After all, he must have seen the people in those rooms as they arrived."

Fleming lowered his head into his hand and pinched. Of course. What the hell had he been thinking? He'd been so eager to get on –

"I've been on the phone to him for the last forty minutes. We've been passing photos back and forward via the net. He doesn't recognise any of the women, including Marcie. He says they never really looked in his direction. Lowered gaze, eastern modesty, that sort of thing. But he did recognise two of the men. I got him to describe them first, then I showed him the photos the Pakistani embassy emailed us. Haider Chamkanni and Idris Kakahel."

Ruby Parker took a sharp breath. "That's – that's excellent work, Toby. Go home and get a few hours' sleep, you've earned it."

She turned to Fleming. "You see, that's the virtue of a dispassionate approach."

"The bloody obvious," Fleming said in bitter self-recrimination.

"And teamwork," she added. "I suppose I'd better ring Celia and tell her to cancel her flight."

"Time to ring Sir Anthony," he said. "Swallow your reservations, Ruby, this is deadly serious. And luckily, I've an idea what to do with those photos of Anya."

Chapter 31: Ghatola Notices the World's Disenchantment

Badrai stood at the top of a flight of stone steps, as she always did in these kinds of dreams. Three knives stuck out of her chest and there were rings under her eyes. "Why did you kill me?" she asked.

Ghatola tried to get to her but something invisible stood in the way. "I didn't. We've been through this. You were already dead."

"You could have helped me get away."

"I would if you'd wanted to, but you didn't. I loved you. Where's Faridun, by the way?"

"In Jahannam."

"Am I going to Jahannam?"

Badrai nodded.

Ghatola awoke listlessly. Only the usual dream. Badrai was supposed to be in Paradise, though you wouldn't know it from those knives and her druggie's eyes. Maybe she only wore them for the dreams, though.

She looked over to the sofa bed where Tasneem slept. It was empty.

"Tasneem?" she called.

No reply. She looked at her clock. Seven-thirty. She got out of bed and went into the kitchen. No Tasneem there, either. All the shops would be shut now, and she hadn't left a note. She sat on the bed to wait and over the next twenty minutes the conviction slowly grew in her that Tasneem had gone for good, unable to cope any more with the way things had turned out. Doubtless she was on her way back to Afghanistan. Good for her.

She stood up and went into the bathroom. She splashed her face with cold water and showered in hot. As she changed into the new clothes Armaghan Jones had bought her as a gift, she realised that she'd be doing her own washing and cleaning from now on. Since she still knew no English – she hadn't been encouraged to learn, which probably didn't bode well for her chances of asylum – she'd probably have to learn to talk to herself as well from now on. It was all the company she was likely to get.

She looked at her clock. Yes, seven-thirty *in the evening*. Another fifteen hours and the black woman or the elderly woman would probably be back with new questions. Everyone knew she'd enjoyed a relationship with Reshtina now. Whatever they publicly admitted, privately they were probably revolted, or they were sniggering, or both.

But then they didn't understand, how could they? It wasn't that she hadn't enjoyed her husband. Of course she had. Rather, she'd known no limits. How could they hope to comprehend that, encountering her here, in this stale cushion of a country?

She used to be a sorceress. She'd had the Ifrits, the Ghuls and the unnamed jinns under her heel. Awar, Dasim, Sut, and Tir she kept in cages hung from the ceiling. The angels threw rose petals beneath her toes, knowing Iblis and Zalambur were her thralls. She could make her human acquaintances forget where, and even who, they were; and the next moment she could encircle them with visions either benign or liable to scare them white. She could induce illnesses. She could cure them. She could heat or cool pans with a sideways glance. Her husband was damp clay in her hands. Through him, and thanks to her own spiritual supremacy, she had the power to cast her enemies into Jahannam. She'd killed men without mercy. She'd expected to go on without disquiet.

When had all that come to an end? Long before she'd left Afghanistan, that was for sure. The first she knew of it was when Balay booted her singed body to bits, but it had started much earlier. The gift had gone out of her and she'd ended up here, in England, where no one even believed in power *per se* any more. The irony was, they believed they'd done women great favours when all they'd done was reduce them to the general mulch.

Mostly, no one anywhere was anything, that was the problem. She wondered if she could run away, maybe catch Tasneem up. It was a long way back to Afghanistan, but Balay was dead, his sons would have given up looking for her by now. True, she could never go back to Pashtunistan, but she might just make it outside in the north, a refugee without a memory, like Reshtina.

Which was when it had all come to an end, of course. Reshtina. Every so often – every thousand years, maybe – someone had the luck and the talent to grow to where they could look down on the mulch with contempt and pity. You'd have to be brought up in the right way: not afraid of the dark. But there could only be a single such person at any given time. If two met, one or the other would have to cede precedence. And the power would go out of the weaker and the stronger would inherit it - and they'd become lovers. It wasn't a question of sex but of spirit.

Yes, Reshtina was still out there somewhere. She felt it intensely. And of course the English knew it. They wouldn't be perpetually asking questions if they thought she was dead. Tasneem didn't matter, any more. The only thing that mattered was getting back to Afghanistan.

So ... if she was going to embark on a journey, she'd need food and water and something to defend herself with. She opened the kitchen drawer, then the cupboard.

There were knives and forks, but they were all plastic. Nothing with a properly sharp edge at all. She began to get a sense of how everyone here saw her. She laughed like she was coughing and picked up a bundle of carrier bags from the corner. As if they'd be able to stop her killing herself, if that's what she wanted! But she didn't. Not yet, anyway.

There wasn't much in the fridge. A malt loaf, a slab of butter, two pickled fish in a jar, carrots, an onion. She put them all in a bag. Now she needed a plan.

England was a small country and an island. Whatever direction you walked in, you'd have to come to the coast eventually. Then you'd just follow the shoreline till you saw France. Crossing the Channel was the only major obstacle. Once you'd done that, all you had to do was tell them you were Afghan and you wanted to go home. They'd be so eager to get rid of you, and so scared you might change your mind, they'd put you on the first flight out. All European countries were the same. The only reason she'd been allowed to stay in England so long was they knew she was part of the AWRB and they thought they could use her. Well, their luck had just run out.

She could hear her alarm jingling in the other room. Magrib, the fourth prayer-time of the day. She followed the sound and switched it off. She put her carrier-bag down and turned towards Mecca and said the Takbir – "God is great" - and the al-Fatihah, then put her palms on her knees and muttered the words she'd been taught in infancy. She stood up and said, "Allah hears those who praise him. O Lord, praise be to you."

She touched the ground with her forehead and said "Glory to God, the most high" three times. She sat back on her heels and bowed right down again and stood up. Then she repeated the entire process, adding a prayer honouring Muhammad and his family.

She sat down on the floor and suddenly she saw God's greatness against her own utter insignificance, the galaxies spread out in all directions endlessly, the infinity of time in front and behind, and her not even a speck. She wasn't a sorceress, she was a nobody. *And all the servants of the Most Merciful are those who walk on the earth in humility and when the ignorant address them harshly, they say words of peace.* She reached into her bag and pulled out a carrot and ate it like a donkey, feeling wretched. She put her hand to her face and felt her grotesqueness.

Suddenly she swelled with terror and she couldn't get started fast enough. She slung her coat over her shoulders and, since she couldn't find anything much of hers, bundled some of Tasneem's clothes into the carrier. She slipped on her shoes and left for the coast.

At five-thirty the following morning, Tasneem turned onto the street where she lived with Ghatola to find the house surrounded by police cars. She blanched and stopped walking, then her training kicked in. She began calculating probabilities, formulating strategies, ascertaining the exits. She turned back the way she'd come and hid beneath the shadow of an oak tree in the shelter of a hawthorn hedge.

The chief problem was they would expect an explanation from her and she didn't yet know exactly what had happened. Relax, she told herself: there are only two possibilities. In either case, she, Tasneem, was in shock. She could stick to Pashto till she worked out which of the two alternatives it was. Unless Armaghan Jones was there. In which case, yes, shock had made her dumb. Yes, that was the best strategy. *Play for time*, as the Americans put it.

The first possibility was that Ghatola had committed suicide. She hoped to God it wasn't that, although it was an increasing likelihood of late. In that case, her story would be that she'd left the house in distress and wandered the streets like a poor helpless child beside herself with grief, not knowing who to turn to or, ultimately, even how to find her way back to where she'd started.

The second possibility was that Ghatola had run away. In that case, she'd gone after her but failed to find her.

Two things were necessary to the success of either story. She needed to look the part. She lay down slowly and rolled methodically in the damp mud. Then she needed to cry. She'd been taught the actor's technique: concentrate on something heart-rending. She forced herself to think back twenty years to the morning her grandfather had backed her dog, Mongoose, into a corner and hit it with an iron rod until its spine snapped and it had to be destroyed. She made herself recall the trusting eyes and the wagging tail as it spied her just before the mercy-gunshot. As always, she burst into tears. She stayed that way for nearly a minute till she'd produced enough salt water to stand out, then she got up and wandered back to her house.

Two police cars stood in front of it, but with their lights off. This was a discreet investigation, not intended to wake the neighbours. The front door was open. She went in to find two policemen and Armaghan Jones in the living room. They turned to her as if she was a burglar. The latter immediately came over and put her arms round her.

"Tasneem," she said gently, "we know where you've been. You only have to answer one question right now. Did you or didn't you find her?"

She shook her head and thought of her dog again. Thank God. From here on, everything would be plain sailing.

Chapter 32: The Afterlife

As al-Maitami cleared the hotel porch he put on a scarf and a Miami Marlins baseball cap. A pair of dark glasses stuck out from his top pocket.

The three women got into the car – as before, Reshtina in the front, Zaituna and Ambrin in the back. The vests were painful to sit in – the sharp edges where the pipes had been tapered to hold the explosive dug in where your legs met your torso - but no one complained. Al-Maitami flipped the sun visor down from the car ceiling.

The two men and the woman who had been to see them in the hotel left in a taxi without wishing them luck or even acknowledging their departure. Once again, they'd become commodities, the more so, Reshtina supposed, as their destiny was now sealed. They were tomatoes in cans, waiting to be ripped open.

Al-Maitami pulled onto the road and handed Reshtina a packet of foil-packed tablets. "Take one of these and pass them back."

"What are they?"

"Travel-sickness pills. We don't want you throwing up in the car. If you feel queasy, there are some purpose-made bags in the pocket on my back seat. Use one and hang onto it."

"It'll stink," Ambrin said. "Couldn't we just throw it out of the window?"

"You're not allowed to do that in this country."

"These belts are agony," Zaituna said. "Mine's digging into my waist. Can't we take them off, just for the journey?"

"No."

"Could we have the CD on?" Ambrin asked.

Al-Maitami leaned over and pressed play. This was a disk his friends had made especially for them, 'to calm everyone's nerves', as they put it. A translation into Pashto of Ibn al-Qayyim's 13th century description of the afterlife.

"And if you ask about its ground and its soil," it said, "it is of musk and saffron. And if you ask about its roof, it is the throne of the Most Merciful. And if you ask about its rocks, they are pearls and jewels. And if you ask about its buildings, they are made of gold and silver bricks. And if you ask about its trees, it does not contain a single one except that its trunk is made of gold and silver."

"Could you switch it up a bit, please?" Zaituna said. "We can't hear it in the back."

He obliged. "And if you ask about its fruits, they are softer than butter and sweeter than honey. And if you ask about its leaves, they are softer than the softest cloth. And if you ask about its rivers, they are of milk with changeless taste, and of wine delicious to those who drink thereof, and of pure honey and fresh water. And if you ask about their food, then it is whichsoever fruits you choose, and the meat of whichever birds you desire."

For some reason, Reshtina began to think about the man she'd helped in the corridor. Her hand trembled. There'd been something about him. Yes, that's right: he was what they were going to London to produce. An excellent specimen of a man about to die. She'd felt compassion for him, as any good Muslim would, and yet here she was, about to replicate his type a thousand times over. She fought back conflicting feelings and hoped al-Maitami wouldn't notice.

"And if you ask about their drink, it is flavoured with ginger and camphor. And if you ask about their drinking cups, they are crystal-clear gold and silver. And if you ask about its shade, the swiftest horseman could ride in the shadow of one of its trees for a hundred years and not escape it."

But no, it wasn't that. The possible absurdity of what they were all about to do might sound a plausible enough pretext, but it wasn't why she was disturbed. It wasn't pity or remorse, but something even deeper and more important. She recalled looking in the mirror only an hour ago, seeing something odd in her own face.

It was the same odd thing.

"And if you ask about its vastness, its lowest citizen has within his kingdom, walls, palaces and gardens such a distance as can hardly be travelled in a thousand years. And if you ask about its encampments, one tent is like a concealed pearl one hundred kilometres in diameter. And if you ask about its towers, they are many-roomed with rivers running beneath them. And if you ask how far it reaches into the sky, then behold the faintest shining star, and those so distant they cannot be seen."

The car turned east to face the just-risen sun and for a moment she was blinded. She noticed a visor above her head, just like al-Maitami's, so she lowered it and found herself looking straight into a mirror. Again, the weirdness of seeing her face as a stranger might, looking down on it from a rooftop.

"You realise vanity's a sin, sister?" al-Maitami said brusquely.

"I want to see Zaituna and Ambrin," she replied.

The two women caught her eyes simultaneously and beamed with gratitude. She noticed she was starting to bleed around her hips, the belt was digging into her so badly. Contoured to a woman's shape? It showed how much Salique, and al-Maintami for that matter, knew about women.

"And if you ask about the clothes of its residents, they are of silk and gold. And if you ask about its beds, its blankets are of the choicest silk. And if you ask about the faces of its residents and their beauty, then they are like the image of the moon. And if you ask about their age, they are thirty-three and in the likeness of Adam, the father of humanity."

"Could I have a drink?" Ambrin said, squirming to change to a more comfortable position. "I'm thirsty."

"We haven't got a bloody drink," he said. "You should have had one before you left. What about all that orange juice?"

"I forgot to bring it."

He laughed. "Your own fault, then."

"And if you ask about their brides and wives, then they are young and full-breasted and have had the liquid of youth flow through their limbs; the sun runs along the beauty of her face if she shows it, light shines from between her teeth if she smiles; if you meet her love, then say whatever you want regarding - "

"I don't like this bit," Zaituna said. "Can we wind it on a bit?"

Al-Maitami sighed and pressed the corner of the forward button. "I shouldn't really be doing this while I'm driving. Here, Reshtina, you do it. You've got to press it in halfway between straight up and straight along, and hold it down for a second."

"And the covering on her head is better than the world and all it contains, and she never ages but only becomes more beautiful. Without an umbilical cord, without childbirth and menstruation, and free of mucous, saliva, urine and other disgusting things. Her youth never fades, her clothing never wears out, no garment - "

Reshtina pressed fast forward.

"And if you ask about the Day of Increase and the visitation of the omnipotent, omniscient one, and the sight of His face – as free from any resemblance to anything as the midday sun or the full moon on a clear night, then listen on the day the messenger calls: 'People of Paradise, your Lord – blessed and exalted – desires you to visit him, so come!' And they will say: 'We hear and obey!'"

Zaituna and Ambrin were crying and smiling at the same time. They interlinked arms and held each other. Reshtina passed her hand back through the gap between the front seats and they both took it and squeezed it so hard she nearly cried out. Ambrin leaned over and kissed it and her tears wet it.

"Finally, they will all reach the wide valley, and the blessed and exalted Lord himself will order his chair to be brought there. Pulpits of light will appear, and pulpits of jewels, gold, silver and pearls. The lowest devotee will sit on blankets of musk, and will not see what those on the higher chairs receive. When they are comfortable, the messenger will call: 'O people of Paradise, Allah has brought you here because he wishes to reward you!' And they will reply, 'What more can he do? Has he not already brightened our faces, loaded us with wealth, set us in Paradise, and saved us from hellfire?'

She looked out of the window and had a strong sense of having been here before. In some strange way, the landscape was more familiar than anything in Afghanistan, and certainly more real than any of the interchangeable sites they'd been through on the backs of lorries, in coaches, stowed away in boxes or simply trudging through with their heads down, since leaving Herat.

But then maybe that's what everyone thought when they were about to die, wherever they were. Maybe you compared this world with the one you were leaving for, and wherever you were it felt more familiar than anything had ever felt before. In a little over four hours, she'd be gone. Everything outside this window, to the four corners of the earth, would be exactly the same, except that there would be no Reshtina, no Zaituna, no Ambrin.

They'd be somewhere better.

"And while the people are wondering, suddenly a brilliant light encompasses all of Paradise. They raise their heads and behold, the Compeller – exalted and holy of names – arrives from on high, sanctifying them and saying, 'O people of Paradise, peace be with you!' And they reply, 'O Allah, you are peace and all serenity comes from you! Blessed are you, O majestic and honourable Lord!' So he – blessed and exalted – laughs, saying, 'O People of Paradise! Where are those who used to obey me without seeing me? This is the Day of Increase!'"

Zaituna vomited into a bag, wiped her mouth with its rim and scrunched it up and sat with it in her lap. It began to seep through the paper onto her jeans. She had blood on her fingertips, presumably from the belt. She looked as miserable and humiliated as Reshtina had ever seen her. Ambrin caressed her shoulder. She took the bag off her as if she was correcting a baby and put it on the floor. Reshtina read her lips in the mirror: 'Mind you don't stand on it'. She was surprised any of them still had anything left in their stomachs although, to be fair, it was probably only gastric juice.

"And they will all give the same reply: 'We are pleased, be pleased with us!' And he will say: 'O people of Paradise, if I were not pleased with you, I would not have brought you here, so ask of me whatever you wish.' And they will cry, 'Show us your face so we may behold it!' So, the Lord – all-powerful and majestic – will remove his veil and sanctify and envelop them in his Light, which would devour them entire had Allah not willed otherwise."

And then there was the Sufi meeting with Ghatola in Kandahar. What had that to do with any of this? Because there definitely was some connection: Reshtina's own face, that meeting and now the mysterious man in the corridor. She tried to think back.

The sheikh had spoken about Allah's command that Ibrahim should sacrifice his son, Ishmael. Shaytan materialised to tell them that they must be mistaken because God didn't approve of murder, but they threw stones at him to drive him away. Yet at the end of the story God himself revealed the same thing.

Meaning?

"And to every single person in turn the Lord – the exalted – will say: 'Do you remember the day you did such and such?' and he will remind him of his evil deeds in the earthly life. And each person will say, 'O Lord, will you not forgive me?' And God will reply, 'You did not gain your place in Paradise except through my forgiveness.'"

God's forgiveness. She suddenly had a vision of herself, Zaituna and Ambrin on a gargantuan slide constructed from Shaytan's body, beginning in Herat and ending in London. And at the bottom, the slaughter of Ishmael, this time without Allah's reprieve ... because they'd deafened themselves to him? She remembered Nangial's words the day they set off. *You're handing yourself over to Shaytan, you realise that?*

It felt like it was all starting to make sense. But how could it? What had the man in the corridor to do with it? His wasn't an abstract connection, as if he stood in for Ishmael or the people of London. She'd tried that and it hadn't worked. No, it was something much more intimate. She was *familiar* with him on some level, just as she felt familiar with the scenery here, just as she felt *un*familiar with her own face.

Merci, he'd said. Thank you.

The car pulled to a halt. They'd been travelling through suburbs for quite some time now, and if Ambrin and Zaituna felt remotely like she did, they were in agony. It was still very early in the morning and there were few cars around and even fewer people.

Al-Maitami switched the engine off and put his sunglasses on. "Get out and go to the front door. The blue one."

They did as they were told, walking past one hedge and skirting another until they were at the end of the short path. The door opened of its own accord and they walked inside without breaking stride. They found themselves in a dimly lit hallway with dark wooden tables and pictures on the wall. A man of about twenty with a woolly beard and a Palestinian keffiyeh bowed to each of them in turn from the waist and said something in what was presumably English. He disappeared into the next room and returned with a tray on which four pint-glasses of fruit juice were perched. Al-Maitami came in and closed the door behind them. The Englishman smiled and produced some more babble.

"He says it's a privilege to meet such courageous, beautiful women," al-Maitami translated in a bored voice. "He says he hopes when he gets to Jannah you've been transformed into houris, so he can 'gaze on you again'. Cheeky bastard, he'll have to be a bloody good boy to get any of you three. You'll be at least two levels higher than him."

The three women were too busy downing their fruit juices to pay the slightest attention to this.

"Could we have another?" Ambrin said, when she'd finished. She suppressed a burp.

"Sure, sure. Now listen, sisters, he's going to give us a room to ourselves when we're ready, and I want you all to get an hour's sleep. No more than that, but it'll make all the difference. You need to be alert, see? And I'm going to bind your wrists together so you don't touch your switches by mistake. That way, you can relax better, yes?"

Reshtina finished her drink and placed it on the tray. She'd never felt weaker. Her body had expelled every fragment of food it had ingested, she was hoarse with retching, she was still bleeding and nauseous from the protrusion of the pipes into her belly. She didn't want al-Maitami to bind her wrists, but she was in no condition to resist.

Then she saw what he was up to. He was Shaytan and this was his last chance to rape Ambrin.

She had to hide the gun again.

Chapter 33: Some of Us Will Die

At precisely 6.15, a chauffeur-driven Mercedes pulled up out-side Scotland Yard and deposited Fleming on the pavement, fresh from a painkilling injection. He found two constables waiting for him with a name badge and a wad of briefs. He identified each remit by colour and mentally ticked it off his list of requests, then unfolded the top one, a memo from Ruby Parker confirming what had already been decided.

> Complete re-think at the highest levels. Defence and Home Secretaries agreed to bury differences & cover both bases simultaneously. 500+ officers to be deployed at your discretion. Good luck, R.

His injury had obviously been forgotten or overlooked in the melee. He flicked through the rest of the papers, mostly advisory notes about availability of equipment, subdivisions of manpower, time and motion projections. There was an itemisation of approvals at the bottom so he didn't have to read anything till later, and only then in the event of a public inquiry.

"Is everyone together?" he asked.

"They're all waiting in the courtyard, sir," the first constable replied.

"Anyone still to come?"

"I believe we've a full house. The vans are waiting."

He emerged into the courtyard to find what looked to be nearly a thousand officers standing in rows facing a make-shift podium, like it was a school assembly. The louring sky was framed by the grey inner walls of the building's offices piled on top of each other. The rumble of conversation ceased as he stepped up to face his audience, and ten hundred jaws set hard.

"Good morning," he said. "I'm Nicholas Fleming and I'm in charge of the 'ground-floor' half of today's operation.

The other half is directed to protecting London's high-rises against what we're fairly sure is an imminent terrorist attack. All the intelligence we've had so far indicates it will take place sometime this week, probably earlier rather than later. The perpetrators may be aware that, after Leeds, we're anticipating something. If so, we believe they've chosen to try and outwit us rather than shelve their plans. But they may not, which is why we're attempting to entrap them as opposed to closing Central London down. The latter option would represent a victory for them anyway, although I accept we're duty-bound to prefer saving lives over symbolic triumphs.

"We don't know exactly what the targets are as yet. However we do have reasons to think they're going to be taken out with suicide bombers, possibly women, possibly no more than three, although in any event they'll spread out so as to maximise casualties. Obviously, for al-Qaeda and its affiliates, propaganda is everything. The more prestigious your target and the more lives lost, the better. So rush-hour is a prime target.

"The other propaganda priority is to go bigger or similar. An attack on a high-rise building would be more impressive than 7/7, and would evoke the Twin Towers. An attack on the Underground would replicate it, and would carry the message that Britain is incapable of learning from its mistakes and thus adequately defending itself. Anything less would represent a reduction of ambition and thus - however extensive the loss of life - a PR own-goal.

"Between seven-fifteen and nine-thirty this morning, and sixteen hundred and nineteen hundred hours, all forty-one Tube stations on *or within* the Circle Line will be exit-only. In other words, all short-range journeys have been suspended. Anyone attempting to buy a ticket from Oxford Circus to Tottenham Court Road, say, will be politely asked to walk. We're concentrating on keeping London running, which means prioritising commuters from outside the area.

"Officers with body-scanning equipment, as detailed in the briefs you've received, will monitor passengers arriving at Victoria, Charing Cross, Waterloo, Blackfriars, Cannon

Street, City Thameslink, Liverpool Street, London Bridge, Vauxhall and Moorgate. Only after examination may they proceed. We're aiming to keep the process as discreet as possible, because the entrapment of the terrorists requires complete confidentiality. We'll be posing as Transport officers. And we're relying on the traditional stoicism of your average British citizen to minimise disruption.

"In the event that we have to evacuate the whole area, we'll shift the crowds by means of police cordons and crowd control barriers. At that point, people will ask you what's happening. You're to tell them there's nothing to worry about, it's a training exercise. Do not elaborate. If we can saturate the crowds with that simple message, everyone should remain calm.

"What do you do if you find yourself confronted by one of the bombers? They're very difficult creatures to stop. They're fanatical and determined, and by the time you've identified one, it's usually too late. It's therefore possible that some of us standing here could be killed or seriously wounded.

"The effective use of your scanning equipment should eliminate identification errors, so some practical advice. Because your main concern is to stop the bomber reaching his detonation switch, grab him from behind by the shins and lift. Or punch him in the face. Either way, instinct should kick in and he'll instinctively use his hands to prevent a fall or further injury, at which point of course, you grab them. Be aware, that might not save you, because explosive belts can be triggered remotely. We've parked signal disrupters around the city centre exclusively for that purpose, but we can't have them going continuously because they'll upset the city's communication systems, so it's a question of letting us know early.

"We've already seen how a shoot to kill policy can end in tragedy when a mistake's made, but if you do feel certain enough, the best place to shoot is the tip of the bomber's nose, or the back of his or her head, just below the skull. Pray God it won't come to that.

"Finally, keep all lines of communication open all the time. Today's a work in progress. We've never been in this sort of situation before so it's likely our plans will have to be revised at some stage. Don't lose concentration, but keep expecting to be redeployed. If you have any questions, ask your section controller. Good luck everyone."

Everyone shouted encouragement to each other, howled and clapped their hands, and for a moment the noise was deafening. Then they began to move towards the exits. Fleming could feel the fear.

At precisely 6.15, an ambulance pulled up behind a police car on the hard shoulder of the A21 southbound carriageway and deposited two paramedics and two nurses on the tarmac. They lifted the collapsed woman, identified a few moments ago as Ghatola Rahman, onto a stretcher and, after ascertaining that her condition wasn't serious, took her to Sevenoaks hospital. She was given a bed in a windowless room with freshly painted walls, a strip-light and a blue carpet.

Twenty minutes after she regained consciousness, Tasneem arrived with Armaghan Jones and two grim looking men, looking distraught. She flung her arms round her. Ghatola returned the hug, tentatively at first but then more firmly.

"We thought you might have been killed!" Tasneem said.

"I woke up and you weren't there."

"I know, I know, I'm sorry, I know."

"What *is* there for us in this country? I'd rather be dead than here."

"Please don't say that. Don't *say* that!"

They held on to each other for another minute, weeping, then one of the men – she guessed immigration officials of some description – coughed discreetly. The door opened and a nurse wheeled in a trolley bearing a television on a video machine.

Armaghan Jones stepped forward and sat on the bed. "Ghatola, these men are with the British Security Services. They need to ask you a question urgently."

"Urgently?"

"They're going to show you a film of four women and three men, taken in a hotel in Dover on the English coast just a few hours ago. They just want you to know if you recognise anyone. It's only a few seconds long and they can freeze-frame and enlarge it if necessary."

She didn't understand, but she realised that, for the purposes of the exercise, she probably didn't need to. She felt Tasneem shiver. When she pulled away, she was pale.

"What's the matter?" Ghatola asked.

She didn't reply. Her eyes turned to the TV screen and the taller of the two men pressed Play. It was low resolution black and white, obviously closed-circuit footage of a hotel reception area. A woman in a niqab passed from left to right with a man, then two more men, talking. Then three women. One in jeans, a woolly jumper and pumps, the next in a long skirt, baseball boots and a coat, and the third in a hoodie, jeans and boots.

She drew a sharp breath and leaned closer. The screen went blank.

"You recognise someone, don't you?" Armaghan Jones said quietly.

Ghatola could hardly contain her emotion. Only the oblique profiles were visible, but even then there could hardly be any mistaking them, especially not in conjunction. "Wh - where did you say it was taken?"

"Dover."

"In - in *England?*"

Armaghan Jones nodded.

"But, no, that's not possible. None of those people was British. *What trick are you trying to play?*"

"It's not a trick. Look at the writing on the desk. It's in English. Look again."

Ghatola couldn't stop trembling. Whatever she said or did now, there was no concealing the fact that she knew. The only question was, should tell them?

But then, why not? These were her best friends and she loved them. She felt a surge of happiness such as she'd never experienced before. Thank God, thank *God* she hadn't died to-night!

"They're three - " she swallowed her emotion " - three women to whom I'm very close. Closer than anyone in the world. They've come to Britain to find me and take me home."

Fleming left the podium and made his way to the front of the building where a car stood with its engine idling, waiting to take him to Oxford Circus. He got onto the back seat next to the Defence Secretary. The transparent partition between the front and the back seats was sealed.

"I trust you didn't tell anyone it's Marcie we're looking out for," Sir Anthony said.

"That was part of the deal, but it wasn't necessary. MI7's as anxious as anyone that that part of the story should remain under wraps."

"I don't want anyone to know it's her unless it's absolutely necessary. That means six or seven people at most. All sworn to absolute secrecy."

Fleming wasn't sure he'd be able to oblige in the longer term, but there was no time to argue. "Understood."

"Excellent. Now, breaking news. We've just found Ghatola Rahman. It appears she knew nothing of Marcie's re-appearance – or at least that's what she's saying."

"Has she identified the three women?"

"We've got names," Sir Anthony said, "if that's what you mean. That doesn't amount to much in terms of recovering background information. When a woman spends all her time indoors, her husband's dead, and her country's seven thousand miles away and stuck in the Stone Age, a biography's hard to come by."

"And yet names are always better than no names."

"Obviously one of them's 'Reshtina Sarbanri'. The others are 'Ambrin wife of Babrak' and 'Zaituna wife of Khush-dil'. They don't have surnames, apparently."

Fleming pushed his index finger into his forehead. "Good God, this is changing all the time. I'm pretty adaptable, but even I'm having difficulty keeping up."

"What does it matter?"

"The lynchpin of today's operation is the hotel receptionist's positive identification of two of the three men that were with Marcie. But what if he was wrong? What if they're not Kakahel and Chamkanni at all? What if all three women were with their husbands?"

"So who was the final woman?"

"You're allowed four wives in Islam."

"So Marcie could be someone's second bloody wife, is that what you're saying?"

"I'm only speculating, sir. It would help if we knew what this 'Babrak' and 'Khushdil' looked like."

"It would seem a bit of a coincidence that they should look like the two Pakistanis. And of course, all three men spoke good English. Haven't we got CCTV footage?"

"A blur."

"They'd have to be pretty cunning. Doesn't all this strike you as the work of trained spies? I don't mean any disrespect, but from what Ghatola Rahman's already told us about her own background, Babrak and Khushdil are most likely farmers or goatherds."

Fleming nodded. "Yes, that makes sense. Sorry, just jitters, I'm afraid. There's a hell of a lot that can go wrong with this sort of defensive strategy. At two million a day, the terrorists can afford to just sit back and wait. We're relying on the behind-the-scenes teams."

The car rounded a corner and an electronic billboard came into view. It showed a Pepsi advert, but then it changed to become a landscape photograph of Anya. Fleming smiled.

"Wait till you see Leicester Square," Sir Anthony said. "It's relentless."

Chapter 34: Soldiers of God

Reshtina's black eye, Zaituna's broken nose and Ambrin's ferocious violation had made it an unforgettable forty-five minutes. They lay on a wooden floor in a puddle of blood with the sun shining on them. Ambrin sobbed, while outside a bird sang.

Ten minutes after al-Maitami staggered out, the Englishman entered in his pyjamas with a bowl of soapy water. His face filled with horror as he probably guessed what had happened, but then al-Maitami reappeared, smiling, doing up his shirt and making string of what were obviously reassurances. Reshtina could guess what he was saying. These women were traitors, they'd never had any intention of doing what they promised. No, they'd come halfway across the world simply to sell out the Movement to the highest bidder. It was his duty, as their controller, to remind them their contracts were binding. This was a war, no room for sentiment. The standard fate of deserters was to be shot. He'd spared them that, but he wasn't going to indulge them. He didn't get to be who and what he was by making allowances.

The Englishman calmed down and knelt by Zaituna to sponge her face. She flinched and turned away. He applied a few gentle wipes to her neck.

Al-Maitami crouched next to Reshtina and brushed her hair from her forehead. "Look, I'm sorry for what I did. I only meant it for your own good. Humility's a virtue, right? You don't seem to realise that." He paused and sighed. "Okay, fair enough, I admit I got carried away. I'm a bad guy and I'm working on it, really. Soon you'll be in Paradise, whereas I'm going to Hell for sure. That's right: Jahannam. From where you are, girl, you'll be able to look down and see me burn, that should cheer you up, yeah?" He swivelled round to address Ambrin and laid his hand gently on her arm. "Listen, baby, you haven't been dishonoured, I have. Nobody in Paradise is going to hold it against you. Soon, that's where you'll be, and you'll be surprised how quickly you forget life's mistakes. Repeat: it wasn't your fault, it was mine. I'm a bad, bad man."

The Englishman asked him a question. He shrugged and let out a stream of babble, then turned back to them and spoke in Pashto.

"He says you've all got to get ready now otherwise you'll be late. You need to let him wash you. I've disabled your detonators, so if you're still feeling a bit put out, don't bother reaching for them or I'll see. Then you won't get me, I'll get you. Just be sensible. You're soldiers of God now and we've got a job to do. Time to put our personal differences aside."

Ambrin hadn't stopped crying in all the time he'd spoken. He hauled her to a sitting position and undid her manacles, then he released Zaituna and Reshtina. They sat and allowed themselves to be washed. They needed a change of clothing, but the Englishman seemed to be ahead of them there too. He left the room and returned with fresh jeans and tops, every bit as hideous as those they had on now.

They allowed al-Maitami to undress and re-dress them as if they were in a bad dream. He grabbed Ambrin's chin. "Stop bloody crying, girl. It's over now. Go on, hit me if you want to. Hit me in the face. I deserve it. Go on, beauty, hit me hard. Hard as you like. I won't hit back, promise."

She looked at the ground and sniffled. Suddenly, Reshtina threw her fist into his eye. He yowled and collapsed into a sprawl. He shook his head like a dog then got up on his elbows and put his fingertips up for a quick assessment. He was bleeding.

"I didn't mean you, you bloody bitch!"

He flushed and tensed as if he was about to kill her. She hoped he'd try. She had the feeling there was more to her than she'd ever realised and it was about to surface. But then the Englishman chuckled, and Ambrin and Zaituna followed suit, and he seemed to lighten.

"Oh, well. I said I could take it. I asked for it. We'll call it even now, yes?"

He didn't seem to notice there was a difference between the smiles. The Englishman's was affectionate. Ambrin's and Zaituna's were wintry, as if they instinctively knew the wind had just altered and this was only the beginning.

He put on his sunglasses and baseball cap and told them to stay ten paces behind him all the way to the city centre. They could join him at the bus stop – he would pay for them - and when he alighted and for final instructions and a fond farewell, but that was all. The CCTV cameras would be watching them all. If they kept apart, it would take the subsequent investigators longer to link him to the bombers, and once they were in Paradise, he'd need every second he could get.

So when he left the Englishman's front door, they counted to ten and set off in guarded pursuit. At first, they walked slower than they usually did because of the pain and the continuing trauma. But then the knowledge of certain death resumed service and they began to feel as light as the kites that used to fly over their village.

He stood at a bus stop and pretended to read a leaflet. They sidled up and pretended not to know him. But then Reshtina broke ranks.

"What are you reading?" she asked.

She couldn't see his eyes behind his glasses, but she didn't need to. He turned away from her.

"Have we enabled the bombs yet?" Zaituna said.

"No," he said in a menacing tone. "And if this is some misguided attempt to be clever, forget it. No one here understands what you're talking about. It's all gibberish to them."

"I understood," Reshtina said. No one laughed.

"Get your pictures out," he said, bringing the leaflet up to cover his lips, "And make sure you've learned your Underground sign. In a few hours time, if you get it right, the entire Arab world will ring with your praises. If you get it wrong, your names, and those of your families, until your seventh cousin removed, will become a byword for shame. Is that what you want, eh? Disgrace?"

The bus came, and they ascended to the top deck. Al-Maitami sat at the front so he could look at the sights. The three women sat at the back, watching him. They put Ambrin in between them so they could comfort her. Reshtina looked out of the window and saw a billboard with alternating pictures. One showed a half-naked woman with what was obviously a bottle of scent. The second showed a little black girl, smiling. There were no words or sign of a product with the child, so what she was meant to sell was impossible to know. Maybe if you were British she meant something.

For a second she had the strange feeling she was connected with the man in the corridor and her own face and all that hopeless mummery. But since what had happened to Ambrin she'd lost all taste for introspection. She was focussed entirely on death and for once it felt good.

On the back seat of a London taxi, Amaghan Jones and Tasneem sat either side of Ghatola so they could comfort her on the journey back. The sun was milky over the knolls flanking the M25, and the cars stood in a queue. Ghatola was as animated as Tasneem had ever seen her. She burst into conversation without warning, then slept for ten minutes and awoke again to pick up talking exactly where she'd left off. She gave all the signs of imminent mental collapse.

Armaghan Jones seemed to notice it too. She held Ghatola's hand in both hers and spoke in the gaps, mainly while she slept, hoping to reach her subliminally.

"You know you can't go home. Not any more, it's too dangerous. For a long time, even *I* wanted to go back to Afghanistan, despite everything. But then I met Ian, and I got on a training course, and one thing led to another, you know? You're still a very attractive young woman, despite your burns – and you can get treatment for that – and *the world's your oyster* as the British say. You've been a teacher in the past, so it's not as if you don't have transferable skills. All you've got to do is learn the language. Learn to speak it, then you can learn to read and write it. We're looking at maybe two, three years. And you've got to go places where you can meet people. There are refugee support groups that can help us with that kind of thing – "

Ghatola awoke with a start. She beamed. "That's *it!*"

"What's 'it'?" Armaghan Jones asked.

"It's *English!* It was staring me in the face all along, and I never realised!"

Tasneem and Armaghan Jones exchanged expressions. Tasneem took Ghatola's other hand and patted it. "Sorry, neither of us is with you, dear. You probably need to explain a little."

"Before we met, Reshtina was caught in a bomb blast. She said she couldn't remember anything. I tried to hypnotise her, but we never got anywhere. All she came out with was this ... babble. Baby-talk, I used to call it. I thought she was putting it on. But whatever it was, that's what English reminds me of. It sounded like English!"

Armaghan Jones looked at the floor, then out of the window. Ghatola fell back into a swoon.

Tasneem felt the blood drain from her face. "Is there a service station nearby?" she asked. "I may need to go to the bathroom."

"Armaghan Jones flipped the partition between them and the driver. "Could we make a toilet break, please?"

"The next set of services isn't for five miles," he replied. "At this rate, that'll be another half hour. As a matter of fact, love, I could do with stopping myself."

Tasneem's mind raced. The truth hit her like a bad egg. Reshtina wasn't even like the others. She was white and her accent ...

Twenty minutes later, they stopped at Thurrock. She made an excuse about wanting to get something to eat and found a payphone booth well away from the possibility of discovery. She couldn't remember Abedrabbo al-Maitami's number so she had to call Idris Kakahel. Her hand shook violently.

"*Reshtina Sarbanri's a British agent!*" she almost yelled when he picked up.

She heard him choke on his own spit. "Wh – *what?*"

The bus dropped them in Regent Street. Everyone queued to disembark, so they all had to stand together for a few seconds, but once they were on the pavement, al-Maitami strode ahead and the three women shadowed him, keeping him just within view.

The pavements were so crowded they had to walk in single file. The traffic was intense and noisy. Fast food stores blasted cooking smells and cars and buses stirred exhaust fumes in. Ten thousand men and women walked unseeingly, clasping newspapers, briefcases, paper cups with lids on, skipping into the gutter occasionally to overtake each other. The sun shone on the gargantuan shops but it was chilly.

Keeping al-Maitami in view wasn't easy, but he seemed to know instinctively when he was in danger of losing them and loitered, looking at a shop display or pretending to daydream, to give them time to catch up. After five minutes of being alternately buffeted and carried along fairly helplessly they saw him halt at a crossroads and turn to face them.

Reshtina realised: this was it. She looked across the road and her stomach turned over as she saw her own Underground sign.

"Come to me, my lambs," he said when they were within hearing distance.

They gathered round him, trembling. Reshtina saw Zaituna was about to ask about the bombs, so she got in first.

"We were all talking in the back of the bus," she said. "We're ready to do our duty. No more selfishness."

"Are you going to enable the bombs now?" Zaituna said.

He smiled. "They were never disabled. Now listen, keep tight hold of your little guide-pictures, but only look at them if you have to. Zaituna, you go up there, and down the steps where you see the sign. Should take about five minutes. Ambrin, beauty, you're down there. Reshtina, you stay here. Count to a hundred slowly then go down the steps over the road. In fifteen minutes, I'll detonate you all automatically, but by that time I don't expect to have to. God is great."

He pulled the peak on his baseball cap down and crossed the road. The women exchanged watery eyes and separated. Reshtina crossed the road by the lights, and began to count to a hundred. She watched al-Maitami go and looked at the pavement in case he turned round to check on her.

Then she set off after him, easing gently through the strangers so as not to arouse his suspicion. When she was within twenty paces of him, he slowed and looked into a shop window. He seemed to struggle with indecision then he went inside. Presumably, he couldn't vacate the area yet in case he had to detonate the bombs. He had a quarter of an hour to go shopping.

She walked to the doorway. A brightly-lit boutique with spotlights, a curving counter and assistants in heels and hairbands. He was one of six customers and he had his back to her. He browsed the lines of men's jackets, lifted two off their racks and went into a changing room, pulling the curtain behind him. This was her chance.

She strode inside the shop so purposefully that the assistants looked at her. She realised that she probably looked more like a thief than a customer, but she didn't care. She heard al-Maitami's mobile ring. She pulled out her pistol and drew the curtain.

He turned round with an expression of indignation, but it changed as he saw the gun. The first bullet tore his arm off – she didn't want to kill him yet - and he smashed against the wall with the force. He looked up at her, bloody and uncomprehending, and she shot him in the face. He'd dropped his mobile. It was still ringing, so she destroyed it. The shop assistants screamed.

Fleming stood a little way back from the main thoroughfare at the junction between Oxford Street and Hills Place, flanked by two army lieutenants. He'd completely miscalculated. Half-closing the Tube had forced everyone to take to the pavement. The volume of pedestrians was twice its usual level, meaning a bomb here would do exactly the same damage as one set off thirty metres below street level. He wore discreet headphones, read notes and sent and received messages. At eight-forty, as tempers frayed at the railway stations and the traffic in the city centre ground to a standstill, he reluctantly issued the order to reopen the Underground. He'd achieved nothing. His phone ran for the fiftieth time.

"Fleming?"

"Cassidy here. Reshtina Sarbanri's just shot a man dead. *Jimmy Deatleberg Co.*, 520 Oxford Street."

"Are you sure it's her?"

"I've seen the footage. A hundred per cent."

"What about the man?"

"Unrecognisable as yet. By that, I mean she blew his head off. Forensics are on their way."

Here she was then, like some creature erupting through the tarmac. There could be no more doubting her purpose, and whatever happened now, their whole past would have to be rewritten. His head went weightless.

"We're in pursuit," Cassidy said.

"Get her picture to everyone." He realised Sir Anthony would eat him alive, but there was no alternative. "Re-close the Underground entrances, make them exit-only. Comb the crowds."

"Shouldn't we start evacuating the city centre?"

He'd been checkmated long ago. Whatever he did now would be a mistake. All he could hope to do was keep casualties to a minimum.

"Stop anyone leaving," he said. "Seal the perimeter. Allow people to come in but not leave."

"Er, I'm not sure I heard that right. You're saying *stop* people leaving?"

"Look, Cassidy, all the research that's ever been done on suicide bombs suggests the damage isn't due to the explosive, but the shrapnel. The more dispersed those surrounding the bomber are, the greater the fatalities. If a bomber's kettled, he'll kill three or four at most."

"So we're accepting defeat?"

"We're trying to limit our losses, yes."

"You realise this is bound to get you in trouble?"

"Just re-issue the order."

Everything, everything was too late. The distinction between generals and foot soldiers fell apart in the general rout and he plunged into the crowds, frantically looking for Marcie. His headset announced Robert Skelton.

"Fleming, this is the Head of Counter-Terrorist Command. I understand you've just issued an order to the effect that everyone's to be sealed in with the bombers? Don't bother answering that because I've countermanded it. My only question is, are you remotely right in the head?"

"It's about containment, sir. It's about whether we want twelve or fifteen casualties or two or three hundred."

"Or none at all, which is my preference."

"How realistic is that? The bombers are here, and now they've already committed a murder in broad daylight, they must know we're onto them. The only reason they haven't detonated their devices so far is because they know they can do so entirely at their leisure. We don't even know what they look like or how many there are."

"And yet I'm fairly sure packing innocent civilians in with them isn't going to win us plaudits in tomorrow's papers. You might want to be crucified, Mr Fleming, but I certainly don't. Good day."

Policemen in plain clothes began putting on luminous jackets and joining hands. Two men began unloading plastic security barriers from the back of a Ford Transit van.

But it was already hopeless. The crowd density was causing the strategy to backfire. The usual noise of vehicles dissipated as drivers switched off their engines and leaned out of their windows, or got out. Everyone began shouting. The alarms in some of the shops went off. Horns parped and Fleming found himself being carried along by the throng. His headset announced the Defence Secretary. He braced himself for an ear-bashing.

"*I thought we had a bloody agreement!*" Sir Anthony raged. "*You said 'understood'! 'UNDERSTOOD'! Now her face is on every police network in town! They'll bloody shoot to kill her on sight, can't you see that?*"

"We've got to weigh scenarios. There's no best case any more, only the least worse."

"This is my daughter we're talking about, and your wife! How long before the press gets hold of it?"

"We can't be continually prioritising the media."

"Get this, Mr Fleming. When all this is over - "

The incoming channel suddenly flicked. 'Emergency' was programmed to override all others.

"We've had another murder," Cassidy said. "A woman, mid-twenties, one of the bombers, not Reshtina Sarbanri."

He drew a sharp breath. "Where?"

After she left the others, Zaituna didn't know where she was walking to or why. She was lost, and the piece of paper al-Maitami had given her was a joke, as useless as anything else in Jannah. She wasn't sure how many thoughts she could fit into fifteen minutes, or what they should be about. She tried to think back to her childhood because she thought she ought to. She tried to think of her husband because she thought it might comfort her. She tried to think of Reshtina and Ambrin, because it was too frightening to know she was alone and lost. She prayed the first chapter of the Qur'an and her mind went blank and flashed red. This, she imagined, was what it was like to fall head-first off a mountain.

She came to Bond Street Underground. Just like al-Maitami said, there was a large entrance leading down. She passed it and walked two corners ahead into a shallow side street with a dead-end. Her tongue felt like a piece of corrugated cardboard. She bent double for a dry retch.

It was dark in here, and cool. There was only one window in the whole road, a grimy-looking single pane in a black wall, possibly the rear of a hotel. Behind it, a set of blinds was drawn. She held onto the sill in an effort to calm her thumping heart – she didn't know how long she had left – and then she made a decision. This was where she'd die.

She looked into the window to examine her reflection and saw she wasn't alone.

That was Reshtina behind her, crying, but there was also a tall man with pale eyes and a serious expression. She wondered who ... then knew. She'd seen him standing just out of sight in the corner of the room the night her little brother died, then again when they'd brought Lalzari home for the last time after she'd stepped on that land-mine.

Azrael. How come she recognised him now but not then?

She saw Reshtina raise her gun. She gripped the window-sill and scrunched her eyes shut.

Then she felt the gentlest impress of the angel's finger on the back of her head.

There were sirens blaring and a chopper roared overhead, and for a crazy three or four seconds it felt like Kandahar again. Reshtina pushed her way along the road against the flow of the crowds, until she came to a fenced-off park with a fountain and ornamental shrubs. She looked inside. It was deserted except for a single woman standing motionless almost at its centre, her head bowed.

She let herself in. Ambrin flinched when she saw her coming but made no attempt to move. They both forced a smile.

"Did you kill him?" Ambrin said.

"Yes."

"And Zaituna?"

Reshtina nodded.

Ambrin wept. "You're coming with us, aren't you? You're not going to leave us alone?"

"Its whole body has to die first. Then, yes."

"Could – could you face me towards Mecca, please?"

Reshtina looked at the sun, gently turned her friend through forty five degrees and took up position behind her, trembling.

Ambrin nodded to say 'ready', and Reshtina fired a bullet through her skull. The corpse slapped hard into the mud.

And lay still. Thank God, there was no need for a second bullet. She knelt over the body, kissed its hair, said the Shahadah falteringly in its ear, and wept.

Fleming calculated Marcie's direction of travel and speed and concluded that if she was killing the bombers, Ballson's Park was where she'd most likely end up.

He arrived there at the head of a CO19 Force Firearms Unit. They closed off the exits and rushed in to find two women, one dead, one sitting up next to a gun with her hands raised. His heart leapt.

"Don't shoot!" he yelled. *"She - she's a British agent!"*

Chapter 35: Political Capital

Ghatola learned the news as soon as she got home and her eyes glazed and she had to find a seat. Tasneem crouched beside her, kneading her knee. They put the TV on because there was nothing else to do, even though Ghatola didn't understand the language. Tasneem saw no harm in it and, in any case, she wanted to gauge how things were panning out.

"So there is no 'Reshtina Sarbanri', nor has there ever been," Ghatola said bitterly, as if to herself.

Tasneem shook her head. "Apparently not."

"Well, in a life punctuated by deceptions and betrayals, this takes the prize. The whole thing was a sordid deception to make the British authorities look good."

"It would seem that way, yes."

"Zaituna and Ambrin weren't terrorists. They were herders' daughters. They can't have been involved willingly."

"So what do you think happened?"

"Obviously, they were inveigled by whoever the hell 'Reshtina Sarbanri' really is and led here like goats at Eid to feed British fantasies. The whole thing reeks."

"I wonder if we'll ever see her again?"

Ghatola laughed. "There are sixty million people in this country, and now we've outlived our usefulness, we'll probably be repatriated anyway. But if I ever do clap eyes on her a second time, I'll slit her miserable little throat without a backwards glance."

At six o'clock that night, they watched the Prime Minister's statement to the country. The TV screen showed a dark-haired man in a grey suit and blue tie step through the doorway of 10 Downing Street and cross the road wearing a smug smile. Cameras whirred and flashed. He straightened his notes on a podium.

"As most of you are now aware, early this morning, a British agent working for MI6 foiled a major attack on central London. As a result of her actions, a terrorist supply-chain stretching across Europe into the Middle East has now been closed down. The agent, who cannot be named for security reasons, infiltrated herself into an al-Qaeda cell in Afghanistan earlier this year and returned to Britain in company with three would-be terrorists, ostensibly to carry out a suicide bombing attack on the capital, scheduled for today. An attack which, had it succeeded, would have killed and seriously injured hundreds of innocent British civilians simply going about their daily business.

"The attacks were aimed at Underground stations in the city centre. Three bombers – of which she was to be one – arrived in the area at 08.30 this morning, along with a controller who had the capacity to detonate their explosive belts remotely. At 08.31, the controller despatched all three women from Oxford Circus with instructions as to which stations to target. He himself remained on hand.

"At 08.35, our agent located and killed the said controller whilst he was apparently browsing designer jackets in Oxford Street, and also disabled his detonation device. She set off in the direction she knew the other terrorists had taken, and at 08.44 killed the first in the vicinity of Bond Street Underground with a single shot to the head. At 08.53, she diverted the second from the same station, eliminating her in the same way, and then surrendered herself to the police by raising her hands. All three women were locked into their explosive belts, which were quickly removed and rendered safe by bomb disposal experts. They would therefore have died anyway.

"Her Majesty's government has already extended its warmest thanks to the agent concerned for her breathtaking courage, determination and dedication to the security of this country and the safety of its citizens. Earlier this afternoon, the Queen also expressed her gratitude in a private message from Buckingham Palace. I am sure everyone listening shares our sentiments, and will wish to join in extending our appreciation and admiration to the agent in question for a mission fully accomplished. Yes, I will take a few quick questions. Nick."

"Prime Minister," said a voice from off-screen, "could you tell us how the agent is recovering from what must have been a pretty hair-raising ordeal?"

"I believe she's being fully debriefed in an MI6 safe-house in the presence of her family. That's all I know at present. Gill."

"I wonder, Prime Minister," an Irish accent said, "if you could tell us why, if the agent in question knew of the existence of terrorists on British soil, she didn't inform the counter-terrorist police forces sooner? Why did she feel the need to do so much of the actual legwork herself?"

The Prime Minister smiled. "As you can imagine, she was being very closely watched by her co-conspirators. And of course, there was no room for error."

"Have you any idea why two of the terrorists apparently targeted the same Underground station – Bond Street?" a man asked. "Why didn't they spread out a little?"

"We don't yet have all the answers, but I believe they may have originally planned to hit three separate stations. Let's just say human frailty may have intervened. They didn't wish to die alone."

"Do you believe they were coerced?" the same man said.

"We're ruling that out. It's very difficult to coerce human beings to make a seven thousand mile journey for something like this. There must have been a strong element of readiness. Nina."

"How far do you think the wars in Afghanistan and Iraq are likely contributors to today's failed attack, and how reasonable is it to expect similar attempts in the future?"

"We have to bear in mind that the coalition forces in Iraq and Afghanistan have a job to do. We're there to help rebuild those countries after years of misrule by tyrannical regimes, and we don't intend to leave until both jobs are completed. Obviously, groups like al-Qaeda and the Taliban have a vested interest in stopping us, and we can expect them to try. So we must be vigilant, but we mustn't allow ourselves to be deterred from doing what's obviously right. Paul - and we'll make this the last question."

"How certain are you that the terrorists in today's foiled bombing are linked to al-Qaeda, rather than one of the other terrorist organisations out there, such as the Taliban or the Haqqani network?"

The Prime Minister smiled. "You've got to understand this has been a very busy twenty-four hours for our agent. There are inevitably going to be some grey areas at this stage. Over the next few days, we can expect the details to become rather clearer. Thank you, everyone."

He gathered up his notes and turned his back on their attempts at just one more question. The screen cut back to the studio and an earnest looking newsreader facing a middle-aged woman with a perm and a black dress across a raised white surface.

"We've got Laila Mustafa, Professor of Middle-Eastern Studies at the University of Sussex, here to discuss some of the implications of what we've just heard. Ms Mustafa - "

Tasneem got up and switched the TV off. She chuckled. "All's well that ends well then."

"I was watching that!"

"What are you getting out of it? You can't even understand English. Besides, it's going to give you an ulcer. I can see what's going through your head. You'd like to kill her."

"That's what I said earlier. But I've done enough killing. See where it's got me. Anyway, she's not worth the trouble. Let Allah deal with her in the afterlife."

"So you're not in love with her any more?"

"There isn't a 'her'! That's the whole *point!*"

"Because I'm sure she'd be up for a little reunion, once she's had a bit of a rest. And I could help you."

"Really," she said sardonically. "You'd do that, would you?"

Tasneem grinned. "Why not?"

"Anyway, forget it. It's not going to happen. I don't want to see her. And If I ever do, I'll probably vomit so hard I'll be no good for anything."

"That's why I'd come in so handy."

Ghatola looked coldly at her. "I said I've had my fill of killing, thank you. If it wasn't so crazy, I'd say Allah meant Reshtina Sarbanri to teach me a long-overdue lesson in humility. From now on, I'm going to do my best to get asylum and then: one day, one step. Armaghan Jones is right. It's time to stop fantasising and live like an adult."

She lay down to sleep, but Tasneem saw she was crying between the sheets, so she got the Nitrazepam and forced her to sit up and take one. Ten minutes later, she was snoring. Tasneem stroked her forehead, dried her eyes with a handkerchief and kissed her left temple.

There was a knock at the door. She jumped. She remembered what Armaghan Jones had taught her: there are plenty of racists in this country, and lots of criminals, and everyone hates asylum-seekers. Only open the door with the chain on.

It was the black woman from British Intelligence. Ruby Parker. Her heart missed a beat. She closed the door, removed the lock and opened it wide.

"What can I do for you?" she asked.

"Is Ms Rahman asleep?"

"Er, yes ..."

"Good, because in that case, I won't have to keep my voice down."

Something was wrong. Ruby Parker was speaking as if she'd come to arrest her, and yet she was alone. You don't arrest someone when you're alone, not unless there's no alternative.

"Keep your voice down about what?"

"About you, Tasneem Babar. Or should I say, Aminah Mohammad? Before you reply, Ms Mohammad, let me tell you I know all about your secret meetings with Idris Kakahel and Haider Chamkanni. My men are in the car, by the way, in case you're thinking of making a run for it. Forget it. It's not in your interests."

Tasneem swallowed loudly. She sat down on a chair. She stared hard at the ground for a full minute. "Don't – don't tell Ghatola, will you?" she said in a defeated tone. "She's suffered enough. She thinks everyone's against her."

"I've no intention of doing so."

"I was only trying to help," she said weakly.

Ruby Parker smiled wryly. "So I hear."

Chapter 36: At the Inquiry

At 9am, fifteen hours after the Prime Minister gave his press statement, Nicholas Fleming sat alone in a wainscoted corridor on the second floor of Westminster Palace. He took a final glance at his notes and replaced them in his inside suit pocket. He wasn't thinking at all of what was about to happen. He expected to be fired. All his thoughts were about Marcie: he still hadn't been allowed to see her, and he hadn't slept.

Big Ben began to toll the hour. As arranged, the door next to him opened and a civil servant in a pinstriped suit emerged.

"The committee will see you now, sir," he said.

Fleming followed him. Inside the room, Tom Purdy and Chris Magee, two elderly backbenchers with cufflinks and Select Committee experience, and Dame Agatha Broughton, a senior civil servant from the Cabinet Office, sat behind a quarter-circular desk with Fleming's chair as its focal point. They stood up as he entered. Tom Purdy gestured for him to sit down and they all followed suit. The civil servant who'd ushered him in sat down to one side with a pen and notepad.

Dame Agatha held her reading glasses upside-down on the desk in both hands. "Now, Nicholas, I'd like to remind you, for the sake of the minutes, that this is only an informal hearing. We've read your report and we don't intend to waste time going over every aspect of it. However, two things do concern us, and we'd like to know more. Firstly, your injury in Leeds and how it may, or may not, have affected your performance on the ground, and secondly, your decision to pack commuters into an area where you believed there would be suicide bombers. And this may be a third thing, although we won't split hairs, we'd like to know whether there was any relationship between the two."

"We may as well begin with the injury," Tom Purdy said. "How far do you think it may have affected your performance?"

"If by 'performance' you mean 'judgement', I don't believe it did. It restricted my ability to cover long distances rapidly on foot, that's all."

"And as evidence of that ...?"

"You should all have received copies of report C67/A, written by Ruby Parker less than twelve hours before the intended attack and forwarded to Robert Skelton immediately afterwards as a matter of urgency. It bears witness that, while wounded, I personally tracked the bombers down to precisely where I predicted they'd be, in Dover. As I claimed at the time, the Southampton corpses were a red herring. Furthermore, at the risk of blowing my own trumpet to pieces, it was probably my contribution that stopped the bombers entering the Underground. Until I intervened, our defences were being scaled down and the remaining manpower was focussed on preventing attacks on high-rises, something the bombers themselves never envisaged."

All three panel members nodded sagely. Chris Magee smiled. "I think we can safely say you've just saved Ms Parker a hauling over the coals, Mr Fleming. It was, after all, she who insisted you be allowed to return to work."

"When, quite frankly, I'd rather have been in bed with a good book and a cup of cocoa. If you believe you're absolutely necessary to saving lives, it's your duty not to spare yourself. And if you believe someone else is, it's your duty not to spare them either. Ruby Parker didn't bring me back to indulge my vanity, of that you can be sure."

"But of course," Dame Agatha said, "if your injury *had* affected your judgement, that might have been gradual, mightn't it, rather than immediate?"

He opened his palms. "It's not impossible."

Tom Purdy looked down at his desk and turned a document. "Which brings us nicely to the kettling."

"You state in your report," Chris Magee said, "that since the rapid spread of shrapnel is the chief cause of fatalities in cases of suicide bombing, the best procedure is to pack the assailant into as confined a space as possible. In support of this thesis, you cite a news article, 'Preventing Suicide Bombing', which appeared in *The New York Times* on December 11, 2005. According to Edward Kaplan, professor of public health at Yale University, confronted with a suicide bomber, I quote: 'the heroic thing to do would be to approach the bomber and hug him or her, sacrificing yourself but saving the lives of many people behind you'. Let the minutes show that I'm quoting a third-party interpretation of Professor Kaplan's findings."

"I think the panel's concern," Dame Agatha said, "is that is by forcing people to rigidly enclose the bombers, you're effectively removing their right to decide their fate for themselves."

"Let me ask you a direct question," Tom Purdy said. "Do you believe, in retrospect, that Robert Skelton was correct to countermand your order to kettle the crowds?"

Fleming was about to reply, but Dame Agatha raised her hand and turned to her colleagues. "I'm afraid that question won't quite do, Tom. 'In retrospect' could be taken to include what Mr Fleming now knows to have happened *historically*. What we want to know is would he have issued the same order ..." She furrowed her eyebrows.

"If you were to find yourself in the same situation today," Chris Magee said, "with a suicide bomber, would you issue the same order?"

"Yes."

"Even though you're forcing people to their deaths?"

"I believe that we're responsible not just for what we do, but for what we don't do."

"Meaning?" Dame Agatha said.

"If I'd kettled the crowd and the bombs had gone off, I'd be responsible for ten, twelve, maybe fourteen deaths. If I'd deliberately declined to kettle the crowds and the bombs had gone off, I'd be responsible for two or three hundred deaths. A difference of say a hundred and fifty, on a conservative estimate."

"I don't see how you arrive at that conclusion," Tom Purdy said.

"Because I could have prevented them, but I chose not to."

Chris Magee drew his chin back. "You 'chose not to' kill fourteen people. Surely you understand there's a difference between direct and indirect responsibility?"

"Not at all. I think you're either responsible for something or you're not."

"Rubbish. There's an obvious difference between letting something happen and causing it."

Fleming frowned. "A moral difference?"

"Of course. If I force you into a position where I know you'll be killed, that isn't the same as allowing you to make a run for it and take your chances."

"It's not about that. It's about numbers of victims."

"No, it's about murder versus manslaughter."

"So you *cause* fourteen people to die, that's murder; you *allow* two hundred to be killed, that's manslaughter, is that right? You're playing with words."

Tom Purdy put his pen down hard and turned to his fellow panellists with a flick of his eyebrows. The room filled with silence.

Dame Agatha leaned forward. "I think the bottom line is, Nicholas, it does seem to us *intuitively* wrong that an officer of the law should be manoeuvring people into a position where he knows they'll be killed. Forget about reason for a minute. It just doesn't sound right, does it?"

"No, it doesn't," he replied. "I'm not disputing that."

"Then the question," Tom Purdy said, "becomes, 'Why does it *seem* so wrong?' Because morality isn't a matter of logic. When things seem wrong, it's usually because they are."

"But that's exactly what I'm saying," Fleming replied. "Yes: *it's wrong*. But there isn't any right option."

The panellists looked at each other again.

"I think we've gone as far as we're going to get," Tom Purdy said. "I can't see us reconciling our differences. You seem to think morality is a numbers game, Mr Fleming, while we on the panel beg to differ. Is there anything further you'd like to say to us before we conclude?"

Fleming filliped the fingers of his right hand and laid his palm on his thigh. He only had one card left but he might as well give it an outing. "This country's currently involved in two wars, Mr Purdy. They're only justifiable if, despite all the thousands of deaths we've caused, yet more would have ensued had we not bothered. Otherwise, they're unpardonable. Mr Purdy, Mr Magee, you both voted to invade Afghanistan in 2001 and go to war with Saddam in 2003. If you have any defence of your conduct that doesn't invoke the principle I acted on when I commanded my men to kettle those crowds, then I'm happy for you to find me guilty."

Dame Agatha smiled. "Thank you, Mr Fleming. That will be all."

Ten minutes later, Fleming stepped out of the building into a broad courtyard where a Thames House car was waiting for him, as arranged. He got into the back to find himself sitting next to Ruby Parker, dressed in a red skirt suit.

"Bloody pen pushers," he said. "It's all so black and white to them."

She looked straight ahead as the car pulled away. "And yet your tone of voice tells me you don't really care."

"I honestly don't. I just want to see Marcie."

"Brace yourself. Two hours ago she cut her forearms. She lost three pints of blood and went into hypovolemic shock. She's in hospital now, unconscious. It's a miracle she didn't die."

"Oh, my God."

"You're aware that she hasn't spoken any English at all since we picked her up? We're not even sure she still understands it."

"I didn't know. I haven't been allowed to see her."

"We're on our way there now."

Chapter 37: The View from Mannersby

Joy thought she might as well wait till dinner to tell her husband. It was when they usually had their battles, after all.

Their dining room was small and carpeted with a low ceiling and polished oak furniture from the century before last. A candelabra stood in the middle of the tablecloth. At ten past six, Sir Anthony sat at one end of the table, Joy opposite him, and Anya and Hawa in between. They ate their minestrone soup in silence.

"I've invited Nicholas to stay for a while," Joy said.

He looked up. "Nicholas ...?"

"Your son-in-law."

He put his spoon down. "Oh, no you don't, Joy. I'm not having him within ten miles of this house. Not after the way he exposed Marcie."

"Exposed Marcie? Or exposed you?"

He chuckled humourlessly. "You're not getting round me that way. I've nothing to feel guilty about."

"He's been suspended from his job. Isn't that enough for you?"

"That wasn't my doing. I've better things to be doing than pursuing vendettas. And no, it isn't, actually."

"I spoke to him yesterday. He's anxious to apologise in person."

"Tell him there's a woman in a padded cell ..." He caught her gaze, but couldn't hold it. "Sorry, Joy."

"*We need all the help we can get!*" she screamed, making everyone jump.

Fleming moved into a bedroom in the east wing. He brought his car, an assortment of clothes, a laptop, photographs of his parents, and Marcie, and a collection of books about farming. He made friends with Hawa, reintroduced himself to Anya, and promised to take them on the London Eye the following week. Sir Anthony braved out his arrival in the Study with a glass of brandy, a fire in the grate and *The Daily Telegraph*. Fleming went to see him half an hour after he arrived. Sir Anthony gestured for him to sit down.

"I've read Agatha's report into the London part of the operation," he said gruffly. "It indicates you're a numbers man when it comes to doing good works. Is that why you put my daughter's photo out, after I bent over backwards to help you on the explicit understanding that you wouldn't?"

"I was trying to save lives, yes."

"There's a word for men like you, Fleming."

"Don't forget, I love Marcie."

"Utilitarians. Charles Dickens said everything that could usefully be said about them in *Hard Times*. Where's your compassion, man?"

Fleming realised he'd been forgiven. "I honestly didn't intend to betray your confidence. Quite the contrary. I acted on the spur of the moment."

"Spontaneity, eh? I suppose you can't be entirely inhuman. Would you like a brandy?"

"Yes, please."

Sir Anthony stood up and poured a fresh drink and refilled his own glass. They sat in silence, looking into the log fire.

"I'm going to see her again tomorrow," Fleming said.

"You know she's on hunger strike now?"

Fleming nodded. "There must be some way of getting through to her. I thought – I thought when I saw her that night in the Grand in Dover, I spotted a glimmer of recognition."

"But not any more."

He swallowed. "No."

"Do you know, Nicholas, if it wasn't for the fingerprint and DNA match, I honestly wouldn't think she was my daughter. There's nothing at all in her eyes. I mean ... apart from hatred."

"Yes, I've had that."

"She even seems to hate Joy. And Anya. What the hell's Anya ever done to anyone? She's just a child."

"It may just be a look."

They fell into silence again.

"How long do you think she can keep it up?" Sir Anthony said. "Do you think it might be permanent?"

"I doubt it. They say the brain never forgets anything. It's all stored in there somewhere. It needs something to access it."

"Those electronic billboards of Anya must have done the trick on some level. She certainly wasn't thinking of Queen and Country, despite what everyone's been told."

"Well, whatever Anya might have done that day, it's stopped working now."

"This may be a long shot, but isn't there supposed to be some woman in the country who knew her in Afghanistan? I know I'm Defence Secretary, but they don't necessarily tell me these things, especially now they know I'm personally involved."

Fleming grimaced. "Ghatola Rahman. They were lovers, apparently."

"I'd heard something of that sort through the grapevine. It's true, then?"

"I've never met the woman and I'm not sure I want to. Ruby Parker told me. She didn't indicate that it was just a working hypothesis either."

"Do you think she could get through to Marcie?"

"*As* Marcie?" Fleming said. "She could get through to Reshtina Sarbanri, and for all I know, she may be doing her damnedest to see her again. I'm sure if we went to see her, she'd sugar us with all sorts of promises about how she'd be able to cure her, and right now, we're so desperate, we'd probably believe her."

"You think it would do more harm than good, then."

"She's in love with Reshtina Sarbanri, not Marcie Hartley-Brown. And Reshtina Sarbanri may well be in love with her. So it's obvious where her interests lie. They'd be off back to Afghanistan before you could say Jack Robinson. Don't forget, the UK Border Police tend to turn a blind eye to refugees leaving. We might very well never see her again."

"Yes, I see. God, it's more complicated than I thought."

"Quite."

"You said you think she might be trying to see Marcie."

Fleming shrugged. "That's conjecture. I only know that if I was in love with someone and I was sure it was reciprocated, if there was any possibility of us getting back together again, wild horses wouldn't keep me away from her. She's quite determined. She was an assassin in Afghanistan."

"An - *assassin*?"

"Apparently."

"Good God, you don't think she'll come here, do you? How did she even get into the country? What the hell's SIS up to, importing contract killers?"

Fleming smiled. "Business as usual, I suppose."

"I wonder if Marcie knows she's around. It might be what's stopping her coming back from the underworld."

"Hope. Yes, I hadn't thought of that."

"I think we ought to have her watched, this Ghatola Rahman woman."

"A private detective, you mean? It can't hurt. We'll go halves."

Chapter 38: Not Sunbathing in Saint-Tropez

As usual, they had to be prepared for her to attack them, even in her straitjacket, so he kept Anya to the rear. The nurse – a burly man with white shoes and a shaven head – went ahead while Amaghan Jones closed the door. Everything was cushioned in here. There was no furniture and no bedding, only a plastic potty, white protected walls and two unreachable windows. It felt like a cross between a bouncy castle and the inside of a coffin.

In the corner, Marcie sat with her arms crossed over her chest by the restraining sleeves, gazing unseeingly at the floor. They'd given her a chador when she was still in her co-operative stage, but that ended six weeks ago when she'd told them about the traffickers. Since then, she'd said nothing and acknowledged no one. A Court Order invoking the 1983 Mental Health Act meant she was being regularly force-fed. Her left eye was black – no one knew how - her skin was grey, her toenails were full of dirt.

"Hello, Marcie," Fleming said. "It's us again."

Armaghan Jones translated.

"Anya's going to tell you about her day out yesterday," he continued. "We went to the Tower of London to collect some materials for her Tudor project at school. I've also got a letter from your mother and father I want to read to you. And of course, I want to remind you that I love you. We all do."

It was like speaking to air. She closed her eyes and although Anya began her narrative, it soon became obvious she was asleep.

"You can stop now, Anya," Fleming said. "I think we've lost her."

"She's getting weaker," the nurse said. "We're not quite sure why. We might have to step up the Ensure."

"Ensure? Isn't that what they use in Guantanamo?"

"It's a balanced meal. And she's not going to know that. We're trying to stop her dying."

"Yes, yes, of course. Stupid question."

After handing over his name badge at the front desk, he stood under the porch and helped Anya on with her coat so they could race through the rain to the car. Armaghan Jones emerged from the electric door with an umbrella.

"Miserable weather," he said.

"I know."

"Would you like a lift anywhere?"

"Thank you, but my husband's coming to pick me up in a minute."

"Can I ask you about Ghatola Rahman?"

She laughed. "Talk about out of the blue. I'm afraid not, no. I'm not allowed to speak about her outside work. Even if I wasn't working for who I occasionally am, it wouldn't be professional."

"I only want to ask, do you think she's making efforts to try and see Marcie? Because that's what might be disturbing her."

She brought her eyelashes together. "I'm not sure I like your tone of voice. What are you implying?"

"It's just a question."

"And you think I'd know about that," she replied tetchily. "You think she'd tell me?"

"I've honestly no idea. I wouldn't ask if I knew the answer."

They stood in silence. Eventually, she said: "I see now. You think that when you say, 'Hello, Marcie, I've come to spend time with you today', I'm actually translating it as, 'I've got another secret message from Ghatola'. Is that it?"

"For God's sake, that never even occurred to me!"

"Why ask, then? Why ask me if I know whether Ghatola Rahman's making efforts to see Marcie? Because if I knew, I'd have to have be for or against, and if I was for, I'd have to be helping her, wouldn't I?"

"Hang on, stop. This isn't fair. You're reading things into my question that I never - "

An old Fiat Panda pulled up and the driver, a small man with grey hair and a chevron moustache, ran round to the passenger door and opened it. Armaghan Jones got in. He kissed her lightly on the cheek, then rushed back, put his seat-belt on and pulled away.

"Why was that lady so angry?" Anya asked.

Two weeks later, it was time for a family conference. Joy, Sir Anthony and Fleming sat in the Living Room on separate chairs, facing each other. Dr Lloyd, a chartered consultant psychologist from the City, sat on the sofa. Geoffrey poured the tea and left them alone. No one was in a hurry to speak, and for a long time the only sound was the ticking of the man-telpiece clock. They all had all the information – they'd stopped the force-feeding, Marcie was dying - it was merely a question of what to do with it.

"Maybe we could hire another translator," Sir Anthony said.

"She already knows what we're saying," Fleming said. "Isn't that right, Dr Lloyd? We probably shouldn't indulge her."

"I think it's analogous to blind-sight," he replied. "She recognises what you're saying, but the reflexive capacity's missing."

"You mean, she doesn't know she knows," Joy said.

"Exactly."

"So what are we going to do, then?" Sir Anthony de-manded. "We can't just leave her to expire."

"What does this private detective of yours say about Ghatola Rahman?" Joy asked.

"How the hell did you find out about that?"

"Anya told me. I don't know how she discovered it, ex-cept that, for obvious reasons, she's interested."

"Good grief."

"Don't you think it's important to put all your cards on the table in this sort of situation?" she snapped. "I understand *you* knew as well, Nicholas. I'm disappointed in you, I won't hide it. Both of you. Sometimes, I think men are hardly different to children."

Sir Anthony shrugged. "We might as well not have bothered, really. There's nothing to report. And I *would* have said if there had been, believe me."

"Nonsense, there must be something."

"She seems reasonably happy. Lives with another refugee of similar age called Tasneem Babar. Goes to the supermarket twice a week, buys a loaf of bread, two cans of mushroom soup, blah, blah, eats at two and seven, bed at ten, goes line-dancing with Armaghan Jones, the cinema with Armaghan Jones, bowling with Armaghan blah, blah. There's not a shred of evidence that she's trying to see Marcie."

"She's no reason to be hanging round with Armaghan Jones any more if she is," Fleming said.

Sir Anthony shifted in his chair. "Although, to be fair, if Armaghan Jones was still seeing Marcie, it would look fairly suspicious."

"Perhaps she is," Fleming replied. "I'm pretty certain we're not the only ones who are trying to communicate with her."

"What if I was to say I want Marcie home?" Joy said. "It would at least mean we could put a stop to that kind of thing."

This possibility had been in the air since the beginning. No one wanted her to die alone in a mental hospital. And Dr Lloyd's theory recommended it.

"My preferred solution," he chimed in. "Bring her into contact with things she knows but doesn't know she knows. Eventually, the brain will reach crisis-point, and it'll have to start acknowledging. It'll be piecemeal at first, but once the floodgates are open ... At least that's my hypothesis. Obviously, you'd have to modify a designated room."

"How long would that take?" Sir Anthony said. "Given that expense is no object. We'd need you on hand to approve everything."

"I'm more than happy to do it for free," Dr Lloyd replied. "My only condition is that you allow me to write it up as a research paper. I wouldn't mention Marcie by name of course, but you could be sure I'd give her my undivided attention."

"How long to get everything in place?" Sir Anthony repeated.

"Timewise – four or five days?"

"And we'd have to a room set aside for Ghatola Rahman," Joy said.

The men looked at each other.

"Excuse me?" Sir Anthony said.

"You hired a private detective to investigate her without telling me, so we don't necessarily have to consult each other. I went to see her yesterday."

"A - and?" Sir Anthony said.

"She wasn't keen to receive me, although she was hospitable enough. She's learning English and she's hoping to apply for British citizenship. Did your PD tell you that?"

"No, he bloody well didn't. It sounds like she's digging in for a long wait."

"She was very cold, despite the tea and cherry bakewells. Afterwards, I spoke to her friend. I say 'friend', I don't know what their relationship was. She asked me on behalf of Ghatola not to visit again. Hardly the behaviour, you might think, of someone who's desperate to worm her way into Marcie's company. However, if I'm persistent and apparently desperate enough, I think she may yet be prevailed on to change her mind. She may be our only hope."

Dr Lloyd leaned forward. "I'm sorry to interject, but this isn't quite on. The aim is to remove her from the circle of mementos of her imagined biography and replace them in a non-coercive way with those of her real one. If we introduce a significant influence associated with the former, it's impossible to guarantee success."

"What's your big game, Joy?" Sir Anthony asked. "Surely you can see Dr Lloyd's logic?"

"She's stuck rigid in her mind set," Joy said, "and she's deteriorating fast. I know you're going to pooh-pooh me, but I'm her mother and I can sense these things. The weaker she gets, the less she'll be able to fight, no matter how many 'mementos' we surround her with."

Sir Anthony nodded as if to express the benefit of the doubt. "So how do you think Ghatola Rahman's going to help?"

"We know we love her, but she doesn't. If she is going to die, I'd like her to know there's someone in the house who does care for her. I'm not interested in what we might think of that person. And if Marcie cares for her too, that's even better. Of faith, hope and love, the greatest is love."

"I'm missing something here," Fleming said. "You say Ghatola Rahman wasn't pleased to see you."

"She apparently doesn't know that Marcie isn't sunning herself in Saint-Tropez, sipping Martinis and boasting about her exploits to wide-eyed expats. She's very bitter. Understandably, she feels she's been used."

He put his thumbs together. "So it appears Armaghan Jones is the soul of discretion. Not that I suggested anything other."

Dr Lloyd sighed. "I did think I was going to get a research paper out of this. I can see the force of what you're saying, Joy, but under the circumstances, I have to withdraw my offer to work for free. I'm sure you understand that."

Sir Anthony shrugged. "As I said earlier, money's no object."

There was a knock at the door. It opened and Geoffrey poked his head round. "There's someone here to see Mr Fleming. Should I ask her to wait?"

"We're in conference here," Sir Anthony said. "Although I think we're just about done. Who is it?"

"Ms Jones. I believe she's Marcie's translator."

Fleming found Armaghan Jones standing in the Dining Room, holding a handbag over her waist and admiring Joy's collection of landscapes. He was pleased fate had given him a second chance and was determined not to wreck it. The key was to speak before she did. He closed the door.

"I apologise for offending you the other day," he said. "In my defence, I honestly wasn't implying what you thought I was. Sometimes the way I say things makes a contrary impression, and I'm insufficiently on my guard against it."

"I came here to say sorry too," she replied quietly. "It was nothing to do with you. I really don't know what came over me. Stress, I guess."

"Oh. Well, let's not play the blame game. Would you care for a cup of tea?"

She smiled. "I have to be getting back home. I just wanted to clear my conscience, that's all."

"I'm glad we're friends again because there's something I need to ask you. Would you teach me Pashto?"

She nodded. "I wondered when you'd ask. I charge ten fifty an hour."

Chapter 39: Fleming Walks Into a Trap

Ghatola and Tasneem arrived at Mannersby in blue chadors the afternoon before Marcie was due. Joy and Sir Anthony stood with Anya on the top of the shallow steps leading to the porch and Geoffrey was there to help with the luggage. The sun shone and the greens and browns of the park seemed to sit next to the blues and whites of the sky in fit proportions, like blobs of paint on an artist's palette.

Fleming was in town, shopping. He expected Joy to introduce him to his wife's former lover later. He wasn't looking forward to it.

Building and renovation work on Marcie's room was expected to finish today. In accordance with Dr Lloyd's advice, it was where she'd been as a child, on the first floor, so bars had to be installed over the window. Hard and sharp edges were filed down and covered over. The bed was removed and a special mattress installed. An outside lock was fixed to her door. A CCTV camera was installed out of sight in the corner, with the monitor hidden in a lockable cupboard in one of the never-visited rooms at the rear of the building.

Joy came down the front steps to welcome the guests and introduced them to her husband and her grand-daughter. Ghatola looked hard at Anya, apparently trying to discern something of the mother. She knew everything now, Joy having ruled there was no point in half-measures. She smiled at the little girl then asked to see Marcie's room before she went to her own.

The builders were finishing off, but Joy explained the modifications and pointed to where the camera was.

"It's for her own safety," she explained.

"Where is her husband?" Ghatola asked, through Tasneem.

"He went out to do some shopping. We thought it might be best if you settled in a little first before you met everyone."

"How much does he know about Marcie and me?"

"I think, everything."

Ghatola blinked slowly and blushed. She stood in silence then said softly, "He must hate me."

"This is about saving Marcie. Besides, I don't know how he feels."

"Marcie and I," she said passionately, in English, "is over. Is finished. No more that way. Friends now" – she broke into Pashto, so Tasneem finished her sentence for her: "What happened in the past cannot be repeated. Marcie must learn to accept who she really is. I will do everything in my power to help her."

Joy seized both her hands in hers and welled up. "Thank you, thank you."

"I will speak to husband when he gets back. With Tasneem only."

Fleming wasn't expecting a trap, but realised he'd walked into one as soon as he heard Ghatola and Tasneem were in the Study - essentially the Hartley-Browns' interview room. He'd been warned that, as a man, he wasn't to attempt a handshake with either woman, so he merely bowed slightly from the waist. Joy introduced them and Ghatola put her hand over her chest and inclined her head a degree. Both she and Tasneem had uncovered their faces and hair for the occasion.

"I'll go and make some more tea," Joy said. She closed the door behind her.

All three remained standing in silence. Fleming didn't feel it was his place to ask them to sit down, and he couldn't very well take a seat alone.

"Well, Ms Rahman, Ms Babar, how are you both settling in?" he asked.

Tasneem translated, then replied: "She says, please call her Ghatola. And you can call me Tasneem."

"Thank you. I'm Nicholas."

Although they'd already been introduced. There followed another five seconds of heavy silence then Ghatola spoke. Tasneem translated:

"When Ghatola and your wife were in Afghanistan together, they were very intimate. She's not prepared to apologise for that, but she wants you to know there will be no repetition. She says you are very lucky to have such a wife."

Fleming smiled. "I accept my need to keep her for myself is selfish, but I can't help it. I'm not the kind who dwells on past infidelities, however. My only concern is with the future. Insofar as you made her happy at a point in her life when she didn't even know who I was any more, I'm deeply grateful. Naturally, I hope you and I can work together on this. Given the extent of my failure so far, I expect to follow orders rather than give them. I'm entirely in your hands."

It was an overlong series of statements that could have gone in any order, such was his surprise at finding himself in sympathy with her. She smiled and put her hand over her chest again and the silence resumed.

"I understand Joy's got a ton of halal food in," he said eventually.

"She's a thoughtful and gracious woman," Ghatola replied, through Tasneem.

Marcie arrived in an ambulance the next morning, and Joy and Sir Anthony stood by with self-conscious hands to supervise the transfer. Two female nurses in pale blue uniforms stretchered the patient to her room, undid her fixings, conveyed her to her mattress and covered her over. She wore a nightie and a dressing gown and her teeth chattered, whether from fear or the cold no one knew. She had been bathed just before leaving the hospital. Her face was shrunken and white, her eyes watery. Her hair had been cut to shoulder-length.

The nurses repeated the practical advice Joy had already heard several times, then handed over the forms to be signed and left. The wind sang in the trees.

Marcie looked at her parents once the talking stopped and furrowed her eyebrows slightly as if trying to place them. She sighed and looked at the ceiling.

Joy sat on the edge of the bed and took her hand. "It's icy," she said. "Anthony, ask Geoffrey to bring the portable gas stove up, will you?"

"Do you think that's wise?"

"I'll stay with her."

"I'll be back in a moment then. I'll bring some more blankets too. Maybe a hot water bottle."

Suddenly, the door burst open and Ghatola and Tasneem entered in a hurry. Tasneem was carrying a holdall.

"Please to let me sit with her," Ghatola said harshly. She uttered a string of Pashto.

Marcie's head switched so fast Joy didn't have time to register what was happening. She dropped her daughter's hand and got to her feet as hurriedly as if it was the scene of a cardiac arrest and the defibrillator was here. Ghatola immediately took her place and put her face next to Marcie's, still talking. Then she stopped dead.

For a second time, all that could be heard was the sound of the wind in the oaks. Marcie's eyes focussed on the face. She put her fingers on Ghatola's burn and brushed them up and down. Then with a snap like a mousetrap, she clutched her and yelped. She whined miserably for a few moments, and broke into a howl as loud as Joy had ever heard before.

Ghatola manoeuvred herself awkwardly into a position where she was holding as much as being held and where she could whisper into Marcie's ear, and they remained this way for ten minutes, while the crying gradually subsided. Eventually, Ghatola turned to Tasneem without releasing her grip and beckoned her forward.

Tasneem knelt on the floor, undid the holdall and passed Ghatola a jar of baby food and a plastic spoon. Ghatola sat Marcie up against the wall, addressed her in a stern tone and slowly began to feed her.

Chapter 40: Planning a Comeback

As soon as Idris Kakahel and Haider Chamkanni learned Marcie was a British agent, they fled to the Norfolk coast. A stolen dory with an outboard motor got them to Holland where they spent what remained of their money on false identification documents and settled in Slotervaart on the edge of Amsterdam, amongst Moroccan and Turkish immigrants. Two days later, Idris Kakahel found work in a kebab house; Haider Chamkanni joined a scrap metal collecting gang. They spent two nights shivering beneath a bridge then snatched a Gucci handbag from a woman sitting outside a café and moved into a bedsit behind Maassluisstraat. They never expected to hear from Tasneem Babar again, nor to return to Pakistan. They were pretty certain they were now on the ISI's Wanted list.

It was in this light that they interpreted the unexpected call. They'd agreed to throw their phones into the North Sea by way of covering their tracks, but neither had. When *Tasneem* showed on Idris Kakahel's display, it was as if death itself had found them.

They didn't pick up. The next morning, at nine, they stood on the Blauwbrug Bridge and reluctantly dropped their Nokias into the Amstel river. It was second best to what they should have done, although better late than never.

But then curiosity got the better of them. Maybe they'd been forgiven, maybe they'd been deemed worthy of a second chance. They were already living outside society. If anything happened to them, it would be weeks before anyone noticed and forever before they cared. What did they have to lose, really?

They saved their money and took a bus to Leeuwarden, ninety miles away, so that if her game was to track their signal as a preliminary to sending the killers in, they'd get a head-start. Idris Kakahel called her from a public telephone booth, while Haider Chamkanni sat on the grass with the traffic whistling by, listening. They each felt afraid to be alone.

"I knew you'd get back to me," Tasneem said. "Where are you?"

They'd rehearsed this one. "Scotland."

"I keep ringing you, but never seem to have your phones switched on."

"We left them behind."

"Whereabouts in Scotland?"

"In a phone booth. We haven't much money. What do you want?"

"To save your skins. Your stock's quite low in Islamabad. Mine too, but thanks to that niqab I wore, no one knows who I am. I'm still looking after Ghatola Rahman and what's more, I've got access to Reshtina Sarbanri now."

"What's her real name?"

She chuckled. "Tush, I really don't want you taking credit for my discoveries."

"Why don't you just kill her then? Up your stock?"

"Because I'm being blamed not only for my own failure but because I'm in charge of comedy duo Idris Kakahel and Haider Chamkanni. If I'm to get anywhere in Inter-Services Intelligence, I have to prove I'm an effective man-manager, not just an effective assassin. I need you to come good."

"So what do you want us to do?"

"Kill them, of course, what else? We're all together in a very big house with lots of empty corridors. I'll give you the signal and you can more or less walk in at your convenience. It'll be as easy as an afternoon stroll."

"And when are we meant to do this?"

"Ring me when you've finished in the Netherlands and we'll set a date and time."

Idris Kakahel blanched. "Wh – what?"

"I can see your international dialling code, moron. You really are very poor spies. No wonder we're in such a mess. I can probably break it down further. There ... yes, what's it like in Leeuwarden and, more to the point, why did you lie to me about being in Scotland?"

"I – we thought you might be going to have us killed."

"I'd hardly have told you I know where you are if I was, would I?"

"No, but - "

"I'm guessing. You're not living in Leeuwarden. You only travelled there because you thought I'd be unable to trace you. You're actually based in Amsterdam, yes?"

"No, no, we're based in Leeuwarden."

"Good. Because that's where the killers are. You're dead meat."

He drew a sharp breath. *"Stop fooling around!"*

"What's the matter?" Haider Chamkanni said from the grass.

"Give me a ring when you're back in Britain," she snapped. "And hurry up because I might change my mind. This is your only chance to make amends."

They caught the last bus back to Slotervaart at five that evening and sat where they could talk. They were dead beat and knew they looked and smelt as if they'd met with bad luck. Sitting as far away from the other passengers wasn't difficult. It seemed to happen of its own accord. Outside, the sea, the lakes and the flat land sped by under a sky made dark by the smoked glass.

"Do you think we should risk it?" Idris Kakahel said.

Haider Chamkanni shrugged. "She knows where we are. She could probably have us killed us at any time. I believe she genuinely is trying to help us."

"I can see her logic. It reflects badly on her if we've screwed up. If we can look good as a team, that's in all our interests."

"On the other hand, maybe we just want to believe she's on our side. Perhaps life here's so awful we'll believe anything."

"It's no worse than anywhere else. Life always feels bad when you're not used to a place. We could get used to it.

Holland's supposed to be one of the most tolerant countries in Europe. We've got documentation too. We just need to be a bit more confident about using it."

"Yeah, but if we turn her down, we're probably not safe here, remember?"

They watched the landscape roll by for a minute.

"If we do decide to leave, how are we going to get back into Britain?" Haider Chamkanni asked.

"There's a Turkish fisherman in Katwijk aan Zee who takes people to the north-east coast. So I'm told. You have to swim the last five hundred yards though. People have drowned."

"How much does he charge?"

"Two thousand Euros. Each."

Haider Chamkanni scoffed. "Where are we going to get that kind of money?"

"Tasneem's always bankrolled us in the past. If we look able and willing, I'm sure she'll find some way of getting the cash to us."

"Maybe."

"It's cold here. I don't like it. I don't want to spend the rest of my life in a jumper and a mac. I want the sun."

"I think if we do take up her offer, we need to do things our own way, show we're as good as she is. She's only a wo-man, after all. She could probably do with a good hiding, truth be told."

Idris Kakahel laughed. "I'm not giving her one. She's supposed to be a black belt."

"Yes, but for her own good she needs to learn humility. Maybe seeing that we're better than her will do it."

"How are we going to pull that off? She herself said it'd be as easy as a stroll in the park. There's not much room for creativity."

"We'll have to find some. I'm still not convinced we're not walking into a trap. If we can do things our own way, maybe we'll find out before it springs."

Idris Kakahel nodded. "I suppose it can't do any harm. We're agreed, then?"

"Back to Britain," Haider Chamkanni replied.

Chapter 41: Kleptomania

Marcie refused to sleep in her own room and since Ghatola wouldn't let her in bed, she slept on the floor beside her. She woke when Ghatola did and trotted after her for the rest of the day, always two paces behind with her head down. She hardly spoke, as if frightened she might come out with something offensive. Ghatola gave up spoon-feeding her. She sat down to meals with the family but ate and drank only when Ghatola reminded her to. She looked glad to be alive but worried it couldn't last. She never smiled. She often flinched.

Ghatola tried always to be in conversation with a family member through Tasneem. She never spoke about herself except to claim similarities or analogies. With Joy, she spoke about Darfur and charitable work, about Anya and Hawa and childhood, about marriage, housekeeping, the weather, the management of the estate, politics, being British, food and drink. With Sir Anthony she spoke about London and his planned biography, ambition, friends and enemies, politics, television. With Fleming, she spoke of Marcie. They had Tom's parents to stay to provide fresh conversational seams, and Celia Demure. Marcie herself sat hunched to one side as if trying to become invisible.

Six weeks after her arrival, Joy and Sir Anthony sat with Dr Lloyd in the lounge. Lloyd wore his loafers and grey suit, differing from the Defence Secretary only in colour fabric, Sir Anthony having preferred black. Joy wore a maroon cardigan and trousers.

"I don't fully understand what's happening to her," Dr Lloyd said. "She's had two personalities so far. Now she's some third thing. Tiny, uncommunicative, petrified ... I'm not sure where it's leading."

"Ideally, we should have Ghatola in here," Joy said.

Sir Anthony folded his hands. "In which case, you'd have to have Marcie, since she's the limpet on the boulder."

"So let me get this straight," Dr Lloyd said. "You never get to see Marcie or her alone, yet they have periods together apart from you."

"I understand what you're implying, Doctor," Joy said. "But you're wrong. Ninety per cent of the time she's awake, Ghatola is with one or more of us: Anthony, myself, Nicholas, even Geoffrey. Marcie doesn't speak, but I'm sure she listens. I'm sure Ghatola herself must find it wearing, even tedious. We're not the world's most riveting family."

"It's early days yet," Dr Lloyd said. "We just have to see what happens. However, I'm a little worried this 'Ghatola' may think she knows more than she does. She's not a professional psychologist, after all. She may end up doing more harm than good."

"Marcie's eating," Joy replied drily. "She's going to live. And if that's all she ever achieves, she has my eternal gratitude."

"Quite," Dr Lloyd said. "But it's an awful lot less than we *can* achieve."

Sir Anthony leaned over to his wife. "The, er, bracelet ...?"

Joy shifted uncomfortably. "What my husband's referring to, Doctor ... There have been a number of disappearances of small items of value in the last three weeks. I lost a bracelet ten days ago, Sir Anthony lost a pair of expensive cufflinks, forty pounds went missing from the kitty in the kitchen."

"You think Ms Rahman or her companion might be thieves?"

"On the contrary," Sir Anthony said. "It's Marcie who's taking them. One of our security consultants saw her. We've also got CCTV footage of her hiding all three things in her room, under the carpet beneath a floorboard I never even knew was creaky."

"But I thought you said she never left Ghatola Rahman's side?"

"All three thefts occurred late at night while Ghatola was sleeping."

"Are you sure? Couldn't she be directing Marcie?"

"Like Fagin, you mean?"

"Not the most judicious comparison. But yes."

Sir Anthony shook his head. "Impossible. She knows about the CCTV in Marcie's room."

"Has she a theory?"

"We haven't had the opportunity to broach it with her," Joy said.

"For obvious reasons," Sir Anthony said. "The question is, do you?"

Dr Lloyd blew air as if he couldn't be expected to come up with something so demanding at such short notice. "Do any of the things she stole have sentimental value?"

"I'm not sure I understand the question, Dr Lloyd," Joy replied. "Do you mean, to Marcie, or to us?"

"Forty pounds is just a wad of cash," Sir Anthony said. "It's got exchange-value, that's all."

"I meant the bracelet and the cuff-links. To her. Did she buy them for you? Was she fond, for example, of wearing the bracelet as a child? Do the cuff-links have symbols on, or are they representations of objects with particular significance for her?"

Joy and Sir Anthony exchanged looks.

"She bought me the bracelet on my fiftieth birthday," Joy said. "That's right."

Sir Anthony shrugged. "The cufflinks are in the shape of footballs. She supported Hertford Town as a teenager."

"Unusual in an adolescent girl, to prefer a lower league team," Dr Lloyd said.

"My influence, I'm afraid," he replied. "One of the heavy responsibilities of being the local MP. Of course, I don't *have* to attend matches, or even show much interest, but it was one of the few areas where she and I converged."

Dr Lloyd smiled. "In that case, I think we have our solution. It looks like she's beginning to turn the corner. We may expect an avalanche the moment she finally remembers who she is. Which could be soon."

Tasneem sat on the floor by the window, cross-legged. Ghatola positioned Marcie on her own bed with her back against the wall. For some reason the hypnotism didn't seem to work in this country, and since straight talking was the next best thing, it would have to be that. She raised Marcie's chin and looked into her eyes. A shaft of sunlight made a striated square on the opposite wall.

"I don't know much Arabic," Ghatola began, "but it's *niyyah* that's important. Intention. Zaituna and Ambrin wanted to stop the war, and in the end they laid down their lives to avoid hurting others. You can forget about them now because I promise you they're in Jannah. You're the one who needs looking after."

"Me?"

"You're not Reshtina Sarbanri. You never were. These people are your real family. You came from England. You're not Afghan. This is your home."

"Are you going to leave me?" Marcie asked weakly.

"No."

"Are you going back to Afghanistan?"

"No."

"We can escape," she said hurriedly. "I'm saving up. I'm going to get us some money. We can go back."

Ghatola scoffed. "To what?"

"Home!"

"I've told you, that wasn't your home. It isn't mine any more either. Even if things weren't as they are, I wouldn't want to return to where I'm hardly allowed out of the house; where, when I am, it's only in a chadri; where, if I miss being bombed by the Americans, the Taliban will get me; where I'm only good for lifting and carrying, cooking meals and having babies. But things *are* as they are. Look at my face and tell me what Afghanistan has to offer a woman like this."

Marcie said nothing. She looked at her knees and wept.

Ghatola put her arm round her. "I still love you, but not in the old way. You're very lucky. You've got a real family and they all care for you. You should be very grateful."

"But I don't know them. How can they be my family?"

"You lost your memory, that's all. It'll come back."

"What if it doesn't? And what if they're not my family?"

"They are."

"How do you know?"

"Ask yourself what you think they're getting out of this. Look around you. Sir Anthony Hartley-Brown is an important politician in one of the most powerful countries in the world. Joy's intelligent, rich and caring; Nicholas Fleming's a handsome, talented young man. Anya's just a child. And they all live in a palace. Why would they be lying?"

"They adopt children. Maybe they want to adopt me."

Ghatola sighed. "You're being stupid now."

"I just don't – feel anything for them. I could pretend they were my parents and my husband, but I'd be acting. I can't spend the rest of my life doing that. The only person I feel anything at all for is you."

"You're not the same as you were in Afghanistan. You used to be the strong one."

"I realised I was much younger than you."

"Rubbish, don't exaggerate. A few years. We knew that from the outset."

"No, you're ancient! Older than the mountains or the seas or the sky! I came half way across the world to find you, but in the end, I couldn't manage it. Yet you found me. You just came back – by magic. And as long as we're together, I feel nothing bad can happen to me."

Ghatola smiled. "I've been told I'm primeval before. It's just an impression I give, nothing more. I married a seventy-three year old. I was in my twenties. I had to learn to think and talk like an old woman or suffer the consequences. That simple. There's nothing magical about it."

"Do you think my parents and the man - "

"Nicholas."

"Do you think they'll let us stay here together?"

"You mean, indefinitely? Probably. They love you. But we've got to move on. It's not good for either of us to keep things as they are. And I don't want to."

"You are going to leave me, aren't you?"

"We've been through this. Not unless you make me."

Marcie put her fingertips to her lips. "How – how could I make you?"

"By being possessive. I love you, but I don't like being stifled. I can't shoulder the responsibility for your well-being alone. I need you to make an effort to remember who you are and love your family back."

"But what if I can't?"

"You can. What do you think of Joy and Sir Anthony?"

"I think they're ... kind. And clever."

"What about Nicholas?"

"He seems nice too."

"Maybe you could fall in love with him. He loves you, after all."

"You mean, he loves who I was."

"Who you *are*. Come on, Marcie - "

"Reshtina."

"*Marcie*. You ought to be able to see it. There isn't much love where there's arranged marriage, but I've seen quite a few Bollywood films, so I know what I'm talking about. Love isn't about the Ashesta Boro or whether you can milk goats and cook rice and give your husband a ten-minute thrill when he finally comes in for the night. It's above things like whether you're modest or lose your temper or even go away for a long time or have an evil reputation. And sometimes even whether you're unfaithful. That's how he loves you."

"Nicholas? You really think so?"

"It's why men often marry women in this culture. He can give you everything I can't. 'Can't' because I don't want to."

"But I don't even speak his language!"

"Well, that's where we're going to begin. Tasneem's been teaching me. She can teach us both. Except you'll learn in world-record time. You know why? Because you already know it. Just keep an open mind. You do still like men, don't you?"

Marcie nodded.

"Good, because you've been lucky with this one."

Chapter 42: Scissors, Paper, Stone

Fleming awoke at seven, as usual, showered and dressed in an open-necked Oxford shirt and a pair of chinos. The weather forecast predicted sun for the third day in a row, which was good because Marcie was most relaxed when the group of them – Ghatola, Tasneem, Marcie, himself and either Sir Anthony or Geoffrey or one of the two security consultants, Jolyon or Benjamin – were walking on the lawn or sitting under the shade of the cedar as if re-enacting the first chapter of *The Portrait of a Lady*.

At breakfast, he found all seven occupants of the house already seated and an unusual looking letter waiting for him. He looked at its shape, shade and postmark before concluding it was a greetings card. He opened it as carefully as the impress stamp in the bottom left hand corner seemed to demand, and smiled. He was wrong.

Mr and Mrs Colin Grimes
request the pleasure of the company of
Mr Nicholas Fleming
at the marriage of their daughter
Yvonne
with
Ashraf Mustafa David Cassidy
at St Bede's Church, Heaton,
on Saturday 25th August 2012
at 1.30pm
and afterwards at
The Fox Inn.
RSVP.

It was part of Marcie being there that nothing that could possibly be remarked upon was passed over. He gave an edited account of how he met Cassidy and Grimes, omitting the connection with Reshtina Sarbanri, and afterwards, went to his room to pen his acceptance of the invite. He drove into the village to post it himself, because he wanted to see whether the house was still surrounded.

A Honda Civic parked on the yellow lines by the Holm Oak and the same two men he'd clocked three days ago in typical security services poses told him it was. Presumably, they thought she might still be a threat till she recovered her memory. There were probably microphones hidden in the house. Given the size of the place, they could be anywhere. He wondered if they'd recruited inside contacts too. That would be standard.

It was a very good reason for being outside in the sun. Over the last three days, he'd noticed Marcie staring at him a lot when she thought he wasn't looking. Maybe it was a good sign, maybe not. She didn't respond to his smiles, except to pretend she hadn't seen them. He wondered if he should spring a little Pashto on her, see what she thought. *Sahaar mo pa kheyr*, perhaps: good morning.

When he got back to Mannersby, he found Geoffrey carrying a trouser-press upstairs. The gloom and silence of the hallway after the bright sunshine and birdsong outside made the house feel as if it ought to be empty, even if it wasn't.

"Where is everyone?" he asked.

"They're outside on the lawn, sir."

"Are you coming?"

Geoffrey smiled. "It's Benjamin today, sir."

Geoffrey considered it funny that Fleming wasn't allowed near the women on his own. It reinforced the already overbearing *Downton Abbey* feel of the place.

"Could you ask him to meet me by the pond in ten minutes?"

"Yes, sir." He paused and added: "Very good, sir", presumably to twist the knife a little more.

Benjamin was fifty-two with dyed black hair and a strong right hook. He'd been a champion swimmer in his twenties. He broke into a trot when he saw Fleming waiting, and the women some five hundred yards further ahead sitting on the grass.

"Thank you for coming," Fleming said. "I realise it's probably not your ideal way to spend a day."

"Mine not to reason why. It'd probably be a lot easier if we could just crack open a few bottles of wine now and again. That's why Islam will never catch on in this country."

"Is Anya with them?"

"I think I can see her, yes."

"I've had an idea. Why don't we get them to play a few games?"

Benjamin laughed. "I've got a pack of cards in my pocket."

"They're Muslims. I don't think they believe in gambling."

"It doesn't have to be. What about Napoleon or Ranter Go Round?"

"For all we know, they might never have seen a pack of cards before."

"How about Pairs, where you put all the cards face down and you've just got to match two numbers?"

"They may not be able to read English numbers. *Sahaar mo pa kheyr!*" he called, when they were within hailing distance.

The four women – Ghatola, Tasneem, Marcie and Anya – turned in surprise. Marcie stood up and blushed. Ghatola said something to her and she sat down again. As usual, they were dressed in their chadors. Tasneem and Ghatola smiled. Anya frowned.

"Where did you learn that?" Ghatola said.

"I've been taking lessons."

"What's it mean?" Anya asked.

"Good morning," he replied.

Once again, he could feel Marcie staring at him. He turned a smile on her, but she'd anticipated him and was already looking at the sky.

"I thought we'd play a few games," he said, sitting down. "Maybe break the ice a bit."

Ghatola nodded. "I think that's a very good idea. I've been hoping you'd suggest it for some time." She turned to Marcie and translated. Marcie looked at him again, without embarrassment this time.

"Have you ever heard of 'Scissors, Paper, Stone'?" he asked.

Anya threw her hand up. *"I have!"*

The three women leaned forward.

He held up his palm. "This is paper."

Anya made a horizontal V with her fingers. "These are scissors."

Benjamin made a fist. "This is a stone."

"It's very simple. Watch me and Anya. Count two, then go, yes?"

She nodded. They gave two beats with their fists then Fleming held up his palm and Anya made the snipping gesture. She laughed.

"You see, Anya wins, because scissors can cut paper. But if she'd made this" – a fist – "I'd have won, because paper can enfold a stone, like so. And that's all there is to it."

The women looked at each other.

"Look, I'll play it with Benjamin," Anya said. "Watch us two."

They played three rounds. Anya won two and lost one.

"So I'm the preliminary heats champ," she said. "Now Ghatola, you play Tasneem. Best of three."

Anya had obviously seen his design. And everyone seemed happy. Ghatola beat Tasneem in two, producing scissors and a rock.

"Now Marcie and Nicholas," Ghatola said solemnly.

Marcie stood up hesitantly and knelt before him. They looked at each other. He produced a scissors to her paper. Then paper to her scissors. Finally he produced paper to her stone. She laughed.

Her reaction was so unexpected a surge of alarm shot through him and he was momentarily thrown. But then he gently took her fist in his palm.

"Paper enfolds stone," he whispered.

Her eyes flashed delight and she smiled. She turned to Ghatola and let out a string of Pashto. The two Afghan women laughed and applauded.

"She says, 'Tell him I want a rematch'!" Ghatola translated.

They played Hide and Seek, Pin the Tail on the Donkey and had six egg and spoon races. Three days later, Marcie slept in her own room. Under cover of darkness she returned the cuff links, the bracelet and the wad of money. She awoke early to hunt Nicholas down then followed him from room to room grinning, gesticulating and speaking in inexact English. After four days, they walked across the parkland without chaperones. They held hands. He told her he loved her in Pashto.

Sir Anthony, Joy and Ghatola sat with Armaghan Jones and Dr Lloyd in the Living Room with the usual tea and fairy cakes, and watched the couple embrace under the Ash tree.

"They never seem to kiss," Sir Anthony said.

Armaghan Jones, on the sofa next to Ghatola, quietly began translating the conversation.

"Five days ago she wasn't even speaking to him," Joy retorted. "Rome wasn't built in a day. Personally, I believe she's almost cured."

Dr Lloyd wagged his finger and sighed. "I think we may be getting ahead of ourselves."

"What do you mean?" Sir Anthony asked.

"Only that, arguably, the woman he's with out there isn't his wife. Sooner or later, she'll remember who she is and it could be harrowing. Apart from anything else, the restored Marciella Fleming might be too traumatised to return his feelings. She might have altered in all sorts of ways. He might find he no longer loves her. People rarely recover from a long bout of amnesia without some sort of fallout."

"So you think this could be a kind of Indian summer before a nuclear winter?" Sir Anthony said.

Dr Lloyd removed a cake from its casing. "I certainly think the two of them need to be more cautious."

Ghatola spoke to Dr Lloyd.

"She says she disagrees with you, Doctor," Armaghan Jones said. "Since when was true love ever cautious?"

Dr Lloyd smiled. "Which is why its course never runs smoothly. But in this case, that could turn out to be a huge understatement. I hope not, but I'm not optimistic."

"My time here is now at an end," Ghatola announced, in English. "Marcie does not me need any more. She loves Nicholas. That is very good."

Joy and Sir Anthony looked at each other. Joy nodded.

Sir Anthony put his cup and saucer on the teapoy. "Joy and I have talked this over and we'd like to ask you formally to come and live with us. Marcie's extremely attached to you, so is Anya, so are we all, and you'd be a welcome addition to the family. We have lots of spare rooms, as you know, and it wouldn't preclude you in any way from having an independent life, getting a job, getting married if that's what you want, even raising a family."

"I don't know much about Afghanistan," Joy said, "but from the little I've learned, it's normal for extended families to dwell under the same roof. We'd love to have you live here, but I realise it might sound a big step. It isn't. In this country, people often live lonely, disconsolate lives in places where they feel scared to go out after dark. Coming from such a tight-knit community, you might find that even more difficult than it sounds. We could give you all the benefits of a proper home."

"Of course, everything we're offering applies to Tasneem too," Sir Anthony said. "We realise you're both in the same boat and we're equally attached to her."

"Don't give us an answer now," Joy said. "Take a day or so to think about it. But I do hope you'll say yes. Now, if you'll all excuse me, I have to get Anya from her other grandparents and Hawa from her piano lessons."

Fleming and Marcie came to where the summer house was and sat down outside it. He put his arm round her and she laid her head on his shoulder. She was in one of her long taciturn moods, so they sat noiselessly watching the clouds.

He judged they'd been there for ten minutes when he heard the slow mumble of a woman's voice, with sufficient number of pauses to make it clear she was inside the summer house on a phone.

Tasneem Babar?

So that's who their inside contact was! Naturally, it had to be one of Ghatola, Armaghan Jones or her. Everyone else had been attached to the family too long and had too much to lose.

It didn't necessarily mean she was hostile. They'd probably persuaded her she was acting in everyone's best interests, because that's how they normally worked. For all he knew, they might even be right. He wondered whether she was the idealistic type or whether they'd had to pay her.

Why hadn't Marcie noticed the babble? It wasn't exactly whispered.

Of course. Because she had one ear on his shoulder, the other beneath her headscarf.

Perhaps he could catch a snippet of the report, see what they were up to. He strained to hear, then frowned.

That wasn't English. It wasn't even Pashto.

So she couldn't be speaking to who he thought she was. Maybe she had other refugee friends, that would be the likeliest explanation.

He memorised two of her phrases. He could Google them later, see what they brought up.

It was another twelve hours – Marcie's prescribed bedtime - before he was alone again. He sat on the armchair in the corner of his room and took out his Smartphone. He typed the two phrases up as phonemes using various combinations of letters, and hoped against hope that someone, somewhere in the world had uploaded the same obscure word-strings plus either a translation or the correct script. He knew in advance he was asking the virtually impossible.

After ten minutes, he was on the verge of giving up. His next move – though it would have to wait till tomorrow – was to search Tasneem's room. It might simply be, as he believed, that she was working for British intelligence. But there were other possibilities, some of which were probably unforeseeable now, a few of which might mean Marcie was in danger. He couldn't take any chances.

Suddenly, the door opened. He looked up to find himself facing Tasneem herself. He felt his heart inflate uncomfortably against his ribs. She wore a coat and she was pointing a gun at him.

The first thing he noticed when he'd assessed the situation – as he'd been trained to – was that it didn't have a silencer. He raised his hands. He should pretend complete ignorance.

He grinned. "Er, what's going on? Is that real?"

"I need your help," she replied.

He noticed she was in no hurry to close the door, and put it down to amateurism. Which might have two opposed consequences. She might be so nervous she'd shoot him without thinking. Or he might be able to distract and overpower her.

But then the reason for her apparent negligence became clear. Marcie and Ghatola stepped into the room behind her, also in coats. Both seemed to have been crying.

"You need to help Tasneem, Nicholas," Ghatola said. "I beg it. You are only one who can aid."

"Please," Marcie said.

Tasneem turned her gun round and handed it to him by the barrel. "You have to trust me," she said. "As I'm now trusting you. All will be revealed later, I promise."

Chapter 43: Aminah Mohammad, R&AW

Now he was in possession of the gun, he was torn between two choices. He could demand a full explanation, thus proving to Marcie that he didn't trust her; or he could make do without, proving he did. The problem was the wild card, Tasneem Babar. There was no telling what her agenda was, or whether Marcie really knew what was happening.

But she'd given him the gun, that had to count for something.

"What do you want me to do?" he asked.

"I need to get out of here and away," Tasneem said. "I need your car and you to drive it."

He reached into the wardrobe and pulled his overcoat on. His keys were in the pocket. "Come on, then."

"We will be chased," she whispered, as they descended the stairs. "You need to be fast."

They left the house and descended the steps onto the forecourt. It was dark and chilly. "I'm afraid I'm not much good at imitating *The Transporter*," he said. "I tend to fret unduly about cyclists and hedgehogs. I'm being serious."

"I can't drive," Tasneem said.

"I've hardly ever been in a car," Ghatola said.

He passed Marcie his keys. "Here."

She looked at them incredulously. "*Me?*"

"We both know you know what to do," he replied, as he got into the passenger seat. Tasneem and Ghatola slipped into the back. "Seatbelts everyone – reach above you and clip in at your waists. Marcie, get behind the steering wheel. I'll guide you through the first few steps. It's an automatic, if that means anything. I bought it with you in mind."

She let herself into the driver's seat looking petrified. She grabbed the steering wheel at quarter to three. He adjusted her gently to ten to two.

"This is the key," he said. "Put it in the ignition – here – and turn. Right, now you don't have to worry about that any more. Headlights here, full beam. On the floor there are two foot pedals. The one on your right speeds it up, the one on your left brakes. This handle here is your handbrake."

"Did – did Marcie know how to drive?" she asked.

"You *are* Marcie," he replied.

"Then, do *I* know how to drive?"

He remembered her last outing when the police had tried to close the M1. "Pretty much."

Suddenly there was a screech as the tyres took hold and they sped off across the lawn. She swerved to clear the estate gates and the two nearside wheels left the ground. They came back to earth with a bump to find themselves travelling along a country lane at fifty climbing.

He wondered how long it would be before Tasneem Babar decided she wanted to walk and whether, given the likelihood of them all dying in the next five minutes, it was academic. What the hell had he unleashed, and why had he thought it a good idea? He gripped the armrest.

They were being followed. Two cars, neither quite as swashbuckling as Marcie, both with their full beams on, losing ground. If they were who he thought they were, they weren't going to put up with being outrun. They'd probably already called the helicopter and when it arrived everything would be over.

He heard one of the back doors slam shut, and when he turned round, Ghatola was alone, weeping hard. They turned a blind corner – luckily, there was nothing coming. But there was another one ahead, and the entrance to a disused quarry to their left. He'd walked this road a good ten times over the last few weeks and knew it intimately.

"Marcie, slow down," he said gently.

She took her eyes off the road momentarily to look at him and obeyed. She was pale.

"Pull in here," he told her.

She veered off the road into the quarry and stopped. He extinguished the headlights and watched their pursuers hurtle past at breakneck speed.

"Bring it a little further in till it's under that tree, then cut the engine and get out."

She did as he ordered and stood with Ghatola as he tore up hazel shrubs, ivy stems and sycamore branches and used them to cover the car. The sky was so thick with cloud it was impossible to tell where the moon was, or even if there was one. The wind was rising.

"We seem to have lost Tasneem," he remarked drily, at last.

"Thank you," Ghatola said as if there was nothing to explain. "We must now walk back, yes?"

"I have the feeling time's of the essence," he replied. "And I'm not sure a ten-mile hike's going to do either of you any good, especially considering it's way past Marcie's bedtime. I'll ring for a taxi and we'll disembark before we get home. We'll pretend we've walked, if necessary." He brushed the dirt off his coat sleeves. "I don't suppose either of you is prepared to tell me what's going on?"

The two women looked at each other.

"I don't know," Marcie said.

Ghatola shook her head. "And I not believe."

They arrived back to find the house surrounded by cars and a light on in every room, including the hallway. The front door was wide open. A group of men in suits watched them approach, then one peeled off and came to meet them. He spoke into a two-way radio then lowered it.

"Nicholas Fleming, right?"

"And who might you be?" Fleming replied.

"Just checking. Go on in. These women with you?"

"You've had this house under observation for how long? And you still have to ask?"

The man put his palms up. "Hey, just being polite. You'll find the boss waiting for you in the Lounge, I believe. Good luck."

"Thanks."

He allowed the two women to precede him into the house then the room and found Sir Anthony in his favourite wingback chair with a double brandy and Ruby Parker standing, feet apart, in front of the fire. Neither looked pleased to see him. The chandelier was fully lit bathing everything in an unforgiving stil de grain yellow. Ghatola and Marcie went straight to the sofa, apparently oblivious to everyone else. They drew their feet up and huddled together with glazed eyes like survivors of a natural disaster. He closed the door behind them.

"I brought the ladies in," he said, "because they seem to know what's going on. Which I presume goes for you two as well. Is anyone going to tell me, or should I just go to bed and forget this ever happened?"

"Sit down, Nicholas," Sir Anthony said.

He perched on the sofa next to his wife and Ghatola, although they might have been on the moon for all the mental proximity he felt to them.

"You've just helped a foreign agent escape," Ruby Parker said.

He shrugged. "Pity, but then you've been having this building watched for weeks. If you'd bothered to tell me, perhaps I'd have thought twice. Who was she working for?"

"India."

"What was her interest?"

"Pakistan."

Fleming sighed. "Are you going to give me the full story, or are you just going to throw me tidbits?"

"Aminah Mohammad, aka, Tasneem Babar, was a senior agent in India's equivalent of MI6, the modestly-named Research and Analysis Wing. Two years ago she infiltrated Pakistan's Inter-Services Intelligence agency with a brief to prove its active involvement in terrorism so irrefutably it would become an international pariah. She attached herself to Idris Kakahel and Haider Chamkanni and began taping conversations with them. Initially she hoped to lure them to Britain in a bid, which she would have foiled, to assassinate Ghatola Rahman, thus provoking a major international incident. But then she discovered that Reshtina Sarbanri was coming to London to carry out a suicide bomb attack.

"In fact, she decided from the outset there was to be no bombing. In order to understand why she made up her mind to shield Ghatola and Marcie, it may be as well to understand India's special relation to the AWRB, but I'll come to that in a moment. In any case, when the group met up in Dover, she contrived to be alone with the three women as they got into their explosive belts and defused each in turn. On the day of the planned attack, there were R&AW agents waiting on all thirty-two of London's bridges to prevent them jumping into the Thames, since that's what they'd been ordered to in the event of a failure.

"Everything went wrong when she learned Marcie was a British agent. She needed everyone alive for India to come up trumps and that wasn't going to happen. She knew that no matter what information she handed over, the British government would prefer taking the credit for foiling the attacks to publicly castigating Pakistan, and that would mean burying all alternative accounts. So she warned her contacts to flee on a 'he who fights and runs away lives to fight another day' basis. Sooner or later, they'd entrap themselves again, and this time she'd be on hand to expose them.

"She came to our attention just afterwards. We revised all security clearances as per policy and she turned up in a file so obscure it hadn't even been digitalised. One of the founders of the Afghan Women's Reparation Brigade: an India-founded, India-funded organisation – however much its members might think otherwise. New Delhi apparently sees militant feminism as a bulwark against Pakistani Islamism and the conflict in Afghanistan as a proxy war. Some factions of the R&AW believe Pakistan's using the country as a recruitment ground for the invasion of Jammu and Kashmir after the withdrawal of ISAF troops. And they want to be ready, which means enlisting global sympathy in advance by whatever means possible."

"So what was she doing at Mannersby?"

Ruby Parker frowned. "I was coming to that. Seven weeks ago – as you probably know from the news - an American journalist by the name of Timothy Meades was captured by the Taliban. By that time, we'd joined the dots sufficiently to work out what 'Tasneem' was up to: her prolonged absence the night before the attacks were due, the appearance of a fourth woman of her size and stature in the Grand that night, and of course the shattered remnants of Abedrabbo al-Maitami's mobile phone. He'd entered her into his address book by name.

"We converted her to the idea of bringing Idris Kakahel and Haider Chamkanni back to Britain to kill Ghatola and Marcie as a way of re-ingratiating themselves in Islamabad. The idea being that if we caught them red-handed, the Pakistani government might reluctantly broker the release of Mr Meades. It was one option we were pushing amongst others. We had the house surrounded so tightly no one inside was ever in any real danger. Unfortunately, the two ISI agents dragged their feet after Idris Kakahel formed a relationship with a Turkish woman and time ran out. Timothy Meades was beheaded this afternoon, as you've probably heard.

"At this point, I think Aminah Mohammad believed we might start considering what alternative use we could put her to, and she decided to escape. She had reasonable cause for suspicion because it's the sort of thing that happens in intelligence. She phoned the Dienst Speciale Interventies, the Dutch anti-terrorist police, and had Idris Kakahel and Haider Chamkanni apprehended just as they were finally about to leave for Britain, then I believe she came to see you.

"In fact, we'd already decided to let her go. It's much better for her self-esteem and her future career if she's thought to have broken out on her own. The car chase was staged, as was the helicopter that appeared half an hour later, as are the radio messages the Indian embassy is doubtless listening in to right now, designed to produce the effect that we're none too happy at having lost her. In a couple of hours, she'll board a fishing boat for the continent and if all goes to plan, she should be back in New Delhi by the weekend."

"You'll be happy to know she left you all a present," Sir Anthony said drily. "Don't worry, they've been checked by the bomb-squad."

He nodded at the coffee table, where three identically gift-wrapped rectangles stood. Fleming picked them up and handed Marcie and Ghatola two. He tore the third open himself.

A hardback book. *Infidel* by Ayaan Hirsi Ali.

"Her desert island choice, apparently," Ruby Parker commented.

Fleming laughed. "I think I'll turn in, unless anyone's got anything else they'd like to say to me. I wish we'd been able to save Timothy Meades, but the house isn't in danger and I'm not in hot water. Small mercies."

"Is it okay for Joy to come in?" Sir Anthony asked. "We're done talking top secret, yes?"

"She could have come in at the outset," Ruby Parker replied.

He rang the service bell. "Yes, but you know what the PM's like – *Joy! You can enter now!* Spouses and partners aren't allowed. Ask Joy to join us, will you?" he said impatiently, when Geoffrey shimmered into view.

Joy walked in, sat down next to Ghatola and put her arm round her. "I understand how you're probably feeling," she said. "I'll stay up with you tonight and we can talk or not, as the mood takes you."

"I think Marcie needs some rest," Fleming said.

She was asleep, her unopened gift lying by her side. He shook her gently and helped her from the room. As soon as they were outside, she opened her eyes wide and grinned.

"I really, really *enjoyed* tonight, Nicholas!" she said.

An hour later he lay in bed unable to sleep. She'd enjoyed tonight, good. Yet Marcie had never called him Nicholas, except when she was angry. But they were getting there.

Suddenly the door opened and closed – but not quickly enough to conceal the entrant, whose silhouette stood out for a moment against the dim light of the corridor.

"Marcie?"

She took off her nightie and slid into bed beside him. It took him a second to recover his breath, by which time she'd put her arm round him. They stroked each other's flesh. They kissed each other's hair. They stared into each other's irises and corneas, marvelling at the movements, colours and the veins that told of their humanity. They combined first frenetically, then tenderly, solemnly, happily, then selflessly with tears of gratitude joining in long blue runnels. Just before dawn they fell asleep.

He awoke twenty minutes later to find a space next to him. She was on the other side of the bedroom, facing the sun through the drawn curtains and washing her feet and arms in a bowl. She put it to one side and stood up muttering, then put on his dressing gown, touched her forehead twice to the ground and sat up on her heels. He watched her go through the prescribed motions again until she'd finished. She undressed, climbed back into bed and put her arm round him again.

"But I thought - " he began.

She kissed him lightly on the lips and smiled.

"Love is greater than memory," she said.

Chapter 44: Going With Bishop Butler

Fleming, Ghatola, Joy and Sir Anthony sat not quite facing each other and listened to the clock on the mantelpiece as the only thing capable of mitigating the oppressive silence. A tea set and a full pot of Earl Grey stood ready for use, whatever the verdict. Three extra chairs had been brought in at a day's notice and now stood vacant, awaiting the interviewers and the interviewee. It was raining outside, and though midday in the middle of summer, almost dark.

"Of course, it's a very inexact science, Psychology," Sir Anthony said.

No one replied. Suddenly, there was a noise of voices in the corridor. Marcie entered the room in a blue dress and pumps, looking solemn, followed by Dr Lloyd and Professor Sir Randolph Jones, a bald, stout man in a waistcoat with a watch-chain and trainers, from Oxford Brookes University. Marcie took the vacant chair next to her mother. The two professionals, after a theatrical show of mutual deference, took the others.

Professor Jones fanned his face with his notebook. "It's a very rough science, Psychology. Sometimes I think we're only half a degree better than shamans."

"Given that caveat," Dr Lloyd said. "It's probably safe to say Marcie's cured."

"What does that mean in practical terms?" Fleming asked.

"That there's going to be no crisis as she reverts to being who she was. She already remembers large parts of her former life. She – sorry, I'm talking about you in the third person here," he told her, "I hope you don't mind – just chooses not to reject her present for-want-of-a-better-word 'personality'."

"So you were wrong?" Sir Anthony said.

Dr Lloyd accepted the cup Joy passed him. "I'm deferring to my colleague's greater experience, but the short answer's yes. That happens in science, of course. Unlike in shamanism there are no unassailable dogmas."

"The problem is," Professor Jones said, "far too much of modern Psychology's still a thrall to John Locke. For Locke, personal identity was based on memory. You are who you are because you have the memories you have. Which seems a reasonable conclusion. Memory's one of the few things that sets you apart from others, after all. There's only one problem with it. It's complete nonsense."

"It sounds sensible to me," Joy said. "What on earth's wrong with it?"

"Well, a generation later, in the eighteenth century, an Anglican Bishop called Joseph Butler pointed out that memory presupposes personal identity, so it can't be used to establish it. 'My memory', as opposed to some random subjective picture of a past occurrence, assumes an already established notion of me."

"Then what's the alternative?" Fleming asked.

"That the self's actually a public notion," Professor Jones said. "Sure, it's got a subjective element, but that's not its defining characteristic. Necessary but not sufficient, as we sometimes say."

Dr Lloyd finished his tea and put the cup and saucer back. "To come back down to earth a bit, three things made the difference. The most important was when you took Marcie out of what was effectively a well-meaning version of solitary confinement. Then you, Ms Rahman, kindly consented to help. Finally, you managed to get Anya's other grandparents on board. You may not have realised this, but Penny and John have spent a long time with her. So the situation she came back to was vastly more harmonious than the one she left. The world's reconciled to her when previously she thought it was irreconcilable."

"So what now?" Sir Anthony said.

"I don't think that's for either of us to say," Professor Jones replied.

"This may sound silly," she said after a pause, "but I think I'd like a honeymoon."

Ten minutes later, she and Fleming stood alone at the French window looking out across the park. The sun had unexpectedly broken through, making half a rainbow beyond the old gate in the boundary wall. She watched Ghatola and Joy amble by, deep in conversation, while Hawa threw a hoop in front of them then retrieved it. The grass sparkled.

"I think she's decided to stay," she said. "I'm so glad."

"Me too."

They watched them for another minute, then she said: "I think I'd like to go somewhere friendly. America, maybe."

"You mean, for our honeymoon?"

"Or Sweden, or Norway. I'd like to climb a mountain before I get too old."

"There's a long way to go till we reach that stage."

She turned to him. "If you've anything you want to do in life, it's no good putting it off. You've got to do it now. Who knows where we'll be tomorrow?"

"You and I, you mean?"

"I love you, Nicholas. Nothing in life can come between us. But bad things happen."

"We'd have to do a bit of training."

"I think I could manage that."

She suddenly saw herself on top of her mountain, her husband sitting beside her. She had a staff in her right hand. The sky was blue, the air crisp and the view stretched over all seven continents. There was no way down, none, and she was elated.

Books by James Ward

General Fiction
The House of Charles Swinter
The Weird Problem of Good
The Bright Fish
Hannah and Soraya's Fully Magic Generation-Y *Snowflake* Road Trip across America

The Original Tales of MI7
Our Woman in Jamaica
The Kramski Case
The Girl from Kandahar
The Vengeance of San Gennaro

The John Mordred Tales of MI7 books
The Eastern Ukraine Question
The Social Magus
Encounter with ISIS
World War O
The New Europeans
Libya Story
Little War in London
The Square Mile Murder
The Ultimate Londoner
Death in a Half Foreign Country
The BBC Hunters
The Seductive Scent of Empire
Humankind 2.0
Ruby Parker's Last Orders

Poetry
The Latest Noel
Metals of the Future

Short Stories
An Evening at the Beach

Philosophy
21st Century Philosophy
A New Theory of Justice and Other Essays

CPSIA information can be obtained
at www.ICGtesting.com
Printed in the USA
LVHW092024120721
692489LV00013B/222/J